SHADOW WOMAN

THE REAL CREATOR OF SHERLOCK HOLMES

John Allen

© 2017 by John Allen

Allen & Allen Semiotics, Inc.

Long Beach CA

ISBN: 978-0-984271665

Initial editing by Byron Case

Later editing by Heather Osborn

Cover artwork by Dean Williams

Cover design by redbat design

I dedicate this book to Byron Case, Missouri inmate #328416, and all other innocent men and women imprisoned for crimes they did not commit.

Sir A. Conan Doyle, the eminent spiritualist of whom we read in Sunday papers, the author of a number of exciting stories which we read years ago and have forgotten, what has he to do with Holmes?

T. S. Eliot, *The Criterion*, 1929

TABLE OF CONTENTS

Chapter 1
Cold Case

A cold case is an unsolved, inactive investigation into a crime or other similar mystery. A cold case becomes interesting and potentially solvable when new evidence or new technology becomes available.

During the previous century, a number of notable individuals have speculated about the authorship of the Sherlock Holmes adventures. None of them, however, has dared suggest any name other than Arthur Conan Doyle. Those incompletely formed speculations of the previous century have long since lapsed into obscurity. The Case of the Unknown Ghostwriter has gone stone cold.

Here, we breathe life into a mystery that many would prefer left dormant.

T.S. Eliot

Thomas Stearns Eliot—best known by his initials, T.S.—was a poet, playwright, essayist, publisher, literary critic, and Sherlock Holmes aficionado. He was also the first person of note to question Arthur Conan Doyle's involvement with the world's most famous literary detective. In 1929, the year prior to Arthur's death, Eliot wrote a review of *The Complete Sherlock Holmes Stories* for *The Criterion* magazine. In that review, Eliot pondered the unusual relationship between Holmes and his presumed creator.

> Perhaps the greatest of the Sherlock Holmes mysteries is this: that when we talk of him we invariably fall into the fancy of his existence. [Wilkie] Collins, after all, is more real to his readers than Cuff; [Edgar Allan] Poe is more real than Dupin; but Sir A. Conan Doyle, the eminent spiritualist of whom we read in Sunday papers, the author of a number of exciting stories which we read years ago and have forgotten, what has he to do with Holmes?

For those interested in poking this beehive, Eliot's observation can be condensed and sharpened to inquire: "What has Arthur Conan Doyle to do with Sherlock Holmes?" A careful reading of the entire excerpt, however, suggests that Eliot was more likely describing a lack of public curiosity about Holmes's creator than he was expressing doubts about Arthur's involvement in Holmes's creation. Eliot may nonetheless have been troubled by the authorship question. Consider his appendage to his claim that every writer owes something to Holmes: "I am not sure that Arthur Conan Doyle is not one of the great dramatic writers of his age."

Why the convoluted, indecipherable, double negative from someone so adept with words? Just what was Eliot driving at?

Rex Stout

Charlotte Brontë feared that her work would be rejected if publishers knew its author to be a woman. She feared also that her work, if actually published, would be judged by harsher standards. She therefore wrote, at least initially, under the pen name Currer Bell.

Though Charlotte could easily write under the name of a man, she soon discovered that she could not write as a man would write. Those who reviewed *Jane Eyre* (1847) quickly recognized the writer's sex. "The writer is evidently a woman," wrote G. H. Lewes in his review for *Fraser's Magazine*. "But, man or woman, young or old, be that as it may, no such book has gladdened our eyes for a long while."

"Whoever may be the author we hope to see more such books from her pen," read the *Westminster Review*, "for that these volumes are from the pen of a lady, and a clever one too, we have not the shadow of a doubt."

"I wish you had not sent me *Jane Eyre*," William Makepeace Thackeray wrote to a colleague. "It interested me so much that I have lost (or won if you like) a whole day [...] Who the author can be I can't guess, if a woman she knows her language better than most ladies do, or has had a 'classical' education. [...] Some of the love passages made me cry [...] I don't know why I tell you this but I have been exceedingly moved and pleased by *Jane Eyre*. It is a woman's writing but whose?"

Charlotte finally agreed that she could not, try as she might, write as a man. Responding to complaints from her publisher about her depiction of male characters, she wrote, "Probably you are right. In delineating male character I labour under disadvantages: intuition and theory will not always adequately supply the place of observation and experience. When I write about women I am sure of my ground—in the other case, I am not so sure."

Charlotte Brontë is of great interest to us, not because she wrote the Sherlock Holmes adventures, but because she helps us understand the woman who did write them. Yes, a woman wrote the Sherlock Holmes adventures. We subconsciously recognize her as such because both she and Charlotte, when delineating male character, necessarily had to labor under disadvantages.

Rex Stout was the first to speak publicly about the female mind lurking behind the Holmes adventures. Stout created the larger-than-life fictional detective: Nero Wolfe. Honored by The Mystery Writer's of America as a Grand Master, and nominated Best Mystery Writer of the Century, Stout's words carried a prominence difficult to ignore. It was therefore a turning point in Sherlockian research when he spoke before the prestigious Baker Street Irregulars and declared that Watson was a woman.

Ellery Queen's Mystery Magazine of April 1946 reprinted Stout's heretical speech, introducing it with this intentionally overwrought lament worthy of Stout himself.

> The most controversial, the most blasphemous, by all odds the most sensational Sherlockian revelation of our decade (indeed of our generation, if not of all time) was Rex Stout's "Watson Was a Woman." This bombshell was flung orally within the sacred precincts of the Murray Hill Hotel, during the meeting of the Baker Street Irregulars on January 31, 1941. The flinger, of course, was Rex Stout, who was invited to attend that fateful session as Guest of Honor, but who finally departed, head high and beard bristling,

the Guest of Dishonor. Yes, it was a profane night in which Holmesian history was born: Who of the innermost circle will ever forget Mr. Stout's first wolfish pronouncement—the savage glee with which he blithely disclosed that Watson Was a Woman? Who among those shocked sycophants of Sherlock will ever forget the pure Holmesian horror that set in, like a sort of literary rigor mortis, when the creator of Nero Wolfe pronounced those terrible and terrifying words—WATSON WAS A WOMAN!

"You will forgive me for refusing to join your commemorative toast [to] the second Mrs. Watson," began Stout, "when you learn it was a matter of conscience. I could not bring myself to connive at the perpetuation of a hoax. Not only was there never a second Mrs. Watson; there was not even a first Mrs. Watson. Furthermore, there was no Doctor Watson."

"Please keep your chairs," he added with a flourish.

Stout explained that the discomforting realization hit him suddenly as he was simply reading the stories once again for the enjoyment they provided. Good conscience demanded that he review the Sacred Writings in their entirety, in an entirely new light. From the very beginning, it was clear that only a woman could have thus written of Holmes, "It was rare for him to be up after ten at night, and he had invariably breakfasted and gone out before I rose in the morning."

"I was indescribably shocked," Stout declared. "How had so patent a clue escaped so many millions of readers through the years? That was, that could only be, a woman speaking of a man. Read it over. The true authentic speech of a wife telling of her husband's –"

With his pause, he allowed the collective imagination of his audience to run wild. He followed with another quote from the suddenly feminine Watson:

The reader may set me down as a hopeless busybody, when I confess how much this man stimulated my curiosity, and how often I endeavored to break through the reticence which he showed on all that concerned himself.

"You bet she did," professed Stout. "She would. Poor Holmes! She doesn't even bother to employ one of the stock euphemisms, such as, 'I wanted to understand him better,' or, 'I wanted to share things with him.' She proclaims it with brutal directness, 'I endeavored to break through the reticence.' I shuddered, and for the first time in my life felt that Sherlock Holmes was not a god, but human—human by his suffering."

The *coup de grace* came when Stout read Watson's petulant description of breakfast with Holmes.

> I rose somewhat earlier than usual, and found that Sherlock Holmes had not yet finished his breakfast [...] my place had not been laid nor my coffee prepared. With [...] petulance [...] I rang the bell and gave a curt intimation that I was ready. Then I picked up a magazine from the table and attempted to while away the time with it, while my companion munched silently at his toast.

"That is a terrible picture," Stout commiserated, "and you and I know how bitterly realistic it is. Change the diction, and it is practically a love story by Ring Lardner. That Sherlock Holmes, like other men, had breakfasts like that is a hard pill for a true disciple to swallow, but we must face the facts. The chief thing to note of this excerpt is that it not only reinforces the conviction that Watson was a lady—that is to say, a woman—but also it bolsters our hope that Holmes did not through all those years live in sin. A man does not munch silently at his toast when breakfasting with his mistress; or, if he does, it won't be long until he gets a new one."

In the same issue of *Ellery Queen's Mystery Magazine*, Kurt Steel, a professor from New York University, refuted Rex Stout's claims. Sort of.

> For this heresy, Dr. Stout has been shamefully abused. It is not my purpose here to defend him.

What I shall do is to demonstrate that his research, if carried beyond the point where he carelessly dropped it, proves not what he was at pains to set forth but almost precisely the opposite.

Stout cites passages from *A Study in Scarlet* that do sound suspiciously as if they flowed from the pen of a yearning, uneasy, petulant female. We can, I think, accept his analysis of this story, but unhappily he overlooked the far richer implications of another tale.

Kurt Steel sees a woman's hand only in the first two Holmes adventures, *A Study in Scarlet* and *The Sign of Four*. He concludes, therefore, that a woman initially posed as Watson, but stepped aside after being thoroughly ignored by Holmes.

Alan Bradley and William Sarjeant, on the other hand, see a woman's hand throughout the Canon. In an interesting twist, they argue that it was Holmes, not Watson, who was the woman. In their *Ms. Holmes of Baker Street: The Truth about Sherlock* (1989), they compile Canonical statements by Holmes himself to prove their point. A few proffered quotes will suffice.

> "Let me see—what are my other shortcomings. I get in the dumps at times, and don't open my mouth for days on end. You must not think I am sulky when I do that. Just let me alone, and I'll soon be right."—*A Study in Scarlet*

> "You know my methods in such cases, Watson. I put myself in the man's place"—*The Musgrave Ritual*

> "I trust that age does not wither, nor custom stale, my infinite variety."—*The Empty House*

> "Three days of absolute fast does not improve one's beauty, Watson."—*The Dying Detective*

> "Put on your hat, Watson."—*The Second Stain*

The last of those quotes may not, at first blush, seem particularly apt, but Bradley and Sarjeant cleverly make it so. "What man ever orders another to put on his hat," they ask, "and what wife ever fails to do so?"

Bradley and Sarjeant rely also on Dr. Watson to make their case for them. According to Watson, Holmes had an "extraordinary delicacy of touch," "curious gifts of instinct," and an "almost hypnotic power of soothing." Holmes furthermore "had a cat-like love of personal cleanliness," "an abnormally acute set of senses," and he "affected a certain quiet primness of dress." Perhaps most curiously, Holmes spoke in a "high, somewhat strident voice."

Constrained as they were by their playful premise that Holmes and Watson were living and breathing individuals, Stout, Steel, Bradley, and Sarjeant failed to recognize the significance of their observations. In their playfulness, they raised important questions that we herein investigate. Who was this person whose *nom de plume* was Doctor Watson? Where did she come from? What was she like? Why did she do it?

D. Martin Dakin

The consensus has long been that the early Holmes adventures are excellent, that the later tales pale in comparison. In his book, *Arthur Conan Doyle* (1985), Don Richard Cox attributes the obvious decline of the last two anthologies to Arthur's weariness.

> It should be clear to anyone who reads *The Case Book of Sherlock Holmes* and *His Last Bow* that the volumes are much weaker than those preceding them. [...] When one looks at [...] how much effort the man expended in his energetic life one cannot complain about the decline of these later Holmes adventures. Doyle wrote four novels and fifty-six stories to satisfy a public constantly demanding more Holmes. Even though he himself tried to end the series twice, he was also persuaded twice to renew the episodes of the characters for whom he no longer had a great deal of interest. One should therefore not be

surprised by the gradual decline in the Holmes cycle,
but rather marvel at the fact that Doyle could sustain
its quality so successfully for the forty years he wrote
the adventures.

Sherlockian scholar D. Martin Dakin, in his *Sherlock Holmes
Commentary* (1972), goes further. Much further. In the chapter
entitled "The Problem of the Case Book," Dakin makes obvious his
suspicions about the authorship of the last collection of Holmes
adventures. "This, the last series of Holmesian adventures," he
writes, "demands a general consideration [...] since serious
questions both of authorship and authenticity arise." He declares two
adventures, *The Blanched Soldier* and *The Lion's Mane* (both 1926),
to be "pseudonymous stories" and "pure inventions." He declares
another, *The Mazarin Stone* (1921), to be "spurious." He holds one
story in particular, *The Three Gables* (1926) in such low regard that
he paints it with all three of these insults, declaring, "Never has a
feebler story insulted the memory of the great detective."

Dakin argues that nine of the twelve stories in *The Case Book*
may have been written by someone other than the person who
wrote the early stories. He stops shy of naming names, declaring
such an undertaking "a mystery worthy of Holmes himself."

To be clear, Dakin wrote his book as a Sherlockian scholar
playing a long-accepted game. The game presumes that Holmes and
Watson were flesh-and-blood individuals, that Watson wrote the
adventures (at least most of them), and that Arthur Conan Doyle was
no more than Watson's literary agent. Dakin's observations about
authorship are nonetheless interesting, regardless of whom the
different authors might be.

In 1994, Oxford University Press published and annotated the
entire Sherlock Holmes Canon in nine volumes: one volume for each
of the four novels, and one volume for each of the five anthologies.
The last of those volumes, the one dealing with the dreaded *Case
Book*, was introduced by literary scholar and critic W.W. Robson.
Somewhat reluctantly, Robson picked up the gauntlet thrown down
twenty-two years earlier by Dakin.

But it is not possible to go any further without confronting what D. Martin Dakin calls 'The Problem with the Case-Book." Bluntly, it has been held that not only are some of these stories inferior in quality, but they are not the genuine work of Doyle.

Robson concedes "there are circumstances which make the suggestion of pseudonymity plausible", and he proposes a means of resolving the issue:

> We may wonder what would be the result of stylometric analysis of the Holmes stories, the kind of treatment that has been given to the Platonic Dialogues, the plays of Shakespeare, or the Epistles of St. Paul. Even without this (and we must remember that such analyses are disputed and controversial) it is hard to believe that any careful reader of the Case-Book would be prepared to testify that they all came from the pen of Conan Doyle.

Sherlockians are naturally reluctant to accept any challenge to the integrity of the Canon. Walter Pond, for example, responded to Dakin with his essay "A Plea for Respect for the Canon."

> All Sherlockian scholarship must be based on the thesis that [...] the stories which the Canon comprises are reports of the great detective's cases written by Dr. Watson, and that Sir Arthur Conan Doyle was Dr. Watson's literary agent. Once this thesis is abandoned, the foundation of Canonical research is undermined and Sherlockians will find themselves adrift on uncharted seas.
>
> For this reason, it is deeply disturbing that some commentators have arrogated to themselves the right to determine [...] which of the stories are genuine and which are not [...] The conclusion would be inevitable that Sir Arthur [...] participated in a

fraud when he placed the stories for publication. This, of course, is unthinkable.

In this volume, we explore the unthinkable.

Martin Gardner

Martin Gardner was, in the view of many, an exemplar of twentieth-century skepticism, hypercritical of all manner of bunk, claptrap, and pseudoscience. He wrote a multitude of books on mathematics, science, literature, philosophy, religion, and stage magic. He was a fan of Sherlock Holmes but disapproved of Arthur's descent into spiritualism. He therefore edited T.S. Eliot's observation about Arthur and Sherlock to create a juicy epigraph for his essay "The Irrelevance of Conan Doyle," found in his 1981 collection *Science: Good, Bad, and Bogus*: "What has that eminent Spiritualist ... to do with Sherlock Holmes?" The ellipses are in the original. It is an eye-catching, but unscholarly, introduction to what is otherwise a fascinating work.

Gardner's basic argument is that Arthur was simply too gullible to have created a character as rational and scientifically minded as Sherlock Holmes.

> Like the scientist trying to solve a mystery of nature, Holmes first gathered all the evidence he could that was relevant to the problem. At times he performed experiments to obtain fresh data. He then surveyed the total evidence in light of his vast knowledge of crime, and of sciences relevant to crime, to arrive at the most probable hypothesis. Deductions were made from the hypothesis; then the theory was further tested against new evidence, revised if need be, until finally the truth emerged with a probability close to certainty. [...] Nothing could be more remote from the mind-set of [Doyle]. Doyle spent the last twelve years of his life in a tireless crusade against science and rationality. It is a period usually glossed over quickly in biographies of Doyle, but, in view of today's explosion of interest in spiritualism and all things

occult, it is good to review it as an object lesson. Above all, it provides overwhelming evidence that Doyle had almost nothing to do with either Holmes or Watson. [...] There is scarcely a page in any of Doyle's books on the occult that does not reveal him to be the antithesis of Holmes. His gullibility was boundless. His comprehension of what constitutes scientific evidence was on a level with that of members of London's flat-earth society.

Gardner provided no examples of Arthur's credulity, but such examples are not difficult to find. In *The History of Spiritualism* (1926), for example, Arthur discusses the astounding power of ectoplasm and its importance to spiritualism. Spiritualism is the belief that those of us remaining on earth can communicate with our forebears who have passed into the spirit world, but can do so only through an especially gifted person called a medium. Ectoplasm is the material through which the spirits make themselves visible to us. In spiritualism's Victorian heyday, the best mediums exuded ectoplasm, hence spirits, from their "natural orifices." Of ectoplasm, Arthur wrote:

> The substance itself emanates from the whole body of the medium, but especially from the natural orifices and the extremities, from the top of the head, from the breasts, and the tips of the fingers. [...] The substance occurs in various forms, sometimes as ductile dough, sometimes as a true protoplasmic mass, sometimes in the form of numerous thin threads, sometimes as cords of various thickness, or as a broad band, as a membrane, as a fabric, or as a woven material, with indefinite and irregular outlines.

Arthur believed that female mediums could exude "psychic rods" from whatever natural orifice they might have beneath a tabletop, and that these rods could become firm enough to lift the table. He described this titillating phenomenon in his *Edge of the Unknown* (1930).

> In the Belfast experiments this same ectoplasm was used for the making of rods or columns of power, which protruded from the body of the unconscious girl, and produced results such as raps, or the movement of objects, at a distance from her. Such a rod of power might be applied, with a sucker attachment, under a table and lift it up, causing the weight of the table to be added to that of the medium, exactly as if she had produced the effect by a steel bar working as a cantilever and attached to her body.

Most mediums were female. They were investigated by some of the most famous scientists of the time, virtually all of who were male. Given Victorian sensibilities, and given that ectoplasm was exuded from all the "natural orifices," this gender dichotomy might have posed a problem of propriety. Fortunately, the female mediums and the male investigators were willing, for the sake of research, to overcome all obstacles. If science demanded that the medium perform in the nude or take her investigator as a lover, so be it. If science demanded that Arthur fondle the ectoplasmic phallus of a female medium, how then could Arthur decline? He describes one such fondling in his *History of Spiritualism*.

> The author has frequently seen ectoplasm in its vaporous, but only once in its solid, form. That was a sitting with Eva C. under the charge of Madame Bisson. Upon that occasion this strange and variable substance appeared as a streak of material six inches long, not unlike a section of umbilical cord, embedded in the cloth of the dress in the region of the lower stomach. It was visible in good light, and the author was permitted to squeeze it between his fingers, when it gave the impression of a living substance, thrilling and shrinking under his touch.

There was no possibility of deception on this occasion.

It is difficult to imagine Sherlock Holmes agreeing to participate in such a performance, much less failing to recognize the charade for what it was.

Another example of Arthur's gullibility comes from his *Wanderings of a Spiritualist* (1921), a book about his speaking tour of Australia and New Zealand. He learned of a particular fox terrier that had "a power of thought comparable, not merely to a human being, but even [...] to a clairvoyant." The dog had, allegedly, often demonstrated his remarkable ability by barking out the number of coins in a person's pocket. When Arthur put the dog to the test, it began barking but would not stop. Arthur nonetheless expressed confidence in the dog's supernatural abilities, attributing its poor performance to age and excitement. He concluded his anecdote with the distinctly non-Sherlockian musing: "One wonders how many other dogs have human brains without the humans being clever enough to detect it."

Though Gardner was correct about Arthur's extreme credulity, and though Gardner promoted rational thought over wishful thinking, his argument that Arthur could not have created Sherlock Holmes is terribly flawed. Gardner recognized that Arthur's focus on spiritualism occurred late in life, well after the creation of Sherlock Holmes, yet he failed to address the possibility that Arthur simply changed during the intervening years. To the contrary, Gardner himself made a case that creative people can and do undergo such life-altering transformations. In the same essay in which he declared Arthur irrelevant, Gardner explained that several notable British scientists, including Oliver Lodge and William Crookes, were also caught up in the spiritualism craze, yet he did not deny either of them their youthful scientific accomplishments. In a statement against interest, Gardner carelessly began his essay with a seemingly prescient quote from Sherlock Holmes: "There are some trees, Watson, which grow to a certain height and then suddenly develop some unsightly eccentricity. You will see it often in humans."

Though Gardner's basic argument is flawed, his conclusion is spot on.

> It was not, I think, Doyle who made this pair immortal. It was the other way around. Holmes and Watson, intent on guarding their privacy, permitted Sir Arthur Conan Doyle to take credit for inventing them. In doing so, they conferred upon him that earthly immortality that his authentic but undistinguished writings could never have provided.

Martin Gardner is the only person so far to have loudly and unequivocally claimed that Arthur Conan Doyle did not create Sherlock Holmes, but because no one pursued the evidence to its logical conclusion, the case has gone cold. It is now time to apply some heat.

Chapter 2
Corpus Delicti

Corpus delicti, Latin for "body of offence," is the principle of jurisprudence dictating that a crime must have occurred before anyone can be charged with committing it. No one, for example, should be charged with larceny unless an investigation has established that property has actually been stolen.

Almost universally, the public accepts without question that Arthur Conan Doyle authored each of the sixty adventures in the Sherlock Holmes Canon. D. Martin Dakin expressed concerns about the relative quality of the later stories; Rex Stout argued that a woman wrote the stories; Martin Gardner took issue with Arthur's gullibility. None of them, however, offered evidence sufficiently substantive to support a charge of literary fraud. None of them identified a corpus delicti.

Here we shall.

The Three Gables

It is not particularly surprising that Dakin, Cox, and others are troubled by *The Case-Book of Sherlock Holmes* (1927). Not only are all the tales in that final Holmes anthology of low quality, one of them, *The Three Gables*, is overtly racist. Dakin derided Holmes's behavior in that story.

> But the falsest note of all is struck in his cheap gibes at the Negro Steve Dixie. No admirer of Holmes can read these scenes without a blush. For Holmes was a gentleman; and one thing no gentleman does is taunt another man for his racial characteristics.

On the same subject, Cox was even blunter:

> Holmes's venomous remarks about Steve Dixie, the black prizefighter, are viciously racist and very untypical of a man who has usually displayed compassion and concern for humanity. There is not only no justification for Holmes's comments, there is

no real good explanation for them either. These kinds
of racial slurs do not occur anywhere else in Doyle's
writing; it is not at all clear how they found their way
into the mouth of a character as sophisticated and
honorable as Sherlock Holmes.

In the opening scene of *The Three Gables*, a large, menacing black
man bursts into 221B Baker Street and threatens Holmes with a
beating should Holmes involve himself in the Harrow case. Watson
describes the intruder as a savage with a broad face, flattened nose,
dark eyes, and a huge knotted lump of a fist, which he places under
Holmes's nose. "Were you born so?" asks Holmes, "Or did it come by
degrees?"

Throughout the scene, Holmes treats the intruder with the same
dismissive, insulting air. One exchange epitomizes the unsettling
writing:

> "I won't ask you to sit down, for I don't like the smell
> of you, but aren't you Steve Dixie, the bruiser?"
> "That's my name, Masser Holmes, and you'll get
> put through it for sure if you give me any lip."
> "It is certainly the last thing you need," said
> Holmes, staring at our visitor's hideous mouth.

Holmes then turns the tables on Dixie by threatening to tie him
to an unsolved murder, at which point the pugilist turns submissive
and even agrees to assist Holmes in future investigations. After
Dixie's obsequious exit, Holmes says, "I am glad you were not forced
to break his wooly head, Watson."

Such overt racism is not to be found anywhere in the early
Holmes adventures. To the contrary, one early adventure takes a
bold stand in support of interracial marriage. For those who believe
that Arthur wrote each and every one the Holmes tales, the contrast
is simply inexplicable. For those willing to entertain the notion that
Arthur did not write every story, the contrast is enlightening.

In *The Yellow Face* (1893), Grant Munro is a financially successful
shop merchant who lives in the countryside with his wife, Effie. He
seeks out Holmes to solve a mystery surrounding her. He has several

times witnessed a strange yellow face staring at him from an upstairs window of a nearby, recently rented cottage. The yellow face began appearing not long after he had agreed to a request by Effie for a large sum of money, no questions to be asked. Since that agreement, she has been sneaking off to visit the cottage. When he confronts her, she begs him not to pursue the issue, for their lives are at stake.

Holmes suspects that Effie's first husband is living in the cottage and blackmailing her. In Munro's company, Holmes and Watson force their way into the cottage. Rather than finding a blackmailing ex-husband, they discover a young black girl wearing a yellow mask.

> "My God!" [Grant Munro] cried, "what can be the meaning of this?"
>
> "I will tell you the meaning of it," cried [Effie Munro], sweeping into the room with a proud set face. "You have forced me against my own judgment to tell you, and now we must both make the best of it. My husband died at Atlanta. My child survived."
>
> "Your child!"
>
> She drew a large silver locket from her bosom. "You have never seen this open."
>
> "I understood that it did not open."
>
> She touched a spring, and the front hinged back. There was a portrait within of a man, strikingly handsome and intelligent, but bearing unmistakable signs upon his features of African descent.
>
> "This is John Hebron, of Atlanta," said the lady, "and a nobler man never walked the earth. I cut myself off from my race in order to wed him; but never once while he lived did I for one instant regret it. It was our misfortune that our only child took after his people rather than mine. It is often so in such matches, and little Lucy is darker far than ever her father was. But, dark or fair, she is my own dear little girlie, and her mother's pet."

We will forgive Effie's misunderstanding of inherited genetic characteristics, and make our way quickly through her too-lengthy monologue. She left her little girl in America, in the care of a Scotswoman, because the little girl's health precluded travel, never for a moment intending to abandon her. She met Grant Munro, fell in love with him, and accepted his proposal of marriage. She failed to mention her previous marriage, or her daughter, because she feared her new husband might leave her. She schemed to have the Scotswoman bring her daughter to England, and to set up house nearby. To prevent suspicion, she had her little girl wear a mask whenever looking out the window. Even she realized it was a stupid thing to do.

> "If I had been less cautious I might have been more wise, but I was half crazy with fear lest you should learn the truth. [...] And now to-night you at last know all, and I ask you what is to become of us, my child and me?" She clasped her hands and waited for an answer.
>
> It was two long minutes before Grant Munro broke the silence, and when his answer came it was one of which I love to think. He lifted the little child, kissed her, and then, still carrying her, he held his other hand out to his wife, and turned towards the door.
>
> "We can talk it over more comfortably at home," said he. "I am not a very good man, Effie, but I think that I am a better one than you have given me credit for being."

Grant Munro carrying his new child

Sherlockians rate *The Yellow Face* as one of the most disappointing adventures in the Canon. Cox, for example, disparages Holmes's efforts as no more creative than that of a lowly Scotland Yard detective.

> The case is nevertheless one of the least satisfying [...] because the case is "solved" largely through strong-arm tactics. Holmes has a theory (which he quite uncharacteristically reveals to Watson *before* he knows it is valid), but he is wrong. In the end, Holmes and Watson, and Munro simply force their way into the cottage; even Lestrade could have done that.

Rather than writing a top-notch detective story, the author seemed more interested in using Holmes's popularity to advance a case for interracial marriage, perhaps even to chastise Americans for their country's anti-miscegenation laws. American publishers could hardly withhold a Sherlock Holmes story from their eager readers, but they could attempt to mitigate Grant Munro's acceptance of the black child into his family. In the British editions, Munro thinks for "two long minutes" before accepting the child. In the American editions, Munro needs "ten long minutes."

The open-mindedness of *The Yellow Face* is a century ahead of its Victorian time. Its author willfully and knowingly injected an inflammatory social issue—interracial relations—into a Sherlock Holmes story, sacrificing the quality of the story to the point to be made. Rather than diminish and denigrate a character because of that person's race, the author challenged readers, who might be troubled by thoughts of interracial marriage, by establishing the progressive views of Grant and Effie Munro as the morally superior ones.

Such a public display of support for interracial marriage is, by itself, quite remarkable. The author, however, did not stop there. *The Yellow Face* argues not simply that all races should be *treated* as equal, but instead that all races *are* equal. Watson's description of the portrait of John Hebron is particularly telling: the author perceived people of African descent to be just as "handsome and intelligent" as people of European descent. The author was not just a humanitarian, but also an egalitarian to boot.

The Yellow Face is an extraordinary story by an extraordinary person. It cannot possibly share the same author as *The Three Gables*. Though both stories are part of the Canon, they force a conclusion that Arthur must have put his name to at least one Sherlock Holmes adventure that he did not write. *The Yellow Face* and *The Three Gables*, taken together, constitute the corpus delicti for at least one case of literary fraud.

Wisteria Lodge

The Three Gables is not the only late Holmes adventure to include racial slurs. *Wisteria Lodge* (1903) is also tainted by two of its passages. In the first of them, the author introduced multiple bizarre objects that serve both to heighten the horror and to lead the reader astray. One of those incidental objects is a desiccated creature made indistinguishable, by the author, as either a monkey or a black infant.

> He held up his candle before an extraordinary object which stood at the back of the dresser. It was so wrinkled and shrunken and withered that it was difficult to say what it might have been. One could but

say that it was black and leathery, and that it bore some resemblance to a dwarfish human figure. At first, as I examined it, I thought that it was a mummified negro baby, and then it seemed a very twisted and ancient monkey.

In the second of the passages, the author employed a racially charged word to describe a minor character. The usage is gratuitous, since the character has nothing to do with the crime. Just as the author introduced an indistinguishable "dwarfish human figure" to lead the reader astray, we are later introduced to a grotesque racist stereotype for the same purpose.

[T]he cook, from the evidence of one or two tradespeople who have caught a glimpse of him through the window, was a man of most remarkable appearance—being a huge and hideous mulatto, with yellowish features of a pronounced negroid type [...] and was captured last night after a struggle, in which Constable Downing was badly bitten by the savage.

The Arthur Twidle image accompanying the story depicts a monstrous ape-like creature.

The "hideous mulatto" from *Wisteria Lodge*

In his *New Annotated Sherlock Holmes* (2004), Leslie S. Klinger provides background and context for the term *mulatto*.

> In the strictest terms, a mulatto was said to be the child of one black parent and one white parent. Reflecting the racial climate of the day, there were further terms that specified one's mixed lineage to an even greater degree: a "quadroon" (one-quarter black) was a child of a mulatto and a white, while an "octoroon" (one-eighth black) was the child of a quadroon and a white. The child of an octoroon and a white was finally considered to be white, according to Brewer's *Dictionary of Phrase and Fable,* whose listing of "Negro Offspring" tellingly only presents situations in which a white man would mate with a "negro" or mixed-race woman. The word "mulatto" was derived from the Portuguese diminutive of *mulo,* or mule, the crossbred offspring of a male donkey and female horse.

A mule is not the result of an interracial union. A donkey and a horse are not simply different races within a common species. They have different numbers of chromosomes; they are entirely different species. A mule is therefore a genetic hybrid, an animal that is not quite a horse and not quite a donkey.

The interspecies connotation of *mulatto* makes the term even more loathsome. It recalls one of the most heated racial debates of the nineteenth century: polygenism versus monogenism. The monogenists argued that the Bible reveals all people to be of one blood, each and every one descended from Adam and Eve. The polygenists, on the other hand, argued that the Bible relates only the story of Caucasians, that God created all other races separately. Some polygenists extended their argument so far as to declare that the different peoples constitute different species. Any child of a mixed marriage would therefore represent a hybrid species; it would be a mulatto.

The author of *The Yellow Face* chose to describe John Hebron as black man of African descent, anticipating, by a century, today's social conventions. *Wisteria Lodge*, we can safely assume, was authored by the same person who wrote *The Three Gables*.

Arthur's Racism

Given Arthur's long-ignored racist attitudes, he may be the person who authored *The Three Gables* and *Wisteria Lodge*, but he could not have penned *The Yellow Face*. Cox was simply incorrect when he wrote, "There is not only no justification for Holmes's comments, there is no real good explanation for them either. These kinds of racial slurs do not occur anywhere else in Doyle's writing."

Arthur's public and private writings are littered with gratuitous racial epithets. Arthur had no qualms, for instance, about peppering his writing with the even-then odious term *nigger*. That word appears in at least fourteen of his works, beginning no later than 1879, when he was twenty years old, with the short story "The Mystery of Sasassa Valley." His usage continued throughout his life, the last recorded instance was at age sixty-eight, when he used the word in his novel *The Maracot Deep*.

Arthur's most disturbing published work is an 1882 piece he wrote for the *British Journal of Photography*. "On the Slave Coast with a Camera" tells of his 1881 journey along the west coast of Africa, as ship's surgeon aboard the *S. S. Mayumba*. That article is filthy with racial slurs, just three examples of which follow.

> I had a beatific vision of strange negatives. The luxuriant growth of the African forest; the haughty grace of the untamed savage as he trod his native wilderness, or yearned in his simple untutored way for a slice of the calf of your leg.

> A great deal has been said about the regeneration of our black brothers and the latent virtues of the swarthy races. My own experience is that you abhor them on first meeting them, and gradually learn to dislike them a very great deal more as you become better acquainted with them.

> I had a great desire to "astonish the natives" by representations of their own hideous faces.

Within private correspondence, Arthur was even less restrained. In a letter sent from Africa to family friend Charlotte Thwaites Drummond, he wrote, "Here we are steaming from one dirty little port to another dirty little port, all as like as two peas, and only to be distinguished by comparing the smell of the inhabitants, though they all smell as if they had become prematurely putrid and should be buried without necessary delay."

Arthur was apparently so pleased by the supposed cleverness of the last sentiment that he incorporated it into "On the Slave Coast with a Camera."

> I had the privilege, while at Duke Town, of taking the portrait of a native prince. His highness did me the honor of informing me that it was wonderfully unlike him. The delight of his retinue, however, at seeing the ugliness of their lord so faithfully represented more

than assuaged my wounded photographic feelings. It was an excellent likeness; but the monarch probably missed the smell of premature putridity which was so characteristic of the original, and yet could not be transferred to paper.

Arthur's sense of racial superiority was hardly limited to blacks; even his own brother-in-law, writer Ernest William Hornung, did not measure up to Arthur's racial purity standard. Hornung and his mother were born in England, but his father had emigrated there from Hungary. When attending one of Arthur's cricket matches, Hornung met Jean Leckie, a young woman who seemed to take a particular interest in Arthur. Louise, Arthur's wife, was not in attendance but at home, slowly wasting away from tuberculosis. Hornung realized not only that Jean and Arthur were acting unseemly by appearing in public together, but that the two were having an affair. He refused to accept Arthur's rationalization that the relationship was platonic. Arthur seethed over the exchange in correspondence with his mother, who attempted to calm him. In reply to her soothing words, he wrote:

> But to tell me not to feel hurt is, with all respect to you, Mammie, simple nonsense. I do and must feel hurt. And I don't feel better by contemplating the fact that William is half Mongol half Slav, or whatever the mixture is.

In his 1924 autobiography *Memories and Adventures*, Arthur delves further into his time aboard the *Mayumba*. In the chapter entitled "The Voyage to West Africa," he reveals that he met Henry Highland Garnet, the famous abolitionist and U.S. Minister to Liberia. Though failing to mention Garnet by name, Arthur speaks surprisingly well of him. "The most intelligent and well-read man whom I met on the Coast was a negro, the American Consul at Monrovia," he wrote. "This negro gentleman did me good, for a man's brain is an organ for the formation of his own thoughts and also for the digestion of other people's and it needs fresh fodder."

Unfortunately, despite Arthur's claim to the contrary, meeting Henry Highland Garnet did him no good whatsoever, at least in terms of understanding his fellow man. It was not long after the meeting that Arthur wrote his unenlightened article for the *British Journal of Photography*. Nor did Arthur learn much in the many years between the publication of that racist article and his autobiography. In the very chapter just referenced, the one in which Arthur romanticized meeting with Henry Highland Garnet, Arthur reported, "At some small village, the name of which I have forgotten, there came off a tall young Welshman in a state of furious excitement; his niggers had mutinied and he was in fear of his life."

In the final year of his life, Arthur's racism intersected with his belief in the paranormal. *The Edge of the Unknown* includes his theory on how heavy lead coffins in a West Indian vault moved about, seemingly by supernatural means.

> [A]ll psychic phenomenon seem to show that the disembodied have no power of their own, but that it is always derived from the emanations of the living, which we call animal magnetism or other names. Now this vault with its absolutely air-tight walls was particularly adapted for holding in such forces [...] To bring in these weighty leaden coffins the space must have been crowded with over-heated Negroes, and when the slab was at once hermetically sealed, these effluvia were enclosed and remained behind, furnishing a possible source of that material power which is needful for material effects.

Arthur's private and public writings reveal that he was appalled even by the thought of kissing a black person. In a letter to another family friend, Amy Hoare, Arthur described the passengers aboard the *Mayumba*, saving his description of the two African passengers for last.

> Our other passengers are a negro Wills (the doctor was quite right, he is rolling in money—he is an unmitigated cad though, fancy pressing a lady to take

a toothpick after dinner)—and a brute of a negress, bearing the aristocratic old name of Smith, a vile dirty woman. She is to marry a black missionary when she gets out if I don't poison her first—fancy anyone kissing those thick cracked purple lips—ugh!

In his 1929 book, *Our African Winter*, Arthur discussed the missionaries then operating in Africa. Since he was there to promote spiritualism as the only religion that could save mankind, he was not particularly complimentary of missionaries of more traditional faith.

The worst, however, appeared to be the American Missions with their four-square evangelical dogmas and their hobnobbing with the blacks. One apparently trustworthy witness told me how he had seen a female missioner (non-British), of not too mature an age, kiss all the black adult boys who had assembled upon the platform to meet her train. The witness said that the sight made him physically sick, and certainly from the expression of his face I thought that a mere memory of it was about to have the same effect.

Arthur's scorn toward anyone who might associate with "the blacks," let alone kiss them, makes a simple matter of determining which of the conflicting Sherlock Holmes stories Arthur may have written. The author of *The Yellow Face* recognized people of African descent as handsome and intelligent; Arthur saw them as "hideous," "primitive," and in need of "regeneration." The author of *The Yellow Face* believed in interracial marriage; Arthur was repulsed at the thought of kissing a black woman. Plainly, Arthur could not have written *The Yellow Face*, though he put his name to the story.

A Beautiful Mind

The Congo Free State (1884-1908) was anything but free and anything but a state. From 1884 until 1908 it was a large area of Central Africa privately controlled by Belgium's King Leopold II. Leopold, a self-proclaimed humanitarian and philanthropist, was considerably more interested in the region's ivory, rubber, and minerals than in the well-being of its native population, which he saw as but a disposable means to a lucrative end. Somewhere between 15% and 40% of the population succumbed to Leopold's humanity.

One notable individual to speak against the atrocities of Leopold's reign was Arthur Conan Doyle, who wrote and had published, in 1909, a long pamphlet entitled *The Crime of the Congo*. Therein he made a passionate and compelling case for international intervention. As a frontispiece to this publication, he used a montage of nine Congolese, each missing a hand. Such mutilation was one of the punishments for failing to meet a rubber-collection quota.

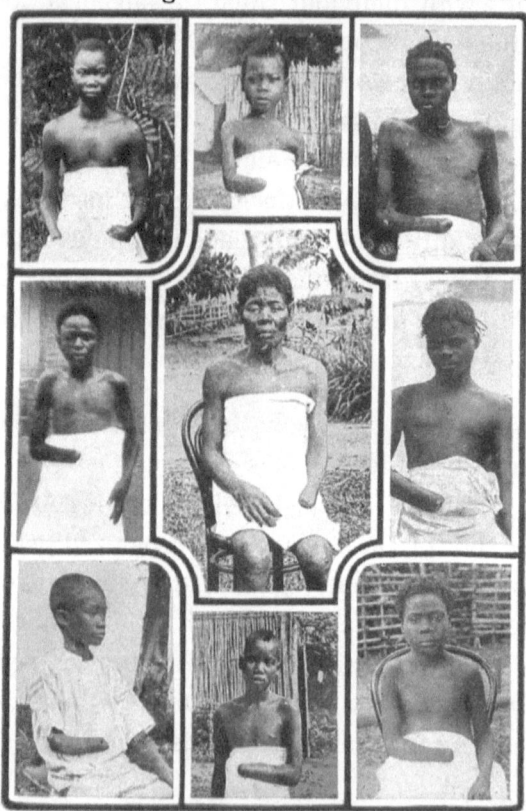

Frontispiece to *Crime of the Congo*

Arthur has been properly credited for his efforts to put an end to the atrocities in the Congo. With respect to issues of race, he was as enlightened as most other European males of his time. Though he did not consider people of other races to be his equal, he was appalled by the cruelty too often inflicted upon them. By the standards of his day, he may have been considered a humanitarian. By any standard, though, he was no egalitarian.

In *Our African Winter*, regarding the poorly clothed blacks, he observed:

> I do not know why these men should wear more than a loin-cloth. It seems an offence against nature to turn the dark, clean-cut Adonis into the poor shambling scarecrow with tattered overcoat and shabby peaked cap. [...] Personally I am not in favour of educating them, though they educate very easily. What is the use of educating people when there is really no room for the educated? Does it not breed discontent and thwarted ambition where there was apathy if not content before? It seems to be a cruel thing to do.

He revealed his tolerance for occasional whippings of black prisoners.

> I was allowed to go over and see the prisoners. Mr. Noah had certainly some curious animals in his ark. There were no whites or Indians—all were negroes. [...] And yet they were well treated [...] There is very little punishment—only four floggings last year. The intelligent men were being taught trades and I saw articles of furniture made by them. The Missions might perhaps learn something from this method of taming the savage.

Arthur's qualified humanitarianism is, for the most part, the best that we can expect from our favored historical figures. Thomas Jefferson, for example, kept slaves both before and after introducing the phrase "all men are created equal". In Query XIV of his *Notes on the State of Virginia* (1785), he reveals conflicting emotions about emancipating the slaves, but is unambiguous regarding their beauty and intelligence.

> The first difference which strikes us is that of colour. [...] And is this difference of no importance? Is it not the foundation of a greater or less share of beauty in the two races? [...]
>
> Comparing them by their faculties of memory, reason, and imagination, it appears to me, that in memory they are equal to the whites; in reason much inferior, as I think one could scarcely be found capable of tracing and comprehending the investigations of Euclid; and that in imagination they are dull, tasteless, and anomalous. [...]
>
> I advance it therefore as a suspicion only, that the blacks, whether originally a distinct race, or made distinct by time and circumstances, are inferior to the whites in the endowments both of body and mind. [...] This unfortunate difference of colour, and perhaps of faculty, is a powerful obstacle to the emancipation of these people.

Abraham Lincoln, before freeing the slaves, publicly declared their inequality. In the fourth Lincoln-Douglas debate, he made his case forcefully and unequivocally.

> I will say, then, that I am not nor have ever been in favor of bringing about in any way the social and political equality of the black and white races—that I am not, nor ever have been, in favor of making voters or jurors of negroes, nor of qualifying them to hold office, nor to intermarry with white people; and I will say in addition to this that there is a physical difference between the White and black races which will ever forbid the two races living together on terms of social and political equality. And inasmuch as they cannot so live, while they do remain together, there must be the position of superior and inferior,

and I, as much as any other man, am in favor of having the superior position assigned to the White race.

Stephen Jay Gould, that egalitarian Harvard professor of natural history, wrestled with the flawed-hero problem of Charles Darwin. To Gould's discomfort, Darwin made clear in *The Descent of Man* (1871) and elsewhere that he believed blacks to be an inferior race.

> At some future period, not very distant as measured by centuries, the civilised races of man will almost certainly exterminate and replace throughout the world the savage races. [...] The break will then be rendered wider [...] between man in a more civilised state [...] and some ape as low as a baboon, instead of as at present between the negro or Australian and the gorilla.

In his essay "The Moral State of Tahiti—and of Darwin," which appears in *Eight Little Piggies* (1993), Gould addresses how we might accept the shortcomings of our heroes.

> How can we castigate someone for repeating a standard assumption of his age, however much we may legitimately deplore that attitude today? Belief in racial and sexual inequality was unquestioned and canonical among upper-class Victorian males— probably about as controversial as the Pythagorean theorem. [...] I see no purpose in strong criticism for a largely passive acceptance of common wisdom. Let us rather analyze why such potent and evil nonsense then passed for certain knowledge.
>
> If I choose to impose individual blame for all past social ills, there will be no one left to like [...] Though I hold no shred of sympathy for active persecutors, I cannot excoriate individuals who acquiesced passively in a standard societal judgment. Rail

instead against the judgment, and try to understand what motivates men of decent will.

Gould contrasts Darwin's shortcomings with Darwin's humanism, shown here in Darwin's *Voyage of the Beagle* (1839)

> On the 19th of August we finally left the shores of Brazil. I thank God, I shall never again visit a slave-country. To this day, if I hear a distant scream, it recalls with painful vividness my feelings, when passing a house near Pernambuco, I heard the most pitiable moans, and could not but suspect that some poor slave was being tortured, yet knew that I was as powerless as a child even to remonstrate. I suspected that these moans were from a tortured slave, for I was told that this was the case in another instance. Near Rio de Janeiro I lived opposite to an old lady, who kept screws to crush the fingers of her female slaves.

Lydia Maria Child presented an image and description of such thumbscrews in her 1836 work, *An Appeal in Favor of that Class of Americans Called Africans*.

> The thumbs are put into two round holes at the top; by turning a key a bar rises from C to D by means of a screw; and the pressure becomes very painful. By turning it further, the blood is made to start; and by taking away the key, as at E, the tortured person is left in agony, without the means of helping himself, or being helped by others.

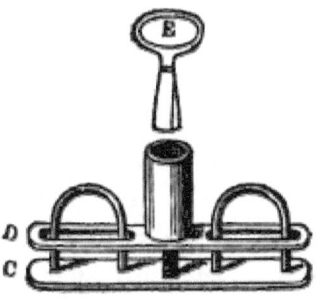

Patented thumbscrew

An honest belief in the equality of all mankind carries with it a tremendous burden. Not only are we brothers and sisters across race, we are siblings across time. We must acknowledge that, given similar circumstances, we would have behaved just as did our forebears. The most we can hope for is that we would not have been among the subjugated, that we would instead have been among the few who campaigned against the maltreatment of our fellow humans. Only with an inflated sense of moral superiority can we possibly imagine ourselves somehow seeing more clearly than a Thomas Jefferson or an Abraham Lincoln.

We therefore examine Arthur's racist attitudes not to denigrate him, but to differentiate him from the person who wrote *The Yellow Face*. That unidentified author saw much further than could Doyle, Darwin, Jefferson and even Lincoln, looking forward to a day when men and women of different color would marry, when they would raise their children as fully fledged humans, rather than as mulattos. She conceived a man such as John Watson, and a man such as John Munro, who would be hurt by any suggestion that he might love his wife's mixed-race child less than his own.

If Arthur could not have written such an enlightened tale, who did?

Chapter 3
The Usual Suspect

In the 1942 movie *Casablanca*, police captain and Nazi collaborator Louis Renault is the only person to witness Rick Blaine shoot and kill the villainous Major Heinrich Strasser. The tension builds as Captain Renault's officers appear on the scene. "Major Strasser has been shot," he tells them. After sharing furtive glances with Rick, he adds: "Round up the usual suspects."

There is only one usual suspect in this case of the shadowy author, and that is Arthur Conan Doyle. His name appears on every byline and title page in the Sherlock Holmes Canon, and it is unsurprising that nearly everyone takes his authorship as an obvious fact. Holmes observes, however, that "there is nothing more deceptive than an obvious fact."

The case for Arthur's authorship of each and every Holmes adventure is already burdened by contrasts between an early adventure, *The Yellow Face*, and two later adventures, *The Three Gables* and *Wisteria Lodge*. Arthur's authorship of any story, however, Holmesian or otherwise, should be questioned in light of his tendency to prevaricate and his willingness to claim credit for the work of others.

The Pestilent Quack

The earliest of Arthur's known fraudulent writings may be his "pestilent quack" letter of 1879. While still a medical student, Arthur served as an assistant to Dr. Reginald Ratcliff Hoare of Birmingham. In a letter to his mother, Arthur boasted of lying about a neighboring doctor:

> There is a pestilent little quack here, or rather a firm, Smith and Hues. The latter is a qualified man but a sleeping partner. Smith is the perfect type of quack. I have written out a most preposterous case and sent it to the Lancet in Hues' name. It is told most gravely and scientifically. If the Doctor sees anything about an eel in the Lancet that is the letter. R R is in ecstasies about it.

The "R R" to whom Arthur refers is Reginald Ratcliff, Dr. Hoare himself. "The Doctor" to whom Arthur refers is Dr. Bryan Charles Waller, a family friend and patron. *The Lancet* is a highly regarded medical journal published still today. Its editors apparently did not find Arthur's letter to be written "most gravely and scientifically," despite Arthur's high praise for his own writing, since the journal declined to print it.

Arthur was a cocksure young man. Though he was only a medical student, an assistant in Birmingham for less than a month, he deemed the neighboring Dr. Smith to be a quack in need of comeuppance. Arthur decided to correct a perceived shortcoming by use of fraud and defamation. Without compunction, Arthur bragged of his deed to Dr. Hoare, who reportedly received the news in encouraging fashion. Arthur bragged also to his mother, and requested that she relay his act of dishonesty to their family patron. Given Arthur's lack of concern for any disapproval, we can presume that such behavior on his part was neither unexpected nor unrewarded.

Chugging Poison

Not long after his "pestilent quack" letter, Arthur submitted an article to the *British Medical Journal* describing his purported experimentation with gelsemium, a poisonous flowering shrub of North America and Asia. In its issue of 20 September 1879, the journal published Arthur's article, perhaps killing a patient or two in the process.

> Several years ago a persistent neuralgia led me to use the tincture of gelsemium to a considerable extent. I several times overstepped the maximum of the text-books without suffering any ill effects. Having recently had an opportunity of experimenting with a quantity of fresh tincture, I determined to ascertain how far one might go in taking the drug, and what the primary symptoms of an overdose might be.

Neuralgia is mild-to-excruciating nerve pain triggered by pressure as gentle as smiling, washing, or a breeze on the skin. It was sometimes treated with exceptionally small doses of gelsemium. As was then the practice, Arthur expressed his doses in minims, one of the smallest units of liquid measure. There are 80 minims in a U.S. teaspoon, 60 in a British teaspoon.

Arthur referred in his article to "a case described some time ago in which 75 minims proved fatal." Six years earlier, a different *Lancet* article attributed a death to 120 minims of gelsemium. A different letter to the *British Medical Journal* summarized twenty-five deaths from gelsemium poisoning, the smallest lethal dose of which was 60 minims. Clearly, anyone ingesting 60 minims of gelsemium would be risking his life.

Arthur claimed to have started his experimentation with 40 minims, incrementing that amount six times each day. This grew to 90 minims by day four, 150 minims by day five, and 200 minims by day seven. If Arthur had ingested six doses a day throughout the course of his experiment, as he claimed, he would have ingested forty-two doses by the end of day seven, any one of which might have been fatal. Each of the eighteen doses during the last three days of his experiment would have been at least twice the lethal dosage Arthur reported in his own article.

Far more suspicious is the total quantity of gelsemium that Arthur alleged he ingested. Assuming evenly increasing dosage increments between his specified breakpoints of 40, 90, 150, and 200 minims, Arthur must have ingested more than 4,400 minims over seven days. Such behavior would not be scientific; it would be suicidal.

History has not verified Arthur's hypothesis that humans can quickly develop a tolerance to gelsemium. There remains no established pharmacological basis for ingesting gelsemium as a treatment for neuralgia, or for any other affliction, as gelsemium is no longer included in U.S. or British pharmacopeias. Gelsemium is a deadly poison that should never be ingested in any quantity, for any reason.

Not only should the reported dosages have prompted skepticism before now, so should have the reported symptoms. Arthur reported giddiness on day four, severe headaches and diarrhea on day five, and severe depression on day seven. The diarrhea became "so persistent and prostrating" that he gave up his experiment. Arthur could not have known that, more than a century later, H.T. Fung and four colleagues would summarize the symptoms of 58 known cases of gelsemium poisoning. From their article, "Two cases of *Gelsemium elegans* Benth. poisoning," found in the October 2007 issue of *Hong Kong Journal of Emergency Medicine*. The symptoms, listed in order of their frequency, follow.

> Dizziness - 100% of the cases
> Limb weakness - 86%
> Nausea & vomiting - 67%
> Breathing difficulty - 48%
> Blurred vision - 47%
> Impaired consciousness - 21%
> Convulsion - 21%
> Renal dysfunction (kidney damage) - 17%
> Abdominal pain - 12%
> Mydriasis (dilated pupils) - 12%
> Hepatic dysfunction (liver damage) - 10%
> Bradycardia (slow heart rate) - 7%

Arthur's list and Fung's list of symptoms have no more than one symptom in common. While hepatic dysfunction occurred in only 10% of the cases studied by Fung, it could be consistent with Arthur's diarrhea.

Arthur's other symptoms (giddiness, headaches, and depression) are not among the thirteen symptoms reported by Fung. More telling still is Arthur's failure to report any of the symptoms most frequently reported by Fung. Arthur did not report being dizzy, though each and every one of the 58 people in Fung's survey did. Arthur did not report any weakness of limb, any vomiting, any difficulty breathing, blurred vision, impaired consciousness, or convulsion. Whatever gave Arthur a depressing case of the runs, it almost certainly was not gelsemium. Yet he managed to have printed, in a respected medical journal, false information about surviving large, lethal doses of gelsemium. By encouraging other doctors to experiment with gelsemium, or to prescribe it for their patients, he put lives on the line.

As will be found time and time again, it was risky then, and still is today, to take Arthur at his word.

Arctic Follies

After a year as Dr. Hoare's apprentice, Arthur signed on as ship's surgeon aboard the Arctic whaler *S.S. Hope*. He penned letters to his mother, kept a logbook, and wrote a ten-page magazine article about his experiences. The log was posthumously published as *Dangerous Work: Diary of an Arctic Adventure* (2012). The ten-page article appeared in the January 1897 edition of the *Strand Magazine*, as "Life on a Greenland Whaler." Arthur later used that article as Chapter IV of his autobiography, *Memories and Adventures*. All three sources provide purportedly truthful anecdotes that are sometimes conflicting, frequently suspicious, and occasionally absurd.

According to a log entry for 7 April, Arthur managed to fall into the Arctic Ocean five times in three days. Though any single dunking in Arctic waters can be quickly fatal, Arthur managed to survive all five without missing a beat. Based on a log entry of 5 April, the last of those alleged five occurred after killing a seal. He provided details for the *Strand* readers:

> I had a narrow escape once through stepping backwards over the edge of a piece of floating ice while I was engaged in skinning a seal. I had wandered away from the others, and no one saw my misfortune. The face of the ice was so even that I had no purchase by which to pull myself up, and my body was rapidly becoming numb in the freezing water. At last, however, I caught hold of the hind flipper of the dead seal, and there was a kind of nightmare tug-of-war, the question being whether I should pull the seal off or pull myself on. At last, however, I got my knee over the edge and rolled on to it. I remember that my clothes were as hard as a suit of armour by the time I

reached the ship, and that I had to thaw my crackling garments before I could change them.

It is a terrific story, particularly if true. It seems suspicious, though, that Arthur would have been allowed to wander off alone, particularly if he had already fallen into the freezing water four times in two days. Arthur, however, not only claimed to have separated himself from all other potential witnesses and rescuers, but to have done it so thoroughly that no one heard his calls for help. It is suspicious as well that he placed himself on a narrow ledge between the seal and the sea. That ledge could not have been wider than an arm's length, lest Arthur would have been unable to reach the flipper after so carelessly falling into the ocean for the fifth time in four days.

Arthur appears not only to have prevaricated in a magazine article and in his autobiography, but in his own log as well. Another entry, one for 31 March, provides a possible explanation as to why he might do such a thing. It reads, "I started a story 'Journey to the Pole,' which I intend to be good."

Arthur wasn't simply recording facts as they occurred; he was compiling material for a story that he intended to be good, by hook or by crook.

Looney Tunes
One tall tale from Arthur's time aboard the *Hope* involves smashing someone on the head with a saucepan, and the cartoonish consequences thereof. This account appeared in *The Strand*.

> There was only one man on board who belonged neither to Scotland nor to Shetland, and he was the mystery of the ship. He was a tall, swarthy, dark-eyed man, with blue-black hair and beard, singularly handsome features, and a curious reckless sling of his shoulders when he walked. It was rumoured that he came from the south of England, and that he had fled thence to avoid the law. He made friends with no one, and spoke very seldom, but he was one of the smartest seamen in the ship. I could believe from his

appearance that his temper was Satanic, and that the crime for which he was hiding away may have been a bloody one. Only once he gave us a glimpse of his hidden fires. The cook—a very burly powerful man— the little mate was only an assistant—had a private store of rum, and treated himself so liberally to it that for three successive days the dinner of the crew was ruined. On the third day our silent outlaw approached the cook with a brass saucepan in his hand. He said nothing, but he struck the man with such a frightful blow that his head flew through the bottom, and the sides of the pan were left dangling round his neck.

It was as if Wile E. Coyote attempted to hit the Roadrunner with a frying pan, only to end up with his own head protruding through the bottom the pan. Though little birdies twittered above his head, Wile E. Coyote would be fine. So too would the drunken cook in Arthur's tale:

The half-drunken and half-stunned cook talked of fighting, but he was soon made to feel that the sympathy of the ship was against him, so he reeled back, grumbling, to his duties while the avenger relapsed into his usual moody indifference. We heard no further complaints of the cooking.

Savior

After his voyage aboard the *Hope*, Arthur went on to earn his medical degree, then sign on as ship's surgeon aboard the *S. S. Mayumba*, for its voyage along the west coast of Africa. In his autobiography, he claimed to have saved that ship from disaster.

The *Mayumba* departed for Africa from Liverpool but, due to a gale, was forced to spend the first night in nearby Holyhead. The next day, the *Mayumba* made its way down the Irish Sea. The narrowest gap through which the ship would steam would be St.

George's Channel, the forty-mile-wide gap between Ireland and Wales. The Irish side of the channel was protected by a lighthouse that sits on one of the many Tuskar Rocks, seven miles off the Irish coast. As the *Mayumba* steamed southward through St. George's Channel, the lighthouse would have been on the starboard side of the ship, the right-hand side. [...]

The next day, in vile and thick weather, with a strong sea running, we made our way down the Irish Sea. I shall always believe that I may have saved the ship from disaster, for as I was standing near the officer of the watch I suddenly caught sight of a lighthouse standing out in a rift in the fog. It was on the port side and I could not imagine how any lighthouse could be on the port side of the ship which was, as I knew, well down the Irish coast. I hate to be an alarmist, so I simply touched the mate's sleeve, pointed to the dim outline of the lighthouse, and said: "Is that all right?" He fairly jumped as his eye lit upon it and he gave a yell to the men at the wheel and rang a violent signal to the engine-room. The lighthouse, if I remember right, was the Tuskar, and we were heading right into a rock promontory which was concealed by the rain and fog.

Arthur's anecdote is pure fiction, a bold-faced lie. Arthur's contemporaneous account of the passage, provided in an October 1881 letter to family friend Amy Hoare, offers a far less novelistic version.

Here goes for an account of all we have done, said and suffered—more particularly the last, though really it all amounts to very little—I could write a large and interesting book about what we have <u>not</u> seen, and done. We have not seen shoals of porpoises or flying fish, which are the proper things to see on such voyages, neither have we seen sea serpents or

> water-spouts or drifting wood from wrecks—in fact
> we have been done out of all amusements. [...] That
> evening we sighted the Tuskar light on the Waterford
> coast—ah, the dear old country, excuse a pensive
> tear.

At the time of the voyage, Arthur described no near-fatal passage; instead, he described one that was outright boring. Only much later, in his autobiography, did he invent the tale of saving the *Mayumba* from crashing against the Tuskar rocks.

This is not the first time Arthur's different tellings of the same event have been noted. Russell Miller, in his *Adventures of Arthur Conan Doyle* (2008), commented somewhat more generously on Arthur's fabulism.

> Conan Doyle was not above a little judicious literary
> embroidery. He would claim in his autobiography
> that he saved the ship from running into rocks off the
> Irish coast only a few hours into the voyage when, in
> thick fog, he alone caught sight of the Tuskar
> lighthouse through the murk and alerted the first
> mate that they were heading straight for it. Yet he
> made no mention of this incident in his letters nor in
> an article about the voyage published in the *British
> Journal of Photography* shortly after his return.

"A little judicious literary embroidery" is certainly less offensive to Arthur's acknowledged legacy than "a big fat lie."

His Unipod

For Arthur, the paucity of truth was never an impediment to publishing. In the *British Journal of Photography* article "On the Slave Coast with a Camera," Arthur claimed to have brought with him a new type of camera stand, that he credited himself with inventing.

> I took a stout ash tripod and also one of my own
> invention, which has already been described in the
> Journal. It simply consists of a single stout stick, fitted

with a strong iron spike and a ball and socket joint. The difference in weight I have found to be no small consideration in a climate which is hot enough to render the weight of a napkin upon your knee at dinner time utterly unbearable.

In his previous article for the journal "After Cormorants with a Camera" (1881), he more thoroughly described his unipod.

I had two stands—one a short ash tripod, the other an invention of my own, which I have found of great service in working the moorlands of Scotland. It simply consists of a stout walking-staff four feet long and shod with iron. This fitted to the camera by means of an adjustable ball-and-socket joint. The advantages which I claim for this simple arrangement are not only its lightness (a consideration which will have weight with every practical worker in the open air) but also its cheapness, and the facility it affords for the focusing of a moving object. By it free movement is secured in every direction, both horizontal and vertical, while four inches of iron spike are sufficient to guarantee perfect steadiness.

He wrote, in a later letter to family friend Charlotte Drummond, that his invention had come to the attention of professional photographers.

So I have the pleasant prospect of a roomful of photographers clamouring to see my negatives & my wonderful unipod stand—which has been described so often tho' mortal eye has never seen it.

If Arthur actually had invented and constructed a unipod camera stand, how could nobody have seen it? His articles for the *British Journal of Photography* recount using the unipod to photograph cormorants in the company of friends, and of taking the device aboard a ship bustling with crew and passengers. He expressed a preference for his unipod over other stands, but said nothing about being secretive with its use. Some mortal eye must have seen it, if indeed it did exist.

In *The Unknown Conan Doyle: Essays on Photography* (1982), Richard Lancelyn Green and John Gibson hint at their reservations.

> Doyle does not appear to have belonged to any photographic society, nor to have known many of the leading photographers of the day. There is, though, a proposed visit which is mentioned in a letter to Mrs. Drummond which is also of interest as it throws some light on his self-designed unipod. That, it seems, existed more tangibly on paper than it did elsewhere. [...] The letter will help to show how Doyle composed his articles. He was obviously free to enhance them with reports of spectacular photographs and success in difficult shots. He also appears to have re-shaped his own experiences to suit the occasion.

To reshape one's experiences does sound more respectable than falsifying articles for incremental fame and fortune.

Photographic Foibles

Arthur's apocryphal photographs and negatives mentioned in the *British Journal of Photography* comprised a source of some concern for Green and Gibson, who wrote:

> No photographs by Doyle are known to exist from this period, though there is one which shows Bush Villa, his house in Southsea, which may be by him (or possibly of him). Either the photographs did not exist, in which case he demonstrated an extremely fertile imagination, or they did exist as stated but were subsequently either lost or destroyed by chemical decomposition.

Adopting Green and Gibson's polite verbiage, Arthur's imagination was not just fertile, but superlatively fertile. His essays on photography included detailed discussions of equipment that he could not have owned and sophisticated techniques that he could not have employed. Consider just three excerpts from his various articles.

> I selected for the journey a folding, bellows-body, half-plate camera, by Meagher, with half-a-dozen double backs. These I had made according to the American plan, with the slides drawing entirely out.

> The plates were of my own manufacture. They were made by the boiling method of our worthy chief Editor, and, being exquisitely sensitive, they enabled me to get many instantaneous exposures. [...] They are lighter, less expensive, less liable to admit light owing to the fact of their not opening in the centre, and, finally, are far more easy to manage when there is any wind. The latter may seem rather a fanciful advantage at first sight, but I can recall instances in my own modest photographic career where great events hung on this single fact.

> I have found no method of emulsification so good as that recommended by Mr. W. K. Burton, but not, I believe, originated by him. This process consists in dropping the nitrate of silver in crystals into the bromide solution and shaking until the crystals are entirely dissolved. The emulsion thus formed will always be found to be ruby red by transmitted light.

The question is not whether Arthur could write technically of photography, it is whether his articles on the subject were truthful as represented. Financial considerations alone suggest otherwise. He could not have afforded the many cameras and lenses that he implied were his. He certainly did not have sufficient money to have equipment custom-made "according to the American plan," nor to manufacture his own plates. He did not have the funds or facilities to experiment extensively with emulsification methods.

During the period in which he wrote his photography essays, he still relied on supplements to his meager income from his fledgling medical practice. "I have no money," he added as a pleading postscript to one letter to his mother, herself struggling with financial difficulties. Arthur's father had been institutionalized for alcoholism, epilepsy, and resultant behavioral issues, which left Arthur's mother alone to subsidize or directly care for her seven surviving children.

Not until 1891, six years after his last photographic essay had been published, was Arthur able to raise sufficient funds to purchase even the most rudimentary photographic equipment. "I sold my eye instruments for £6.10.0," he wrote his mother, "with which I shall buy photographic apparatus, so we may have been able to start a hobby without any outlay." That letter privately belied what Arthur publicly claimed. One does not "start a hobby" involving an area in which one is already expert, owns expensive equipment, has access to sophisticated facilities, and possess a large and impressive portfolio.

Medical Braggadocio
Robert Heinrich Herman Koch was a German physician and a pioneering microbiologist. In 1882, he identified the bacterium that causes tuberculosis. In August of 1890, as the keynote speaker at a medical conference, he mentioned in passing that he had managed to cure guinea pigs of tuberculosis and, more significantly, that he anticipated he would be able to extend his cure to humans. By that November, Europe was abuzz with speculation that Koch had cured human subjects of the dreaded disease.

Koch attempted to keep his research secret, but he was quickly overwhelmed by pressure from the public, his colleagues, his government, and his own ambition. On 13 November he announced, in *Deutsche Medizinische Wochenschrift* (*German Medical Weekly*), that he had rid humans of tuberculosis bacilli through a series of injections of a specific fluid, the contents of which he kept secret. The *British Medical Journal* issued a special printing of their magazine the next day to provide an English translation of Koch's announcement.

In *Memories and Adventures*, Arthur claimed to have been

suddenly and inexplicably overcome by an impulse to travel to Berlin and witness Koch's cure in action. "I felt so sure of my ground," he wrote, "and so strongly about it that I wrote a letter of warning to 'The Daily Telegraph,' and I rather think that this letter was the first which appeared upon the side of doubt and caution. I need not say that the event proved the truth of my forecast." He signed his letter:

> I am, Sir, your obedient servant,
> A. CONAN DOYLE, M.D.
> Central Hotel, Berlin, Nov. 17

In his autobiography, he claimed to have arrived home in Southsea "two days later." That would be on 19 November, and therein lays one of many substantial problems associated with his story. Arthur was a member of the Portsmouth Literary and Scientific Society, the meetings of which were newsworthy, at least locally. The 22 November issue of *The Hampshire Telegraph* noted the most recent meeting, which took place four days prior, the one that occurred on 18 November. The title of the speech given that night was "The Philosophy of Cookery." The *Telegraph* also listed the attendees. Arthur could not have been in, or returning from, Berlin on 18 November, for he was instead that evening in attendance of a meeting of the Portsmouth Literary and Scientific Society, listening to someone philosophize about the culinary arts.

Either *The Hampshire Telegraph* incorrectly placed Arthur in Southsea on 18 November, or Arthur did not write from the Central Hotel in London on 17 November and then return to Southsea two days later. Given Arthur's proclivity for prevarication, it is easier to trust the *Telegraph*.

If Arthur did not actually travel to Germany, however, one might wonder where he gained so much insight into Koch's cure that he could discredit it so thoroughly. The answer, as it turns out, is simple. Arthur obtained the insight from Koch himself, at least from Koch's announcement. Recall that Koch announced his cure in a German medical journal on 13 November, and that the *British Medical Journal* provided a translation on the 14th. Arthur had everything he needed, three days before sending his letter from the Central Hotel to the *Daily Telegraph*.

Arthur's letter enumerated nine medical concerns with Koch's so-called lymph, the curative substance to be injected into the patient. Eight of the nine had already been addressed by Koch's announcement. Arthur, for example, cautioned that Koch's lymph did not actually kill the tuberculosis bacteria; it merely killed the tissue encapsulating the bacteria. Koch had already conceded this point in print. There was no need to race all the way to Berlin. Any adept writer could have thus plagiarized Koch's announcement, just as Arthur did.

Petty Libel

During the Boer War, Arthur served for a short time as a volunteer doctor at the Langman Hospital in Bloemfontein, South Africa. In *Memories and Adventures*, he wrote snidely of Dr. Robert O'Callaghan, the man selected by the Langmans as chief surgeon for their hospital.

> When we were complete we were quite a good little unit, but our weakness was unfortunately at the head. Dr. O'Callaghan had been a personal friend of Langman's and had thus got the senior billet, but he was in truth an excellent gynæcologist, which is a branch of the profession for which there seemed to be no immediate demand. He was a man too who had led a sedentary life and was not adapted, with all the will in the world, for the trying experience which lay before us. He realized this himself and returned to England after a short experience of South African conditions.

Arthur was openly arrogant about the arrangement in a letter he sent his mother from the hospital. From *A Life in Letters*, 20 April 1900:

> But it is most certain that there would have been a complete breakdown if I had not been here, so it is as

well that I did not go with the Yeomanry. [...] O'C goes
home and very glad I shall be to see the last of his fat
body.

After more than a century, the diary of Charles Blasson has been
published, and it reveals quite a different story. Blasson was a
dresser at the hospital, a senior medical student, more qualified than
an orderly, less qualified than a doctor. From Ken Cooper's *Aide-de-
Camp to Conan Doyle: The Boer War Diary of Charles Blasson*, entry
for 16 April 1900, we finally learn why Dr. O'Callaghan departed
early.

> Mr O'Callaghan is leaving as soon as a man can be got
> up from Cape Town to take his place. He told us the
> reason he was leaving was that the rest of the staff
> would take no precautions against typhoid and
> therefore he refused to have the responsibility upon
> his shoulders.

O'Callaghan did not leave because he was overweight and unable
to cope. Pictures of the hospital staff show none of them to be obese,
with Arthur as full-figured as any of them. Blasson's diary reveals
that O'Callaghan left because no one else on the medical staff, Arthur
included, would take the necessary precautions to prevent a typhoid
outbreak at the hospital.

As an example of the lax standards that Blasson was unable to
change, we know also from Blasson's diary that everyone, patients
and staff inclusive, was being served from the same kitchen. This was
utter folly since flies were known even then to transmit typhoid from
the mouths of infected patients to the food of patients and staff not
yet infected. Even Arthur wrote in his autobiography of the flies
trying to get into the mouths of the diners.

O'Callaghan's concern turned out to be justified, and Arthur's
lack of attention to proper sanitary conditions unfortunately turned
out to be deadly. Typhoid did break out in the hospital soon after
O'Callaghan departed, and it did spread throughout the staff. In his
diary, Blasson recorded the toll on the staff as of 8 June 1900: one
orderly, one nun, and one dresser had died of the disease; six

dressers and one nun had been invalided home. Seven out of the twenty orderlies were lost, as were two out of the three nuns. As each cleaner fell, the challenge of maintaining sanitary conditions increased. Uninfected patients and staff became increasingly vulnerable to mounting filth and swarming flies, and the toll continued to climb. Charles Blasson eventually died of the disease during a subsequent outbreak.

We are no longer bound by Arthur's autobiography to understand Dr. O'Callaghan's service to the Langham Hospital, nor by Arthur's denunciation of the doctor as an overweight gynecologist. O'Callaghan's obituary in the *British Medical Journal* tells us that Dr. O'Callaghan was an accomplished surgeon.

> We have to record with regret the death, after a short illness, of Mr. R. T. A. O'Callaghan, Surgeon-Gynaecologist to the French Hospital, London. [...] Robert Thomas Alexander O'Callaghan [...] held the appointments of House-Surgeon to the Children's Hospital, Dublin; Resident Surgeon to the Meath Hospital, Dublin; and House-Surgeon to the Stockport Infirmary. ...
>
> He was [...] appointed Surgeon to the Chelsea Hospital for Women, but did not long retain that office. In January, 1900, when the Langman Hospital was presented for service in the South African war by Mr. John L. Langman, Mr. O'Callaghan was appointed Senior Surgeon. He proceeded with that hospital to South Africa. He served with it for some time, and returned home from Bloemfontein before the conclusion of the war. For his services in connexion with this hospital his name was mentioned in dispatches, and he received the medal and clasps. At the time of his death he held the appointment of Surgeon-Gynaecologist to the French Hospital, London.

Arthur attempted to diminish O'Callaghan's contribution to the hospital, omitting that O'Callaghan was a highly qualified surgeon— much more so than Arthur himself. It simply galled Arthur not to be chosen to head the hospital, and then, of all things, to be lectured about sanitary procedures! Later, Arthur was particularly irked that O'Callaghan received credit for the otherwise fine performance of the hospital. After returning home, Arthur added this postscript to a March 1901 letter to his mother.

> [P.S.] Fancy the Official Gazette said the "The Langman Hospital under the capable command of Mr O'Callaghan had done &c &c." It will end by him being Knighted!

Dr. O'Callaghan attempted to prevent a deadly outbreak of typhoid at the Langham Hospital. Arthur rewarded the surgeon's efforts by falsely tainting his legacy.

Undue Credit

Published in 1926, Arthur's two-volume *History of Spiritualism* is the most substantial of his twenty books on the occult. Though his name, and his name alone, appears on the title pages and covers, he was not the book's only author, and perhaps not even the primary author. We get but a hint of Arthur's collaborator from the preface to Volume I.

> It was clear that such a work needed a great deal of research—far more than I in my crowded life could devote to it. [...] Under these circumstances I claimed and obtained the loyal assistance of Mr. W. Leslie Curnow [...] I had originally expected no more than raw material, but he has occasionally given me the finished article, of which I have gladly availed myself, altering it only to the extent of getting my own personal point of view. I cannot admit too fully the loyal assistance which he has given me, and if I have not conjoined his name with my own upon the title-

page it is for reasons which he understands and acquiesces.

Perhaps, if the name of the actual author did not appear on the title page of any Holmes adventure, it was for reasons that the actual author understood, and to which she acquiesced.

A Brief Biography

Arthur was born in Edinburgh in 1859 to Charles Altamont Doyle and Mary Josephine Doyle, the third of nine children, and the older of two boys. His father was a civil servant eventually institutionalized for alcoholism. Arthur was much closer to his mother, to whom he wrote persistently and frequently. She saved his letters, and it is from them that we know much about Arthur that would have otherwise remained secret.

In 1868, when he was nine years old, Arthur's parents sent him two hundred miles south to Hodder House, a Jesuit preparatory school. He spent two years there before advancing to a Jesuit college, Stonyhurst, where he spent five years before moving to a Jesuit university in Austria. After a year abroad, he returned home to study medicine at nearby Edinburgh University. During his eight-year absence, he had been allowed home for Christmas no more than twice, possibly not even once.

As part of his medical training, Arthur served three times as a doctor's assistant, as already noted, and twice in the position of ship's surgeon. Following a brief, failed partnership with George Turnavine Budd in Plymouth, he set up his own practice in the Portsmouth suburb of Southsea, where he began writing books and short stories to supplement his meager income.

It was there, in Southsea, early in 1885, that Arthur allegedly first met Louise Hawkins. By August, they were married. Eight months later, the first Sherlock Holmes adventure was complete. "Arthur has written another book," Louise wrote to Arthur's sister, "a little novel about 200 pages long, called 'A Study in Scarlet.' It went off last night. We have no news of Girdlestone yet, but we hope that no news is good news. We rather fancy that 'The Study in Scarlet' may find its way into print before its elder brother."

Multiple rejections and delays followed before that groundbreaking mystery, *A Study in Scarlet*, was published in the 1887 edition of *Beeton's Christmas Annual*. In February of 1890, the second Holmes novel, *The Sign of Four*, began serialization in *Lippincott's Magazine*.

Subsequent to five years of married life and the arrival of daughter Mary Louise, Arthur and Louise had a brief stay in Vienna, where Arthur intended, at least initially, to further his medical education. The couple returned to England after two months, rather than the intended six, settling in London where Arthur established a short-lived practice as an eye specialist.

The first Sherlock Holmes short story appeared in *The Strand Magazine* in July of 1891. Unlike the first novel, the short stories were met with immediate success. Since Arthur's other writings were also beginning to sell, he abandoned medicine completely, moving his family to the London suburb of South Norwood.

By the end of 1893, Louise had given birth to Arthur Alleyne Kingsley, *The Strand* had published twenty-four Holmes adventures (anthologized in *The Adventures of Sherlock Holmes* and *The Memoirs of Sherlock Holmes*), Holmes had tumbled to his apparent death in the Reichenbach Falls, and Louise had been diagnosed with tuberculosis. Declared terminal, Louise followed Holmes to Switzerland, in the hope that the cold, thin air might spare her.

Louise somehow survived her consumption (as tuberculosis was then frequently called), at least temporarily. After two winters in Switzerland, she and Arthur spent the next in Cairo before returning to England, eventually settling into a custom-built country house called Undershaw. As Louise slowly deteriorated, Arthur began an affair. Supposedly platonic, that affair with the much younger Jean Leckie continued throughout the last nine years of Louise's too-short life.

Arthur and Jean married a year after Louise succumbed to her tuberculosis. Arthur moved out of Undershaw, and the new couple settled into a different country house. Mary and Kingsley were sent away to school while Arthur and Jean produced three children of their own: Denis, Adrian, and Jean.

Long a believer in the paranormal, Arthur dedicated his later years to convincing the world of the legitimacy of spiritualism, the belief that we earth-bound humans can communicate with our spiritual forebears who enjoy eternal, joyous lives in the great beyond. He joined those on the other side in 1930, after seventy-one years on this material plane.

A Hateful Relationship

After the first two Holmes novels, *A Study in Scarlet* and *The Sign of Four*, Arthur contracted with *The Strand* for six Holmes short stories, and he intended no more than that. It was, at that point, far from clear that the serial rights to the anthologies would make him rich. Though Holmes was rapidly becoming popular, Arthur balked when *The Strand* requested an additional six stories. On 14 October 1891, he wrote his mother about his reluctance to supply them.

> "The Strand" are simply imploring me to continue Sherlock Holmes. I enclose their last. The stories brought me in an average of £35 each, so I have written by this post to say that if they offer me £50 each, <u>irrespective of length</u> I may be induced to reconsider my refusal. Seems rather high handed, does it not?

The Strand agreed to a higher rate. Less than a month later, on 11 November, Arthur updated his mother on his stunning headway.

> I have done five of the Sherlock Holmes stories of the new Series. They are 1. The Adventure of the Blue Carbuncle 2. The Adventure of the Speckled Band 3. The Adventure of the Noble Bachelor 4. The Adventure of the Engineer's Thumb 5. The Adventure of the Beryl Coronet. I think they are up to the standard of the first series, & the twelve ought to make a rather good book of the sort. I think of slaying Holmes in the sixth & winding him up for good & all. He takes my mind from better things.

Arthur's mother was appalled. To discourage her son's thoughts of literary homicide, she provided him an alternative plot. On 6 January 1892, Arthur wrote to say that he would use her story, but that he would not do any Holmes adventures after that, for he was eager to get back to his historical fiction.

> During the holidays I finished my last Sherlock Holmes tale "The Adventure of the Copper Beeches" in which I used your lock of hair, so now a long farewell to Sherlock. He still lives, however, thanks to your entreaties. I must now return with a rush to Louis the fourteenth and get those poor Huguenots out of France.

It was too late, though. Holmes had become too popular. *The Strand* pleaded for more. "They have been bothering me for more Sherlock Holmes tales," he wrote on 4 February. "Under pressure I offered to do a dozen for a thousand pounds, but I sincerely hope that they won't accept it now." *The Strand*, of course, accepted. Their readers demanded more of Holmes. They cared not a whit about Arthur getting his Huguenots out of France.

By the end of 1892 Arthur was once again plotting Holmes's demise. J. M. Barrie, the creator of *Peter Pan*, in his *The Greenwood Hat* (1938), recorded an instance he had with Arthur after appealing for help on a play. On the subject of their collaboration, Barrie inserted this tantalizing parenthetical: "(I sat with him on the seashore at Aldeburgh when he decided to kill Sherlock Holmes.)"

Arthur gave voice to his homicidal urges to war artist and correspondent Frederic Villiers, who wrote of the conversation in his *Peaceful Personalities and Warriors Bold* (1907).

> I happened to call upon Sir Arthur in England one morning. He received me in his usual hearty and breezy manner, but I could see there was something weighing heavily upon his mind. I discovered that he had finally come to the conclusion that his old and valuable friend Sherlock Holmes must die. [...] He was quite perplexed as to how he should get rid of

Holmes. His publishers wished for more of the astute detective, but he was getting tired of the gentleman, and wanted to devote his attention to war adventures. [...] But first of all he must settle what manner of death Sherlock Holmes should die.

"A man like that mustn't die of a pin-prick or influenza. His end must be violent and intensely dramatic."

I could see that my dear friend of many happy monthly parts was doomed. The author of his being was inexorable on this point, and I left the house with a touch of sadness in my heart.

It came to a head in 1893. On 6 April, Arthur informed his mother that he was done with Holmes, that he would "never never" write of him again. "I am in the middle of the last Holmes story, after which the gentleman vanishes, never never to reappear. I am weary of his name." But even then, Holmes did not die. Whatever "last Holmes story" Arthur may have been writing never saw the light of day.

While Arthur's purported motivations for wanting Holmes dead are numerous and confused, it is clear that he had come to resent the man with more than a little vehemence. Less than three years after Holmes disappeared into the depths of the Reichenbach Falls, Arthur was still somehow cursed by the ghost of the detective, writing, as if to convince himself that Holmes is really gone. "Poor Holmes is dead and damned. I couldn't revive him if I would (at least not for years), for I have had such an overdose of him that I feel towards him as I do towards *pâté de foie gras*, of which I once ate too much, so that the name of it gives me a sickly feeling to this day."

For the remainder of his life, the resentment seethed barely beneath the surface, occasionally boiling over. Biographer Charles Higham reported, in *The Adventures of Conan Doyle* (1976), that Arthur, after being knighted for his defense of British honor in the Boer War, exploded in fury at the mention of Sherlock Holmes.

He was widely congratulated on his knighthood. [...] When a parcel containing some exquisite handmade shirts arrived at his suite, he was pleased until an anonymous note fluttered to the floor. Reading it, he shouted out so loudly that the children present started to cry. It contained the words, "With greetings to Sir Sherlock Holmes."

Even during the final phase of his life, when he was a leading proponent of Spiritualism, Arthur would not tolerate any mention of Sherlock Holmes. Samuel Rosenberg recorded these words spoken by an acquaintance of Arthur's, a fellow occultist who had born witness to this type of outburst:

> Conan Doyle *hated* Sherlock Holmes and *hated* to be reminded of him. He would grow very angry when inevitably, some person in an audience would ask him about his detective stories when he was talking about the occult or something else he considered far more important. Very angry. Y'know, he preferred his rather juvenile romances like *Micah Clarke* and the *Brigadier Gerard* nonsense.

Also according to Rosenberg, the widow of Arthur's son, Adrian, explained that no one was to ever mention Holmes's name in his father's presence: "My late husband told me that once, when he violated the unspoken rule *never* to mention Sherlock Holmes, his father became *livid* and shouted: 'Don't mention that *name* to me! I forbid it! I *hate* him!'"

Arthur considered the Holmes adventures "a lower stratum of literary achievement," ungraciously using those very words in his autobiography to describe the character who had made him famous and wealthy. But Arthur wanted to be remembered for his *Micah Clarke*, his *White Company*, his *Sir Nigel*, and *Rodney Stone*. Of course he came to resent, and then to hate, Holmes, to say nothing of the woman who created him. When Arthur and his second wife, Jean, were in need of funds, he begrudgingly conceded to the demand for more Holmes. Many years later, Martin Dakin finally gave voice to what had become obvious to everyone, baldly stating there is a "Problem with the Casebook," declaring that those later stories flowed from a different pen.

Chapter 4
Crime Scene

Edmond Locard was known as the "Sherlock Holmes of Paris." In 1912, he founded the Laboratoire de Police Scientifique, the world's first forensic lab, and is today most remembered for his exchange principle, the theory that a perpetrator will always leave something of him at the crime scene.

> Wherever he steps, whatever he touches, whatever he leaves, even unconsciously, will serve as a silent witness against him. Not only his fingerprints or his footprints, but his hair, the fibers from his clothes, the glass he breaks, the tool marks he leaves, the paint he scratches, the blood or semen he deposits or collects. All of these and more, bear mute witness against him.

In an investigation of literary fraud, the crime scene consists not of a physical location, but of the text written by someone other than the person claiming credit. According to Locard's exchange principle, a ghostwriter must leave something of himself in his work, perhaps notes in his manuscripts, or tells in his writing style. Possibly, the author even intentionally leaves clues to his identity, engaging in a game of literary cat and mouse.

Evidence abounds in the Sherlock Holmes Canon that the early adventures were written by someone other than Arthur Conan Doyle. The manuscript for the first short story, *A Scandal in Bohemia* (1891), is particularly revealing. Careful examination provides startling results.

The *Scandal* Manuscript

Most of the early Sherlock Holmes manuscripts have been lost, destroyed, or sold in pieces. Of the first twenty-three Holmes manuscripts, only two survive and only one is available for public viewing.

The manuscript for *A Study in Scarlet* (1887) has been destroyed, dispersed, or tucked away.

The manuscript for *The Sign of Four* (1890) was sold at auction in 1996, to an anonymous collector, for $519,500. Images of two different first pages for that manuscript are available online, but the other pages are unavailable to the public.

The manuscript for *A Scandal in Bohemia* is maintained at The Harry Ransom Center, University of Texas at Austin, and represents the earliest Holmes manuscript that can be reviewed and evaluated. The Ransom Center provides a quality online image of each page.

The *Scandal* manuscript consists of thirty pages from two different stocks of lined paper. Pages 1 through 12 have thirty-nine horizontal lines. The rest have thirty-four horizontal lines. All of the story text is written between the horizontal lines. Pages 1 through 12 therefore have a maximum of thirty-eight lines of text; the remaining pages have a maximum of thirty-three.

All pages have one slightly ragged vertical edge, as if torn from a journal or exercise book.

There are multiple indications that the pages were written in the same order that they appear. The text flows smoothly across the pages; incomplete sentences on one page are completed on the next. The page numbers, which appear in the upper margin, are in proper sequence, even across the changes in paper stock. The pinholes or staple holes, at the upper left of each page, align. The manuscript does not seem to be the patchwork of two different writers, except in one obvious aspect—it was written by two different hands.

The manuscript has clearly changed ownership several times, but the early history of its travels is unknown. Randall Stock, in the limited edition *Bohemian Souls* (2011), suggested that Arthur must have sold it before 1913, the year that many of Arthur's manuscripts were bound for sale. By 1916, Arthur routinely had every Holmes manuscript bound. The *Scandal* manuscript, however, was still unbound when it turned up in the 1940s. Under the presumption that Arthur would have had it bound in 1913, or after 1916, had he still owned it, this makes sense.

There is, however, an alternative explanation. Perhaps Arthur did still possess the manuscript, but had good reason to not sell it. Perhaps the manuscript revealed something he wanted to remain secret.

The Second Hand

At least two people were involved in the physical act of writing the *Scandal* manuscript. Pages 1 through 12 are in the recognizable hand of Arthur Conan Doyle. Pages 13 through 19 are in a different, yet-to-be-identified hand. Pages 20 through 30 return to Arthur's handwriting. The second handwriting coincides with the change in paper stock.

Arthur's handwriting is tight and legible. It never varies. The only noticeable flaw is that his left margin grows with each line, slanting down and to the right. There are few corrections to his text, with seldom more than two words replaced or inserted per page.

The second handwriting style is less disciplined. It is more wild and variable. Its left margins, though, are more constant. Corrections by this hand are strikingly infrequent.

Arthur's handwriting on page 2; unknown handwriting on page 17

The earliest explanation for the different handwriting is incorrect and suspiciously so. It was the result of one of Arthur's many biographers, John Dickson Carr, preparing an undated, unaddressed, affidavit in which he did "testify" that both handwritings are Arthur's.

> Sir Arthur Conan Doyle, as a schoolboy at Stonyhurst, cultivated two styles of handwriting—his own famous script, and another, more angular style which he adopted to rest his hand. This appears in his school and college letters, where his mother sharply criticizes the second handwriting, and he explains how he came to adopt it. Indeed, the second handwriting may be seen in the letters as late as his days at Norwood, and in his Norwood notebook. Having examined dozens of examples, I can testify that the second handwriting which appears in 'A Scandal in Bohemia', and which appears to be an interpolation by someone else, is actually by Conan Doyle himself.

Carr was one of only two biographers granted access to the Conan Doyle papers, and he worked under the close supervision of the protective Adrian Conan Doyle. We know that Carr wrote his letter sometime after viewing the family papers, since he referenced them. That sets the earliest date not much before 1949, the year in which Carr's biography of Arthur first appeared.

Randall Stock argued that Carr's letter was written no later than 1950. In that year, a leading dealer in detective fiction catalogued the *Scandal* manuscript as "the entire manuscript in the writing of the author, showing the use of 'two fists.'" In either case, Carr's affidavit seems to have been written very near the middle of the previous century.

Richard Lancelyn Green's *Reflections on a Scandal in Bohemia* (1986) suggests that Carr wrote the affidavit to enhance the value of the manuscript, and that he did so at the behest of whomever it then belonged. Green dismissed Carr's "resting hand" hypothesis, noting that Arthur did not use it when deliberately writing in two different handwriting styles for the Holmes adventure *The Reigate Squires* (1893). Stock pointed out that, in the *Scandal* manuscript, the two writers are distinguishable not only by their handwriting but also by their indentations and capitalization. Neither Green nor Stock, however, mentioned two other discriminators. Arthur's left margin increases incrementally line by line, as he progresses down the page, and he placed his page numbers near the very top of the paper. The other writer's left margin is more nearly constant, and the page numbers rest just above the first horizontal line.

It is unreasonable to assume that Arthur would change his margins, indents, capitalization, and pagination simply because his hand needed some rest. The "resting hand" hypothesis is humbug. A review of the manuscript's ownership history helps understand the origin and purpose of that humbug.

Green speculated, in *Reflections on a Scandal in Bohemia*, that Adrian first sold the *Scandal* manuscript to Charles Scribner's and Sons, but Green provided neither dates nor details. In 1943, Scribner sold the manuscript to Carroll Atwood Wilson, a collector of rare books and one of the original Baker Street Irregulars. Wilson died in 1947 and his executors sold most of his collection, most likely including the *Scandal* manuscript, back to Scribner. In 1948, Scribner sold the Conan Doyle items from Wilson's collection to Lew David Feldman, a dealer in detective fiction, who, in October of 1948, advertised the manuscript for sale. In 1951, Frederic Dannay, one of the two cousins behind the Ellery Queen enterprise, purchased the manuscript from Feldman. In 1958, Dannay sold the manuscript to the University of Texas at Austin, where it remains today, in the Harry Ransom Center.

The scenario for Carr's affidavit now seems to be as follows. Carr was working on his biography of Arthur Conan Doyle when Adrian granted him access to the family papers. Around the same time, Scribner interested Feldman in the Conan Doyle items that it had acquired from Wilson's estate, the *Scandal* manuscript among them. Feldman, concerned about the manuscript's provenance, asked about the second handwriting. Scribner, having most likely purchased the manuscript originally from Adrian, contacted the seller again regarding the second handwriting. Adrian cherry-picked family papers for Carr, and had Carr "testify" that the second hand was simply Arthur's resting hand. Since Carr was, at that time, one of the most renowned authors of detective fiction, his judgment was accepted at face value. His affidavit thereafter accompanied the manuscript.

While a few details of this scenario may be erroneous, only some modest variation of it makes sense, both with respect to the manuscript's provenance and the timing of Carr's affirmation. Carr probably believed in the accuracy of his testimonial, but it is difficult to believe that Adrian did. In a 1962 letter to the University of Texas, Adrian offered an entirely different explanation for the second hand, just as false and suspicious as the first.

> In the holograph manuscript of 'A Scandal in Bohemia', you may have noticed some five or six sheets not in my father's handwriting, occur in the middle of the manuscript, and I thought that you might like to know that this is the handwriting of his sister Lottie, to whom, when my father's hand became tired, he would dictate. This happened on very rare occasions and among the family collection of manuscripts there are only two which carry one or two sheets in dictation in his sister's handwriting.

This too is humbug. Brian Pugh's comprehensive *A Chronology of the Life of Sir Arthur Conan Doyle* (2014) establishes that Lottie was in Portugal when the second hand was applied to the *Scandal* manuscript. She did not return to England until the year after the story was published. Furthermore, Randall Stock pointed out that Richard Lancelyn Green and Peter Blau each compared the second handwriting in *Scandal* against Lottie's handwriting, and each concluded that the hands do not match.

Stock declared the case of the mysterious second hand unsolved. It seems, however, that the solution should be readily at hand. Recall that Carr explained he personally witnessed dozens of instances of the second hand among Arthur's letters: "Indeed, the second handwriting may be seen in the letters as late as his days at Norwood, and in his Norwood notebook. Having examined dozens of examples, I can testify that the second handwriting [...] is actually by Conan Doyle himself." Those letters, unfortunately, are apparently no longer available for comparison. It is almost as if they have been hidden.

Cut-and-Paste Alterations

Nine of the manuscript pages, nearly one third of them, have been physically altered by cutting, tearing, pasting, taping, or post publication emendation. "Singularity is almost always a clue," observes Holmes, and the physical alterations to the *Scandal* manuscript are singular indeed, for none of them add, subtract, or change even a word of the story's text.

Someone altered the *Scandal* manuscript by cutting through page 14, twice, from side to side. One cut isolated the top margin, and that portion is now missing. A second cut isolated the first three lines of text. Someone then pasted that three-line segment over the bottom margin of page 13.

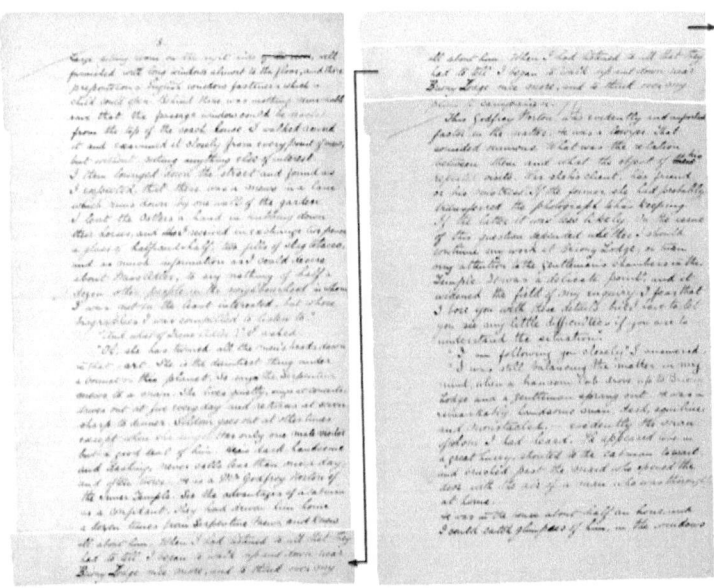

Three lines cut from the top of page 14
were pasted onto the bottom of page 13

The cut-and-paste alterations do not, in any way, change the text. Their purpose is therefore a mystery, as is the identity of their perpetrator. Randall Stock, in his analysis of the manuscript, noted the alterations but offered no explanation. We are therefore left to imagine.

The most probable reason is that there is something written in the bottom margin of page 13 that we are not supposed to see. Though nothing is written in the bottom margin of any of the twenty-seven pages in which the margin remains visible, it is difficult to believe that page 13 was not an exception. Why would someone desecrate a valuable manuscript, thereby reducing its sale price, if not to avoid incurring an even greater cost? It is tempting to suspect a cover-up, in the most literal sense of the word.

Our suspicion grows by observing that pages 3 and 4 are altered in similar fashion. The first cut isolated the top margin of Sheet 4, and that portion is now missing. A second cut isolated the first two lines of text, which were then pasted over the bottom margin of page 3.

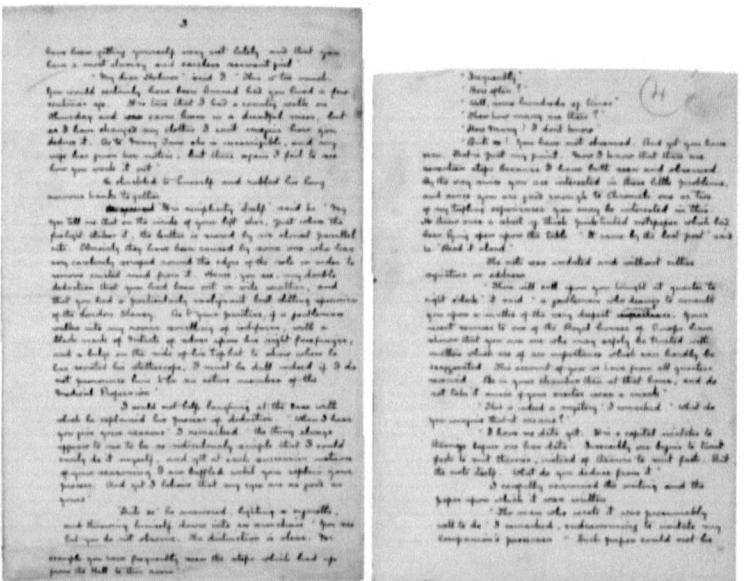

Two lines cut from the top of page 4, pasted onto the bottom of page 3

Careful examination of the online images reveals that the two lines of relocated text do indeed cover handwriting in the bottom margin of page 3. One small, barely noticeable, piece of that handwriting somehow managed to escape being covered. It seems to be a portion of a lowercase descender, such as that associated with g, j, p, q, or y, peeking out from beneath the pasted two-line segment, just beneath the word "which." Previously unnoticed, it is difficult to see in any image of reduced quality and size, such as that above. An enhancement of the critical segment is therefore provided below.

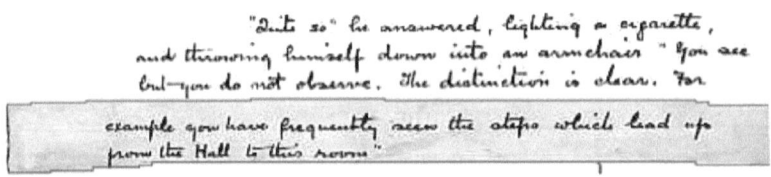

Bottom of page 3 (enhanced), showing lowercase
descender near bottom edge

This tiny segment of handwriting is actually quite distinctive. The bottom seems to have shot off the paper, having begun higher and to the left, where it is now hidden beneath the two lines of text from page 4. It is unlike any lowercase descender used by the owner of the second handwriting, the lowercase descenders of which almost always slope down and leftward—the orientation of that hand's text. Arthur's handwriting is more vertical, but his lowercase descenders never turn the opposite way. The handwriting seems to belong to a third party, perhaps the publisher or the literary agent.

Despite being able to see only a portion of a single lowercase descender, we may still be able to recover the entirety of what was covered up on pages 3 and 13. Whoever tried burying it for all time could not have anticipated the development of today's noninvasive, nondestructive radiology technology. Such technology is now routinely used to examine any desired cross-section of the human body. It has also been used to examine each of the thirty exceptionally fine layers of paint that Leonardo da Vinci used to create the *Mona Lisa*. Whether such an examination will ever be conducted on the *Scandal* manuscript, and what it might reveal, remains to be seen.

A Tear-and-Trash Alteration

Given that the perpetrator hoped to forever conceal the content of the lower margins, he should not have merely pasted over it, but torn the offending text from the bottom of the page and destroyed it, as he did with page 19, the last of seven written in the second hand. It is ripped from side to side, along a line three quarters of the way from the top. The excised portion is missing, presumably destroyed long ago.

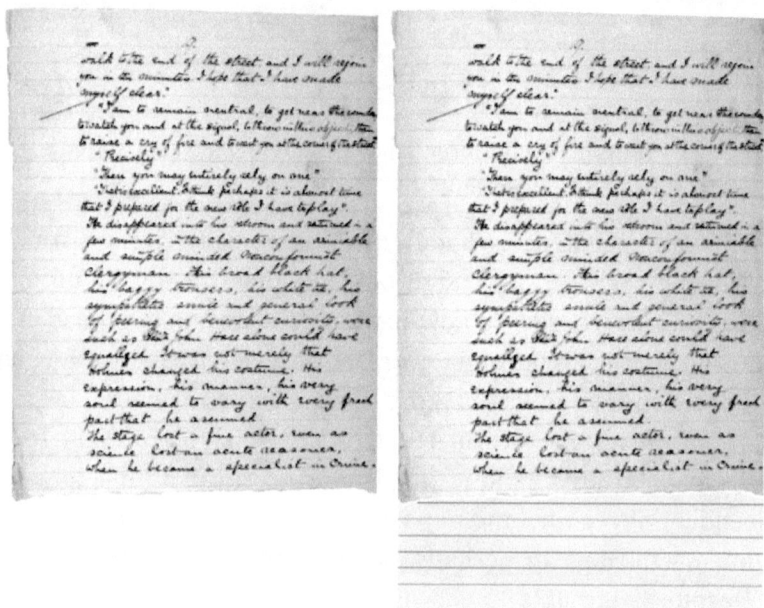

Page 19, current condition (left) and reconstructed (right)

We know that no story text was lost as part of this alteration, since the flow of text from page 19 to 20 is identical to what was published in *The Strand*. The last paragraph on page 19 is complete. The first line beneath it is absolutely blank, and the second is most likely blank. Blank lines are used sparingly in the manuscript. One exists on page 1 after the story's title, another is used on page 11 before the beginning of Part II, another appears on page 26 before the beginning of Part III, and one exists on page 30 before the concluding paragraph of the story. Nowhere else does the owner of the second hand interrupt the text with a blank line. The one or two blank lines following the last paragraph on page 19 are evidence that role of the owner of the second hand was at that point ended.

We can know also that Arthur did not include on that missing segment any part of the story that was later deemed unworthy of submission to the publisher, since the standard means of instructing the publisher to ignore text is to mark through it, as Arthur did elsewhere in the manuscript.

Given that the perpetrator of the cut-and-paste alterations intended to hide a third party's handwriting at the bottom of two other pages, we can presume that the same perpetrator tore off the bottom of page 19 to hide even more extensive handwriting by that third person.

"The more *outré* and grotesque an incident is," explains Holmes, "the more carefully it deserves to be examined, and the very point which appears to complicate a case is, when duly considered and scientifically handled, the one which is most likely to elucidate it." Taking Holmes's advice, we should consider why anyone would damage something so valuable as the manuscript of the very first Sherlock Holmes short story.

The perpetrator must certainly have understood that his desecrations would seriously degrade the value of the manuscript. We can therefore conclude that something damaging did indeed exist on the bottoms of the three pages. We can presume, therefore, that the perpetrator needed money badly enough to sell the manuscript despite its damaging content, and concluded that it would be more profitable to damage the manuscript than make public the entirety of the three pages in question. Whatever that third hand revealed must have been threatening indeed.

Tear-and-Tape Alterations

Pages 12, 23, and 28 of the *Scandal* manuscript are torn from side to side, approximately one third of the way down. In each case, the tear cleanly separated the first paragraph from the remainder of the text. Just beneath the tear line on page 23, someone has written *23½*, assigning the two portions contiguous pagination. Just beneath the tear line on page 28, *28a* serves the same purpose.

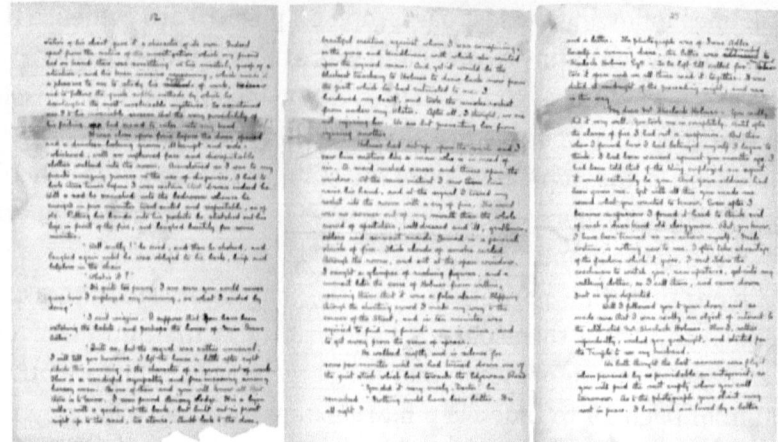

Pages 12, 23 and 28, torn and taped

The tear-and-tape alterations offer us important dating information. While we cannot establish when the pages were torn, we can infer something about when they were taped. Cellophane tape, the world's first transparent tape, was invented by Dick Drew of the 3M Corporation in 1929. On 8 September 1930, Drew sent the first roll of Scotch™ Cellophane Tape to a prospective customer. That customer wrote back with perspicacious advice: "You should have no hesitancy in equipping yourself to put this product on the market economically. There will be a sufficient volume of sales to justify the expenditure."

Arthur died on 7 July 1930, two months before Drew sent his first roll of transparent tape to a foresighted customer. Arthur may have torn the pages, but he did not repair them.

The cut-and-paste alterations might be explained away as actually enhancing the value of the manuscript, since they may have hidden something substantially more costly than a reduction in the manuscript's sales price. That explanation, however, fails when it comes to the tear-and-tape alterations; the use of transparent tape precludes any effort to hide something beneath.

"It is impossible as I state it," observed Holmes, "and therefore I must in some respect have stated it wrong."

A Forged Signature

At the end on the story, on Sheet 30, we find Arthur's signature and the address of his medical practice. The evidence suggests that the signature block is a forgery, added well after *A Scandal in Bohemia* was published. The first and most obvious indication is the reduced intensity of the signature block. The print seems lighter than that of the rest of the text. The difference is, admittedly, slight.

Signature on the final page of the *Scandal* manuscript

This image, as is each image in this work, is presented in shades of gray. The Harry Ransom Center's online images have a yellow component that cannot be captured in a grayscale document. Every pixel of a grayscale image has a quantifiable value ranging, from 0, for pure black, to 100, for pure white. Grayscale values are an objective measure of any shade difference.

The darkest pixel in the letter "D" that begins the word "Doyle" is approximately 60% black. The darkest pixel in the letter "e" that ends the word "title" (just above the "D" in "Doyle") is approximately 75% black, making it objectively darker than the signature block.

Another means of comparing shades is to convert the image to pure black and white. In this conversion, all pixels darker than a specified threshold will become completely black, and all others will become completely white. The image below shows the results for three different thresholds: 30%, 50%, and 70%.

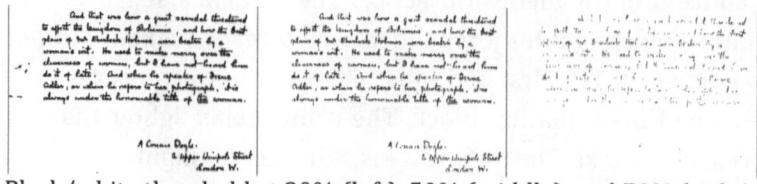

Black/white threshold at 30% (left), 50% (middle), and 70% (right)

At a threshold of at least 70% black, the difference in shade becomes apparent. The signature block disappears, while most of the story's text remains, showing us that the text of the story is objectively darker than the signature block.

A different writing implement was used for the signature block than for the last paragraph of the story. Whoever used that different pen managed a reasonable, if imperfect, forgery of Arthur's signature. He failed, in particular, to accurately mimic Arthur's distinctive "D."

Christie's auction house published a catalog of Conan Doyle papers they hoped to sell on 19 May 2004. That catalog reveals five examples of Arthur's signature, dating from 1893 (two years after the *Scandal* manuscript was written) to 1916. In the image below, those five signatures are displayed beneath the signature from the last page of the *Scandal* manuscript.

Arthur's signature from *Scandal*, 1893, 1894, 1903, 1905, and 1916

Each of the authentic signatures show a "D" with a loop on top that extends to the "o" that follows. The "D" from the manuscript signature is materially different. It has no loop, much less one that extends to the following "o." It is more vertical. It has no irregularity along its lower edge, as does each "D" in the authentic signatures. Similarly, both the "l" and the descender of the "y" are closer to a vertical orientation in the manuscript signature than in the authentic signatures.

One might argue that Arthur's signature merely evolved over time, but that argument must overcome a serious hurdle. The address beneath the manuscript's signature—2 Upper Wimpole Street London—dates it sometime after or concurrent with the others, not before them.

Arthur and Louise left Southsea in December of 1890. After spending the Christmas season with his mother, the couple spent two months in Vienna so that Arthur might further his medical education. On 24 March 1891, the couple moved into a rented flat at 23 Montague Place, directly across from the British Museum. It was on 1 April of that year when Arthur took occupancy of the office at 2 Upper Wimpole Street, just a mile distant from his newly rented home, to operate his short-lived eye practice. In his autobiography, he claimed that he wrote A Scandal in Bohemia from the consulting room while awaiting his first patient, who was never to come.

> Every morning I walked from the lodgings at Montague Place, reached my consulting-room at ten and sat there until three or four, with never a ring to disturb my serenity. [...] I felt that Sherlock Holmes, whom I had already handled in two little books, would easily lend himself to a succession of short stories. These I began in the long hours of waiting in my consulting-room. [...] It was as well, for not one single patient had ever crossed the threshold of my room.

Arthur apparently assumed that no one would remember or discover the interview he gave in 1892, to World: A Journal for Men *and Women*. In that interview, he alleged that he had to give up the medical practice because it left him too little time for writing.

> [Arthur] very soon found out the evident incompatibility between the desk and the consulting-room. He was compelled to attend his patients in the morning, and spend most of the afternoon at the [Royal Westminster Ophthalmic] hospital, so no time remained for his writing but a portion of the night. For months he struggled to combine the two wholly dissimilar avocations; but in the end his health began to give way, and, after mature consideration, he resolved "to throw physic to the dogs," and to rely entirely on the profits of his books and articles."

The autobiographical legend is further tarnished by a letter sent to Arthur by his literary agent, A. P. Watt, in which Watt acknowledged receipt of *A Scandal in Bohemia*, the first Sherlock Holmes short story. Watt's letter is dated 31 March, the day before Arthur moved into his office on Upper Wimpole.

> I am in receipt of yours of today's date and will take the story which has also arrived to the Strand Magazine, as none of the other periodicals can use more than 7,000 words at the outside. I note that you propose to write a series, and that you will entrust the sale of it to us.

The *Scandal* manuscript was out of Arthur's hand before he moved into his office. He could not possibly have added the signature block from his consulting room on Upper Wimpole. That he wrote the story there, waiting for patients who never came, renders that portion of his autobiography as much a work of fiction as *Scandal* itself.

The signature block was added to the *Scandal* manuscript almost certainly to buttress its provenance. The person who forged it unwittingly relied on *Memories and Adventures* when specifying the address. We can therefore conclude that the signature block was added after the autobiography's 1924 publication, and perhaps after Arthur's death in 1930.

A Provisional Theory

"One forms provisional theories and waits for time or fuller knowledge to explode them. A bad habit," Holmes concedes, "but human nature is weak."

Based on the evidence we have recovered from the text and physical condition of the *Scandal* manuscript, we can envision a scenario that explains how the manuscript came to be in the state in which it now exists. The scenario begins with someone preparing a foul copy manuscript for what would be the first Sherlock Holmes short story, *A Scandal in Bohemia*. Only after the foul copy manuscript was completed did Arthur become involved, transforming it into the fair copy that is now on display at the Harry Ransom Center. At some point, the actual author relieved Arthur of the drudgery by copying the second-hand portion in a second exercise book. Arthur then completed the task, continuing to use that same book. He did not add his name or his yet-to-be business address on the final page.

The foul copy was eventually disposed of. The fair copy was sent to Arthur's literary agent, A. P. Watt, who received it on 31 March 1893. Watt managed to place *A Scandal in Bohemia* not only with *The Strand Magazine*, but also with multiple American publications.

After *The Strand* no longer needed the *Scandal* manuscript, they returned it to Arthur. Sometime before, during, or after publication, someone wrote something in the bottom margins of pages 3 and 13, and in the lower quarter of page 19. In the absence of sophisticated imaging techniques, all that can be seen of that writing today is the fragment of a descender at the bottom edge of page 3.

Whatever was written on the bottom of those three pages may have been cause for Arthur to be protective of the manuscript, keeping it from the binders even as many of his other manuscripts were bound in 1913. The irony is that his efforts to hide the *Scandal* manuscript caused it to be the only one of the first twenty-three to be publicly available today.

For whatever reason, Arthur could not bring himself to sell or destroy the *Scandal* manuscript. Nearing the end of his life, he devised a plan to keep it in the family for at least another generation. He prepared a will in which he apportioned his literary rights: one half would go to his second wife Jean; the other would be split equally among their three children. This apportionment included the *Scandal* manuscript, which was to be sectioned out accordingly, one portion including the note added to page 3, another including notes on pages 13 and 19.

To further protect against any of the family members from selling the manuscript, Arthur made his dividing lines not between pages, but amidst them. He tore through page 12 just beneath the first paragraph. The first portion therefore includes one partial page and the troublesome note in the bottom margin of page 3.

He then tore through page 23 just beneath the first paragraph, making the second portion the most interesting to us. It includes two partial pages, any notes near the bottoms of pages 13 and 19, and all of the text written in the second hand.

Finally, Arthur tore through page 28 just below the first paragraph. The third portion therefore consists only of four complete pages and two partial, and includes no troublesome notation whatsoever.

The fourth portion is the least interesting, consisting of only two complete pages and one partial page. It did not even include, at the time, Arthur's signature or the address of his consulting room.

The tearing of the manuscript could make sense only to someone, such as Arthur, who hoped to negate its sale value. Manuscripts were routinely divided, by complete pages, to increase their value. The total value of the individual pages might easily exceed the value of one complete manuscript. No one, though, would attempt to increase the value of a manuscript by ripping any single page from side to side, much less three of them.

Arthur's plan worked, at least for a decade. Jean respected his wishes and never allowed the manuscript to be sold. After she died, however, Arthur's plan fell apart. Their sons, Denis and Adrian, needed whatever money could be brought in by the fractured and contaminated manuscript's sale. In *The Man Who Created Sherlock*

Holmes, Andrew Lycett gave a telling description of the two profligate sons.

> Denis and Adrian (and the latter in particular) were both spendthrift playboys. Denis married Nina Mdivani, who claimed to be a Georgian princess. (Her brothers made a habit of marrying and discarding a succession of Hollywood actresses and American heiresses.) Adrian took a more sober Danish woman, Anna Andersen, as his wife, but lived in a chateau in Switzerland, surrounded by Ferraris and mistresses.
>
> These two sons used the Conan Doyle estate as a milch-cow. Because neither man ever did anything useful in his life, they both took pleasure in making things more difficult for anyone who tried to write about their father.

Georgina Doyle treated them only somewhat more gently in *Out of the Shadows* (2004). She quoted from a letter sent by Adrian's widow to John Doyle, Arthur's nephew and Georgina's husband.

> I feel their upbringing was all wrong from the start; they were never educated to any definite profession and that is a catastrophe for any man [...] They were fundamentally not bad men, but destiny seemed against them because they never had to stand on their own feet and were somehow not able to cope with reality.

Jean died in June of 1940. By 9 January 1943, Carroll Atwood Wilson owned the full Scandal manuscript. We can now guess what happened to it around that time. One of the two brothers, more likely Adrian, decided to sell the manuscript for whatever he could get. His mother's portion of the manuscript was now available, Denis would go along with the plan (for a share of the proceeds), and Lena Jean could be convinced to contribute her portion as well.

For Adrian, the major problem was not the three torn pages. Transparent tape had been available since shortly after his father's death, so he could easily repair the three torn pages in a fashion not anticipated by his father. The issue was instead the notes at the bottoms of Pages 3, 13, and 19. Those notes revealed that *A Scandal in Bohemia* was written by someone other than his father, a disclosure that would seriously degrade the value not only of the manuscript but the entire estate.

Just as his father had devised a simple plan to keep the manuscript from being sold, Adrian devised a simple plan to make the manuscript sellable once again. He taped pages 12, 23, and 28 back together, then cut the first two lines from page 4 and pasted them over the damaging note at the bottom of page 3. He cut the first three lines from page 14 and pasted them over the damaging note at the bottom of page 13. When he got to page 19, there was simply too much text to cover up, so he simply ripped off the bottom quarter.

It was merely by habit that Adrian worked from the beginning to the end. Had he worked from back to front, he would have realized early on that it would be easier to simply tear off the offending portion of any page rather than covering it up. He needlessly "repaired" five pages instead of three, but what's done was done. There was no going back.

Even with the most damaging notes covered up, or disposed of, there was still the problem of seven pages of text written in the second hand. That text could not be removed or covered up, even though it pointed to some level of involvement by someone other than his father. Adrian therefore tricked John Dickson Carr into affirming that the second handwriting was Arthur's resting hand. Adrian further puffed up the provenance by forging his father's signature beneath the last line of the story, and by adding the address of his father's consulting room.

Had Adrian disposed of each damaging note by tearing off the bottoms of the offending pages, and had he added just his father's signature to the last page, he probably would have gotten away with it for all time. However, by pasting over the bottoms of Pages 3 and 13, he left the hidden text potentially readable by technology he could not have then possibly imagined.

Adrian was aware of the creation story that Arthur told in *Memories and Adventures*, that Arthur had opened his eye practice in London to great expectations but not a single patient. Having nothing but time on his hands, Arthur wrote *A Scandal in Bohemia* and the other Holmes short stories soon to follow. Adrian, however, did not take into account the contemporaneous interviews that falsified not only the father's autobiography, but also the son's forgery.

Like so many before and after him, Adrian made the mistake of taking his father at his word.

Chapter 5
Shadow Woman

The 1955 movie *The Usual Suspects* revolves around Keyser Soze, a shadowy mastermind of near mythical reputation. Under interrogation, one of the usual suspects says of Soze, "Nobody believed he was real. Nobody ever saw him or knew anybody that ever worked directly for him [...] You never knew. That was his power."

The Keyser Soze in our case of literary deception is Arthur's first wife, the shadowy Louise Hawkins Conan Doyle.

A Tubercular Family

Jeremiah Hawkins was a landowner and farmer who worked the land in Minsterworth, Gloucestershire. His brother died without heir, and his unmarried sister was beyond childbearing age. The task of preserving the family line therefore fell on Jeremiah's shoulders. He dutifully married Emily Butt, the daughter of a neighboring farmer just across the River Severn. She was only nineteen years old; Jeremiah was fifty.

Despite their age difference, the two were fruitful and they did multiply. Over the next fourteen years Emily gave birth to seven children. She was pregnant, nursing, or both, for a decade and a half. In the end, she outlived her husband, which was to be expected, and outlived four of her children, which was tragic. Only one of her children, Louise, would provide grandchildren, neither of who would marry. That branch of the Hawkins family tree came to an end, unremarkable in its entirety unless Louise turns out to have created Sherlock Holmes.

Louise, born in 1857 on the family's farm in Wales, was the sixth of Emily and Jeremiah's seven children. Five of the seven would die before their time, perhaps in each case from tuberculosis.

In *Out of the* Shadows, Georgina Doyle tells us that Mary, Louise's oldest sibling, died at age thirty-six not long after moving to New Zealand. "Poor Mary must have endured a painful voyage, dying of a disease of the bone in two vertebrae which she had suffered for several months, and also an abscess on the brain." Mary's symptoms are consistent with tuberculosis of the spine, such as that suffered by Mark Twain's wife, Olivia Clemens.

Jeremiah, hereafter referred to as Jeremy to minimize confusion, was Louise's oldest brother. Georgina Doyle tells us that he died at age forty-seven of "diarrhoea lasting five days and long-standing general debility." His symptoms are consistent with a persistent tubercular infection that spread to his abdomen. One of the classic symptoms of abdominal tuberculosis is long-standing diarrhea, and another certainly is general debility.

Charles died at an unknown age, presumably so young as to not leave any genealogical mark or record other than his date of birth.

John, Louise's only younger sibling, died at age twenty-five, a resident patient of Dr. Arthur Conan Doyle. John succumbed to cerebral meningitis, a common secondary infection of tuberculosis.

Because tuberculosis ran in families, people long believed it to be hereditary. After Robert Koch's identification of its bacterial origin, people came to understand that families shared the disease because they breathed the same air and ate the same food. Tuberculosis of the lungs usually spreads through the air, and the extrapulmonary forms can spread via contaminated milk.

Bovine TB affects a broad range of mammalian hosts, including cows, badgers, and humans. Not only did infected cattle spread bovine TB among their own herd, badgers spread the disease from herd to herd. This was a particular problem in rural Victorian Britain where the badgers were drawn to the oil cakes used to feed the cows, where the milk was not pasteurized, and where neither the cows nor their milk was tested for TB.

Since each of the Hawkins children, other than John, had been born on a farm, *Mycobacterium bovis* provides a feasible explanation for Mary's spinal affliction, Jeremy's debility and fatal diarrhea, and Charles apparent childhood death. Even children such as John, born and raised in a suburban area, were at risk of bovine TB from the milk imported and consumed.

Thomas Dormandy explained all this in *The White Death: The History of Tuberculosis* (2000).

Tuberculosis may infect any part of the body, but most commonly occurs in the lungs (known as pulmonary tuberculosis). Extrapulmonary TB occurs when tuberculosis develops outside of the lungs. [...] General signs and symptoms include fever, chills, night sweats, loss of appetite, weight loss, and fatigue, and significant finger clubbing may also occur. [...] In many people, the infection waxes and wanes. Tissue destruction and necrosis are often balanced by healing and fibrosis. Affected tissue is replaced by scarring and cavities filled with caseous necrotic material. [...]

Intestinal tuberculosis [...] in children was the typical presentation of the bovine strain. It could be an agonisingly painful illness, a succession of episodes of acute or subacute intestinal obstruction [...] Death was often due to progressive malnutrition and general debility.

The bovine organism may also have been responsible for nearly half of all cases of tuberculosis meningitis, the most rapidly fatal form of the system; and it was probably a frequent cause of tuberculosis of the bones and joints, the genitourinary system, the cervical lymph-nodes and lupus vulgaris. In some parts of the world it was—and still is—the chief killer of babies and young children.

Louise would suffer from multiple forms of tuberculosis, including pulmonary and, late in life, laryngeal. When her doctor determined that her pulmonary tuberculosis had turned "galloping and wasting," he explained to Arthur that there was little hope, particularly given her family history.

Louise and John

When Louise was only two years old, her father retired from farming and moved the family to Leckhampton Road, an affluent street in an affluent suburb of the affluent English town of Cheltenham. The 1861 census records John being born there and Louise living there, noting that she was a "Scholar." The notation indicates that Louise was already attending school or being formally educated, though she was only three years old.

Louise's father is described as a retired farmer, wealthy enough to afford a governess and a house servant. As late as 1866, local directories record Jeremiah still living on Leckhampton Road. Sometime before 1870, however, the family might have fractured. Local directories show that Jeremiah had returned to Minsterworth. The 1871 census reveals that the blind, seventy-six-year-old Jeremiah was living separately from his forty-five-year-old wife.

Emily, the mother, was by then living with, or perhaps just visiting, her sister, Louise's aunt, in Whitchurch, one hundred miles to the north of Jeremiah. None of her children are listed as living with her.

Mary, aged twenty-four, and Emily, aged sixteen, were living with their father on his farm in Minsterworth; under "Rank, Profession, or Occupation," the census records Mary as "housekeeper" and Emily as "daughter."

Jeremy, aged twenty-three, was living in the Barnwood House Hospital, a private asylum in Gloucester. Joseph, aged twenty-one, was working as a civil engineer, far away near the Bristol Channel in Neath. The mysterious Charles may have moved to Australia or New Zealand.

John, aged eleven, was at Camden House School in Bristol. Herbert Fry, in *Our Schools and Colleges* (1868), described the school thusly:

> Bristol, Camden House School, Kingsdown. Instructs in Classics, Mathematics, French, German, &c., boarders at Forty to Fifty Guineas, day boys at Twelve to Sixteen Guineas per ann[um]. William Benham, Ph. D., Master.

Interestingly, in the Sherlock Holmes Canon, Camden House is located directly across the street from 221B Baker Street, being the eponymous structure of *The Empty House* (1903). In reality, Camden

House School was tantalizingly close to the Badminton School for Girls, just a mile distant. At the same time that John Hawkins was the second youngest of twenty-three resident "scholars" at Camden, thirteen-year-old Louise Hawkins was the youngest of twenty-three resident "pupils" at Badminton.

Established in 1858 by Miriam Badock, Badminton was an independent boarding and day school for girls. An advertising flyer from 1861 summed up the curriculum:

> Mrs. William F. Badock superintends the education of a limited number of Young Ladies. The general course of Study includes French (which is made the medium of conversation) with a sound English Education comprising Writing, Arithmetic, Grammar, Composition, Elocution, Biblical Knowledge, Geography, Ancient and Modern History, Natural Philosophy, Botany, Astronomy, Calisthenics, Deportment, Plain and Fancy Needlework.

Nigel Watson, in *Badminton School: The First 150 Years* (2008), wrote of the school:

> Girls could also learn German and Italian for an extra fee. Latin was added three years later. [...] The inclusion of science was unusual. The subject was often ignored in girls' schools although it scarcely fared any better in many boys' schools of the period. When Badminton began, it was the responsibility of William, Miriam's husband, who gave lectures and conducted elementary experiments in an amateur laboratory.

When Dr. Watson first meets Holmes, Holmes is busily at work in a chemistry laboratory. After Nigel Watson mentioned the laboratory at Badminton, he explained that excellent instruction was provided there:

The school was among the earliest to enter girls for the Junior and Senior Cambridge Local Examinations. When the local committee asked Mrs Badock to send in pupils for the exams, she had no hesitation, calling for volunteers from among the girls. Her daughter remembered that "it was considered a most advanced and dangerous thing to do and there was great excitement about it." Competitive examinations, remember, were regarded as injurious to female health. All those first entrants passed. They were taught largely by unqualified staff because women could not graduate from an English university until 1878. One girl at the school in the late 1880s recollected that there was only one mistress on the staff with a degree. [...] Mrs Badock was by all accounts an outstanding maths teacher.

According to the 1871 census, the oldest resident student at Badminton was nineteen years of age. Assuming Louise attended Badminton until she was just as old, she would have spent six years there, graduating in 1877.

Similarly, the 1871 census records the oldest resident student at Camden House to have been seventeen years of age. Assuming John attended Camden House until he was just as old, he too would have spent six years there, just a mile from Louise, graduating just when she did.

Louise and John appear together again four years later, in 1881, at least according to one interpretation of *The Stark Munro Letters* (1895). The book is purportedly a semi-autobiographical epistolary novel based on Arthur's young adult life. In *Memories and Adventures*, Arthur explained, "I drew in very close detail the events of the next few years [...] I would only remark, should any reader reconstruct me or my career from that book, that there are some few incidents there which are imaginary."

In the novel, in 1881, Arthur (in the guise of Stark Munro) is riding on a train, sitting across from an elderly lady (obviously Louise's mother), Louise herself (in the guise of Winnie LaForce), and one of Louise's brothers (called Fred), who was "a year or two older." Arthur's fellow travelers have given up housekeeping, finding life more pleasant living in apartments. The trio is traveling to Southsea (Birchespool in the novel) to take up residence there. Suddenly, the brother experiences an epileptic fit, kicks Arthur in the leg, and thereby frightens his sister and mother. Arthur saves the day by tearing open the epileptic's collar, unbuttoning his waistcoat, and holding his head down on the seat. After a heel crashes through the carriage window, Arthur sits across the knees and holds on to the wrists. In gratitude, Louise's mother gives Arthur her card, and Arthur promises to call on her should he ever be in Southsea.

As of October 1884, Emily, Louise, and John Hawkins were indeed living in Southsea, at No. 2, Queen's Gate, as close to the English Channel as one could reside in Southsea. In March of 1885, John would suffer cerebral meningitis, become Arthur's resident patient, die soon thereafter, and be buried on the twenty-seventh of the month.

The Stark Munro Letters raises multiple issues of interest to us in our search for Holmes's creator. First and most obviously, the book calls into question Arthur's claim of when and under what circumstances he first met Louise. In *Memories and Adventures*, Arthur glosses over the issue.

> In the year 1885 [...] I was married. A lady named Mrs. Hawkins, a widow of a Gloucestershire family, had come to Southsea with her son and daughter, the latter a very gentle and amiable girl. I was brought into contact with them through the illness of the son, which was of a sudden and violent nature, arising from cerebral meningitis.

Arthur explained that he volunteered to accept the son as a resident patient. Not long thereafter, in the same paragraph, the son succumbed while under Arthur's roof, and the police investigated, but only briefly.

> The family were naturally grieved at the worry to which they had quite innocently exposed me, and so

our relations became intimate and sympathetic, which ended in the daughter consenting to share my fortunes. We were married on August 6, 1885, and no man could have had a more gentle and amiable life's companion.

Arthur said nothing about meeting them earlier on a train. In fact, it is clear that he claimed to have never met any of them before being asked to care for the ailing John Hawkins. The date of their meeting in *The Stark Munro Letters*, however, is nearly specified. The letter in which Stark Munro tells his pen pal of the epileptic encounter is dated 7 March 1882. The contents of the letter place the encounter no earlier than two days previous. We are left with a discrepancy of three years. Did Louise and Arthur first meet in March of 1882 or three years later, early in 1885?

Louise and Arthur

Arthur managed to compress the entirety of his engagement and marriage into a single paragraph, one he used mostly to discuss Louise's mother and brother. Louise is not even mentioned by name, there or anywhere else in Arthur's autobiography. Instead, on the rare occasion when Arthur does refer to her, he relies on impersonal nouns such as "gentle and amiable girl," "the daughter," "my wife," or (on multiple occasions) "the invalid." Consider, for example, Arthur's justification for leaving Louise behind with his sister, whom he did name, while he toured America: "In the meantime, Lottie's presence and the improvement of the invalid, which was so marked that no sudden crisis was thought at all possible, gave me renewed liberty of action."

Such rude autobiographical treatment of his first wife, Louise, resulted probably from demands of his second wife, Jean. Louise was ultimately purged not just from Arthur's autobiography, but from the family papers as well. Initial biographies were written under the supervising eye of Adrian Conan Doyle, youngest son of the second marriage. Because of the great purge, later biographers were left with little material about Louise. Limited to information presumably spoon-fed by Adrian, the biographers consistently damned Louise with faint praise.

One of the earliest of Arthur's biographers, John Dickson Carr, set the disparaging standard by describing Louise, in *The Life of Sir Arthur Conan Doyle* (1949), as a domesticated, unenlightened, fawning personality, thrilled to listen as Arthur talked down to her.

> Of Louise, twenty-seven years old—"Touie," her nickname was—he saw a great deal. Though not beautiful, she was of a type which appealed to him; the round face, the wide mouth, the brown hair, the wide spaced blue eyes, shading to sea green, which were her finest feature. Her gentleness, her complete unselfishness, roused all his protective instincts. Louise, or Touie, was what they called a home-girl, loving needlework and an armchair by the fire. He met her in sorrow; and ended by falling deeply in love. Towards the end of April they were engaged.

Carr wrote that the two settled into Arthur's medical office and residence where, in the upstairs sitting room, they passed their free time.

> "Shall we read aloud together, my dear," he would suggest, "and improve our minds? Say Gordon's Tacitus? Or perhaps, in a lighter vein, Boswell's Johnson or Pepy's [*sic*] Diary?"
>
> "Oh, do!" cried Touie, who would have been just as eager to hear him read in Sanskrit if he had possessed that accomplishment.

Charles Higham, in *The Adventures of Conan Doyle* (1976), was more direct and thorough with his derision.

> Louise was not gifted or well-read, but she made the ideal Victorian housewife, with sewing, mending, and cleaning her chief interests. [...] When he was racked by some complex question of metaphysics, Louise

could fix a cup of tea. When he came home from a long walk or from a séance, or sank back pale and exhausted from writing some horrific story, she could ease off his shoes and massage his feet and brow. He loved her with all the passionate adoration of a Victorian man for a little woman who adored him worshipfully. For this tormented genius, as brooding and abstracted as Poe behind the respectable mask of a sports-living *Times* reader, the relationship worked perfectly.

Martin Booth was exceptionally spare with his words, at least when it came to Louise. Without ever mentioning their meeting or wedding, he dispatched her with a single sentence in *The Doctor, the Detective and Arthur Conan Doyle* (1997).

His marriage was happy, if perhaps unexciting, Louise playing her part as doctor's spouse and housewife, welcoming patients, entertaining visitors and not intruding upon either her husband's creative or his social existence.

The Man Who Created Sherlock Holmes (2007) deals with Louise more fairly than had the earlier biographies. There, Andrew Lycett records:

Arthur found himself drawn to Louise, a quiet jolie-laide woman with wispy brown hair, an appealing rounded face and soft green eyes. Almost twenty-seven at the time of her brother's death, she was two years older than Arthur. Her helplessness and his nagging guilt combined as aphrodisiacs.

Lycett portrayed Louise as a helpless *jolie-laide*, a French term (literally "pretty-ugly") used to describe someone who is somehow attractive despite being not conventionally beautiful. Photographs present Louise in variable fashion. She could be pretty, but she was neither beautiful nor particularly sophisticated in terms of aesthetics.

Louise (right) and Arthur (center) at South Norwood

In *Out of the Shadows*, Georgina Doyle provides a particularly alluring photograph of Louise attired in an all-black dress with long sleeves and a high collar. Louise's back is turned three-quarters to the camera, and her head turned only slightly, allowing her face to be lit in almost perfect profile. Her hair is straight and tied up, revealing the curve of her back and a pleasing figure, even soon after childbirth. On her left hip she holds her baby Mary, plump, bald and dressed in an overly long white gown. The contrast between the two consecutive members of the same lineage, particularly in black and white, is striking.

Though Arthur's biographers tend to dismiss Louise's intellect and sophistication, no one has ever questioned her kind and gentle nature. Her daughter Mary provided Arthur's biographer Pierre Nordon this touching recollection, from *Conan Doyle* (1966):

> My mother was a tiny little woman with dainty hands and feet, and lovely shadowy eyes that always seemed to see beyond what she was looking at. There was a gentle all-lovingness about her that drew the

simple folk, children, and animals to her, as to a magnet. She had the quiet poise that comes rather from the wisdom of the spirit than from the knowledge of the world, and there ran through her a bright ripple of fun, that would glint in the eyes, and hover round her mouth. It was a sense of fun rather than a more sophisticated sense of humour, because Mother never smiled at a joke at anyone else's expense. At such moments a shadow passed over her face, and her silence would rebuke the joker. But she loved the comical aspects of life and the unconscious humour in people and things.

Mary, Kingsley, and Louise

Georgina Doyle, widow of John Doyle and thereby daughter-in-law to Arthur's only brother, Innes, had access to family knowledge unavailable to other biographers. Her biography focused, at least more than did the others, on Louise and her two children, and she aptly entitled it *Out of the Shadows: The Untold Story of Arthur Conan Doyle's First Family*. Louise has indeed been a shadowy figure, but Georgina's book brings some light.

The Doyle family adored Louise. Again and again I
have had clear indication of this: from my husband,
John, whose inherited knowledge of her came from
her daughter, Mary, and also indirectly from Innes;
from Claire Oldham [daughter of one of Arthur's
sisters]; and from Barbie Foley through her mother-
in-law, Ida [another of Arthur's sisters]. Between
them, down through the years, they have kept alive
the memory of a beautiful, charming, and unaffected
woman, who had a warm, gentle, and loving
personality.

Georgina Doyle was the first biographer to paint Arthur with
something other than a completely flattering brush. She was also the
first to suggest that Louise was not quite the vapid homebody that
Arthur's biographers portrayed. Georgina noted, for example, that
the 1861 census recorded the young Louise as a "Scholar." The
notation means that Louise was already attending school or being
formally educated, though she was only three years old. Everyone
though, including Georgina Doyle, seems to have missed the obscure
entry in the 1871 census, the one listing Louise as a resident student
at the prestigious Badminton School for Girls.

Louise and Arthur were wed at St. Oswald's Church, Thornton-
in-Lonsdale, Yorkshire, on 6 August 1885. After John's death in
Southsea, Louise had been sent north to await the wedding as a guest
of Arthur's mother. Arthur arrived no earlier than two days before
the marriage, having spent the previous months in Southsea,
working on his dissertation, bowling, and playing cricket.

Within days of the wedding, Arthur was in Ireland, unable to stay
long off the cricket field. Most biographers who bother to mention
Arthur's foray into Ireland claim that Louise and Arthur
honeymooned there. Some suggest that Arthur managed to fit in a bit
of cricketing. Both positions amount to little more than speculation;
no evidence places Louise in Ireland with Arthur. Only Andrew
Lycett seems to have considered the alternative.

So Louise may have spent the first week of married life involuntarily bonding with her new mother-in-law at Masongill Cottage. This would have been in keeping with Arthur's unthinking presumptions about the relative merits of his sporting life and her emotional needs.

When Arthur returned to Southsea, his fellow bowlers threw him a celebratory dinner. The 18 September issue of Portsmouth's *Evening News* described the fête.

> Presentation to a Southsea Doctor. At the Bush Hotel last evening a presentation was made of a handsome dinner service by members of Southsea Bowling Club to their popular President, Dr Conan Doyle. Mr T. Reynolds [...] alluded to the recent marriage of their President, and wished him every happiness in his future career. The dinner was a slight token of the esteem in which Conan Doyle was held by members, not only in his capacity as President but for his private character.

It seems obvious that Louise was not invited, particularly since Arthur's mates wished only "him every happiness." As a member of the fairer sex, Louise was excluded also from the meetings of the Portsmouth Literary and Scientific Society, the major social organization in the area. Geoffrey Stavert, in *A Study in Southsea* (1987), described the social climate that then prevailed.

> This was the period, of course, when Queen Victoria's reign still had another twenty years to run; when men were men and women knew their place. [...] A certain amount of chauvinist piggery, therefore, was only to be expected. Ladies were not eligible to become members of the Literary and Scientific Society. They could attend the meetings, and often did in quite considerable numbers, but only as guests. This meant, however, that since they were only

guests they were not allowed to speak; they could not raise questions or join in any discussion.

By 1887, the dues-paying membership of the Society dropped to precipitously low numbers, and the few remaining members considered the previously unthinkable: perhaps women should be allowed to join if they paid the same dues as men. The editor of the *Hampshire Post* wrote of the prospect, with barely contained distaste.

> Whether the ladies will care to be taxed in this way, for the bare recognition of their equality with men, when they know very well, without any payment at all, that they are greatly superior, remains to be seen. But, since they are admitted with gentlemen to witness the performances, there is no reason why they should not be asked, the same as in the case of gentlemen, to pay for the privilege. The subscription will of course confer upon them the right of participating in discussions, but we sincerely trust that they will refrain.

Sherlock Holmes was born eight months after Louise married Arthur, as though a month premature. We already learned of the delivery from the April 1886 letter the proud parents sent to Arthur's sister. "Arthur has written another book," Louise wrote, "a little novel about 200 pages long, called 'A Study in Scarlet.' It went off last night." Also in that letter, Louise mentioned that everyone else had gone off to church and that she and Arthur were left "alone in our glory."

Arthur was an apostate Catholic and Louise a nonconformist Protestant. At least, the Badminton School was nonconformist in its teachings. Nigel Watson wrote of the school's religious leaning while describing its move to Worcester Terrace, where Louise attended: "A number of staunch Anglican residents were appalled that they not only had another nonconformist family in their midst (one was already living on the Terrace) but also a nonconformist school."

It is interesting that Louise would brag of missing church when all those about her were in attendance. Sherlock Holmes seems equally indifferent to religion, first discussing the subject in his twenty-fifth published adventure. Arthur's questioning led him to a life committed to spiritualism. Louise, on the other hand, seems to have regained a more conventional faith sometime before she died, apparently being baptized and adopting a new name. Though born Louisa and preferring Louise, the name on both her death certificate and her casket is Mary Louise Conan Doyle.

On 28 January 1889, while still living in Southsea, Louise gave birth to a daughter named, not surprisingly, Mary Louise Conan Doyle. Astonishingly, Arthur seems never to have informed his mother that Louise was pregnant. We learn of that shocking withholding of vital information in a letter Arthur sent his mother on the day of his daughter's birth.

> Toodles [Louise] produced this morning at 6.15 a remarkably fine specimen of the Toodles minor, who is now howling her head off in the back bedroom. [...] Forgive me for not telling you dear. I knew how trying the suspense would be, and thought that on the whole it would be best that you should learn when it was too late to worry yourself.

Consumption

Given that Arthur's mother had weathered nine pregnancies of her own, his excuse of protecting her is suspect. Perhaps Arthur withheld the information because he realized from the beginning that Louise's pregnancy would be unusually risky. Though Arthur never acknowledged it, Louise may have been consumptive even when they married. He subsequently assured his mother that Louise and the baby were doing nicely. He wrote her again on 14 February, seventeen days after the birth, informing her that Louise was not yet sitting up, but might soon try. On 26 February, four full weeks after the birth, Arthur offered an encouraging announcement: "Touie & baby came down yesterday."

Suspicious episodes appear yearly after Louise's hushed up pregnancy. In 1890, according to *Memories and Adventures*, Arthur claimed he became suddenly interested in Koch's proposed cure for tuberculosis. "I could give no clear reason for this, but it was an irresistible impulse and I at once determined to go." Since we now have reason to believe that Arthur did not actually travel to Berlin, we should be skeptical of his claim that he had only recently become interested in cures for tuberculosis.

In 1891, after having settled in the London suburb of South Norwood, Arthur informed his mother that he had purchased a tandem tricycle. The cycle had two large side-by-side wheels and a small trailing wheel. Arthur sat between the large wheels, above and behind the axle. Louise sat somewhat lower, in front of the axle. Arthur was proud of how fast and far he could propel them both. He described to his mother one particular challenging outing: a trip through Woking, Reading, and Chertsey before returning home. He did not mention that the distance would have been seventy-five miles. "We both find it very healthy exercise," he wrote. "I don't know when we have been in such good condition."

On one instance at least, Louise became too tired to continue. Arthur sent her home on a train and continued without her.

The cycling may have been an effort to force fresh air deep into Louise's tubercular lungs. Climbing, horseback riding, sailing, and cycling were all considered preventative and curative exercises, since each allegedly forced air into the lungs. Hobart Amory Hare discussed the benefits of such exercises to consumptives in his *A System of Practical Therapeutics* (1891).

> [W]here the character of the country permits it, ascents proportionate to the age and strength of the individual should be prescribed. These ascents should be made with slow and measured steps, in order to avoid fatigue to the respiratory organs; and there should be occasional rests by the way. To expand the lungs as much as possible, especially while climbing, the elbows should be made to approach each other behind the back, and a walking-

stick be supported between them; or the arms may be folded behind the back, with or without a stick being thrust through. Even without this the head and trunk should be kept erect and the shoulders well thrown back. Whether walking on a level or climbing the patient must be instructed to breathe deeply and slowly. He must take a long breath, hold it as long as possible without causing distress, and let it out slowly. [...]

Walking or other exercise—let it be repeated— whether for prophylaxis or for cure, should never be permitted to pass the point of gentle and pleasant fatigue. A wealthy patient in the city or country may have his carriage follow him while he walks. Riding on pony-, donkey-, or horse-back, on tricycle or bicycle, is also a good form of exercise. "One brisk ride is (sometimes) worth a dozen lazy walks;" and Sydenham, echoed by Rush, declares a journey on horseback to be a sure cure for consumption.

Early in 1892, Arthur wrote to his mother that he intended to have his small family spend the next winter on the Riviera. That region had long been believed to be an ideal wintering ground for consumptives. The tubercular Dr. James Henry Bennet described, in *Winter and Spring on the Shores of the Mediterranean* (1875), how he went there "to die in a quiet corner [...] like a wounded denizen of the forest." Dr. Bennet survived and spread the word.

With the assistance of sunshine, a dry, bracing atmosphere, a mild temperature [...] I have found pulmonary consumption in this favoured region, especially in its earlier stages, by no means the intractable disease that I formerly found it in London and Paris. After fifteen winters passed at Mentone, I am surrounded by a phalanx of cured or arrested consumption cases.

When arguing for the Riviera, Arthur explained, "We shall work better & be better in the Riviera than here." The use of the plural *we*, as in "we shall work better", is particularly tantalizing. Certainly Arthur was referring to his writing; was he referring also to Louise's?

Later that year, in an interview for *The Strand*, Arthur pontificated about climatological health benefits, but not of the temperate Riviera. He spoke instead of the freezing Arctic.

> What a climate it is in those regions! We don't understand it here. I don't mean its coldness—I refer to its sanitary properties. I believe, in years to come, it will be the world's sanatorium. Here, thousands of miles from the smoke, where the air is the finest in the world, the invalid and weakly ones will go when all other places have failed to give them the air they want, and revive and live again under the marvellous invigorating properties of the Arctic atmosphere.

Still later that year, Arthur did explore for therapeutic air, but in neither the Riviera nor the Arctic. Instead he traveled to Norway in the company of family and friends, and apparently in the absence of Louise. She is never mentioned among the travelers, perhaps understandably so, since she was at that time pregnant with Kingsley. Arthur learned to ski while in Norway, and boasted later that he introduced the sport to Switzerland.

While in Norway, Arthur visited St. George's Leprosy Hospital in Bergen, on the southwest coast of the country. Leprosy and tuberculosis are similar diseases in several respects. Leprosy is a chronic infection caused by *Mycobacterium leprae*. Tuberculosis is a chronic infection caused by *Mycobacterium tuberculosis*. The bacteria are quite similar in appearance, in their ability to hide inside their host for decades, and in the nature of their symptoms when they burst forth. Classic symptoms of leprosy include granulomas (nodules) of the skin, eyes, nerves, and respiratory tract. Tuberculosis is most commonly associated with masses (tubercles) formed within the lung, but the scrofulous form exhibits grotesque masses on the neck.

Bergen is of interest also because it was renowned for the quality of its cod liver oil, which is known also (not surprisingly) as Bergen oil. In 1848, physicians at the Hospital for Consumption and Diseases of the Chest in Chelsea tested cod liver oil as a treatment for tuberculosis. They gave 542 phthisic patients cod liver oil three times a day. (Phthisis, pronounced *thigh sis*, was the medical term for pulmonary tuberculosis.) Another 535 phthisic patients were used as a control group. Of those provided cod liver oil, 18% had all or nearly all of their symptoms disappear while 19% deteriorated or died. The comparative numbers for the control group were 6% and 33%. The study suggested that cod-liver oil increased the chances of improvement by a factor of three and cut the chance of further deterioration by nearly half.

Beyond its leprosy hospital and its high-grade cod liver oil, Bergen might have been of interest because the city was the disembarkation point for anyone traveling between London and the Tonsaassen Sanatorium. The hospital for consumptives was located 2000 feet above sea level in the mountains of Norway. Richard Douglas Powell, the person who would later offer Louise her terrible prognosis, described the sanatorium in his 1899 *Sanatoria for Consumptives*.

> There are verandahs or balconies on every floor. The furniture is simple. The lighting is by electricity. Ventilation by open windows, day and night, summer and winter. There are said to be good water-closets and baths. The waste water is carried into a brook. In winter the sewage is covered with earth.
>
> The establishment is open throughout the year. It was built in 1881, and has been a winter station since 1885. No advanced cases are admitted. Treatment is by open air, in the verandahs or balconies, or in the pavilions in the woods. Patients who are fit for it take plenty of exercise. There is a very complete apparatus for hydrotherapy, with vapour baths, needle baths, ferruginous, hot and cold baths, etc. Patients in summer have friction with water at 15° to

20° C, or douches [showers]. In winter, dry friction and partial ablutions are substituted. Five or six meals are provided daily, with alcohol in great moderation. Cod-liver oil and specifics are little used. The sputa are put into a cask with [a solution] of ferrous sulphate, and after a month are burnt. Patients bring their own bedcovers and pillows. Mattresses are disinfected by brushing with [a corrosive sublimate] followed by solution of washing soda. Rooms are rubbed with bread and then washed with soap and water. There is one nurse.

In 1893, Louise and Arthur considered visiting, perhaps moving to, the South Pacific. Robert Louis Stevenson had moved there already after finding that the cold, clean air of Switzerland's Davos Platz did not cure his tuberculosis. Stevenson mentioned the impending visit in a letter to Arthur.

Delighted to hear I have a chance of seeing you and Mrs. Doyle; Mrs. Stevenson bids me say (what is too true) that our rations are often spare. Are you Great Eaters? Please reply.

As to ways and means, here is what you will have to do. Leave San Francisco by the down mail, get off at Samoa [...] We are in the midst of war here; rather a nasty business, with the head-taking; and there seem signs of other trouble. But I believe you need make no change in your design to visit us. All should be well over; and if it were not, why! you need not leave the steamer.

Louise did not follow Stevenson to Samoa, but she did follow him to Davos Platz. By September of that year, 1893, her tuberculosis became too obvious to ignore. In his autobiography, Arthur claimed the turning point came after they had returned from an earlier trip to Switzerland.

I now come to the great misfortune which darkened and deflected our lives. I have said that my wife and I had taken a tour in Switzerland. I do not know whether she had overtaxed herself in this excursion, or whether we encountered microbes in some inn bedroom, but the fact remains that within a few weeks of our return she complained of pain in her side and cough. I had no suspicion of anything serious, but sent for the nearest good physician. To my surprise and alarm he told me when he descended from the bedroom that the lungs were very gravely affected, that there was every sign of rapid consumption and that he thought the case a most serious one with little hope, considering her record and family history, of a permanent cure. With two children, aged four and one, and a wife who was in such deadly danger, the situation was a difficult one. I confirmed the diagnosis by having Sir Douglas Powell down to see her, and I then set all my energy to work to save the situation. The home was abandoned, the newly bought furniture was sold, and we made for Davos in the High Alps where there seemed the best chance of killing this accursed microbe which was rapidly eating out her vitals.

Almost nothing here withstands scrutiny. One deception is his claim that he "set all his energy" to save her. They had returned from Switzerland near the beginning of September, meaning that her terminal diagnosis must have been in that month. Yet, instead of making for Davos, Arthur set off on a lecture tour throughout England and Scotland. Through October, November, and early December, he gave somewhere between eighteen and twenty-one lectures. Also during that period he attended several meetings of the Upper Norwood Literary and Scientific Society, joined the British Society for Psychical Research, and hung out at the all-male Reform Club in London.

Arthur's most poignant lie, however, is the plural pronoun in his claim "we made for Davos in the High Alps." According to a residence list provided in the *Davoser Blätter*, Louise and her sister Emily were residents of the Curhaus Davos as of 2 November. Arthur was not with them. He was still in England, only then beginning his lecture tour, and having no intention of cutting it short. "My wife has fallen ill," he wrote to his lecture agent Gerald Christy, "and has had to go to Davos. Of course, I shall let no private matter—however urgent—interfere with my engagements." He signed his unfaithful letter "Yours faithfully, A Conan Doyle."

Arthur joined Louise in Davos by Christmas. During her remaining thirteen years, however, Arthur managed to frequently remove himself from her, both physically and emotionally. In 1894, he absented himself from Switzerland and Louise for nine months. In 1895, he indulged Louise with his company somewhat more, returning to England perhaps only twice that year.

Arthur longed for England. After two years in the Alps, the disintegrating couple wintered in Egypt. There, Arthur left her behind twice to sail up the Nile, hoping to join Kitchener's army as it prepared to invade Sudan. Thereafter they returned to England. Within a year, they settled into an expensive, expansive, custom-designed mansion called Undershaw, located in the village of Hindhead, forty miles southwest of London. Arthur rationalized the move by declaring that the slightly elevated English air would be better for Louise than the high-altitude cold air of Switzerland, or the balmy, sea-level hot air of Cairo. "If we could have ordered Nature to construct a spot for us we could not have hit upon anything more perfect," he wrote his mother.

The 10,000 square-foot, fourteen-bedroom house included a generator for electric lighting, a dining room large enough to seat thirty, a billiards room, a grand staircase with shallow steps to ease Louie's ascent, and doors that swung in both directions to ease her coming and going. Arthur's wood-paneled drawing room featured weapons, stuffed birds, walrus tusks, and trophies. No room in the house, however, was large enough for a grand piano. Louise settled for an upright.

Arthur and Louise moved into Undershaw in October of 1897. The very next month, Arthur had the temerity to allow Jean, his second wife in waiting, to dine there with his family.

Chapter 6
Calling Cards

A Death's-Head Hawkmoth is easily distinguishable by the pattern, on its thorax, of a human skull. This interesting creature, when threatened, emits a loud squeak and flashes its brightly colored abdomen. It raids bee colonies of their honey by mimicking their scent. It flies faster than any other moth, and it hovers over flowers to drink the nectar. In the 1991 thriller *Silence of the Lambs*, Buffalo Bill places a Death's-head Hawkmoth in the throat of each of his victims. It is his calling card.

In *The Pink Panther* series of movies, the Phantom leaves behind a monogrammed white glove after each successful burglary.

In *Home Alone* (1990), the Wet Bandits leave the water running after burglarizing the homes of people on vacation.

In the Sherlock Holmes adventures, the author left behind distinctive calling cards. Three of those calling cards stemmed from a propensity for puzzles (eschewed by Arthur), a fascination for Mark Twain (a person of no interest to Arthur), and the unique use of function words.

Sidney Paget

English illustrator Sidney Paget was the man who drew the now-iconic illustrations that accompanied *A Scandal in Bohemia* upon its publication in the July 1891 edition of *The Strand*. He had no involvement with the first two Holmes adventures, the novellas *A Study in Scarlet* and *The Sign of Four*, but he did illustrate the next thirty-eight tales. So renowned did he become for his contribution to the Sherlock Holmes mythos that his original "Holmes and Moriarty in Mortal Combat" illustration sold, in 2004, for $220,800.

Sidney Paget and his first Watson and Holmes illustration (left); July 1891
cover of *The Strand* (right)

There is, within *A Scandal in Bohemia*, an apparent allusion to
Paget. Holmes receives a note requesting his assistance. He gives
Watson the opportunity to study the note and offer any thoughts.
Watson observes that the paper on which the note is written "is
peculiarly strong and stiff." Holmes then picks up the conversation.

> "Peculiar—that is the very word," said Holmes. "It is
> not an English paper at all. Hold it up to the light."
> I did so, and saw a large *E* with a small *g*, a *P*, and
> a large *G* with a small *t* woven into the texture of the
> paper.
> "What do you make of that?" asked Holmes.

Holmes poses the question to the readers as well as to Watson.
The letters PgGEt nearly comprise an anagram for Paget's last name.
If one covers the descender of g, one sees *PaGEt*. It is an imperfect
result, but as Holmes elsewhere concedes, "I can discover facts,
Watson, but I cannot change them."

The Harry Ransom Center has, by generously opening the
Scandal manuscript to the public, changed the facts. Watson's

original sentence from page 5 of the manuscript reads somewhat differently than that printed in *The Strand*, and in critical detail. "I did so," reads the manuscript, "and saw a large *E* with a small *a*, a *P*, and a large *G* with a small *t* woven into the texture of the paper."

*"Peculiar—that is the very word" said Holmes "It is not an English paper atall. Hold it up to the light"
"I did so and saw a large E with a small a, a P, and a large G with a small t woven into the texture of the paper*

A large *E* with a small *a*, a *P*, and a large *G* with a small *t*

As the letters are written in the manuscript, but not in any printed version of the story, they do form a perfect anagram for *PaGEt*. It seems that the author was alluding to her story's illustrator, Sidney Paget, after all.

An allusion is a figure of speech in which a writer refers indirectly, perhaps covertly, to a person or an event. It is the writer's role to determine how obvious or obscure the allusion will be. It is the reader's role to recognize the allusion, or to miss it. Allusions can therefore be envisioned as covert puzzles to be detected and solved by the readers. The word "allusion" in fact derives from the Latin verb *ludere*, meaning "to play with" or "to jest." The author of *A Scandal in Bohemia* has been playing with us for more than a century.

The unknown author could have expected that this story would be placed in *The Strand*, which had already received Arthur's *The Voice of Science* in January, and published it in March. Standard practice at *The Strand* was to include illustrations with its stories, one of the magazine's hallmarks since its first edition ran in January of 1891. *The Voice of Science* had been accompanied by five illustrations, each by Walter Stacey. Furthermore, the author would have known of Paget as an illustrator, at least of Henry Marriott Paget, Sidney's older brother, who was, at the time, more widely recognized for his illustrative talent. More to the point, Henry Paget provided illustrations for Arthur's already published novel *Micah Clarke*.

Henry Marriott Paget illustrations from the 1890 Silver Library Edition of
Micah Clarke

The youngest of the three Paget brothers was Walter, prolific
contributor of illustrations both for magazines and popular novels,
including *Robinson Crusoe* and *Treasure Island*.

Walter Paget illustrations from *Robinson Crusoe* (left)
and *Treasure Island* (right)

A careful comparison of the three brothers' works suggests that the author of *A Scandal of Bohemia* expected the story to be illustrated by Walter rather than Sidney. The anagram for *PaGEt* would have been far too obscure unless the illustrator's last name actually appeared somewhere in the illustrations. Sidney signed his illustrations "SP," and none of his ten illustrations for *Scandal* reveal his last name. Similarly, Henry also signed his illustrations with his initials, and his "HMP" is visible on the two images from *Micah Clarke*. Of the three brothers, only Walter's signature included the entirety of their last name. As can be seen on his illustrations for *Robinson Crusoe* and *Treasure Island*, Walter signed his illustrations "Wal Paget."

Even in the absence of insight into the possible *PaGEt* anagram, Arthur's biographers have long accepted that *The Strand* actually intended all along to commission Walter, not Sidney, to illustrate its Sherlock Holmes series. Different biographers offer various explanations for the confusion, but all agree it was merely by accident that Sidney came to be the illustrator. One common version holds that an editor simply forgot Walter's first name and sent the offer to "Mr. Paget the Illustrator," which Sidney then opened and accepted.

It seems as if the editors at *The Strand* unwittingly thwarted the author's aim to plant an allusionary anagram into the story. They not only changed the *a* to a *g*, they commissioned the wrong illustrator. The latter mistake has long been recognized, the former only now comes to light. The search for the cause of the anagram error is enlightening, so we return to Holmes's analysis of the note received in *A Scandal in Bohemia*.

> "Peculiar—that is the very word," said Holmes. "It is not an English paper at all. Hold it up to the light."
>
> I did so, and saw a large *E* with a small *g*, a *P*, and a large *G* with a small *t* woven into the texture of the paper.
>
> "What do you make of that?" asked Holmes.
>
> "The name of a maker, no doubt, or his monogram rather."

"Not at all. The *G* with the small *t* stands for Gesellschaft, which is the German for Company. It is a customary contraction like our Co. *P* of course stands for *Papier*. Now for the *Eg*. Let us glance at our *Continental Gazetteer*." He took down a heavy brown volume from his shelves. "Eglow, Eglonitz—here we are, Egria. It is a German speaking country—in Bohemia, not far from Carlsbad."

Holmes and Watson see that *Eg P Gt* is a watermark indicating that the paper is another fine product of Egria Papier Gesellschaft or, in English, the Egria Paper Company. The author invented and named the company such that its watermark would include an imprecise anagram for Paget. The editors of The Strand must have assumed that the earlier *a* in the manuscript was an error, since Egria clearly begins with Eg, not Ea. It is certainly not clear, however, that the *a* in the manuscript was erroneous. The textual discomfort introduced by the letter *a* may have been intentional.

Consider, as evidence of this suggestion, that Eglow and Eglonitz are made-up names. No location anywhere on Earth is, or was, so named. A search of the thirty million books already scanned (at the time of this writing) as part of the Google Books project turns up not a single instance of either word prior to its appearance in Scandal. Not only are the words invented, they are listed in incorrect alphabetic order; Eglonitz should have preceded, not followed, Eglow. As Holmes scanned the entries in the Continental Gazeteer (as it is misspelled in the manuscript), he should have read "Eglonitz, Eglow—here we are, Egria."

But Egria is also an error. That so-called country, which we are informed is "in Bohemia, not far from Carlsbad," was actually Eger, a region of northwestern Bohemia, now a district of the Czech Republic. There is also a city of Eger within the district of Eger, not far from Carlsbad (which also lies within the district of Eger). Eger was previously known as Egra, but it is now more commonly known as Cheb. In an interesting twist, the Latin name for Eger is Agria, which is strikingly similar Egria, different only by an A.

The multiple alphabetical and geographical errors are simultaneously too simple and too sophisticated to be happenstance. They were introduced intentionally, to some end, then undone by editors who changed an *a* to a *g* and hired Sidney instead of Walter.

The Sherlock Holmes stories are riddled with long-unrecognized puzzles, allusions, incongruities, and irony. While Arthur was obviously bright and well-educated, he seems unlikely to be the person who created the second layer of storytelling that lies beneath the surface of the Sherlock Holmes adventures. In fact, he seems to have unwittingly eliminated himself as the person responsible for the subtext.

In "Sidelights on Sherlock Holmes," Chapter XI of *Memories and Adventures,* Arthur had a perfect opportunity to explain that he had buried allusions, puzzles, incongruities, and irony amidst the stories, assuming he had been the person who buried them. Such insight would certainly have been an interesting sidelight on Sherlock Holmes, whom Arthur otherwise ignores throughout his autobiography. We will not, however, find any such revelation therein, nor in any of his other writings, interviews, speeches, and personal correspondence. It is as if Arthur was oblivious to them.

"The first object of a novelist is to tell a tale," Arthur explained during a 1894 interview with W.J. Dawson, "If he has no story to tell, what is he there for? Possibly he has something to say which is worth saying, but he should say it in another form."

"When a man invents he usually gives essentials for his story and no more," Arthur advised in his Our *Second American Adventure* (1924). "A novelist, for example, does not give details which have no bearing upon his plot."

Arthur believed that allusions, incongruities, and mathematical subtleties had no place in a story. He seems unlikely to be the person who left behind the puzzling calling cards scattered throughout the Holmes adventures.

Mark Twain

Not only does Holmes detect and explain the watermark for Egria Papier Gesellschaft, he determines, based on the note's writing style, the sender's nationality.

"And the man who wrote the note is a German. Do you note the peculiar construction of the sentence— 'This account of you we have from all quarters received'. A Frenchman or Russian could not have written that. It is the German who is so uncourteous to his verbs."

The verb in Holmes's sample sentence appears at the very end, rather than near the middle of the phrase. Such late appearance of verbs is characteristic of the German language. By using Holmes's observation, the author seems to be alluding to Mark Twain. Twain preceded *Scandal* by eleven years in poking fun at the German language. In 1878, he hiked through Europe so that he could write a travelogue of his adventures. The resulting work, *A Tramp Abroad*, was published in 1880. In a lengthy appendix entitled "The Awful German Language," Twain complained about Teutonic placement of verbs.

Surely there is not another language that is so slipshod and systemless, and so slippery and elusive to the grasp. [...] There are ten parts of speech, and they are all troublesome. An average sentence, in a German newspaper, is a sublime and impressive curiosity; it occupies a quarter of a column; it contains all the ten parts of speech—not in regular order, but mixed; it is built mainly of compound words constructed by the writer on the spot, and not to be found in any dictionary—six or seven words compacted into one, without joint or seam—that is, without hyphens; it treats of fourteen or fifteen different subjects, each enclosed in a parenthesis of its own, with here and there extra parentheses, making pens within pens: finally, all the parentheses and reparentheses are massed together between a couple of king-parentheses, one of which is placed in the first line of the majestic sentence and the other in the middle of the last line of it—*after which comes the*

verb, and you find out for the first time what the man
has been talking about.

The italics are in the original.

It may be mere coincidence that Mark Twain and Sherlock
Holmes each poke fun at the placement of German verbs. There is,
however, evidence that Holmes's creator intended *A Scandal in
Bohemia* to allude to Mark Twain: the author had already done so in
A Study in Scarlet. That earlier tale alluded not to Twain's *A Tramp
Abroad*, but to his much more famous work, *Tom Sawyer*. The scene
in *Study* now of interest to us involves Holmes's attempt to lure the
killer to 221B Baker Street by advertising the discovery of a gold
ring. He and Watson are surprised, instead, by the arrival of an old
woman who claims the ring belongs to her daughter Sally.

> "And your name is –?"
>
> "My name is Sawyer—her's is Dennis, which Tom
> Dennis married her—and a smart, clean lad, too, as
> long as he's at sea, and no steward in the company
> more thought of; but when on shore, what with the
> women and what with liquor shops –"
>
> "Here is your ring, Mrs. Sawyer," I interrupted, in
> obedience to a sign from my companion; "it clearly
> belongs to your daughter, and I am glad to be able to
> restore it to the rightful owner."

Had the custom been for a groom to adopt his bride's last name,
rather than vice-versa, then Sally Sawyer would have been married
to Tom Sawyer.

In 1893, shortly before Holmes plummeted into Switzerland's
Reichenbach Falls, Arthur and Louise traced Mark Twain's footsteps
through Switzerland, just as Twain had vividly described them in *A
Tramp Abroad*. In *The Final Problem*, published soon afterwards,
Holmes and Watson also follow a portion of Twain's route, a portion
hiked just months earlier by Arthur and Louise.

So critical is Mark Twain to understanding the origin of the
Sherlock Holmes Canon that he will, in the final chapters of this book,
lead us to Holmes's creator. Arthur, however, had absolutely no

interest in the man. In his *Through the Magic Door* (1907), Arthur gave us a tour of his personal library. He browsed the shelves, selected book after book, holding each in his hand as he described it.

> Come through the magic door with me, and sit here on the green settee, where you can see the old oak case with its untidy lines of volumes. Smoking is not forbidden. Would you care to hear me talk of them? Well, I ask nothing better, for there is no volume there which is not a dear, personal friend, and what can a man talk of more pleasantly than that? The other books are over yonder, but these are my own favourites—the ones I care to re-read and to have near my elbow. There is not a tattered cover which does not bring its mellow memories to me.

For 231 pages, Arthur droned on about his favorite books and authors, writing more to impress than to illuminate. A few excerpts will suffice to make the painful point.

> I remember the late James Payn telling the anecdote that he and two literary friends agreed to write down what scene in fiction they thought the most dramatic, and that on examining the papers it was found that all three had chosen the same. It was the moment when the unknown knight, at Ashby-de-la-Zouch, riding past the pavilions of the lesser men, strikes with the sharp end of his lance, in a challenge to mortal combat, the shield of the formidable Templar. It was, indeed, a splendid moment! What matter that no Templar was allowed by the rules of his Order to take part in so secular and frivolous an affair as a tournament? It is the privilege of great masters to make things so, and it is a churlish thing to gainsay it. Was it not Wendell Holmes who described the prosaic man, who enters a drawing-room with a couple of facts, like ill-conditioned bull-dogs at his heels, ready to let them loose on any play of fancy?

What would we not give for a portrait of one of Murat's light-cavalrymen, or of a Grenadier of the Old Guard, drawn with the same bold strokes as the Rittmeister of Gustavus or the archers of the French King's Guard in "Quentin Durward"?

We have left our eighteenth-century novelists— Fielding, Richardson, and Smollett—safely behind us, with all their solidity and their audacity, their sincerity, and their coarseness of fibre. They have brought us, as you perceive, to the end of the shelf. What, not wearied? Ready for yet another? Let us run down this next row, then, and I will tell you a few things which may be of interest, though they will be dull enough if you have not been born with that love of books in your heart which is among the choicest gifts of the gods. If that is wanting, then one might as well play music to the deaf, or walk round the Academy with the colour-blind, as appeal to the book-sense of an unfortunate who has it not.

Arthur touched on 137 authors, ranging from Joseph Addison to William Wordsworth. He discussed Percey Bysshe Shelley, but not Mary Shelley, whose *Frankenstein* is several times alluded to in *The Final Problem*. Arthur mentioned authors recognizable still today, such as Dickens, Poe, and Stevenson, but did not hesitate to throw in obscure writers such as Hippolyte Taine, Françoise-Marguerite de Sévigné, John Collis Snaith, and Dmitry Sergeyevich Merezhkovsky.

Nowhere in *Through the Magic Door*, however, did Arthur have a single word for Mark Twain, much less Twain's *A Tramp Abroad* on which so much will hinge.

Stylometry

When, in *Scandal*, Holmes infers certain facts about a note's author from the style in which the note was written, he is anticipating the now burgeoning field of stylometry. The online *Oxford Living Dictionary* defines *stylometry* as "the statistical analysis of variations in literary style between one writer or genre and another." The term comes from the Polish philosopher Wincenty Lutoslawski and his *Principes de stylométrie* (1890). Lutoslawski developed stylometric techniques not to expose shadowy authors, but to establish the proper chronology of Plato's writings.

Stylometry in the modern era began with an effort to properly attribute authorship of *The Federalist Papers*. The *Federalists* consist of a series of articles, published between 1787 and 1788, to promote ratification of the U.S. Constitution. Under the pen name Publius, the papers were generally considered to be the writing of Alexander Hamilton, James Madison, and John Jay. After Hamilton died, his paperwork revealed his private claim to most of the papers, including twelve that seemed more in the style of Madison, who later also claimed credit for each of those twelve.

Based on scholarly examination of the texts, Douglass Adair concluded, in 1944, that Hamilton authored fifty-one of the papers, Madison twenty-six of them, Jay five, Hamilton and Madison, working in concert, the remaining three. Adair confirmed as well that Madison wrote each of the twelve disputed papers.

Statisticians Frederick Mosteller and David Wallace carried Adair's work further, using stylometric analysis. They presented their pioneering methods in a 1963 paper titled "Inference in an Authorship Problem." Using the *Federalists* as their test case, they applied statistical methods to the relative frequencies of commonly used words. They determined that Adair had been correct about the disputed papers: Madison wrote all of them. In their paper's conclusion, Mosteller and Wallace exhibited the caution that is the hallmark of trained statisticians.

> We may go too far in these conclusions [...] but they should serve to stimulate thought, even if they later require revisions. [...] Our data independently supplement that of the historian. On the basis of our data alone, Madison is extremely likely, in the sense of degree of belief, to have written the disputed *Federalists*, with the possible exception of No. 55, and there our evidence is weak, suitable deflated odds are 80 to 1 for Madison.

As part of their work, Mosteller and Wallace identified and evaluated twenty words most likely to discriminate the works of Hamilton from those of Madison.

although	as	at	by
commonly	consequently	considerable	destruction
enough	innovation	language	of
on	there	*upon*	vigor
voice	while	whilst	would

They took particular note of *upon*, italicized in the list above. In the known writings of Hamilton, *upon* appears at the rate of 32 times per 10,000 words. In the known writings of Madison, it appears barely at all, only 2 times per 10,000 words. The rarity of that word in the disputed documents therefore weighed heavily in Madison's favor.

Not only were Mosteller and Wallace surprised by the differential usage of *upon*, they discovered that simple, common words are more useful discriminators than more descriptive content words. "We were surprised that in the end," they wrote, "it was the utterly mundane high-frequency function words that did the best job. Though we love them for their lack of contextuality, their final strength was as unexpected as it was welcome."

Most words can be classified as either content words or function words. Content words are the high-status nouns, adjectives, verbs, and adverbs. They are people, teeming masses, innocent victims, murder weapons, bloodstains, and crime scenes. They stab wildly, utter a last gasp, and die grotesquely.

Function words, on the other hand, are the lowly prepositions, pronouns, conjunctions, articles, and auxiliary verbs that, by themselves, provide no information. Function words exist only to serve content words.

Consider, for example, a standard typing exercise: *The quick brown fox jumped over the lazy dog*. The sentence works as a typing exercise because it contains at least one instance of each letter in the alphabet. It is of passing interest to us because it consists primarily of content words. Removing its function words makes the sentence only slightly ambiguous: *Quick brown fox jumped lazy dog.*

Shakespeare's most famous line, on the other hand, is a grand mass of function words: *To be or not to be, that is the question.* Removing the function words leaves but a one-word sentence with zero context: *Question.*

The Victorian mathematics professor, Lewis Carroll, most famous for *Alice's Adventures in Wonderland* (1865), clearly understood the relationship between content words and function words. Linguist Itziar Laka observed (in her essay "Jabberwocky, or the poetry of function words") that Carroll (in his poem *Jabberwocky*) used a nonsense word in place of each content word, but left each function word untouched:

'Twas brillig, and the slithy toves
Did gyre and gimble in the wabe;
All mimsy were the borogoves,
And the mome raths outgrabe.

Even though the stanza has not a single recognizable content word, the function words still give us a sense of the story. We don't know who or what the toves were, but we know that they were slithy, and we know they were slithy sometime in the past. We know also that they gyred and they gimbled in some place called the wabe. Each and every one of the borogoves, by comparison, were mimsy. And those raths, those mome raths, they were outgrabed.

In *The Secret Life of Pronouns* (2013), linguist James W. Pennebaker estimates that the average English speaker has a vocabulary of 100,000 unique words. The overwhelming majority of those are content words; fewer than 500 are function words. The lowly function words, nonetheless, constitute more than half of the words actually uttered or typed. Everyone uses them in distinctive fashion. Authors leave them behind, unconsciously, like fingerprints on a knife.

When we examine the function words in *A Scandal in Bohemia*, and in the other early Holmes adventures, and compare their frequencies against those found in Arthur's non-Sherlockian works of fiction, we are in for more than a few surprises. According to my stylometric analysis of the Holmes Canon and Arthur's writing, someone other than Arthur Conan Doyle wrote the early Holmes adventures and has left literary fingerprints all over the stories.

The word *the* is the most frequently used word in the English language. It constitutes almost twenty-five percent of the words in the previous sentence. It belongs to a part of speech called articles, of which there are only three: *the*, *a*, and *an*.

James Pennebaker is the Regents Centennial Professor of Liberal Arts and Chair of the Department of Psychology at the University of Texas at Austin. That university is, coincidently, home to the Harry Ransom Center, discussed previously herein as the current owner of the *Scandal* manuscript. Pennebaker, in his own words, has "become intrigued by how people reveal themselves in their everyday spoken and written language." In his *Secret Life of Pronouns*, he provides insight into gender preference for the part of speech called articles.

> Across hundreds of thousands of language samples from books to blogs to everyday informal conversation, men consistently use articles at higher rates than women. [...] Articles are used with nouns—especially concrete, highly specific nouns. A person who uses an article is talking about a particular object or thing. Guys talk about objects and things more than women do. They talk about the broken carburetor, the wife, and a steak on the grill for dinner. [...]
>
> Women use social words at far higher rates than men. Social words refer to any words that are related to other human beings. ... Women do, indeed, think more and talk more about other people. [...] Women disproportionately talk about other people and men talk about, well, carburetors and other objects and things.

A Scandal in Bohemia is 8,606 words long; the word *the* makes 446 appearances. That is an average of 518 instances for each

10,000 words. By comparison, the non-Holmes short stories attributed to Arthur use the word *the* at a rate of 596 instances for each 10,000 words. Though it may not seem so, it is a remarkable difference. Had the *Scandal* author used *the* as frequently as did Arthur, *Scandal* would have had an additional 78 instances of *the*, and an additional 78 nouns to accompany them. That would be five more articles and five more nouns for each of the story's fifteen pages in *The Strand*.

Scandal is not the only anomaly. Twenty of the first twenty-six Holmes adventures use the word *the* at a rate lower than Arthur's average. *The Yellow Face* is particularly noteworthy. Not only did it promote the issue of interracial marriage a century before its time, it did so while using *the* at a spare rate of just 431 instances per 10,000 words. That is nearly a 30% difference from Arthur's norm.

The first adventure, *A Study in Scarlet*, is also quite interesting with respect to its usage of *the*. *Study* is a novella composed of two distinct, poorly integrated stories. Part I constitutes the first Holmes tale, beginning with Watson's first meeting with Holmes and continuing through Holmes's apprehension of the murderer. It is written in the first person, present tense. Part II, specifically labeled as such, begins suddenly, without segue. Written in the third person, past tense, it tells a story of Mormon treachery in Utah. In the final paragraph of the Utah tale, an aggrieved party pursues his prey from Utah to St. Petersburg to Paris to Copenhagen and, finally, to London, where Holmes awaits to explain how he solved the mystery. The final sentence of the final paragraph of Part II is among the worst segues in the history of western literature.

> Again the avenger had been foiled, and again his concentrated hatred urged him to continue the pursuit. Funds were wanting, however, and for some time he had to return to work, saving every dollar for his approaching journey. At last, having collected enough to keep life in him, he departed for Europe, and tracked his enemies from city to city, working his way in any menial capacity, but never overtaking the fugitives. When he reached St. Petersburg, they had

departed for Paris; and when he followed them there, he learned that they had just set off for Copenhagen. At the Danish capital he was again a few days late, for they had journeyed on to London, where he at last succeeded in running them to earth. As to what occurred there, we cannot do better than quote the old hunter's own account, as duly recorded in Dr. Watson's Journal, to which we are already under such obligations.

In the Holmes portion of *A Study in Scarlet*, the word *the* appears at a rate of 546 times per 10,000 words. In the Utah portion, *the* appears at a rate of 618 times per 10,000 words.

If we could discriminate the gender of two writers based only on their use of the word *the*, then we would conclude that the first Holmes adventure is the work of two authors, one female and one male, the male presumably being Arthur. We would conclude further that the female author wrote the Holmes portion of the novella and Arthur wrote the Utah portion. We would conclude still further that the female author wrote the majority of the next twenty-five adventures, and that Arthur wrote but a few of them.

It is dangerous, however, to base stylometric conclusions on any single word, even if that word is *the*. Mosteller and Wallace used twenty marker words to discriminate the works of Hamilton from those of Madison, even though the single word *upon* seemed to tell the story by itself.

There are a number of other function words that seem to differentiate the early Holmes adventures from Arthur's other short stories. The relative usage of *that*, for example, is even more suggestive that someone other than Arthur wrote the early Holmes adventures. On average, *that* appears 22% more frequently in the early Holmes short stories than it does in Arthur's non-Holmes short stories. Twenty-five of the twenty-six early Holmes adventures use *that* at a rate in excess of Arthur's average. The word *that* appears 23% more frequently in the Holmes portion of *Study* than it does in the Utah interlude. Most remarkably, the word *that* appears 53% more frequently in *The Yellow Face* than in Arthur's short stories.

The function words *very, many, another, and,* and *of* behave in similar fashion. In fact, applying a statistical method (adapted from Mosteller and Wallace) to Arthur's one hundred most frequently used function words leads to the same inescapable conclusion. Someone other than Arthur wrote the early Sherlock Holmes adventures.

Chapter 7
Accessory after the Fact

In its original, 16th century meaning, "fact" meant a noble or evil thing done. Shakespeare used the word fourteen times, always in the negative sense. In *Henry VI, Part II*, the witches were caught not in the act, but in the fact.

> Dealing with witches and with conjurers:
> Whom we have apprehended in the fact;
> Raising up wicked spirits from underground,
> Demanding of King Henry's life and death,

By Victorian times, the word "fact" had taken on its current meaning of actuality, retaining its old meaning mostly in matters of law. An accessory after the fact was then, and is still today, someone who assisted a perpetrator to avoid capture or punishment after the offense had already been committed.

Jean Leckie met and began dating Arthur while he was still married to Louise, after the early Holmes tales were already published. She therefore cannot be Holmes's creator, or the author of the early adventures. She did, however, play a substantial role in perpetuating Arthur's literary fraud.

Jean and Arthur
Jean Elizabeth Leckie was born on 14 March 1874, the second of five children born to James Blythe and Selina Leckie. She was more than fifteen years younger than the man she would marry, and more than seventeen years younger than the woman she would supplant. As Georgina Doyle observed, "What chance did forty-year-old, sick Louise stand against healthy, twenty-two-year old Jean? It would appear none whatsoever."

Other than missing Jean's age by one year, Georgina Doyle was correct. For the last decade of Louise's consumptive life, Arthur frequently left Louise behind to carry on his affair elsewhere with Jean.

Jean was raised in a fashion typical of young women springing from prosperous Victorian families. Taught to sing, ride, and chase the hounds, she was formally educated in Dresden, returned to London for music instruction at the renowned Guildhall School of Music, then moved to Florence for training under vocal maestro Vincenzo Vannini. No later than 15 March 1897, we know she was back in England, for that was the day that Arthur marked as the beginning of their relationship. That was after Arthur and Louise arrived from Cairo, and before they moved into Undershaw.

John Dickson Carr and Pierre Nordon described Jean in lofty terms. Carr, who thoroughly diminished Louise, gushed over Jean.

> Miss Jean Leckie was just twenty-four. Even the not-very-expert photography of the time reveals her extraordinary beauty. But the colouring of that beauty it cannot show; the dark-gold hair, the hazel-green eyes, the delicate white complexion, the changes of the smile. [...] Despite her delicacy (slender, with small hands and feet), she was an expert horsewoman who had been trained to ride from childhood. [...] We see her across the years as quick of sympathy, impulsive, strongly romantic: the slender neck rises from a lace gown, and the eyes (read their expression, even in a photograph) tell her character. [...]
>
> Conan Doyle was no plaster saint. Anyone who has so far followed his life will have seen that. He was violent, he was stubborn, he was often wrong-headed, he did not easily forgive injury. And yet, with his particular background, upbringing, and beliefs, we can foresee exactly what he did. He could not help being in love with Jean, or she with him. But there it must stop.

Carr's suggestion that Arthur's ten-year affair with Jean was purely platonic may indeed have been the case. When Arthur discussed Jean with his biological family, he consistently maintained as much, and no surviving document proves otherwise. On the day of Jean's death, however, their son burned all of Arthur's love letters to her, hiding forever an untold number of secrets.

Pierre Nordon used his praise of Jean as another opportunity to denigrate Louise.

> Jean was entirely different from Louise: charming, dignified, sensitive, and demonstrative, she had an ease of manner which came from the advantages she was born to. This woman who might have been the heroine of a novel by George Meredith aroused in the mature Conan Doyle an intensity of passion he had never before experienced. For ten years she was his mystical wife, and he her *cavaliere servente* and her hero; they were years of sometimes painful emotional tension for him, providing a test of his chivalry which he was better fitted to meet than any man of his generation, and which he may even have desired. Like a lamp under a parchment shade, this enduring passion lit up the unexpected paths of his public life during those ten years.

Georgina Doyle took issue with such lofty portrayals as those from Carr and Nordon. Though she did not have access to the Conan Doyle archives, as they did, she was not writing under the watchful eye of Adrian. She made her stance abundantly clear.

> When Carr described Jean Leckie, he used extravagant terms, to the detriment of Louise. We must remember that his description was influenced by Adrian Conan Doyle, for Carr and Pierre Nordon were the two writers he allowed to fully examine the family archives. Adrian was sometimes over-enthusiastic, and he was intent on presenting his own one-sided viewpoint; naturally he would be his mother's champion. Mary [Louise and Arthur's daughter] believed firmly that the blame lay with Adrian for the virtual obliteration of her own mother

as part of Arthur's life. A picture has emerged of Jean as a romantic heroine, possessing all the qualities that Louise lacked. Arthur has been presented as a noble hero, torn by hopeless love for a worthier woman but steadfastly refusing to abandon the stern duty of standing by, and looking after, his sick wife. I think this is humbug. [...]

Carr eloquently pleaded for her with an appealing complexion, and what he called a changing smile. He stated that she possessed an extraordinary beauty, but this is not borne out by photographs. In fact, she was rather sharp-featured, with a small mouth and intensely soulful eyes. She had lovely clothes and luxuriant hair but she was not a beauty. I have heard again and again from members of the Doyle family that Jean was gushing and affected and a woman who craved limelight.

Andrew Lycett walked the line between the two views.

Jean had a trim figure, searching green eyes and cascading golden hair, her only possible blemish being a small, downturned mouth that brought out a pinched quality in her features. [...] Arthur must have sensed that Jean would provide the support he needed as he geared up for the next period in his life when, secure at home, he would play a more public role in the nation's affairs. He did not intend to desert his wife: that would be alien to his nature. But while she remained alive and he had no physical outlet for his sex drive, Jean Leckie would offer him an idealized romance. This was an understandable option for a man such as Arthur who, for all his blunt physicality, had an unusual capacity for living in his mind. It would also let him off the moral hook, for he would convince himself that, so long as he was chaste, this type of dalliance was acceptable.

Lycett's observation about Jean's pinched features is interesting. Victorians seldom smiled when posing for pictures, but Jean's images do seem unnecessarily dour. Louise's images, on the other hand, usually reveal the hint of a smile. Given the comparative circumstances of the two women, one might expect the reverse.

According to Innes's diary, Jean was at Undershaw frequently. She dined there on 26 November 1897, just a month after Arthur and Louise had moved in, then again on 22 December, joining Arthur for a walk and some tea, and again on 26 December.

The Undershaw guest book was crammed with signatures every weekend, but none of Arthur's biographers gives credit to Louise as a hostess. Mary, fortunately, left a charming description of her gracious and unflappable mother.

> Well I do remember one occasion when Mother's poise was put to the test with a vengeance. Daddy had asked a well-known authoress of that time, who was staying at the Royal Huts Hotel, to come in and have Sunday evening supper with us—and had then forgotten all about it. Nobody knew, so there was no extra place set. We were half way through the meal, when the front door bell pealed, the dining-room door was thrown open to Miss Helen Mathers, and in she sailed resplendent in a pink evening dress and pearls.
>
> I can see the picture now—Daddy's half-turned head, jaw dropped with amazement, and the little feather of hair on the crown of his head sticking straight up as it always did when he was tired or agitated. Mother rose and took the situation in hand. She came forward with a calm sweetness and a charming little dignity all her own—only that telltale glint in the eye told me what she was thinking. She greeted the unexpected guest, and proceeded to put everyone at their ease by her own refusal to be embarrassed or appear to be taken aback. We all took

our cue from her, started talking naturally and soon the position was restored.

Mary and Kingsley saw much more of their mother than they did of their father. Arthur made frequent and lengthy trips to London and other locations, for business and secret meetings with Jean. Mary noted that he "invariably brought a small posy of flowers back for [Louise], or some charming little trinket. It was beautiful to see his gentleness with her." Arthur later, in a letter to his mother, rationalized this behavior: "If I cannot give her my full love I can at least give her every material pleasure with a full hand."

In December of 1897, Arthur and Louise staged such a large costume ball that it required two venues: Undershaw, and the Beacon Hill Hotel in nearby Hindhead. Innes described the affair in his diary.

> Dance was a great success. All costumes were wonderfully good. Nearly 200 people. Everything right except that the band stole all the cigars. Our house party was Touie [Louise], Lottie, Mrs Trevor, Arthur, Trevor, Wood, Bartley, Williams, Archie and I. At hotel were mother, Nem, Connie, Tootsie, K.H., Misses Lecky and Driver, Mrs. Ford, Mrs. Boulnois, Ford, Stone, Driver.

Arthur was dressed as a Viking, Jean as Queen Mary. Arthur's sister Lottie met Jean there for the first time, apparently under false pretenses. The meeting is preserved by a note from Lottie to Jean: "I hope that next time we meet you will remember that all my friends call me Lottie and that I hate being Miss Doyle to anyone I like."

Lottie seemingly did not realize that Jean was destined to replace Louise. Jean's parents, on the other hand, were certainly aware of the possibility. For Christmas, they gave Arthur a diamond and pearl pin-stud. The following February, Arthur visited them at their home and dined with them. Not long thereafter Jean moved out of her parent's home and into a flat with two friends.

In early 1900, with the second Boer War well underway. Arthur volunteered as a civilian doctor for a privately run field hospital in

Bloemfontein, South Africa. Hoping to rent Undershaw during his absence, he sent Louise and the children to Naples, so that they could be near his sister and her husband. Louise's absence allowed Jean to be the one to see Arthur off as he set sail for Africa. According to Carr, Jean had told Arthur she would not be there because she could not endure the parting; Arthur learned only later that she had been standing on the dock as his ship pulled out. According to Nordon, Jean had Arthur's cabin filled with flowers.

While at the Langham Hospital, Arthur spent much of his time working on his book *The Great Boer War* (1900), and taking furloughs from the hospital, hoping to witness combat. He departed for good before his contract expired. Letters to his mother make clear that he longed to see her and Jean; his behavior evidenced no particular desire to see Louise or their children. On 23 June, he stated explicitly that there were only two reasons for wanting to return to England: one was to kiss his mother, the other he left to her imagination. Upon disembarking in London, he debated whether he should "recall Touie [Louise] & the family to Undershaw." The massive house had not been rented, and that seemed to be the only reason he considered bringing them back. "It seems absurd to pay highly for rooms abroad when that fine house is empty."

If he visited Undershaw soon after his return, he must have done so only briefly. During the last half of August, he played cricket in London and Cambridgeshire. His brother-in-law, Willie Hornung, stumbled into Jean at one of the matches and became aware of their relationship. Hornung later, in private, expressed his disapproval to Arthur, resulting in the previously discussed racist insult by Arthur.

Arthur ran for office in an unsuccessful effort to represent an Edinburgh district more than 430 miles north of Undershaw. During the final months of 1900, he split his time between London and his family estate. He did spend Christmas at Undershaw, presumably with Louise, Mary, and Kingsley, but this was likely a small comfort to them, as he had managed to separate himself from them for most of the year.

Arthur's contemporaneous letters provide insight into the nature of his liaisons with Jean. He encouraged Louise to travel or to visit her family. Whether she did or not, he would plan a golf vacation on the pretense of needing to recover his health, of which he frequently complained, as if he was the one slowly dying of tuberculosis. He would then arrange lodging for a fortnight in a remote, tranquil location such as the North Countree, New Forest, or Ashford Forest. There, Arthur would be joined by Jean, a chaperon, and, frequently, his mother.

In February of 1901, Arthur stayed in Ashford Forest with Jean and her brother Malcolm. His mother did not join him on that occasion, but she wrote to him there and he responded. He invited her to his next liaison, to take place elsewhere since Ashford Forest had become too well known among their friends. He fretted that Louise had decided not to spend a month in France, that she planned instead to visit her mother in Torquay.

The 1901 census recorded that Arthur settled once again on Ashford Forest. His mother joined them at the Ashford Forest Hotel. The same census reveals that Louise's sister Emily cared for Mary and Kingsley at Undershaw while Louise visited her mother in Torquay. Curiously and sadly, the census recorded the occupation of both Louise and her mother as "Living on own means."

The year 1901 turned out to be yet another in which Arthur spent most of his time away from Louise. In January, he played golf in Ashford Forest. In February he met Jean there. In March, he met Jean and his mother there. In April he seems to have rendezvoused with Jean there yet again, and travelled also to Cromer for still another golfing vacation.

Throughout early- and mid-May, Arthur socialized in London, dining with Winston Churchill at the House of Commons, presiding over the Ladies Dinner given by the Authors' Club, attending the annual dinner of the Society of Authors, and feasting at another dinner in the Gray's Inn. He also played cricket on the 16th, 17th, 18th, 20th, 23rd, 24th, and 25th.

Any cricket match could last three days and each was a major social event. We know that Jean had taken a flat in London, and that she had attended at least one cricket match, since that instance caused a rift within the family. We have no reason to doubt that Jean attended matches prior to that instance, and we have direct evidence that she at least hovered about afterward.

The cricket season continued in June. Arthur played every day from the 3rd through the 8th, always at locales well away from Undershaw. Around the 10th he was at Undershaw for at least a day before setting forth for more cricketing on 13, 14, 17, 18, 24, 25, 26 and 29 June.

In July, Arthur attended more dinners in London, and he took a 25-mile balloon ride from the Crystal Palace to Kent. Jean won a bronze medal as a vocalist during her public examination for the London Academy of Music, and we can be confident that Arthur attended.

Early in August he took a four-day vacation to Southsea with Louise and the children. After performing his husbandly and fatherly duties, he traveled to Norwich for a cricket match on the 9th and 10th. Jean was then staying thirty miles away, at the Marlborough Hotel in Southwold. On the 16th, 17th, 24th and 31st, Arthur played cricket at Lord's Cricket Ground in London, much closer to Jean's flat.

Thus did the three of them pass Louise's remaining years. Louise would stay at Undershaw or visit family. Arthur would socialize in London, or play cricket, or take golfing vacations to secluded locales. He would always be emotionally closer to Jean, and conspire to be physically closer as well. When writing to his mother, he spoke of Jean only in lofty tones: "Dear J is a model of good sense and propriety," "No man can owe a greater debt to a woman," and "There never was anyone with a sweeter and more unselfish nature."

Louise's presence, on the other hand, had become an annoyance. In a letter to his mother, he gave what he described as a trivial but typical example of Louise's exasperating behavior. He discovered that several of his pipes had been cleaned, and he presumed that she had cleaned them. He was touched by the gesture, so he mentioned it to her, only to be shocked to learn that George, the family's bootblack, had cleaned them. Arthur was appalled by the thought of a lowly bootblack cleaning his pipes. "It was he who had cleaned them all, the things I had to put between my lips," he wrote in anger.

Arthur was more explicit about his growing frustration with Louise in a later letter to his mother. Her reply prompted him to backpedal a bit.

> You must have misunderstood something which I
> said. I have nothing but affection and respect for
> Touie. I have never in my whole married life had one
> cross word with her, nor will I ever cause her any
> pain. I cannot think how I came to give you the
> impression that her presence was painful to me.

In another letter, Arthur simply conceded that he had grown weary of being married to someone so ill: "I have lived for six years in a sick room and, oh, how weary of it I am." Remarkably, he claimed to have suffered from Louise's disease more than she did: "It has tired me more than her." It would hardly be the first or last instance in which he minimized Louise's affliction. His letters are littered with self-comforting claims that "Touie [Louise] keeps very fit," "is in very good form," "is in excellent form," "keeps bright and well," "has been in bed for a week but rather as a prevention than a cure," "is wonderfully well save for her poor voice which has almost gone."

"I do think that in spite of all she is the happiest woman I know," Arthur wrote, but it must have been obvious that Louise was wasting away. "Touie has lost weight considerably," he finally conceded, noting that "for two years there has been a steady drop." As an experienced physician, he must have known that her laryngitis was evidence that the bacteria had escaped her lungs, that they were coursing through her blood vessels, and already consuming other parts of her body. Even as Arthur downplayed her illness, he complained of "feeling rather run down" or "low." His proposed cure was usually another vacation.

The year 1906 began for Arthur and Louise as had the previous eight. Arthur absented himself from Undershaw as Louise wasted away. In January he again ran for office, this time to represent Harwick, 380 miles to the north. Again he lost. In March, his *Brigadier Gerard* opened as a comedy in four acts at the Imperial Theatre in London. In April, he dined at a Pilgrim's banquet at the Savoy Hotel, dined with Lord Milner at the Hotel Cecil, and then met with the Jewish Territorial Organization. Each event was in London, conveniently close to Jean's flat.

At the end of May, it was Innes, not Arthur, who escorted Louise and Mary to London to see Arthur's *Brigadier Gerard* play. That outing seems to have been the last time Louise left Undershaw, other than to be buried. She deteriorated even more quickly after that outing. The infection spread beyond her larynx to her brain. She suffered bouts of delirium. She became paralyzed on her left side.

On 8 June, Arthur was at the Grand Hotel, in London. On the 11th, he presided at the Authors' Club, in London. On the 15th, he unveiled a memorial table to Henry Fielding at Widcombe Lodge in Bath. On the 30th, he attended the Golf Club Exhibition near home.

Louise died barely four days later, at 3 AM, on 4 July 1906. Arthur was at her side, weeping.

Arthur eventually came clean about his true feelings regarding the marriage. He did so while spreading the word of spiritualism. He described the great beyond as an idyll where a person's etheric body resembles the living one, absent all imperfections, and where individuals pursue the same interests and hobbies they had on Earth. From *Our American Adventure* (1923):

> The usual information is that any nutrition is of a very light and delicate order, corresponding to the delicate etheric body which requires it. Then there was the question of marriage, and the old proposition of the much-married man, and which wife he should have. As there is no sexual relation, as we understand it, this problem is not very complex and is naturally decided by soul affinity."

In *Our Second American Adventure* (1924), Arthur spoke more to the point: "True marriage carries on, but the tepid or cold marriage dissolves." He not only abandoned Louise in this world, he hoped to avoid her for all eternity.

Arthur deluded himself until the very end that Louise was unaware of his relationship with Jean. As was usually the case, he thought too highly of his cleverness and too little of everyone else's. Of course Louise knew of his love for Jean; everyone knew. He told his siblings of the affair and they told their spouses. He told even

Innes, who was particularly close and kind to Louise. Arthur frequently left Louise behind, provided baubles when he returned, then schemed to leave yet again. He told his mother that he disposed of Jean's letters by burning them or burying them, presumably at Undershaw. Jean lodged near the scenes of Arthur's frequent diversions, and she appeared in public with him. She was so bold as to visit Undershaw, walk and ride there with Arthur, and dine with the family.

As the end neared, Louise called seventeen-year-old Mary to her bedside. Mary told Pierre Nordon of that conversation.

> Finally the sand began to run out, and it became clear she would not remain with us much longer. Some two months before the end she called me in for a talk. She told me that some wives sought to hold their husbands to their memory after they had gone—that she considered this very wrong, as the only consideration should be the loved-one's happiness. To this end she wanted me not to be shocked or surprised if my father married again, but to know that it was with her understanding and blessing.

Georgina Doyle offered inside information about that sorrowful discussion between a dying mother and her teenage daughter. She reported that Mary told John (Georgina's husband) that Louise mentioned Jean Leckie by name.

Jean's Revenge

Louise would have certainly been appalled by the treatment that Mary and Kingsley suffered at the hands of their father and his new wife. The two children were separated when they most needed one another. Kingsley was sent to Eton for his schooling, Mary to Dresden for singing lessons. Mary soon suspected that she would not be allowed to see Kingsley, even at Christmas. Two of her early letters to Kingsley reflect her anger, disappointment, and pain.

> My boy—if I don't come home for Xmas there will be words—for the girls I travelled out with are

returning for 3 weeks and coming back again after.
[... there] is no reason why I shouldn't, unless they
want to clear us both out [...] and have it to
themselves for Xmas. We are a bit of a mistake now.
But never mind old chap, we'll stand together
whatever happens.

When Mary pressed Arthur on the matter, he told her that he did
not expect to see her for another nine months. He accused her of
being weak for even asking to come home. She wrote again to
Kingsley.

I can't think why my father is so hard—I have not had
one gentle word, or sign of love from him since
Mother died. One would have thought it would be
otherwise. But no—life has all gone to make him a
very hard man.

In a subsequent letter, she painfully accepted that she and
Kingsley were no longer wanted, writing, "It's for all the world as if
they didn't care. [...] But at least they might hide it more decently."

Kingsley too was disappointed by Christmas. He had been sent to
an aunt's home for the holiday season and allowed home for
Christmas itself, but made to feel unwelcome. Mary exchanged
"words" with Jean over the matter, and wrote again to Kingsley.

I feel alternately angry and sad for you. I consider the
least Daddy and Jean could have done, considering
they denied you me—your natural companion—was
to have made you as at home and happy in the New
Life as possible. And in neglecting you like that, I
consider they have let slip a very important duty. I'm
disappointed in both of them.

Arthur and Jean's treatment of Louise's children was simply
cruel without cause. Mary, for example, had arranged to have
Kingsley visit her in Dresden, and she hoped also to travel to Berlin
to see an opera that she had been studying. Having no money of her

own, she turned to her father, by then one of the richest men in England, for the £20 necessary. He sent her a £10 check and a note, claiming that he could not afford to pay for both the opera and Kingsley's trip to Dresden. He left Mary to choose one or the other.

Intrepid Mary somehow managed both. While Kingsley was in Germany, he received a letter from Arthur berating him for a slight against Jean. Jean had apparently given Kingsley flowers or left flowers in his room, and he had not properly thanked her. In his groveling reply, Kingsley apologized profusely. He asked Arthur and Jean to provide him with a list of all his faults, so that he could improve on them.

Kingsley joined the military, suffered a neck wound during the battle of the Somme, and died of flu just a few days before the end of the war. He died unwed and without children. Only Mary could extend Louise's bloodline. She spent her life alone, however, both figuratively and literally. Though Arthur had arranged for his sisters to interact with potential suitors, neither Arthur nor Jean ever made the same effort for Mary. Instead, they kept her financially dependent on them. As Jean bore Arthur two more sons and another daughter, Mary became only more isolated.

When the couple toured Australia and New Zealand, along with their three shared biological children, they left Mary behind, alone. They forsook her again when they visited America, twice, then again when they traveled the length of Africa.

We learn from Mary's writings that both Jean and Arthur cautioned her against marriage. Regarding Arthur's advice, she wrote:

> He didn't concur with the Victorian view that women should marry at all costs—for he thought the unmarried woman, with her freedom, was a whole lot happier than a woman married to the wrong man and, he added, "The worst of it is, the poor things can never tell till they have married the chap!"

Jean insisted that a man should never marry a woman of equal intelligence, so Mary should wait for someone brighter than she was.

This she did, it would seem, living a quiet, lonely, unremarkable life, trying to please. She followed her father as he turned towards the paranormal, and she worked in the bookstore that he opened to promote the spiritualist cause. Later in her life, she recalled fondly her talks with him, noting that he had a lovely mind and the capacity to see many points of view. For some time after his demise, she participated in séances longing to speak with him again.

Just weeks before his death, Arthur (presumably with Jean's involvement) drew up the will that would be the final affront to Louise and her children. He bequeathed Mary some cash, only a portion of the farm property that had previously belonged to Louise, and an £8000 war bond that proved worthless. He excluded Mary from the real wealth of his estate, the copyrights to his writings. That asset he divided in two, bequeathing half to Jean and half to be split among the three children from her womb. Mary's much earlier observation to Kingsley, that "in all future dealings it is Jean and not Daddy with whom I shall have to reckon with," proved prescient.

Mary died, unmarried and childless, on 12 June 1976, whereupon the bloodline of Louise Conan Doyle came to an end.

None of Arthur's more recent biographers doubt that family papers were cleansed of documents relating to Louise. Of the purge, the editors of *A Life in Letters* wrote: "Very few letters have survived from 1885 and the next two years, driving Conan Doyle's biographers to other sources for some momentous things happening in his life."

Andrew Lycett addressed the document dispute between two of the three children born to Jean and Arthur.

> Feeling the need to defend himself against suggestion that he had been hoarding jointly owned material, [Adrian] told [his sister] Jean that he had been charged by their mother to burn two boxes of her love letters from their father. On the day of her death he had gone to Windlesham and though aware of the sacrilege, had carried out her instructions.

Lycett himself witnessed the continued culling of papers from family archives.

> Imagine my astonishment when on one of my early visits to the British Library's manuscripts room I found Charles Foley at a nearby table. I learned that he was going through all the letters Dame Jean [the younger Jean] had left to the Library with the intention of withdrawing significant numbers. He was apparently allowed to do this under article 6 of Dame Jean's will. [...] When I asked Foley about his criteria for selection, he declined to answer, saying this was a matter for him and his co-executor. However, I acquired a list of seventy-five items Foley intended to remove from the library. Ninety percent were letters from Conan Doyle to his mother.

Russell Miller, author of *The Adventures of Conan Doyle* (2008), speculates thusly about the motive for destroying and suppressing the documents: "[N]one of Touie's letters survive—it is possible they were destroyed after Conan Doyle's death because Jean wanted to be seen as the great, unrivalled, love of his life."

But perhaps there was something even more substantial in those letters, something that would materially threaten Arthur's legacy and the value of the family's inheritance.

Chapter 8
Modus Operandi

Modus operandi, typically abbreviated M.O., is a Latin term meaning "mode of operation." With respect to a series of crimes, it refers to the methods consistently employed by the perpetrator—a kind of methodological fingerprint. Identifying the M.O. is often key to identifying the culprit.

With respect to Sherlock Holmes adventures, there emerges a distinctive M.O. The author embedded within the tales frequent allusions to literary and historical personalities. The allusions range from simple, obvious, and undeniable to complex, subtle, and revealing. The most meticulous and nuanced of them have gone unrecognized until this work before you.

Allusions

Samuel Rosenberg was, most decidedly, an interesting fellow. His pattern recognition ability led to his role as a World War II photo analyst, and one of his assignments was to make a photographic record of the liberated Nazi death camps. After the war, he served as an official photographer for the founding of the United Nations. Being an omnivorous reader with a prodigious memory, he found employment as a literary consultant for MGM studios, protecting them against plagiarism lawsuits. He was subtle neither in his physical nor his literary presence. Standing six feet three inches tall and weighing more than three hundred pounds, his friend Buckminster Fuller affectionately dubbed him "history's most massive reader." His best-known and most reviled work, *Naked Is the Best Disguise* (1974), appalled many fans of Sherlock Holmes and Arthur Conan Doyle.

In *Naked*, Rosenberg made public his discoveries of previously unrecognized allusions interspersed liberally throughout the Sherlock Holmes Canon. Within *A Study in Scarlet*, for example, Rosenberg identified the character of Constable Harry Murcher as an allusion to Henry Murger, a French novelist and poet, distinguished for *Scènes de la vie de bohème*, a book based on Murger's own experiences as a desperately poor writer. There can be little doubt that Rosenberg is correct in his identification. Soon after the passing mention of Harry Murcher in *Study*, we find Watson reading Henry Murger's *Scènes de la vie de bohème*, its author's name unmentioned.

Rosenberg deserves credit also for identifying, in the same work, Torquay Terrace in Camberwell as an allusion to Elizabeth Barrett and Robert Browning. The murderer lodged at Madame Charpentier's boarding house on Torquay Terrace in Camberwell. In real life, there is no Torquay Terrace anywhere in Britain, much less in Camberwell. There is, however, a town named Torquay not far from Plymouth, and there is a district in south London called Camberwell. Elizabeth Barrett spent several years in Torquay, under doctor's orders, in the hope that the sea air would cure or ameliorate her tuberculosis. Robert Browning was born in Camberwell.

In addition to identifying the allusion to the Brownings, Rosenberg went to great lengths to show that Holmes's discovery of a rare book in *Study* is intentionally parallel to Robert Browning's discovery of a rare book in his own *The Ring and the Book* (1868).

Rosenberg argued that the Holmes adventures are awash in allusions to famous people including (but hardly limited to) Giovanni Boccaccio, Napoleon Bonaparte, John Bunyan, Charles Dickens, Dionysus, General George Gordon, Herman Melville, Friedrich Nietzsche, Plato, Edgar Allan Poe, William Shakespeare, Mary Shelley, Socrates, Harriet Beecher Stowe, and Oscar Wilde. Many of the allusions are difficult to deny, such as those of Harry Murcher and Torquay Terrace in Camberwell. Others seem strained beyond credibility.

Had Rosenberg limited himself to identifying and substantiating allusions, his book might have been better received by Sherlockians, and more insightful research might have followed. Rosenberg, however, ventured into psychosexual analysis of Holmes's presumptive creator. He attributed each and every one of the allusions to Arthur's repressed sexual impulses, going so far as to coin the term *Conan Doyle Syndrome*. His foray into these murky waters allowed his detractors to disparage, dismiss, and ignore his work.

Richard Lancelyn Green, perhaps the most respected of all Sherlockians, wrote Rosenberg's obituary for the 19 January 1996 issue of *The Independent*.

> The presence of Friedrich Nietzsche at the Reichenbach Falls in 1877 was the premise for Rosenberg's theory that Sir Arthur Conan Doyle based the character of Professor Moriarty on the German philosopher and that Doyle's detective stories were the "pre-Freudian psycho-dramatic confessions" of a "self-revealing allegorist" [...] Although never an invested Baker Street Irregular and often scornful of "orthodox Sherlockian ducks" and "Bakerstreetniks", he contributed an expanded version of a chapter of his book to *Beyond Baker Street* (1976), gave several lectures on the "Conan Doyle syndrome," and wrote introductions to facsimile editions of *The Hound of the Baskervilles* and *The Return of Sherlock Holmes* published in 1975.

In his final paragraph, Green turns the subtitle of Rosenberg's, book, *The Death and Resurrection of Sherlock Holmes*, against Rosenberg.

> [H]is other essays and studies concentrated on characters such as Frankenstein [...] Herman Melville, St Nicholas, Perseus, Dr Albert Schweitzer, Lot's wife, James Joyce, Medusa, and Sigmund Freud, but it is for his book on Sherlock Holmes—which was not so much 'resurrection' as 'desecration'—that he will be best remembered.

Despite Rosenberg's impolitic speech and his fixation on Arthur's presumed sexual proclivities, he deserves substantial credit and consideration for being the first to recognize the scope of the allusions in the Canon, and for being the first to attempt a comprehensive explanation of them.

Incongruities
In literature, the best allusions are those that are difficult to recognize, difficult to solve, then suddenly obvious and indisputable when realized. The Harry Murcher and Torquay Terrace allusions are good examples. They were certainly difficult to recognize; both remained hiding in plain sight for eighty-seven years, until Rosenberg spotted them. They were difficult to solve; Rosenberg relied on his unique pattern-matching skills and his vast literary knowledge. Now that Rosenberg has identified and explained them to us, they are suddenly obvious.

"The world is full of obvious things," explains Holmes, "which nobody by any chance ever observes." The author of the early Holmes adventures wrestled, as all allusionists must, with the problem of being simultaneously invisible and obvious. If the allusions were too obvious, there would be no challenge; if they were too invisible, there would be no purpose. A variety of cues were therefore used to focus additional attention on some of the allusionary passages. One commonly used cue is incongruity.

In *A Scandal in Bohemia*, for example, the author alluded to the story's illustrator by having Watson offer an anagram of Paget: "I did so and saw a large *E* with a small *a*, a *P*, and a large *G* with a small *t* woven into the texture of the paper." Holmes then offers an explanation for the letters, requiring the lowercase *a* be swapped with a lowercase *g*. The well-meaning editors recognized the incongruity, then unwittingly destroyed the allusion.

In *A Study in Scarlet*, the author alluded to Elizabeth Barrett via the seaside town of Torquay and to Robert Browning via the London district of Camberwell. Via the incongruous placement of Torquay Terrace in Camberwell, the readers are cued to the Brownings reference. Sherlockian scholars repeatedly commented on the fictitious nature of Torquay Terrace in Camberwell but failed to recognize its significance. It was the impolitic Rosenberg, so often scornful of "orthodox Sherlockian ducks" and "Bakerstreetniks," who first spied the incongruity as one of several allusions to the Brownings.

Also in *Study*, the author used an incongruity to cue her allusion to Henry Murger. The character Harry Murcher never actually appears in the adventure. He is merely mentioned in passing by Constable John Rance. While Rance describes how he discovered the body, he explains: "At one o'clock it began to rain, and I met Harry Murcher—him who has the Holland Grove beat—and we stood together at the corner of Henrietta Street a-talkin'."

While Holland Grove and Henrietta Street both exist in London, they do not cross. Instead, they are separated by three miles and the river Thames. Constable John Rance could not have met Constable Harry Murcher at the corner of Holland Grove and Henrietta Street, yet neither the infinitely astute Holmes nor the less perceptive Watson took any notice of the incongruity. They are not supposed to. The author did not intend the incongruity for them, but for the readers, and Samuel Rosenberg was the first of us to catch on.

Interconnections

When Watson first meets Holmes in *A Study in Scarlet*, Holmes is in a laboratory developing his own forensic test, one he hopes will become known as the Sherlock Holmes test.

> This was a lofty chamber, lined and littered with countless bottles. Broad, low tables were scattered about, which bristled with retorts, test-tubes, and little Bunsen lamps with their blue flickering flames. There was only one student in the room, who was bending over a distant table absorbed in his work. At the sound of our steps he glanced round and sprang to his feet with a cry of pleasure. "I've found it! I've found it," he shouted to my companion, running towards us with a test-tube in his hand. "I have found a re-agent which is precipitated by haemoglobin, and by nothing else." Had he discovered a gold mine, greater delight could not have shone upon his features.
>
> "Dr Watson, Mr Sherlock Holmes," said Stamford, introducing us.
>
> "How are you?" he said cordially, gripping my hand with a strength for which I should hardly have

given him credit. "You have been in Afghanistan, I perceive."

"How on earth did you know that?" I asked in astonishment.

"Never mind," said he, chuckling to himself. "The question now is about haemoglobin. No doubt you see the significance of this discovery of mine?"

"It is interesting, chemically, no doubt," I answered, "but practically –"

"Why, man, it is the most practical medico-legal discovery for years. Don't you see that it gives us an infallible test for blood stains. Come over here now!" He seized me by the coat-sleeve in his eagerness, and drew me over to the table at which he had been working. "Let us have some fresh blood," he said, digging a long bodkin into his finger, and drawing off the resulting drop of blood in a chemical pipette. "Now, I add this small quantity of blood to a litre of water. You perceive that the resulting mixture has the appearance of pure water. The proportion of blood cannot be more than one in a million. I have no doubt, however, that we shall be able to obtain the characteristic reaction." As he spoke, he threw into the vessel a few white crystals, and then added some drops of a transparent fluid. In an instant the contents assumed a dull mahogany colour, and a brownish dust was precipitated to the bottom of the glass jar.

"Ha! ha!" he cried, clapping his hands, and looking as delighted as a child with a new toy. "What do you think of that?"

"It seems to be a very delicate test," I remarked.

"Beautiful! Beautiful! The old guaiacum test was very clumsy and uncertain. So is the microscopic examination for blood corpuscles. The latter is valueless if the stains are a few hours old. Now, this appears to act as well whether the blood is old or new. Had this test been invented, there are hundreds of men now walking the earth who would long ago have paid the penalty of their crimes."

"Indeed!" I murmured.

"Criminal cases are continually hinging upon that one point. A man is suspected of a crime months perhaps after it has been committed. His linen or clothes are examined and brownish stains discovered upon them. Are they blood stains, or mud stains, or rust stains, or fruit stains, or what are they? That is a question which has puzzled many an expert, and why? Because there was no reliable test. Now we have the Sherlock Holmes test, and there will no longer be any difficulty."

His eyes fairly glittered as he spoke, and he put his hand over his heart and bowed as if to some applauding crowd conjured up by his imagination.

"You are to be congratulated," I remarked, considerably surprised at his enthusiasm.

"There was the case of Von Bischoff at Frankfort last year. He would certainly have been hung had this test been in existence. Then there was Mason of Bradford, and the notorious Muller, and Lefevre of Montpellier, and Samson of New Orleans. I could name a score of cases in which it would have been decisive."

This passage is laden with allusions, none of which has been previously identified (even by Rosenberg), all cued by the incongruity of Holmes's claim that the ratio of blood to water "cannot be more than one in a million." Anyone bothering to check will discover that the ratio cannot have been anywhere near so low, that Holmes was in error by at least an order of magnitude.

At least three of the many allusions thus cued interact with one another: the Sherlock Holmes test, Mason of Bradford, and Lefevre of Montpellier. All three deal with poisons, the very means by which murder is accomplished in *A Study in Scarlet*.

The first of the allusions is to the Marsh test, represented in *Study* as the Sherlock Holmes test. The Marsh test, developed in 1836 by chemist James Marsh, is an extremely sensitive forensic method for detecting the presence of arsenic, an odorless, largely tasteless poison commonly used for controlling rats and, all too frequently, for dispensing with unloved and unwanted humans. Prior to the creation of the Marsh test, arsenic poisoning was easily mistaken for cholera, since the two afflictions share many of the same symptoms. So common had become the nefarious use of arsenic that the French referred to the chemical as *poudre de succession*, inheritance powder.

The Marsh test was the first toxicological test ever to be used in a murder trial. In 1840, Marie-Fortunée Lafarge née Chappelle was convicted of the fatal arsenic poisoning of her husband, after the Marsh test revealed arsenic in the deceased's organs. Her case was a sensation in its day, being one of the first trials publicized via daily newspaper reports, and being the very first to rely on toxicological forensic evidence. Unhappy in her marriage, Madame Lafarge twice purchased arsenic, purportedly to kill rats, and many times, allegedly, added the poison instead to her husband's food and drink.

Found guilty, Madame Lafarge wasted no time in writing her memoirs. In 1841, publisher Henry Colburn turned out an English-language version of the two-volume *Memoirs of Madame Lafarge; Written by Herself.* The foreword to that book, prepared by its editors, mentions the conflicting results obtained from the Marsh test, initially negative, then positive (and damning). The foreword mentions also that the verdict depended on the Marsh test detecting identical concentrations to the Sherlock Holmes test's purportedly "one in a million":

> [T]he world, astonished by this sudden change, and terrified to behold the most mysterious problems of the heart, the most grand and precious interests of humanity, the life and honour of a creature fashioned in the likeness of God, resting on the chemical analysis of the millionth portion of an atom of matter, demanded—"Where is truth or certainty? Are we to

believe the science of yesterday, the science of to-day,
or the science of to-morrow?"

The second of the interconnected allusions is to Mason of
Bradford. In 1858, a Bradford confectioner attempted to save money
by replacing sugar with plaster of Paris, but he inadvertently used
arsenic instead. Hundreds died in what is known as the Bradford
sweets poisoning case. Masons at the time frequently used plaster of
Paris to coat and repair their handiwork, and their occupation is one
of several possible sources for the Mason in "Mason of Bradford."

The Lancet, in its edition of 6 November 1858, detailed the
circumstances of the mass poisoning in Bradford. The quality of the
writing is, by itself, worthy of a read.

> A serious misfortune has occurred, and a great crime
> has been committed, of which the law will take no
> cognizance. A hecatomb of victims has fallen beneath
> the careless error of an inconsiderate lad. A sacrifice
> so vast has rarely fallen to the share of any one shop-
> boy before his time. Many a druggist's lad has slain
> his one, two, or three victims; this boy counts the
> dead by dozens. Twelve pounds of arsenic have been
> manufactured into sweet lozenges, and sold
> broadcast to the first comers amongst the unhappy
> population of Bradford. Very sweet and toothsome
> bon-bons they were, and withal flavoured warmly
> with a comforting savour of peppermint; and so they
> went off briskly from the hands of the vendor in the
> market-place on these late cold and foggy days.
> Honest wholesome lozenges of this variety are not to
> be sold at less than thirteenpence the pound. But
> these were fraudulent trash at the best; their basis
> should have been "daff"—that is, plaster of Paris.
>
> It is a dreary sequence of crime following
> intended fraud. The druggist's boy, Goddard, sent the
> lozenge-maker, Hardaker, white arsenic instead of
> daff, for he had mistaken the casks, and so these poor

souls in Bradford were purchasing their cheap and deadly lozenges at sixpence and sevenpence per pound. One ounce contained about twelve or fourteen lozenges, and each lozenge is calculated to contain eight or ten grains of arsenic—poison for two. A classic poet would picture the Fates hovering over this fatal stall, with all their snakes uncoiled, darting their poison at the fated wretches who were tempted to their death. As they passed away, each to his home, full of market thoughts and mundane troubles, so the pangs of sickness and death seized them. It is not yet known how many have perished. Some fifteen or more are reported dead, and 167 persons suffering.

When the truth was known, bellmen carried the warning through the town, and every household was quickly advertised of the dreadful poison that lurked in these sweets. It was a timely warning to many. But peppermint lozenges are not purchased to be kept in store; they soon vanish before the eager appetites of the little ones at home. And many a sad story is already told of a father and mother unconsciously tempting to a painful death the dearest of their innocents. To many the warning brought only terrible anticipations, too soon realized; to others it confirmed the assurances which death had already given. The public appetite for tragedy will be fed for many days with affecting details of this catastrophe.

The tragedy has been retold many times across the years. In 1887, the very year in which *A Study in Scarlet* first appeared in *Beeton's Christmas Annual*, a reminder appeared in *Mr. Punch's Victorian Era* in the form of a macabre cartoon.

"The Great Lozenge-Maker"

The third of the interacting allusions is to Lefevre of Montpellier, the poisoner Madame Lafarge herself, the woman convicted based on the Marsh test. Not only is she identified early in *Study* as Lefevre of Montpellier, she is identified late in the same adventure as Leturier of Montpellier: "The forcible administration of poisons is by no means a new thing in criminal annals. The cases of Dolsky in Odessa, and of Leturier in Montpellier, will occur at once to any toxicologist."

These two names, Leturier and Lefevre, are telling. Leturier is tantalizingly close to *le tueur*, French for "the killer." Similarly, Lefevre is tantalizingly close to *la fièvre*, French for "the fever." While imprisoned, Madame Lafarge suffered the recurring fevers of her tuberculosis, just as Louise Conan Doyle would suffer her own. And as icing on this allusionary cake, Madame Lafarge was sentenced to life imprisonment at the Maison Centrale prison in Montpellier.

Madame Lafarge wrote another book in her cell, *Heures de Prison* (1854), published two years after her death. It focused on her miserable prison existence. In its July 1854 edition, *The Ladies' Companion and Monthly Magazine* reviewed that book, mentioning more than once Lafarge's feverish, consumptive condition.

> Arrived at the prison of Montpellier, [she] was removed to a dismal cell [...] She had not been many weeks in confinement, before a severe attack of fever brought the necessity of medical advice. M. Pourche was called in—he became interested in his patient, and remained from that time forth one of her firmest friends. Gradually this illness gained more and more upon her—her strength failed—the pains in her head grew insupportable—a burning iron seemed to eat into her brow—she could no longer leave her bed, and she prayed only for death. [...] Soon the very chance of recovery seemed gone. Her mind wandered—she had constant fainting fits—violent spasms seemed to tear her very being asunder, and she became frequently delirious. This part of the book is terrible. [...]
>
> Madame Lafarge arrived at the prison of Montpellier on the 11th September, 1841. In the early part of 1848, her health for the second time declined, and again the burning fever seized, never again to quit her. In the second month of 1851, she was suffered to leave the prison of Montpellier for the Maison de Sante of St. Remy. She arrived there a living skeleton. On the 7th of September, 1852, she died.

There is but one person who was convicted of killing via poison, who suffered the fevers of consumption while imprisoned at Montpellier, and who was the first person to be proven guilty based on a forensic toxicological test. That person is Madame Lafarge, late of Montpellier, familiar to readers of the Sherlock Holmes Canon as the poisoner Leturier of Montpellier, a.k.a. Lefevre of Montpellier.

Irony

There is a fascinating scene in *A Study in Scarlet* in which Holmes tells the police to not waste any time hunting for Miss Rachel, even though her name was written, nearly complete, on a wall at the crime scene, in the killer's own blood. Watson provides the grizzly details. I add the emphasis.

> [Inspector Lestrade] struck a match on his boot and held it up against the wall.
>
> "Look at that!" he said, triumphantly.
>
> I have remarked that the paper had fallen away in parts. In this particular corner of the room a large piece had peeled off, leaving a yellow square of coarse plastering. Across this bare space there was scrawled in blood-red letters a single word—RACHE.
>
> "What do you think of that?" cried the detective, with the air of a showman exhibiting his show. "This was overlooked because it was in the darkest corner of the room, and no one thought of looking there. The murderer has written it with his or her own blood. See this smear where it has trickled down the wall! That disposes of the idea of suicide anyhow. Why was that corner chosen to write it on? I will tell you. See that candle on the mantelpiece. It was lit at the time, and if it was lit this corner would be the brightest instead of the darkest portion of the wall."
>
> "And what does it mean now that you *have* found it?" asked [Inspector] Gregson in a depreciatory voice.
>
> "Mean? *Why, it means that the writer was going to put the female name Rachel*, but was disturbed before he or she had time to finish. *You mark my words, when this case comes to be cleared up you will find that a woman named Rachel has something to do with*

it. It's all very well for you to laugh, Mr. Sherlock Holmes. You may be very smart and clever, but the old hound is the best, when all is said and done."

"I really beg your pardon!" said my companion, who had ruffled the little man's temper by bursting into an explosion of laughter. "You certainly have the credit of being the first of us to find this out, and, as you say, it bears every mark of having been written by the other participant in last night's mystery. I have not had time to examine this room yet, but with your permission I shall do so now."

Holmes meticulously examines the crime scene, then stuns the detectives by profiling the unknown killer in great detail. As he leaves the scene, the police ask him about the murder weapon:

"Poison," said Sherlock Holmes curtly, and strode off. "One other thing, Lestrade," he added, turning round at the door: "'Rache,' is the German for 'revenge;' so *don't lose your time looking for Miss Rachel.*"

With which Parthian shot he walked away, leaving the two rivals open-mouthed behind him.

Henry Watson Fowler was an English lexicographer—in other words, a writer of dictionaries. The London *Times* described him as "a lexicographical genius." In his *The King's English* (1906), Fowler explains that "any definition of irony—though hundreds might be given, and very few of them would be accepted—must include this, that the surface meaning and the underlying meaning of what is said are not the same."

When Holmes advises the police, and us, to not to waste time seeking Miss Rachel, he is actually offering a challenge to do just the opposite. The author was engaging in literary irony, intending the opposite of the superficial meaning. There was indeed a real Miss Rachel, more precisely a real Mademoiselle Rachel, and she visited Madame Lafarge at the Maison Centrale in Montpellier.

Madame Lafarge was one of the first *causes célèbres*. The daily newspaper reports had been gruesome; the use of forensic evidence was exciting, and its results were debatable. Through her memoirs, Madame Lafarge had sustained widespread public interest in her case even after her conviction, inspiring many supporters to visit her at the Maison Centrale. One of the celebrities to visit was the most famous actress of the day, Elizabeth Rachel Felix, better known as Mademoiselle Rachel, or simply Rachel.

Rachel was born 1821, in Mumpf, near the northern border of Switzerland. Her father was a Jewish peddler and her mother a Bohemian dealer of second-hand clothes. (In *A Study in Scarlet*, Holmes is visited by "a grey-headed, seedy visitor, looking like a Jew pedlar.") As a child, Rachel helped support her family by singing in the streets, but singing was not her strong suit; acting was. She became famous for performing the tragedies of Voltaire, Molière, Pierre Corneille, and Jean Racine. She excelled in her diction and economy of gesture, and she thereby provided a welcome contrast to the exaggerated style of the day. Performing mostly in France, she toured Brussels, Berlin, St. Petersburg, London, and America.

Rachel was known almost as well for her sexual liaisons as for her acting. James Agate writes of her, in his 1924 biography *Rachel*, that she "built no Wall of China around her virtue," but "took as many lovers as had beards that pleased her and complexions that liked her." She had two bracelets, Agate explains, "entirely composed of rings given her by her lovers, so heavy that she could wear only one at a time."

In *Tragic Muse* (1995), Rachel Brownstein writes of Rachel's visit with Madame Lafarge.

> She was touring the provinces in her usual repertoire of tragic roles [...] In the cities outside Paris, the women in the audience were especially enthusiastic: complaints that the tragedienne's visits disrupted family life had already appeared in provincial papers years before. In 1848, the mix of art and politics was particularly heady; at Nîmes the tragedienne was cheered for donating a hundred francs to the unemployed. By visiting an accused murderess in Montpellier she was making another timely gesture

towards the unfortunate [...] The account of the
interview she wrote to her sister Sarah suggests that
both parties were strongly affected. [...] Rachel felt
intense pity for a person who had been married
without love, and condemned by a petty jury. Such a
woman might have done greater things in a different
world, where women had more opportunity, she
wrote to Sarah in an unaccustomed spirit of
revolutionary sisterhood. And she pitied Mme
Lafarge for being a victim of tuberculosis: better a tile
on the head or a bullet in the breast than such a
death, she wrote, in language suggestive of the
revolution.

Neither Madame Lafarge nor Mademoiselle Rachel died from a
speeding bullet or a falling, wind-blown tile. Each was consumed
slowly from within by *Mycobacterium tuberculosis* until she was no
more. We do, however, find this striking parallel in Holmes's
account, in *The Final Problem*, of an attempt on his life.

"I kept to the pavement after that, Watson, but as I
walked down Vere Street a brick came down from the
roof of one of the houses, and was shattered to
fragments at my feet. I called the police and had the
place examined. There were slates and bricks piled
up on the roof preparatory to some repairs, and they
would have me believe that the wind had toppled
over one of these."

Rachel one day, long after her visit to Montpellier, returned, not
to visit Madame Lafarge, but under doctor's orders to breathe in the
supposedly recuperative Mediterranean air. It did not save her, so
she relocated to breathe in the supposedly more recuperative air of
Le Cannet, in the Maritime Alps near the southeast corner of France.
She succumbed there just before her thirty-seventh birthday. Her
wasted body was treated as if she had been royalty: sealed in a lead
box, which was placed inside a walnut coffin, then transported in a

special train car from nearby Nice all the way to Paris. Along the way, she was mourned and honored by an admiring public.

In Marseilles, the Grand Rabbi Isidore presided over a makeshift funeral. In Lyons, the actors of the Grand Theater gathered to pay homage. In Paris, she was laid to rest in a mausoleum in the Jewish section of the Père Lachaise Cemetery. The procession from the Place Royale was nothing short of spectacular, as Brownstein depicted it.

> At 1 o'clock the coffin, draped in white cloth embroidered with silver stars, was finally carried outside and laid on the hearse. [...] Drawn by six horses caparisoned in black, the hearse began its slow progress through the narrow streets [...] At the head of the procession rode eleven municipal guardsman on horseback, followed by thirty on foot [...] Behind the hearse walked Grand Rabbi Isidore of Paris, followed by Jacques and Raphaël Félix, the dead woman's father and brother [...] The dead woman's older son, the grandson of Napoleon I, had remained at his school in Switzerland. [...]
>
> Some six hundred carriages and thirty to forty thousand people on foot followed the hearse. According to one newspaper account, several detachments of cavalry were on hand to keep order. By the time the procession reached the cemetery, over one hundred thousand mourners surged forward dangerously toward the open grave, and the wrought-iron gates had to be closed to control the crowd.

Among the celebrities in the procession was Henry Murger, author of *Scènes de la vie de bohème* and allusionary target of *Study's* Harry Murcher.

We do not need to speculate much about whether the author of *A Study in Scarlet* truly had Rachel in mind when alluding to Henry

Murger and Madame Lafarge. The handwriting is on the wall, both literally and figuratively.

Holmes's caution that we not search for Miss Rachel comes at the end of Chapter 3. The next words we see are those of the title for Chapter 4: "What John Rance Had to Tell." John Rance is the constable who discovers the dead body in the abandoned house, the man who met and spoke with fellow constable Harry Murcher on the night of the murder. Just as Harry Murcher is an obvious play on Henry Murger, John Rance is an obvious play on Jean Racine: the French name Jean is cognate with the English name John, and Rance is a near anagram of Racine.

Rachel became famous performing the works of Jean Racine. She played his female leads as no woman had before. One of the characters she portrayed was Monime, from his *Mithridate*. Monime was the wife of Mithridates VI of Pontus, that kingdom surrounding the Black Sea and encompassing parts of what are now Bulgaria, Greece, Turkey, Georgia, Russia, and Ukraine. Mithridates had a fear of poison that was so great that he constantly drank it to build up his immunity. (Poison was central to *A Study in Scarlet*.) When in danger of being captured by Pompey's army, Mithridates attempted suicide by poison but failed, ironically, due to his immunity.

In Racine's play, Mithridates discovers that Monime has fallen in love with one of his sons from an earlier marriage. He provides her with poison that she is to take in his absence, as punishment for the transgression. He then heads off to battle the invading Romans. Just as she steels herself to drink, her hand is stayed when she learns that Mithridates has been stabbed and is near death. He lives long enough to absolve her and her lover, his son, and then sends the two of them forth to continue the resistance against the Romans.

In *Memoirs of Rachel* (1858), Madame de Barrera relates that Rachel's rendition of Monime brought her even more fame and even more fortune.

> *Mithridates* was revived for Rachel who, in the part of Monime, elicited new bursts of admiration. The committee presented her with its first gift, consisting of all the plays in which she had appeared, each

separately and splendidly bound, with her name and the date of her first performance in the part inscribed in golden letters on the back. Shortly after, the committee presented to the gentle and sublime Monime a tiara of gold and precious stones, thus splendidly recording the triumph of the queen even when she falls in the snare laid for her by the wily King of Pontus.

Rachel's career was so intertwined with Jean Racine's that it can be no coincidence, Holmes advising against searching for her as he sets off to question John Rance. It is not coincidence; it is irony.

Double Audience

Fowler noted (lexicographical genius that he was) in his *A Dictionary of Modern English Usage* (1926), that irony anticipates a double audience. Most members of that audience will see only the superficial sense of the text, but an "initiated circle" of readers might recognize the subtlety and complexity. The delight of that double audience, he explained, is "in the secret intimacy set up between the latter and the speaker; it should be added, however, that there are dealers in irony for whom the initiated circle is not of outside hearers, but is an alter ego dwelling in their own breasts."

Though Samuel Rosenberg deserves credit for recognizing the allusionary nature of the Canon, he was not among the "initiated circle" who recognized irony in the tales. He failed, for example, to recognize the irony in Holmes's harsh assessment of Edgar Allan Poe, the issue arising in *A Study in Scarlet*, when Holmes first explains his methods to his new companion, John Watson.

> "You appeared to be surprised when I told you, on our first meeting, that you had come from Afghanistan."
>
> "You were told, no doubt."
>
> "Nothing of the sort. I knew you came from Afghanistan. From long habit the train of thoughts ran so swiftly through my mind that I arrived at the conclusion without being conscious of intermediate

steps. There were such steps, however. The train of reasoning ran: 'Here is a gentleman of a medical type, but with the air of a military man. Clearly an army doctor then. He has just come from the tropics, for his face is dark, and that is not the natural tint of his skin, for his wrists are fair. He has undergone hardship and sickness, as his haggard face says clearly. His left arm has been injured. He holds it in a stiff and unnatural manner. Where in the tropics could an English army doctor have seen much hardship and got his arm wounded? Clearly in Afghanistan.' The whole train of thought did not occupy a second. I then remarked that you came from Afghanistan, and you were astonished."

"It is simple enough as you explain it," I said, smiling. "You remind me of Edgar Allan Poe's Dupin. I had no idea that such individuals did exist outside of stories."

Sherlock Holmes rose and lit his pipe. "No doubt you think that you are complimenting me in comparing me to Dupin," he observed. "Now, in my opinion, Dupin was a very inferior fellow. That trick of his of breaking in on his friends' thoughts with an apropos remark after a quarter of an hour's silence is really very showy and superficial. He had some analytical genius, no doubt; but he was by no means such a phenomenon as Poe appeared to imagine."

Rather than recognize the irony, Rosenberg accuses the author of plagiarism for making Sherlock Holmes so similar to Auguste Dupin. After detailing an impressive list of similarities, Rosenberg stakes his claim.

Some apologists for Conan Doyle have excused his plagiarism, arguing that Sherlock Holmes is a much more interesting character than Poe's Dupin and that Doyle improved Poe's ideas and devices when he used them. I agree in part with these opinions and prefer the Sherlock Holmes stories. But I find this line of defense as unconvincing as the similar argument that a thief deserves to keep stolen money if he invests it more wisely than the person he stole it from.

Some readers, unfamiliar with Poe's work, may presume Dupin is a very inferior fellow. Others, familiar with Dupin, may conclude that Holmes is a product of plagiarism. A different audience, however, may see something in Holmes's words other than insults. This second audience may perceive Holmes's discourtesy to be not an insult but an honor, delivered in the form of irony.

Immediately after this nod (or insult) to Poe and his detective, the author insults Émile Gaboriau and his crime-solving detective.

> "Have you read Gaboriau's works?" I asked. "Does Lecoq come up to your idea of a detective?"
>
> Sherlock Holmes sniffed sardonically. "Lecoq was a miserable bungler," he said, in an angry voice; "he had only one thing to recommend him, and that was his energy. That book made me positively ill. The question was how to identify an unknown prisoner. I could have done it in twenty-four hours. Lecoq took six months or so. It might be made a text-book for detectives to teach them what to avoid."
>
> I felt rather indignant at having two characters whom I had admired treated in this cavalier style. I walked over to the window, and stood looking out into the busy street. "This fellow may be very clever," I said to myself, "but he is certainly very conceited."

Holmes soon thereafter investigates a crime scene in a manner undeniably fashioned after Gaboriau's *L'Affaire Lerouge* (1866), in which the crime scene investigation is described as follows:

> As the old fellow spoke, his little gray eyes dilated and became as brilliant as carbuncles. His face

reflected in internal satisfaction; even his wrinkles seemed to laugh. His figure became erect, his step almost elastic, as he darted into the inner chamber. He remained there about half an hour; then came running out again; once more he disappeared and re-appeared again almost immediately. The magistrate could not help comparing him to a pointer on the scent, his turned-up nose even moved about as if to discover some subtle odour left by the assassin. All the while he talked loudly and with much gesticulation, apostrophising himself, scolding himself, uttering little cries of triumph or self-encouragement. [...] He wanted this or that or the other thing. He demanded paper and a pencil. Then he wanted a spade; and finally he called out for plaster of Paris, some water and a bottle of oil. When more than an hour had elapsed, the investigating magistrate began to grow impatient, and asked what had become of the amateur detective. "He is on the road," replied the corporal, "lying flat in the mud, and laying some plaster on a plate. He says that he is nearly finished, and he is coming back presently.

Consider now the parallel scene in *A Study in Scarlet*.

As he spoke, he whipped a tape measure and a large round magnifying glass from his pocket. With these two implements he trotted noiselessly about the room, sometimes stopping, occasionally kneeling, and once lying flat upon his face. So engrossed was he with his occupation that he appeared to have forgotten our presence, for he chattered away to himself under his breath the whole time, keeping up a running fire of exclamations, groans, whistles, and little cries suggestive of encouragement and of hope. As I watched him I was irresistibly reminded of a pure-blooded, well-trained foxhound as it dashes backwards and forwards through the covert, whining in its eagerness, until it comes across the lost scent. For twenty minutes or more he continued his researches, measuring with the most exact care the distance between marks which were entirely invisible to me, and occasionally applying his tape to the walls in an equally incomprehensible manner. In one place he gathered up very carefully a little pile of grey dust from the floor, and packed it away in an envelope. Finally he examined with his glass the word upon the wall, going over every letter of it with the most minute exactness. This done, he appeared to be satisfied, for he replaced his tape and his glass in his pocket.

Owen Dudley Edwards, in his book *The Quest for Sherlock Holmes* (1983), pointed out the similarity of the texts and called Arthur out, as gently as he could, for stealing from Gaboriau.

The parent passage rather justifies Holmes's rude remarks about Lecoq's energy [...] Conan Doyle would have been a little horrified had he realised how very close indeed his excellent memory had brought him to the original on which he was seeking to improve.

Though Edwards recognized the parallel, he too missed the irony of mimicking someone you criticize. Despite describing Gaboriau's Lecoq as a "miserable bungler," Holmes's creator unabashedly borrowed from Gaboriau's *L'Affaire Lerouge*. This book, however, cannot be the one derided by Holmes, the one in which Lecoq takes six months or so to find an unknown prisoner. Not only does Lecoq play but a minor role in *L'Affaire Lerouge*, the investigation has nothing to do with locating an unknown prisoner. The investigation of Holmes's derision is to be found in Gaboriau's second detective novel, in which Gaboriau promoted Lecoq from an underling to a legendary detective. That novel, *Le Crime d'Orcival* (1867), deals not with the search for an unknown *prisoner*, but instead with the search for an unknown *poisoner*.

Once again we see that our unidentified author was writing for a double audience. "The difficulty," we read in *Le Crime d'Orcival*, "is to seize the beginning; in the entangled skein, the main thread, which must lead to the truth through all the mazes, the ruse, silence, falsehoods of the guilty." Watson first met Holmes as Holmes was searching for an unambiguous test for either blood or poison, depending on the audience. Those readers who recognize that Holmes was testing for poison are likely to recognize as well that Holmes's creator was alluding to *Le Crime d'Orcival*. A key character in that story is introduced in the same fashion as Holmes is introduced in *A Study in Scarlet*.

> Dr. Gendron was well-known in those parts; he was even celebrated, despite the nearness of Paris. Loving his art and exercising it with a passionate energy, he yet owed his renown less to his science than his manners. People said: "He is an original;" they admired his affectation of independence, of scepticism, and rudeness. He made his visits from five to nine in the morning—all the worse for those for whom these hours were inconvenient. After nine o'clock the doctor was not to be had. The doctor was working for himself, the doctor was in his laboratory, the doctor was inspecting his cellar. It was rumored that he sought for secrets of practical chemistry, to augment still more his twenty thousand livres of income. And he did not deny it; for in truth he was engaged on poisons, and was perfecting an invention by which could be discovered traces of all the alkaloids which up to that time had escaped analysis.

Our unidentified author has toyed with us by having Holmes disparage Dupin and Lecoq while borrowing heavily from their creators, urging us to read through all of Lecoq's adventures for an unknown prisoner, knowing there is none to be found. Instead we discover Tabaret (whom Holmes mimics), an unknown poisoner (whom Lecoq is slow in finding), and a laboratory eccentric intent on discovering a test for poisons. As we grasp this tangled skein and attempt to unravel it, it leads us back to the Sherlock Holmes test for blood, from there to the Marsh test for poisons, and then to Madame Lafarge, to Mademoiselle Rachel, Jean Racine, Henry Murger, the Brownings, Edgar Allan Poe, and Émile Gaboriau. We end up where we started, wherever that might have been, for our brilliant author interconnects and entangles as few authors have done before or since.

Chapter 9
Means

Means, motive, and opportunity constitute a simplifying triad for narrowing a list of suspects. In our investigation, "means" relates to the personal attributes that one of our suspects must have possessed to create writings as sophisticated as the Holmes adventures. That person must have been uniquely gifted to devise the interconnected allusions of which we are now becoming aware, and to seamlessly incorporate such clever irony into the stories. Less obvious, and of particular interest here, the creator of Sherlock Holmes had an affinity for math and science not reflected in Arthur's undisputed, non-Sherlockian works.

Blaise Pascal

The author of the Holmes adventures was manifestly fascinated by mathematics. Watson declares Holmes "a calculating machine," Moriarty writes a treatise on the binomial theorem, and Holmes twice drops Euclid's name into casual conversation. These seemingly disjointed mathematical tidbits combine to form a hidden but lasting tribute to one of the most brilliant of all mathematicians, Blaise Pascal.

Pascal invented a calculating machine in 1645, more than two centuries before Watson would declare Holmes to be one, and almost as long before Charles Babbage invented his, in 1822. Pascal also described the fundamentals of the binomial theorem two hundred years before Moriarty was a twinkle in his creator's eye. Pascal even attempted, albeit unsuccessfully, to extend Euclid's axiomatic approach to geometry to human thought and reason. He did so two centuries before Holmes attempted to turn reason into an exact science.

Pascal is also the father of hydraulic theory. In *The Engineer's Thumb*, Holmes is asked by hydraulics engineer Victor Hatherley to investigate the circumstances surrounding his, Hatherley's, missing digit. It was Pascal who invented the hydraulic press that nearly crushed Victor Hatherley and both his thumbs. It was Pascal, also, who invented the syringe, that "tiny piston" that Holmes uses to inject cocaine into his veins.

In *The Final Problem*, Holmes is nearly killed by a team of runaway horses. Blaise Pascal dodged a similar death when his team of runaway horses nearly pulled his carriage off a bridge. Mary Shelley described the event in her encyclopedic work *Lives of the Most Eminent French Writers* (1840):

> One day, in the month of October, he was taking an airing in a carriage-and-four towards the Pont de Neuilli, when the leaders took the bit in their teeth, at a spot where there is no parapet, and precipitated themselves into the Seine: fortunately the shock broke the traces, and the carriage remained on the brink of the precipice. Pascal, a feeble, half-paralytic, trembling being, was overwhelmed by the shock. He fell into a succession of fainting fits, followed by a nervous agitation that prevented sleep, and brought on a state resembling delirium.

So humbling was the experience that Pascal abandoned math, science, and engineering to focus on religion. "I spent a long time in the study of the abstract sciences," he wrote in *Pensées* (1670), "before the little communication that was possible allowed me to quit them in disgust. When I began the study of man, I saw that the abstract sciences are not proper to man." In his *Essay on Man* (1734), Alexander Pope expressed the introspective thought more poetically: "Know then thyself, presume not God to scan; the proper study of mankind is man." *A Study in Scarlet* references Pope and alludes to Pascal when Watson observes, "'The proper study of mankind is man,' you know."

After his religious conversion, Pascal sided with the Jansenists in their dispute with the more powerful Jesuits. He wrote and had published, anonymously, a series of eighteen letters called *The Provincial Letters* (1656-1657), which Louis XIV ordered be collected, shredded, and burnt. The Jansenists fell into further disfavor, and many of them fled to the Netherlands, particularly to Utrecht.

That seemingly irrelevant historical tidbit is actually significant to our investigation, since Holmes, in *A Study in Scarlet*, mentions an untold story involving "the circumstances attendant on the death of Van Jansen, in Utrecht."

Leonardo da Vinci

Holmes's creator did not merely name-drop or allude to mathematicians by name. In *Study,* Holmes's understanding of mathematics dovetails with his understanding of human proportions, key to determining the height of the murderer, for which he inconspicuously credits Leonardo da Vinci.

This takes place during the crime scene investigation adopted from Émile Gaboriau's *L'Affaire Lerouge*, with new elements added so that Holmes can develop a detailed description of the murderer. Holmes examines the word (or partial word) *Rache* that appears on the wall, in blood, and then inspects footprints that appear both inside the house and out. Some of those footprints step directly over a large puddle. Only then does Holmes astound the two Scotland Yard detectives, and the readers, by describing the murderer in substantial detail.

> "There has been murder done, and the murderer was a man. He was more than six feet high, was in the prime of life, had small feet for his height, wore coarse, square-toed boots and smoked a Trichinopoly cigar. He came here with his victim in a four-wheeled cab, which was drawn by a horse with three old shoes and one new one on his off fore-leg. In all probability the murderer had a florid face, and the fingernails of his right hand were remarkably long. These are only a few indications, but they may assist you."

Once Holmes and Watson are alone, Watson asks Holmes how he can be so sure about, among other issues, the murderer's height. Holmes's answer reveals his creator's mathematical acumen.

"Why, the height of a man, in nine cases out of ten, can be told from the length of his stride. It is a simple calculation enough, though there is no use my boring you with figures. I had this fellow's stride both on the clay outside and on the dust within. Then I had a way of checking my calculation. When a man writes on a wall, his instinct leads him to write about the level of his own eyes. Now that writing was just over six feet from the ground. It was child's play."

Though it may now seem obvious that a person's stride length is, to some degree, related to his height, it has not always been apparent. No one other than Holmes seemed the least bit interested in the subject until the late twentieth century, when physical fitness and geriatrics became social issues worthy of scientific studies. Today, we know that a person's stride length, the length of two steps, is approximately 83% of the person's height. The mathematical converse is that a person's height is approximately 1.2 times the length of his stride. We understand that now, but how did Holmes's creator know it more than a century ago?

Not only is Holmes one of the first, perhaps the very first, to use for practical purpose the relationship between height and stride, he is clever enough to do what few people do even today: he cross-checks his results. "Child's play," he says.

It was anything but.

To understand how the author may have gained insight into such arcane matters, we turn to Jean Paul Richter's *The Literary Works of Leonardo da Vinci, compiled and edited from the Original Manuscripts*, published in 1883 and "Dedicated by Permission to her most Gracious Majesty the Queen." The Jean Paul Richter of interest to us here is not the German Romantic writer usually known simply as Jean Paul, but the one born in 1847, who worked as an art historian, a dealer of Italian art, and who was likely the foremost Leonardo scholar of his day.

More than five thousand leaves of Leonardo's manuscripts had been scattered among private holdings throughout Italy, France, and England. Richter somehow gained access to most of those holdings, including those of Queen Victoria, and copied the precious documents using a technique called photogravure, an early photomechanical process for capturing and printing high-quality photographs. He painstakingly transcribed and translated Leonardo's crabbed, backwards-written scrawl. As best he could, Richter then organized Leonardo's entries into the sequence in which Leonardo hoped them to be published, based on indicators Leonardo included to that effect. Richter added editorial notes to help his readers understand Leonardo's entries, the time period when they were written, and the man who had written them. Richter then had this magnum opus published in Italian, German, and English. The end result was the world's first public viewing of Leonardo's astounding manuscripts, and of his sketches therein. All of them were readily available just a few years before someone began writing *A Study in Scarlet*.

On one particularly famous leaf from Leonardo's manuscripts is the likely source of Holmes's insight into determining a man's height from his stride length. It is a seemingly innocuous little entry, erroneous in fact, and apparently misattributed: "4 cubits make a man's height. And 4 cubits make one pace."

The excerpt comes from the text above the sketch known as *Vitruvian Man*. Thanks to Jean Paul Richter, Leonardo's *Vitruvian Man* has become as recognizable as Leonardo's *Mona Lisa*.

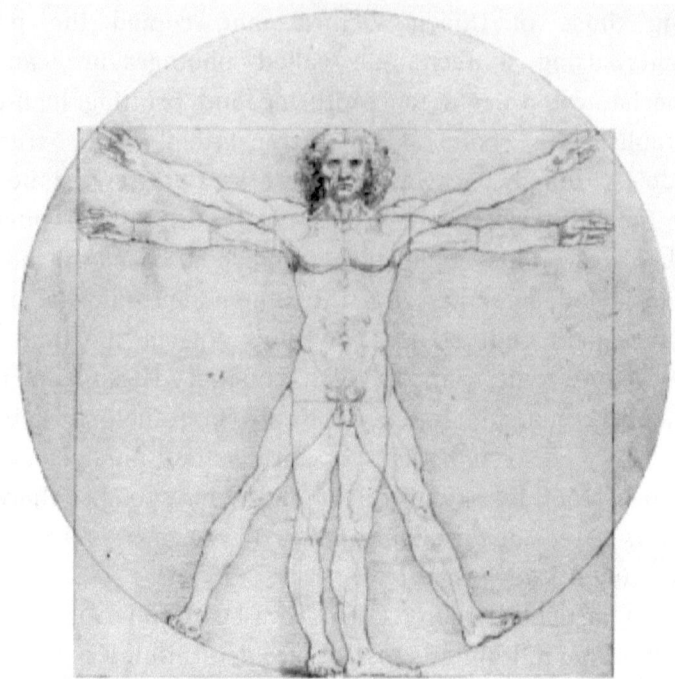

Leonardo's *Vitruvian Man*, circa 1490

It depicts an idealized man in two superimposed positions inscribed within both a circle and a square. Known also as the *Canon of Proportions* and the *Proportions of Man*, the sketch provides a graphical representation an ideally proportioned man. Beneath it, Leonardo put into words his perception of those ideal proportions. His list includes, but is not limited to:

The length of a man's outspread arms is equal to his height.

From the bottom of the chin to the top of his head is one eighth of his height.

The distance from [...] the roots of the hair to the eyebrows is [...] a third of the face.

From the nipples to the top of the head will be the fourth part of a man.

The greatest width of the shoulders contains in itself the fourth part of the man.

From the elbow to the tip of the hand will be the fifth part of a man.

From the elbow to the angle of the armpit will be the eighth part of the man.

The whole hand will be the tenth part of the man.

The beginning of the genitals marks the middle of the man.

From the sole of the foot to below the knee will be the fourth part of the man.

From below the knee to the beginning of the genitals will be the fourth part of the man.

The foot is the seventh part of the man.

In the text above his sketch, Leonardo credited his insight to Vitruvius, the great architect of ancient Rome.

> Vitruvius, the architect, says in his work on architecture that the measurements of the human body are distributed by Nature as follows: that is that 4 fingers make 1 palm, and 4 palms make 1 foot, 6 palms make 1 cubit; 4 cubits make a man's height. And 4 cubits make one pace and 24 palms make a man; and these measures he used in his buildings.

Marcus Vitruvius Pollio is remembered almost exclusively for his ten-volume masterpiece *De architectura*, published sometime around 15 BC. The work details the design of perfectly proportioned structures such as buildings, baths, harbours, and aqueducts. In Volume III, Vitruvius described the perfectly proportioned man who might inhabit or make use of such ideal structures, and appended the text with a sketch that Leonardo improved upon 1500 years later.

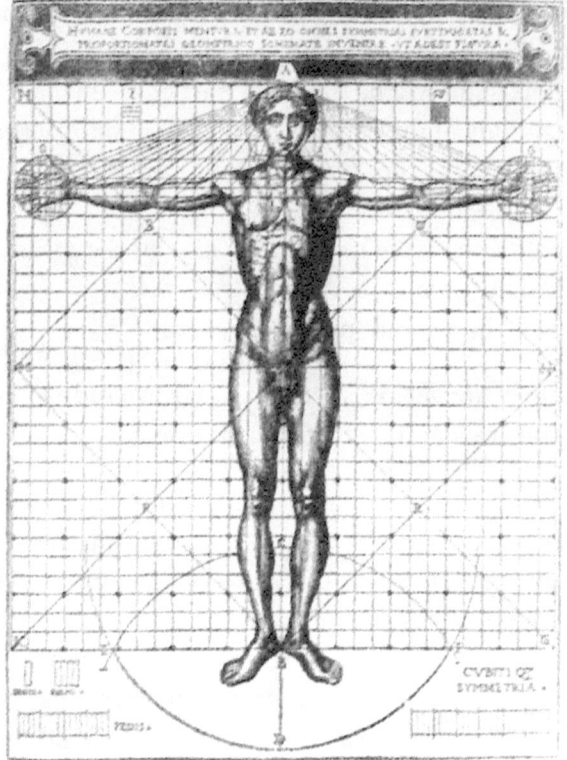

Vitruvius's perfectly proportioned man

Leonardo and Vitruvius each drew their perfectly proportioned man in a static position. The only suggestion of motion is Leonardo's note that Vitruvius declared, "4 cubits make one pace." Since an ancient Roman pace (*passus*) is what Holmes calls a stride (two steps), and since "4 cubits make a man's height," Vitruvius seemingly declared that a perfectly proportioned man has a height equal to his stride. There are problems, however, with Leonardo's note. First, it is wrong. Second, Vitruvius seems not to have claimed such a thing, at least not in the copy of *De architectura* translated by Joseph Gwilt in 1860.

In *De architectura*, a perfect man is declared to be six feet tall: "Moreover, as the foot is the sixth part of a man's height, [the ancients] contend that this number, namely six, the number of feet in height, is perfect." Vitruvius, however, said absolutely nothing about a pace, or a *passus*, or the length of a man's step or stride. If he had, he would certainly have been aware that it was not equal in length to his perfect six-foot man. The standardized Roman *passus* was five feet in length, not six. Rome's perfect man was 1.2 standard strides tall. That ratio is, quite remarkably, identical to nominal height-to-stride ratio so widely accepted today.

We do not know which height-to-stride ratio Holmes believed to be correct, since he chooses not to bore Watson with the figures. We do not know whether he used Leonardo's ratio of 1 to 1, or if he recognized the actual ratio, closer to 1.2 to 1. We have good reason to suspect, however, that Holmes's creator was at least aware of Leonardo's ratio, and of *Vitruvian Man*, in part, because Holmes concludes that the murderer "had small feet for his height."

As you might have noticed, our author endowed Holmes with not just two, but three means of determining the height of the murderer. First, Holmes knows that a person's height is related to his stride. Second, he knows that a person tends to write on a wall at the height of his eye. These two insights he shares with Watson. Third, Holmes knows that a person's height is related to the size of his foot. If the murderer's feet were smaller than normal, there must be a normal.

In *De architectura*, Vitruvius said, "the foot is the sixth part of a man's height." In the text above his sketch, Leonardo restated Vitruvius's ratio as "4 palms make 1 foot [...] and 24 palms make a man." In both statements, Vitruvius's ratio of 1 to 6 is clear. Leonardo, however, disagreed with that value. When it came time for him to declare his own idealized proportion beneath his sketch, he more accurately noted, "The foot is the seventh part of the man." Like the murderer in *A Study in Scarlet*, Leonardo's *Vitruvian Man* "had small feet for his height," at least by the standard of Vitruvius.

The author of *Study* could have most easily given the murderer feet of normal size, and had Holmes determine the murderer's height from any single footprint. There were, at the time, plenty of art and sculpture books that detailed Vitruvius's idealized proportions and encouraged the use of them. Those books, however, said nothing of a person's stride, because Vitruvius said nothing of it. Holmes could have explained to Watson that "the height of a man, in nine cases out of ten, can be told from the length of his foot," but he could not have explained that "the height of a man, in nine cases out of ten, can be told from the length of his stride," unless he had read Jean Paul Richter.

In *The Sign of Four*, Holmes asks Watson:

> "Are you well up in your Jean Paul?"
>
> "Fairly so. I worked back to him through Carlyle."
>
> "That was like following the brook to the parent lake. He makes one curious but profound remark. It is that the chief proof of man's real greatness lies in his perception of his own smallness. It argues, you see, a power of comparison and of appreciation which is in itself a proof of nobility. There is much food for thought in Richter."

Is Holmes referring to the Romantic writer or the Leonardo expert? Why can it not be to both?

Shakespeare's Sere and Yellow

"Let no man who is not a Mathematician read the elements of my work." So forewarned Leonardo near the beginning of his manuscripts.

It appears that our unidentified author not only dared to read Leonardo's elements, but also presumed to expand on them. Given the absence of any precedent, we are tempted to conclude that our author independently developed the mathematics of a man stepping over a puddle. Begin by considering, once again, Holmes's explanation of how he determines the murderer's height, this time including how he approximated the murderer's age.

> "Why, the height of a man, in nine cases out of ten, can be told from the length of his stride. It is a simple calculation enough, though there is no use my boring you with figures. I had this fellow's stride both on the clay outside and on the dust within. Then I had a way of checking my calculation. When a man writes on a wall, his instinct leads him to write about the level of his own eyes. Now that writing was just over six feet from the ground. It was child's play."

"And his age?" I asked.

"Well, if a man can stride four and a half feet without the smallest effort, he can't be quite in the sere and yellow. That was the breadth of a puddle on the garden walk which he had evidently walked across. Patent-leather boots had gone round, and Square-toes had hopped over. There is no mystery about it at all."

To determine whether the killer could easily step over a puddle four and a half feet wide, we will want first to determine his height. By putting a ruler to Leonardo's *Vitruvian Man*, we can determine that his height is 1.075 times the height of his eyes. Since the writing is "just over six feet" up the wall, and since one tends to write at eye level, the murderer must have been just over 6.45 feet tall. We'll call it six feet and six inches, an imposing figure for the time.

Next, we should consider the man's stride length. Holmes measured the stride at the crime scene, and advised us that we can work back to the stride length from the man's height. If the author believed that a man's stride is equal to his height, as per Leonardo, then the killer had a two-step stride length of 6.5 feet, and a single-step length of 3.25 feet. If the author believed instead that a man's stride is only 83% of his height, as is accepted today, then the killer had a stride of 5.4 feet, and a single-step length of 2.7 feet. In either case, the killer could not have stepped over a 4.5-foot puddle without taking an unusually large step.

Two questions now present themselves. First, could a 6.5-foot-tall man who is not "quite in the sere and yellow" make such an unusually large step? Second, would he need to walk around?

The phrase "sere and yellow" is from Shakespeare. *Sere*, also spelled *sear*, means dry and withered. *Yellow* refers to the color change of leaves preceding their fall. Shakespeare coupled the two words in *Macbeth*:

I have liv'd long enough: my way of life
Is fall'n into the sear, the yellow leaf;
And that which should accompany old age,

As honour, love, obedience, troops of friends,
I must not look to have;

The author invoked Shakespeare to distinguish between a young man, such as the murderer in *A Study in Scarlet*, and an old man, such as Macbeth on the verge of battle.

The shortest single step to clear a 4.5-feet puddle would involve placing the toe of one boot at the front edge of the puddle, then landing the heel of the other boot at the far edge. Since, according to Leonardo, a man's foot is one-seventh his height, the murderer's foot was just over 11 inches long, his boot somewhat longer, by an inch, perhaps. We can calculate, therefore, that the killer would need to make a single step of 5.5 feet to clear a 4.5 feet wide puddle.

Geriatric researchers now study how far people can step, since the ability to quickly make a large step is key to safely recovering from a stumble. The researchers define the maximum step length as the distance that the subject can, starting with feet together, step forward and then step back. The maximum step length is somewhat shorter than a single step of the sort one would take over a puddle, but the studies nonetheless provide us with valuable information. According to Brian W. Schultz's "Age-related redistribution of hip and knee kinetics during out-and-back stepping", the maximum step length is approximately 80% of the person's height. For seniors, it drops to 73% of the youthful value, 58% of the person's height.

Based on modern geriatric studies, the 6.5-feet-tall murderer in *Study* would be able to step forward 5.2 feet, from a standing position, and still recover to his original position. Walking towards a 4.5-feet-wide puddle, he should easily be able to make the 5.5-feet step without getting his boot wet, but only if he is in the prime of life. If, on the other hand, he is in his "sere and yellow," his maximum step length will be a mere 3.8 feet, with no way to make the necessary 5.5-feet step. His boot will get soaked, or he will walk around.

We should be utterly astonished. The results attest not only to the accuracy of the unidentified author's insight into human proportions, but also to an ability to apply mathematics in original and surprising fashion, a century before geriatric specialists turned their attention to the subject. By the use of mathematical propensity and acumen, the author properly calculated the size of a puddle that would be small enough for a young man to step over, but large enough that an older one would have to circumvent it.

Child's play indeed.

The Method of Zadig

Holmes does not merely describe the murderer from prints on the ground, he describes also the horse that pulled the carriage that delivered the murderer (and his victim) to the soon-to-be crime scene. "He came here with his victim in a four-wheeled cab," Holmes informs the Scotland Yard detectives, "which was drawn by a horse with three old shoes and one new one on his off fore-leg."

Because of Holmes's observation, we can be reasonably confident that his creator read Thomas Henry Huxley's "On the Method of Zadig: Retrospective Prophecy as a Function of Science," an article that appeared in the August 1880 issue of *Popular Science Monthly*. In it, Huxley expounded on how paleontology, geology, and other historical sciences share an ancient root, with Voltaire providing a little biographical information on Zadig.

> It is said that he lived at Babylon in the time of King Moabdar; but the name of Moabdar does not appear in the list of Babylonian sovereigns brought to light by the patience and the industry of the decipherers of cuneiform inscriptions in these later years; nor indeed am I aware that there is any other authority for his existence than that of the biographer of Zadig, one Arouet de Voltaire, among whose more conspicuous merits strict historical accuracy is perhaps hardly to be reckoned. [...]
>
> Voltaire tells us that, disenchanted with life by sundry domestic misadventures, Zadig withdrew from the turmoil of Babylon to a secluded retreat on the banks of the Euphrates, where he beguiled his solitude by the study of nature. The manifold wonders of the world of life had a particular

attraction for the lonely student; incessant and patient observation of the plants and animals about him sharpened his naturally good powers of observation and of reasoning; until, at length, he acquired a sagacity which enabled him to perceive endless minute differences among objects which, to the untutored eye, appeared absolutely alike.

It might have been expected that this enlargement of the powers of the mind and of its store of natural knowledge could tend to nothing but the increase of a man's own welfare and the good of his fellow-men. But Zadig was fated to experience the vanity of such expectations.

Huxley went on to describe the incident in Zadig's life that exemplifies his method of reason and deduction.

One day, walking near a little wood, he saw, hastening that way, one of the Queen's chief eunuchs, followed by a troop of officials, who appeared to be in the greatest anxiety, running hither and thither like men distraught, in search of some lost treasure.

"Young man," cried the eunuch, "have you seen the Queen's dog?"

Zadig answered modestly, "A bitch, I think, not a dog."

"Quite right," replied the eunuch; and Zadig continued, "A very small spaniel who has lately had puppies; she limps with the left foreleg, and has very long ears."

"Ah! you have seen her then," said the breathless eunuch.

"No," answered Zadig, "I have not seen her; and I really was not aware that the Queen possessed a spaniel."

By an odd coincidence, at the very same time, the handsomest horse in the King's stables broke away from his groom in the Babylonian plain. The grand huntsman and all his staff were seeking the horse with as much anxiety as the eunuch and his people the spaniel; and the grand huntsman asked Zadig if he had not seen the King's horse go that way.

"A first-rate galloper, small-hoofed, five feet high; tail three feet and a half long; cheek pieces of the bit of twenty-three carat gold; shoes silver?" said Zadig.

"Which way did he go? Where is he?" cried the grand huntsman.

"I have not seen anything of the horse, and I never heard of him before," replied Zadig.

The grand huntsman and the chief eunuch made sure that Zadig had stolen both the King's horse and the Queen's spaniel, so they hauled him before the High Court of Desterham, which at once condemned him to the knout [a multi-prong whip], and transportation for life to Siberia. But the sentence was hardly pronounced when the lost horse and spaniel were found. So the judges were under the painful necessity of reconsidering their decision: but they fined Zadig four hundred ounces of gold for saying he had seen that which he had not seen.

The first thing was to pay the fine; afterwards Zadig was permitted to open his defence to the court, which he did in the following terms:

"Stars of justice, abysses of knowledge, mirrors of truth, whose gravity is as that of lead, whose inflexibility is as that of iron, who rival the diamond in clearness, and possess no little affinity with gold; since I am permitted to address your august assembly, I swear by Ormuzd that I have never seen the respectable lady dog of the Queen, nor beheld the sacrosanct horse of the King of Kings.

"This is what happened. I was taking a walk towards the little wood near which I subsequently had the honour to meet the venerable chief eunuch

and the most illustrious grand huntsman. I noticed
the track of an animal in the sand, and it was easy to
see that it was that of a small dog. Long faint streaks
upon the little elevations of sand between the
footmarks convinced me that it was a she dog with
pendent dugs [teats], showing that she must have had
puppies not many days since. Other scrapings of the
sand, which always lay close to the marks of the
forepaws, indicated that she had very long ears; and,
as the imprint of one foot was always fainter than
those of the other three, I judged that the lady dog of
our august Queen was, if I may venture to say so, a
little lame.

"With respect to the horse of the King of Kings,
permit me to observe that, wandering through the
paths which traverse the wood, I noticed the marks of
horse-shoes. They were all equidistant. "Ah!" said I,
"this is a famous galloper." In a narrow alley, only
seven feet wide, the dust upon the trunks of the trees
was a little disturbed at three feet and a half from the
middle of the path. "This horse," said I to myself, "had
a tail three feet and a half long, and, lashing it from
one side to the other, he has swept away the dust."
Branches of the trees met overhead at the height of
five feet, and under them I saw newly fallen leaves; so
I knew that the horse had brushed some of the
branches, and was therefore five feet high. As to his
bit, it must have been made of twenty-three carat
gold, for he had rubbed it against a stone, which
turned out to be a touchstone, with the properties of
which I am familiar by experiment. Lastly, by the
marks which his shoes left upon pebbles of another
kind, I was led to think that his shoes were of fine
silver."

All the judges admired Zadig's profound and
subtle discernment; and the fame of it reached even
the King and the Queen. From the ante-rooms to the

presence-chamber, Zadig's name was in everybody's mouth; and, although many of the magi were of opinion that he ought to be burnt as a sorcerer, the King commanded that the four hundred ounces of gold which he had been fined should be restored to him. So the officers of the court went in state with the four hundred ounces; only they retained three hundred and ninety-eight for legal expenses, and their servants expected fees.

We can be reasonably confident that our unidentified author read Huxley's article about Zadig, because three elements of this tale appear in the Holmes adventures. The first and most obvious is that Holmes reads the hoof prints of the carriage horse in the same fashion that Zadig read the paw prints of the Queen's dog. "There were the marks of the horse's hoofs," explains Holmes to Watson, "the outline of one of which was far more clearly cut than that of the other three, showing that that was a new shoe."

Less obvious from our discussion thus far is that Zadig's deductions seemed so mysterious that "many of the magi were of opinion that he ought to be burnt as a sorcerer." Consider the similar excerpt from *A Scandal in Bohemia*, when Watson visits Holmes after an extended interlude prompted by Watson's marriage.

> [Holmes's] manner was not effusive. It seldom was; but he was glad, I think, to see me. With hardly a word spoken, but with a kindly eye, he waved me to an armchair, threw across his case of cigars, and indicated a spirit case and a gasogene in the corner. Then he stood before the fire, and looked me over in his singular introspective fashion.
>
> "Wedlock suits you," he remarked. "I think, Watson, that you have put on seven and a half pounds since I saw you."
>
> "Seven," I answered.
>
> "Indeed, I should have thought a little more. Just a trifle more, I fancy, Watson. And in practice again, I

observe. You did not tell me that you intended to go into harness."

"Then, how do you know?"

"I see it, I deduce it. How do I know that you have been getting yourself very wet lately, and that you have a most clumsy and careless servant girl?"

"My dear Holmes," said I, "this is too much. You would certainly have been burned had you lived a few centuries ago.

Less obvious still is the common interest shared by Holmes and Huxley regarding the famous paleontologist Georges Cuvier. Wrote Huxley:

> Though Zadig is cited in one of the most important chapters of Cuvier's greatest work [...] it may be justly urged that Cuvier, the great master of this kind of investigation, gave a very different account of the process which yielded such remarkable results. Cuvier is not the first man of ability who has failed to make his own mental processes clear to himself, and he will not be the last. The matter can be easily tested. Search the eight volumes of the "Recherches sur les Ossemens Fossiles" from cover to cover, and nothing but the application of the method of Zadig will be found in the arguments by which a fragment of a skeleton is made to reveal the characters of the animal to which it belonged.

Huxley preceded his article by quoting Cuvier's single mention of Zadig: "*Une marque plus sure que toutes celles de Zadig,*" translated as "A more certain mark than all those of Zadig." The quote is from Cuvier's *A Discourse on the Revolutions of the Surface of the Globe and the Changes thereby Produced in the Animal Kingdom*, translated into English in 1831. Consider this more complete quotation:

> Any one who sees the track of a cleft foot may conclude that the animal who left it is ruminant; and

this assertion is as sure as any other in physics or morality. This footmark alone gives to the observer both the formation of the teeth, the shape of the jaws, the structure of the vertebras, and the form of all bones of the legs, thighs, shoulders, and even the frame of the animal which has passed. It is a more certain mark than all those of Zadig.

Consider now the scene from *The Five Orange Pips*, when Holmes makes his only mention of Cuvier.

Sherlock Holmes closed his eyes, and placed his elbows upon the arms of his chair, with his fingertips together. "The ideal reasoner," he remarked, "would, when he has once been shown a single fact in all its bearings, deduce from it not only all the chain of events which led up to it, but also all the results which would follow from it. As Cuvier could correctly describe a whole animal by the contemplation of a single bone, so the observer who has thoroughly understood one link in a series of incidents should be able accurately to state all the other ones, both before and after.

Attempting to implement Holmes's teaching, we might now attempt to link the series of incidents that leads Holmes to conclude that the murderer could not have been "quite in the sere and yellow." Consider: his creator, a reader of *Popular Science Monthly*, happens on Thomas Henry Huxley's article, "On the Method of Zadig," and is fascinated that people such as Zadig and Cuvier could discern so much from so little. Having already read of Poe's insightful detective, and, more recently, of Gaboriau's, the budding author conjures an even more interesting character.

The author traces Huxley's quote of Cuvier to its source, *A Discourse on the Revolutions of the Surface of the Globe*, and reads at least through page 63 of that 250-page work, for it is on page 63 that Cuvier's only reference to Zadig appears. The author reads of how

Cuvier could with certainty envision an entire animal by examining a single footprint.

Cuvier's words must be placed into the mouth of this new detective! If, as Huxley claimed, all of paleontology, geology, and other historical science is based on the method of Zadig, so too, the author realizes, is the work of Poe and Gaboriau. Thus, in the author's first detective story, the method of Zadig is invoked: a horse leaves one hoof print different from the other three, just as Zadig observed one odd paw print. Stepping beyond Zadig, however, and even beyond Cuvier, Holmes's creator has the detective describe the murderer from his footsteps, and uses mathematics to insure the claims are reasonable.

For anatomical proportions, the author turns to Leonardo's *Vitruvian Man*, just recently made public by Jean Paul Richter's great work, recognizing in Leonardo's notes that a man's stride is proportional to his height, and using the foot-size disagreement with Vitruvius as an advantage. Holmes determines the man's height from his stride length and eye height, and that the man has the smaller feet of Leonardo.

Standing on the shoulders of Zadig, Cuvier, Vitruvius, Leonardo, Poe, and Gaboriau, Holmes's creator sees further than they did. Holmes speaks not only to the murderer's height, based on his footprints, but to the murderer's age as well.

In the second Holmes adventure, *The Sign of Four*, an additional clue appears when Holmes asks Watson if he is up on his Jean Paul. Here she is clearly referring to Jean Paul Richter the author, since the author usually went by the name Jean Paul, then notes that "there is much food for thought in Richter." That would be Richter, the da Vinci expert, since the author eschewed his last name.

In the third Holmes adventure, *A Scandal in Bohemia*, Huxley's telling of Zadig is echoed by Watson telling Holmes: "You would certainly have been burned had you lived a few centuries ago," just as the magi wanted done to Zadig.

The seventh Holmes adventure, *The Five Orange Pips*, has Holmes admire Georges Cuvier's ability to envision an entire animal from a single footprint.

For the creator of Sherlock Holmes, all this was mere child's play.

Chapter 10
Motive

Of motives, Charlotte Brontë cautions, "The study of motives is a strange one, not to be pursued too far by one fallible human being in reference to his fellows." We therefore proceed with due caution.

Irresistible Impulse

"I'm just going to write, because I cannot help it," recorded a sixteen-year-old Charlotte Brontë in her journal. "There is a voice, there is an impulse that wakens that dormant power, which in its torpidity I sometimes think dead." Even at such a young age, she feared that her muse would abandon her. "Why cannot the blood rouse the heart, the heart wake the head, the head prompt the hand to do things like these?"

Charlotte Brontë provides a possible model for understanding why the creator of Sherlock Holmes wrote the early adventures but claimed no credit for doing so. A comparison of their writing suggests the two were similarly motivated to write, to express themselves, to escape the humdrum.

Holmes tells Watson, "I cannot live without brainwork. What else is there to live for? [...] What is the use of having powers, Doctor, when one has no field upon which to exert them?"

Charlotte's eponymous Jane Eyre laments, "I tired of the routine of eight years in one afternoon. I desired liberty; for liberty I gasped; for liberty I uttered a prayer; it seemed scattered on the wind then faintly blowing. I abandoned it and framed a humbler supplication. For change, stimulus."

Holmes pronounces "My mind rebels at stagnation. Give me problems, give me work, give me the most abstruse cryptogram, or the most intricate analysis, and I am in my own proper atmosphere. I can dispense then with artificial stimulants. But I abhor the dull routine of existence. I crave for mental exaltation."

Charlotte's letter to a friend reads, "An account of one day is an account of all. In the morning, from nine o'clock till half-past twelve, I instruct my sisters, and draw; then we walk till dinner-time. After dinner I sew till tea-time, and after tea I either write, read, or do a little fancy-work, or draw, as I please. Thus, in one delightful, though somewhat monotonous course, my life is passed."

"My life," Holmes explains to Watson, "is spent in one long effort to escape from the commonplaces of existence."

Charlotte and her siblings Branwell, Emily, and Anne, spent much of their youth amidst several fantasy worlds, paracosms of their own making. They adopted the personae of their imaginary characters, created detailed maps of their faraway lands, and published three single-issue magazines to be sold within their imaginary cities. The second of those, *The Young Men's Magazine*, is particularly notable, having been actually sold in 2011 for £690,850. Its title page reads:

SECOND SERIES OF THE
YOUNG MEN'S MAGAZINE. NO
THIRD
FOR OCTOBER 1830

Edited by Charlotte Brontë
SOLD
BY
SERGEANT TREE
AND ALL OTHER
Booksellers in the Glass Tow,
Paris, Ross's Glass Town, Parry's G
Town & the Duke of Wellington's Glass Town
Finished August 23 1830
Charlotte Brontë—
August 23
1830

This second series of magazines
is conducted on like
principles with the first. The
same eminent authors
are also engaged to contribute for it.

Charlotte was but fourteen years old when she edited *The Young Men's Magazine*. Writing as Lord Charles Wellesley, a man rather than a woman, she contributed also, as one of the magazine's "eminent authors." An excerpt from Lord Wellesley's "A Day at Parry's Palace" provides shocking insight into "his" potential for violence. Given Charlotte's slight size, mild demeanor, and kindness, she must have been hard pressed to welcome such material into her magazine.

> Parry now withdrew to his study & Lady Aumly to her work room, so that I was left alone with Eater. He stood for more than half an hour on the rug before me with his finger in his mouth, staring idiot like full in my face, uttering every now & then an odd grumbling noise, which I suppose denoted the creature's surprise. I ordered him to sit down. He laughed but did not obey. This incensed me, and heaving the poker I struck him to the ground. The scream that he set up was tremendous, but it only increased my anger. I kicked him several times & dashed his head against the floor, hoping to stun him. This failed. He only roared the louder. By this time the whole household was alarmed: master, mistress, and servants came running into the room. I looked about for some means of escape but could find none.
>
> "What hauve you beinn douing tou de child?" asked Parry, advancing towards me with an aspect of defiance.
>
> As I wished to stop a day longer at his palace, I was forced to coin a lie. "Nothing [at] all," I replied. "The sweet boy fell down as I was playing with him & hurt his self."
>
> That satisfied the good and easy man & they all retired, carrying the hateful brat still squalling & bawling along with them.

In that same issue we find the sophisticated poem "Morning" by Marquis Douro, later King of Angria—actually Charlotte in yet another of her characters. The poem invokes the names of mythological figures Aurora and Philomela. Aurora, the Roman goddess of dawn, heralds the passage of Apollo's fiery horses as they pull his chariot across the sky. Philomela, the Greek lover of song, is transformed into a nightingale after she is raped.

Also found in *The Young Men's Magazine* is a conversation among Lord Wellesley, Marquis Douro, Young Soult, De Lisle, and Sergeant Bud, as they gather in the parlour at Bravey's Inn. Young Soult, a poet who barely escapes beheading, is a Branwell character, as are Sergeant Bud, a lawyer and bookseller, and De Lisle, the greatest painter and portraitist of Verdopolis.

Since she modeled *The Young Men's Magazine* after the real *Blackwood's Magazine*, Charlotte ensured that all the contributors were men. She took care also to include such advertisements as:

The Elements of LYING
By LORD CHARLES WELLESLEY
in one vol., duodecimo
PRICE 2s 6d
With some account of those
who practise it.

SOGAST, a Romance. By
CAPTAIN TREE
in 2 volumes. Oct. Price 20d

Orion & Arcturus, a POEM —
LORD WELLESLEY
Recommendation: 'this is the
most beautiful poem that ever
flowed from the pen of man. The
sentiments are wholly original;
Nothing is borrowed'
Glass T Review

TO BE SOLD: a rat-trap, by

MONSIEUR it can catch nothing
FOR it's BROKEN.

THE ART OF BLOWing
One's Nose, is taught by
Monsieur Pretty-foot at his
house, No. 105 Blue Rose Street,
Glass TOWN

It must be obvious that Charlotte was compelled by some irresistible impulse to write. She wrote because she had to. Upon reaching her twenty-first year, she sent some of her poetry to Robert Southey, poet laureate of England. He advised her to forget writing, to tend instead to her womanly chores.

It is not my advice that you have asked as to the direction of your talents, but my opinion of them, and yet the opinion may be worth little, and the advice much. You evidently possess, and in no inconsiderable degree, what Wordsworth calls the "faculty of verse." I am not depreciating it when I say that in these times it is not rare. Many volumes of poems are now published every year without attracting any attention, any one of which if it had appeared half a century ago, would have obtained a high reputation for its author. Whoever, therefore, is ambitious of distinction in this way ought to be prepared for disappointment.

But it is not with a view to distinction that you should cultivate this talent, if you consult your own happiness. I, who have made literature my profession, and devoted my life to it, and have never for a moment repented of the deliberate choice, think myself, nevertheless, bound in duty to caution every young man who applies as an aspirant to me for encouragement and advice, against taking so perilous a course. You will say that a woman has no need of such a caution: there can be no peril in it for her. In a certain sense this is true; but there is a danger of which I would, with all kindness and earnestness, warn you. The daydreams in which you habitually indulge are likely to induce a distempered state of mind; and in proportion as all the ordinary uses of the world seem to you flat and unprofitable, you will be unfitted for them without becoming fitted for anything else. Literature cannot be the business of a woman's life, and it ought not to be. The more she is engaged in her proper duties, the less leisure will she have for it, even as an accomplishment and a recreation. To those duties you have not yet been called, and when you are you will be less eager for celebrity. You will not seek in imagination for excitement, of which the vicissitudes of this life, and the anxieties from which you must not hope to be exempted, be your state what it may, will bring with them but too much hope.

But do not suppose that I disparage the gift which you possess; nor that I would discourage you from exercising it. I only exhort you so to think of it, and so to use it, as to render it conducive to your own permanent good. Write poetry for its own sake; not in a spirit of emulation, and not with a view to celebrity; the less you aim at that the more likely you will be to deserve and finally to obtain it. So written, it is wholesome both for the heart and soul; it may be made the surest means, next to religion, of soothing the mind and elevating it. You may embody in it your best thoughts and your wisest feelings, and in doing so discipline and strengthen them.

Farewell madam. It is not because I have forgotten that I was once young myself, that I write to you in this strain; but because I remember it. You will neither doubt my sincerity nor my good will; and however ill what has here been said may accord with your present views and temper, the longer you live

the more reasonable it will appear to you. Though I may be but an ungracious adviser, you will allow me, therefore, to subscribe myself, with the best wishes for your happiness and hereafter, your true friend,
    Robert Southey

To this crushing letter, young Charlotte replied with humility and a promise.

At first perusal of your letter I felt only shame and regret that I had ever ventured to trouble you with my crude rhapsody; I felt a painful heat rise to my face when I thought of the quires of paper I had covered with what once gave me so much delight, but which now was only a source of confusion; but after I had thought a little and read it again and again, the proper prospect seemed to clear. You do not forbid me to write; you do not say that what I write is utterly destitute of merit. You only warn me against the folly of neglecting real duties, for the sake of imaginative pleasures; of writing for the love of fame; for the selfish excitement of emulation. You kindly allow me to write poetry for its own sake, provided I leave undone nothing which I ought to do, in order to pursue that single, absorbing exquisite gratification. [...] In the evenings, I confess, I do think, but I never trouble any one else with my thoughts. I carefully avoid any appearance of pre-occupation and eccentricity, which might lead those I live amongst to suspect the nature of my pursuits. [...] I have endeavoured not only attentively to observe all the duties a woman ought to fulfil, but to feel deeply interested in them. [...] I trust I shall never more feel ambitious to see my name in print.

Try as she might, Charlotte was not able to suppress her writing. In her debut novel *Jane Eyre* she implanted thoughts in Jane's head that doubled as a revised, blunt reply to Southey's patronizing advice.

> Who blames me? Many, no doubt; and I shall be called discontented. I could not help it; the restlessness was in my nature; it agitated me to pain sometimes. Then my sole relief was to [...] open my inward ear to a tale that was never ended—a tale my imagination created, and narrated continuously; quickened with all of incident, life, fire, feeling, that I desired and had not in my actual existence.
>
> It is in vain to say human beings ought to be satisfied with tranquility: they must have action; and they will make it if they cannot find it. Millions are condemned to a stiller doom than mine, and millions are in silent revolt against their lot. [...] Women are supposed to be very calm generally: but women feel just as men feel; they need exercise for their faculties, and a field for their efforts as much as their brothers do; they suffer from too rigid a restraint, too absolute a stagnation, precisely as men would suffer; and it is narrow-minded in their more privileged fellow-creatures to say that they ought to confine themselves to making puddings and knitting stockings, to playing on the piano and embroidering bags. It is thoughtless to condemn them, or laugh at them, if they seek to do more or learn more than custom has pronounced necessary for their sex.

In composing Jane's thoughts, Charlotte was writing for a double audience, the smaller part of which consisted of no more than two individuals: Robert Southey and Charlotte herself. Her reading public could not possibly know of her earlier exchange of letters with Southey, for it remained private until two years after her death, when Elizabeth Gaskell provided details in *The Life of Charlotte Brontë* (1857).

The author of the early Holmes adventures seems to have read both the biography and the novel, and to have furthermore realized something about Southey's reply that even Charlotte missed. In *A Study in Scarlet*, our still-unidentified author shockingly alluded not only to Robert Southey, but also to the French playwright Molière.

Consider a scene from *A Study in Scarlet*. As Watson reads from Henri Murger's *Scènes de la vie de bohème*, Holmes returns to 221B Baker Street to report on the progress of his investigation into the murder. "On inquiring at Number 13," he tells Watson, "we found that the house belonged to a respectable paperhanger, named Keswick."

Keswick is never again mentioned anywhere within the Canon. For those Sherlockians playing the game, Holmes's incidental discovery must be taken at face value; Keswick was, and always will be, a professional wallpaperer. Beyond the fictional realm of the Canon, however, Keswick is not a person but a place, a civil parish in the Lake District of northwest England. Samuel Taylor Coleridge lived there, as did William Wordsworth, whom, interestingly, Southey mentioned in his reply to Charlotte. Southey visited Coleridge in 1803 and never left. He was living there when he advised Charlotte to give up writing and tend her housework. Along with Coleridge and Wordsworth, Southey became known as one of the Lake Poets, as famous for that as he was for being Britain's Poet Laureate.

Molière, on the other hand, was not one of the Lake Poets. Born Jean-Baptiste Poquelin in 1622, he was a contemporary of Jean Racine and Nicolas Boileau. In *A Study in Scarlet*, the author alluded to Jean Racine as John Rance, and to Nicolas Boileau via an untranslated quote from *L'Art poétique*. Molière is alluded to much earlier in the story, when the wounded Watson is transported from the subcontinent to England on the troopship *Orontes*. In Molière's *Le Misanthrope* (1666), Oronte asks the pompous Alceste to assess one of his poems, just as Charlotte would later ask Southey to assess one of hers. Alceste does not want to tell Oronte what he really thinks of the poem, but Oronte persists.

ORONTE   Speak to me, I pray, in all sincerity.

ALCESTE   These matters, Sir, are always more or less
          delicate, and everyone is fond of being praised for
          his wit. But I was saying one day to a certain
          person, who shall be nameless, when he showed
          me some of his verses, that a gentleman ought at
          all times to exercise a great control over that itch
          for writing which sometimes attacks us, and
          should keep a tight rein over the strong
          propensity which one has to display such
          amusements; and that, in the frequent anxiety to
          show   their

          productions, people are frequently exposed to act
          a very foolish part.

ORONTE   Do you wish to convey to me by this that I am
          wrong in desiring—

ALCESTE   I do not say that exactly. But I told him that
          writing without warmth becomes a bore; that
          there needs no other weakness to disgrace a man;
          that, even if people, on the other hand, had a
          hundred good qualities, we view them from their
          worst sides.

ORONTE   Do you find anything to object to in my sonnet?

ALCESTE   I do not say that. But, to keep him from writing, I
          set before his eyes how, in our days, that desire
          had spoiled a great many very worthy people.

ORONTE   Do I write badly? Am I like them in any way?

ALCESTE   I do not say that. But, in short, I said to him, What
          pressing need is there for you to rhyme, and what
          the deuce drives you into print? If we can pardon
          the sending into the world of a badly-written
          book, it will only be in those unfortunate men
          who write for their livelihood. Believe me, resist
          your temptations, keep these effusions from the

public, and do not, how much soever you may be asked, forfeit the reputation which you enjoy at Court of being a man of sense and a gentleman, to take, from the hands of a greedy printer, that of a ridiculous   and

wretched author. That is what I tried to make him understand.

ORONTE   This is all well and good, and I seem to understand you. But I should like to know what there is in my sonnet to—

ALCESTE   Candidly, you had better put it in your closet.

The likeness of Charlotte Brontë to Oronte is apparent. Both reach out to someone they respect to evaluate their poetry. The parallels between Robert Southey and Alceste are numerous and striking. Southey and Alceste each avoid commenting on the poem submitted for their critique. Though they have nothing positive to offer, they shy from saying anything negative. Southey cautions Charlotte to "not suppose that I disparage the gift which you possess." Alceste, when asked if the poem is bad, repeatedly hedges with "I do not say that."

Southey and Alceste each offer their would-be protégés the same advice they purportedly offered other nascent poets. Southey claims to be "bound in duty to caution every young man who applies as an aspirant to me for encouragement and advice." Alceste tells Oronte, "a gentleman ought at all times to exercise a great control over that itch for writing."

Southey and Alceste each devoted most of their words to warning of dire consequences that await anyone wishing to become a poet. Southey cautioned Charlotte "But there is danger of which I would with all kindness & all earnestness warn you," and Alceste cautioned Oronte, "that desire had spoiled a great many very worthy people." Each encouraged their aspirants to keep poetry a personal, private avocation, should they insist on writing at all, and passed a blunt, discouraging verdict on the poet appealing for validation.

The responses of Alceste and Southey are so similar that it now seems likely that Southey borrowed from Molière's *Le Misanthrope* when he replied to Charlotte's plea for approval. Astonishingly, our unidentified author recognized the parallels. By introducing the troopship *Orontes* and the paperhanger Keswick, Holmes creator left sufficient clues in *Study* to record, for at least one member of the double audience, her empathy and affinity for Charlotte.

Perhaps it is only coincidental that Holmes's creator chose a ship named so similarly to Molière's Oronte; that Oronte requested feedback on his poetry just as Charlotte Brontë requested feedback on hers; that Robert Southey's reply to Charlotte mirrored Alceste's reply to Oronte; and that Louise decided to name a paperhanger Keswick, the surname being identical to the place name associated with Robert Southey. Coincidence becomes an even more improbable explanation, however, when one learns that there was in fact a paperhanger hanger named Southey.

To pattern Holmes's ennui after Jane Eyre's, Louise must have read Charlotte's eponymous novel, *Jane Eyre*. To make the intricate connections linking the *Orontes* to Molière, Southey, and Brontë, Louise must have read Elizabeth Gaskell's *Life of Charlotte Brontë* and Molière's *Le Misanthrope*. To allude to Southey as a paperhanger named Keswick, Louise must have been familiar with the Lake poets Southey, Coleridge, and Wordsworth. She must also have read the six-volume *The Life and Correspondence of Robert Southey*. From Volume IV of that work, published in 1850, we learn of a letter from Southey to his friend Grosvenor Bedford. The first paragraph follows, the emphasis being mine.

> Keswick, Feb. 15, 1917
>
> My Dear G.,
>
> Do you remember that twenty years ago a letter, directed for me at your house, was carried to a *paper-hanger of my name* in Bedford Street, and the man found me out, and put his card into my hand? Upon the strength of this acquaintance, I have now a letter from this poor namesake, soliciting charity, and describing himself and his family as in the very depth

of human misery. This is not the only proof I have had of a strange opinion that I am overflowing with riches. Poor wretched man, what can I do for him! However, I do not like to shut my ears and my heart to a tale of this kind. Send him, I pray you, a two-pound note in my name, to No. 10. Hercules Buildings, Lambeth; your servant had better take it, for fear he should have been sent to the workhouse before this time. When I come to town, I will seek about if anything can be done for him.

Throughout the early adventures, Holmes repeatedly mirrors Charlotte's sentiments about intellectual restlessness. Charlotte wrote to a friend, "If you knew my thoughts, the dreams that absorb me, and the fiery imagination that at times eats me up, and makes me feel society, as it is, wretchedly insipid, you would pity and I dare say despise me." Holmes tells Watson, "My mind rebels at stagnation. Give me problems, give me work, give me the most abstruse cryptogram, or the most intricate analysis, and I am in my own proper atmosphere. I can dispense then with artificial stimulants. But I abhor the dull routine of existence. I crave for mental exaltation."

Charlotte fumed to a troublesome publisher, "To you I am neither Man nor Woman—I come before you as an Author only—it is the sole standard by which you have a right to judge me—the sole ground on which I accept your judgment. [...] Out of obscurity I came—to obscurity I can easily return." And, again, Holmes's words echo back: "My name figures in no newspaper. The work itself, the pleasure of finding a field for my peculiar powers, is my highest reward."

Who was this author who read and retained Gaskell's *Life of Charlotte Brontë*, Molière's *Le Misanthrope*, and the six-volume *Life and Correspondence of Robert Southey*; who alluded to Southey as a paperhanger from Keswick; who detected the origins of Southey's advice to Charlotte; who interconnected subtle allusions to Southey and Molière to create an even more subtle allusion to Charlotte, and who infused Holmes with a similar intellectual restlessness and a desire for obscurity? Who was this person who kept secret such brilliant work?

Empathy

Why should the first Holmes adventure be entitled *A Study in Scarlet*? The color scarlet is obviously a metaphor for blood, but there is precious little blood spilled in the first murder, the one that prompted Holmes to describe it as "a study in scarlet." The first victim was poisoned, and the only blood to be found was that used to write Rachel's name on a wall, that bloody ink coming from the killer's bloody nose. According to Holmes, that blood has nothing to do with the case. Where, then, is there the blood—the scarlet—to study?

Louise Conan Doyle suffered tuberculosis of the lungs. The classic fatal symptom of that disease is the coughing up of arterial blood the color of scarlet. In his article "At the Deathbed of Consumptive Art," David Morens describes the moment John Keats, the great poet, knew he would soon die.

> In his modest room, a 25-year-old "lapsed" medical student in 1820s Great Britain wakes from a sudden fevered sweat and finds a single drop of blood on the sheet. He has known many patients who spit such bright blood. "It's arterial blood [...] that blood is my death warrant, I must die," he confides to a friend. One of England's greatest poets, the medical student John Keats, never wrote specifically about phthisis. But his life and his works became a metaphor for generations of patients, a metaphor that helped transform the physical disease phthisis into its spiritual offspring, consumption. [...] He died only months after he first spit blood. Autopsy found his lungs completely destroyed. He was 26.

"There's the scarlet thread of murder running through the colourless skein of life," declares Holmes in his first adventure, "and our duty is to unravel it, and isolate it, and expose every inch of it." According to Madame Barrera's *Memoirs of Rachel*, the actress used similar words to describe the imprisoned consumptive Madame LaFarge:

> The poor woman—whether guilty or not, I must call her so—the poor woman was slowly dying of that most terrible of all diseases, consumption. She feels the skein of life's thread unwinding, and, to the very last, she will see, she will feel. It is very dreadful. Better far a bullet in the weak chest, or a tile falling on the aching head some windy day.

Little did Rachel then know that she too would die of "that most terrible of all diseases," that she too would feel "the skein of life's thread unwinding," and that a dying poisoner in a detective story would attempt to write her name in scarlet on the wall of the crime scene.

The early Holmes adventures, particularly the first two novels, are red with allusions to consumptive literary figures. We shall consider just three more.

In *Scènes de la vie de bohème*, the book Watson is reading before Holmes returns with a copy of *De Jure Inter Gentes*, Henri Murger fictionalized his experiences as an impoverished Parisian writer. His novel features two characters, both female, whose afflictions are painted in a flattering light, as was the fashion of the day. The first, Mimi, is a "fair creature, pale as the angel of consumption [...] in whose veins [...] the blood of youth flowed warm and rapid" and "imparted rosy tints to her transparent skin of camellia-like whiteness." She was based on a real Mimi, a flower girl of humble origin who met Murger at an informal club called Bohemia. Unlike the fictional Mimi, the real Mimi succumbed to her tuberculosis the year after taking Murger as her lover.

The second consumptive female in Murger's novel is Francine. Though Francine dies of the disease, she does so fashionably, sentimentally, in grand artistic style.

> When she was alone she said to the doctor. "Oh sir! I am going to die, and I know it. But before I pass away give me something to give me strength for a night, I

beg of you. Make me well for one more night, and let me die afterwards, since God does not wish me to live longer."

As the doctor was doing his best to console her, the wind carried into the room and cast upon the sick girl's bed a yellow leaf, torn from the tree in the little courtyard.

Francine opened the curtain, and saw the tree entirely bare.

"It is the last," said she, putting the leaf under her pillow"

"You will not die until tomorrow," said the doctor. "You have a night before you."

"Ah, what happiness!" exclaimed the poor girl. "A winter's night—it will be a long one."

Jacques came back. He brought a muff with him.

"It is very pretty," said Francine. "I will wear it when I go out."

So passed the night with Jacques.

The next day—All Saints'—about the middle of the day, the death agony seized on her, and her whole body began to quiver.

"My hands are cold," she murmured. "Give me my muff."

And she buried her poor hands in the fur.

"It is the end," said the doctor to Jacques. "Kiss her for the last time."

Jacques pressed his lips to those of his love. At the last moment they wanted to take away her muff, but she clutched it with her hands.

"No, no," she said, "leave it with me; it is winter, it is cold. Oh my poor Jacques! My poor Jacques! What will become of you? Oh heavens!"

And the next day Jacques was alone.

A not-so-noteworthy character in Murger's story is Alexander Schaunard, an underappreciated musician who wishes he had tuberculosis. Caught up in the fanciful, *au courant* belief that consumption is a romantic disease of the artistic class, Schaunard imagines that a tubercular affliction will cause his talent to be properly recognized. In one scene, confronting an unimpressed music publisher, Schaunard makes the point memorably explicit.

> Schaunard reflected that a modest air might injure him in the publisher's estimation. Indeed, a modest musician, and especially a modest pianist, is a rare creation. Accordingly, he replied boldly: "I am a first rate one; if I only had a lung gone, long hair and a black coat, I should be famous as the sun in the heavens; and instead of asking me eight hundred francs to engrave my composition 'The Death of the Damsel,' you would come on your knees to offer me three thousand for it on a silver plate."

After fictionalizing the loss of his beloved Mimi, Murger revealed his impending death in a letter to a friend.

> Do you remember Schaunard, the musician presenting himself to a prospective patron [...] and telling the fat bourgeois that one of his lungs was gone? Of course it was a fib to arouse the patron's compassion. Well, I'm like Schaunard now, except it's not a fib and it's not one of my lungs which is gone but both.

Henry Murger, therefore, is another of *Study*'s many hidden consumptives, identified here after Madam LaFarge and Mademoiselles Rachel.

Elizabeth Barrett, she of the Torquay Terrace allusion, also suffered tuberculosis. In 1845, the little-known Robert Browning began his lovesick pursuit of her. She resisted, but he persisted until, suddenly, in 1846, the two poets eloped to the continent. Just seven months later, she gave birth to their first and only child. Her father disowned her, but the young couple nonetheless lived a fairy-tale marriage, writing poetry in the Italian countryside. Because of the natural brown tone of her skin, Robert called her his "little Portuguese," which gave her the title for her *Sonnets from the Portuguese* (1850), a collection of poems about their love.

Ironically, it was only after Elizabeth's death by consumption in 1861, following many years of illness, that the public learned details of the couple's lives, specifically that her sonnets were autobiographical. Her poetry subsequently soared to new heights of popularity.

Among the countless Victorians drawn to Elizabeth Barrett Browning's poetry was Louise Conan Doyle. Georgina Doyle records that Louise had her own copy of *Sonnets*, marked on those pages of sonnets to which she was particularly drawn. One of them, numbered XIV, is repeated here in its entirety.

> If thou must love me, let it be for nought
> Except for love's sake only. Do not say
> "I love her for her smile—her look—her way
> Of speaking gently,—for a trick of thought
> That falls in well with mine, and certes brought
> A sense of pleasant ease on such a day"—
> For these things in themselves, Beloved, may
> Be changed, or change for thee,—and love, so wrought,
> May be unwrought so. Neither love me for
> Thine own dear pity's wiping my cheeks dry,
> A creature might forget to weep, who bore
> Thy comfort long, and lose thy love thereby.
> But love me for love's sake, that evermore
> Thou mayst love on, through love's eternity.

Despite Arthur's claims to the contrary, Louise was symptomatic when he married her, or became so soon thereafter. Just as Robert loved and married Elizabeth with full awareness her affliction, Louise hoped that Arthur would love her for love's sake, that evermore he would love on, through love's eternity. It was not to be.

Thus, Elizabeth Barrett Browning is another of *Study*'s many hidden consumptives, identified here after Madam LaFarge, Mademoiselles Felix, and Henry Murger.

Charlotte Brontë, she of the Keswick, paperhanger, and *Orontes* allusions, lost each of her five siblings to tuberculosis before being consumed herself, pregnant with her first child. In *Jane Eyre*, Charlotte had Jane lie beside her first friend, Helen Burns, in Helen's final hours.

> Close by Miss Temple's bed, and half covered with its white curtains, there stood a little crib. I saw the outline of a form under the clothes, but the face was hid by the hangings: the nurse I had spoken to in the garden sat in an easy-chair asleep; an unsnuffed candle burnt dimly on the table. Miss Temple was not to be seen: I knew afterwards that she had been called to a delirious patient in the fever-room. I advanced; then paused by the crib side: my hand was on the curtain, but I preferred speaking before I withdrew it. I still recoiled at the dread of seeing a corpse.
>
> "Helen!" I whispered softly, "are you awake?"
>
> She stirred herself, put back the curtain, and I saw her face, pale, wasted, but quite composed: she looked so little changed that my fear was instantly dissipated.
>
> "Can it be you, Jane?" she asked, in her own gentle voice.
>
> "Oh!" I thought, "she is not going to die; they are mistaken: she could not speak and look so calmly if she were."
>
> I got on to her crib and kissed her: her forehead was cold, and her cheek both cold and thin, and so were her hand and wrist; but she smiled as of old.
>
> "Why are you come here, Jane? It is past eleven o'clock: I heard it strike some minutes since."
>
> "I came to see you, Helen: I heard you were very ill, and I could not sleep till I had spoken to you."
>
> "You came to bid me good-bye, then: you are just in time probably."

"Are you going somewhere, Helen? Are you going home?"

"Yes; to my long home—my last home."

"No, no, Helen!" I stopped, distressed. While I tried to devour my tears, a fit of coughing seized Helen; it did not, however, wake the nurse; when it was over, she lay some minutes exhausted; then she whispered—

"Jane, your little feet are bare; lie down and cover yourself with my quilt."

I did so: she put her arm over me, and I nestled close to her. After a long silence, she resumed, still whispering—

"I am very happy, Jane; and when you hear that I am dead, you must be sure and not grieve: there is nothing to grieve about. We all must die one day, and the illness which is removing me is not painful; it is gentle and gradual: my mind is at rest. I leave no one to regret me much: I have only a father; and he is lately married, and will not miss me. By dying young, I shall escape great sufferings. I had not qualities or talents to make my way very well in the world: I should have been continually at fault."

"But where are you going to, Helen? Can you see? Do you know?"

"I believe; I have faith: I am going to God."

"Where is God? What is God?"

"My Maker and yours, who will never destroy what He created. I rely implicitly on His power, and confide wholly in His goodness: I count the hours till that eventful one arrives which shall restore me to Him, reveal Him to me."

"You are sure, then, Helen, that there is such a place as heaven, and that our souls can get to it when we die?"

"I am sure there is a future state; I believe God is good; I can resign my immortal part to Him without any misgiving. God is my father; God is my friend: I love Him; I believe He loves me."

"And shall I see you again, Helen, when I die?"

"You will come to the same region of happiness: be received by the same mighty, universal Parent, no doubt, dear Jane."

Again I questioned, but this time only in thought. "Where is that region? Does it exist?" And I clasped my arms closer round Helen; she seemed dearer to me than ever; I felt as if I could not let her go; I lay with my face hidden on her neck. Presently she said, in the sweetest tone—

"How comfortable I am! That last fit of coughing has tired me a little; I feel as if I could sleep: but don't leave me, Jane; I like to have you near me."

"I'll stay with you, dear Helen: no one shall take me away."

"Are you warm, darling?"

"Yes."

"Good-night, Jane."

"Good-night, Helen."

She kissed me, and I her, and we both soon slumbered.

When I awoke it was day: an unusual movement roused me; I looked up; I was in somebody's arms; the nurse held me; she was carrying me through the passage back to the dormitory. I was not reprimanded for leaving my bed; people had something else to think about; no explanation was afforded then to my many questions; but a day or two afterwards I learned that Miss Temple, on returning to her own room at dawn, had found me laid in the little crib; my face against Helen Burns's shoulder, my arms round her neck. I was asleep, and Helen was— dead.

Charlotte Brontë, then, is yet another of *Study*'s many hidden consumptives.

Equality

The Adventure of the Blue Carbuncle (1892) begins, as do many of the Holmes adventures, with the detective showing off his powers of observation and deduction. Watson arrives at 221B Baker Street to find Holmes contemplating a hat of unknown ownership.

> "You know my methods. What can you gather yourself as to the individuality of the man who has worn this article?"
>
> I took the tattered object in my hands, and turned it over rather ruefully. It was a very ordinary black hat of the usual round shape, hard and much the worse for wear. The lining had been of red silk, but was a good deal discoloured. There was no maker's name; but, as Holmes had remarked, the initials 'H.B.' were scrawled upon one side. It was pierced in the brim for a hat-securer, but the elastic was missing. For the rest, it was cracked, exceedingly dusty, and spotted in several places, although there seemed to have been some attempt to hide the discoloured patches by smearing them with ink.
>
> "I can see nothing," said I, handing it back to my friend.
>
> "On the contrary, Watson, you can see everything. You fail, however, to reason from what you see. You are too timid in drawing your inferences."
>
> "Then pray tell me what it is that you can infer from this hat?"
>
> He picked it up, and gazed at it in the peculiar introspective fashion which was characteristic of him. "It is perhaps less suggestive than it might have been," he remarked, "and yet there are a few inferences which are very distinct, and a few others which represent at least a strong balance of

probability. That the man was highly intellectual is of course obvious upon the face of it, and also that he was fairly well-to-do within the last three years, although he has now fallen upon evil days. He had foresight, but has less now than formerly, pointing to a moral retrogression, which, when taken with the decline of his fortunes, seems to indicate some evil influence, probably drink, at work upon him. This may account also for the obvious fact that his wife has ceased to love him."

"My dear Holmes!"

"He has, however, retained some degree of self-respect," he continued, disregarding my remonstrance. "He is a man who leads a sedentary life, goes out little, is out of training entirely, is middle-aged, has grizzled hair which he has had cut within the last few days, and which he anoints with lime-cream. These are the more patent facts which are to be deduced from his hat. Also, by the way, that it is extremely improbable that he has gas laid on in his house."

"You are certainly joking, Holmes."

"Not in the least. Is it possible that even now when I give you these results you are unable to see how they are attained?"

"I have no doubt that I am very stupid; but I must confess that I am unable to follow you. For example, how did you deduce that this man was intellectual?"

For answer Holmes clapped the hat upon his head. It came right over the forehead and settled upon the bridge of his nose. "It is a question of cubic capacity," said he; "a man with so large a brain must have something in it."

The hat, as it turns out, belongs to one Henry Baker, a tall, well-educated man who presents no evidence of spectacular intellect. What are we to make of this? If head size is related to intelligence, as

Holmes himself believes, and if Holmes is among the most intelligent of all men, why would Mr. Baker's hat fall all the way to Holmes's nose?

The gigantic hat, or Holmes's small head, is not the only affront to our hero's intelligence. In *The Final Problem*, when Holmes first meets his nemesis, he suffers a cruel and heartless comment about the size of his forehead. Moriarty's first words to him: "You have less frontal development than I should have expected."

The London that Holmes prowls is in the heyday of craniology and phrenology. Craniology is the study of skull size and shape. Phrenology is the attribution of intelligence and personality to craniological measurements. A craniologist could tell us whether not Holmes's head was actually smaller than usual or abnormally formed. A phrenologist could, allegedly, tell us all about Holmes's intellect and personality based on the resulting measurements. In *The Mismeasure of Man* (1981), paleontologist Stephen J. Gould offered readers the horribly fascinating history of measuring people to classify them, focusing several chapters on craniologists such as Samuel George Morton.

> Morton's fame as a scientist rested upon his collection of skulls and their role in racial ranking. Since the cranial cavity of a human skull provides a faithful measure of the brain it once contained, Morton set out to rank races by the average sizes of their brains. He filled the cranial cavity with sifted white mustard seed, poured the seed back into a graduated cylinder and read the skull's volume in cubic inches. [...] Morton published three major works on the sizes of human skulls [...] reprinted repeatedly during the nineteenth century as irrefutable, "hard" data on the mental worth of human races. Needless to say, they matched every good Yankee's prejudice—whites on top, Indians in the middle, and blacks on the bottom: and, among whites, Teutons and Anglo-Saxons on top, Jews in the middle, and Hindus on the bottom.

In reality, the primary determinant of adult skull size (and therefore brain size) is not intelligence, but height. Taller people tend to have larger skulls, just as they tend to have larger ribs and femurs. Gould adjusted Morton's data for height and concluded that "Morton's conventional ranking reveals *no* significant differences among races."

> Sizes of brains are related to the sizes of bodies that carry them: big people tend to have larger brains than small people. This fact does not imply that big people are smarter—any more than elephants should be judged more intelligent than humans because their brains are larger. Appropriate corrections must be made for differences in body size. Men tend to be larger than women; consequently, their brains are bigger. When corrections for body size are applied, men and women have brains of approximately equal size. Morton not only failed to correct for difference in sex or body size; he did not even recognize the relationship, though his data proclaimed it loud and clear.

Gould then took the time to finally do what he believed Morton should have done long ago: he reviewed Morton's data, adjusted it for body size, corrected simple arithmetic errors, and applied more rigorous statistical standards.

> Morton's summaries are a patchwork of fudging and finagling in the clear interest of controlling *a priori* convictions. Yet—and this is the most intriguing aspect of the case—I find no evidence of conscious fraud; indeed, had Morton been a conscious fudger, he would not have published his data so openly.

Another of the renowned craniologists was Pierre Paul Broca, a French physician, surgeon, anatomist, anthropologist, racist, and sexist. He is best known for his research of a particular region of the frontal lobe—a region that has since been named Broca's area. Here is Gould, discussing Broca:

> Indeed, one cannot read Broca without gaining enormous respect for his care in generating data. I believe his numbers and doubt that any better have ever been obtained. [...] I spent a month reading all of Broca's major work, concentrating on his statistical procedures. I found a definite pattern in his methods. He traversed the gap between fact and conclusion by what may be the usual route—predominantly in reverse. Conclusions came first, and Broca's conclusions were the shared assumptions of most successful white males during his time—themselves on the top by the good fortune of nature, and women, blacks, and poor people below. His facts were reliable (unlike Morton's), but they were gathered selectively and then manipulated unconsciously in the service of prior conclusions. By this route, the conclusions achieved not only the blessing of science, but the prestige of numbers.

Broca made his conclusions as clear as his data, writing:

> In general, the brain is larger in mature adults than in the elderly, in men than in women, in eminent men than in men of mediocre talent, in superior races than in inferior races. [...] Other things equal, there is a remarkable relationship between the development of intelligence and the volume of the brain.

So entrenched was the perceived link between brain size and intelligence that men of eminence donated their brains to science. These brains were weighed, dissected, and sketched, frequently to the distress of everyone involved. Of five professorial brains in a particular sample of 559 European male brains, only one weighed in among the heaviest 10%, one did not quite make it into the top 50%, and one scarcely outweighed the bottom 20%. Broca, unwilling to let such awkward data interfere with his precious theory, defamed the university that had employed the brains' original owners—a trashing made easier by the fact their university was German rather than French.

> It is not very probable that 5 men of genius died within five years at the University of Göttingen [...] A professorial robe is not necessarily a certificate of genius; there may be, even at Göttingen, some chairs occupied by not very remarkable men. [...] The subject is delicate, and I must not insist on it any longer.

It seems unlikely that Broca would have so belabored his hypothesis had he known his own brain was to weigh in lighter than three of those Göttingen professors. An even sweeter irony is to be found inside the skull of Franz Josef Gall, one of the two founders of phrenology and the author of the six-volume *On the Functions of the Brain and of Each of its Parts: with Observations on the Possibility of Determining the Instincts, Propensities, and Talents, or the Moral and Intellectual Dispositions of Men and Animals by the Configuration of the Brain and Head* (1835). In terms of weight, Gall's brain surpassed only the bottom fifth percentile of brain size.

At the phrenological low end of the abovementioned eminent brain-donors was French poet, journalist, and novelist Anatole France. His brain weighed less than each and every other brain in the sample of 559. On the opposite end of the scale was the exceptionally large brain of Georges Cuvier, fan of Zadig and ideal reasoner in the eyes of Sherlock Holmes.

Broca and the others did not apply their science purely to the ranking of race; they addressed gender as well. Women, whose bodies tend to be smaller than men's, tend to have smaller brains than men, just as shorter men generally have smaller brains than their taller counterparts. Broca understood the fundamental relationship, but nonetheless concluded that women were less intelligent than men, because, well, they just were.

> We might ask if the small size of the female brain
> depends exclusively upon the small size of her body.
> [...] But we must not forget that women are, on the
> average, a little less intelligent than men, a difference
> which we should not exaggerate but which is,
> nonetheless, real. We are therefore permitted to
> suppose that the relatively small size of the female
> brain depends in part upon her physical inferiority
> and in part upon her intellectual inferiority.

When discussing female intelligence, French sociologist Gustave Le Bon pulled no punches. Gould refers to Le Bon as the "chief misogynist of Broca's school." Le Bon's 1879 article for *Revue d'Anthropologie* gives some sense of his attitude.

> In the most intelligent races [...] there are a large
> number of women whose brains are closer in size to
> those of gorillas than to the most developed of male
> brains. This inferiority is so obvious that no one can
> contest it for a moment; only its degree is worth
> discussion. All psychologists who have studied the
> intelligence of women, as well as poets and novelists,
> recognize today that they are the most inferior forms
> of human evolution and they are closer to children
> and savages than to an adult, civilized man. They
> excel in fickleness, inconstancy, absence of thought
> and logic, and incapacity to reason. Without doubt
> there exist some distinguished women, very superior
> to the average man, but they are exceptional as the
> birth of any monstrosity, as, for example, of a gorilla
> with two heads; consequently, we may neglect them
> entirely.

Because Morton, Broca, Le Bon, and most other white male scientists of the day had an inviolate theory of their own superiority, their facts became sufficiently malleable to diminish people of different race or sex. Holmes's creator recognized the flawed science, and she mocked its perpetrators by giving Sherlock Holmes a small head with an unimpressive forehead. Henry Baker, as it turns out, needs a large hat not just because he is intelligent, but also because he is tall, as Watson reveals when he first meets him: "I saw a tall man in a Scotch bonnet."

More than on the incongruity of Holmes's small head, to defend minorities and women against pseudoscientific claims of intellectual inferiority, Holmes's creator relied on data, just as she had her creation rely on data. "As to Holmes," she had Watson report, "I observed that he sat frequently for half an hour on end, with knitted brows and an abstracted air, but he swept the matter away with a wave of his hand when I mentioned it. 'Data! data! data!' he cried impatiently. 'I can't make bricks without clay.'"

To understand where Holmes's creator obtained the data, we consider yet again Holmes's first listing of unsolved crimes: "There was the case of Von Bischoff at Frankfort last year. He would certainly have been hung had this test been in existence. Then there was Mason of Bradford, and the notorious Muller, and Lefevre of Montpellier, and Samson of New Orleans."

We suspect already that Mason of Bradford refers to the Bradford sweets poisoning case of 1858, and we are confident that Lefevre of Montpellier alludes to the consumptive poisoner Madame Lafarge. It is equally likely that Von Bischoff of Frankfort is none other than Theodor Ludwig Wilhelm von Bischoff, German physician, biologist, and author of *Das Hirngewicht des Menschen: Eine Studie* (1880). Though his book has yet to be translated into English, its English title would be *The Brain Weight of Man: A Study*. Von Bischoff compiled a database of 906 brain weights, each accompanied (when possible) by the age, sex, height, weight, and cause of death of its previous owner.

Von Bischoff tabulated and indexed each and every one of his measurements in his book. We can still examine those data today, to see what they reveal about the relationship among brain size, height, and gender. Presenting the data in graphical format, which von Bischoff did not do, is particularly revealing.

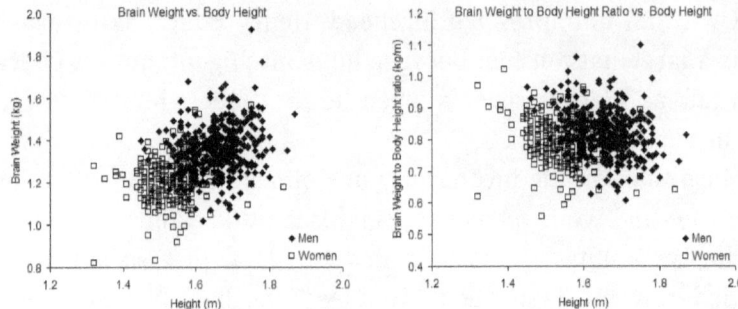

The plot on the left presents von Bischoff's brain weights along the vertical axis, versus the corresponding body heights along the horizontal. Data points for men are solid diamonds, for women open squares. It is immediately obvious that women tend to be shorter and have smaller brains. This should come as a surprise to no one.

The plot on the right presents the same data in slightly different format. The horizontal axis still represents body height. The vertical axis, however, no longer presents the brain weight directly. Instead, it presents the ratio of brain weight divided by body height. On average, the human brain weighs 800 grams for each meter of body height, regardless of gender, regardless of height. When thus plotted, von Bischoff's data make obvious that there is no difference in brain weight between men and women, once body size is taken into account.

Even without a plot, Von Bischoff recognized the strong relationship. He claimed to be the first to recognize it.

> For each body size of adult male and female persons a variety of brain weights occur; large individuals often have light, small brains. If, however, if one looks at a large number of observations, one becomes all but certain that an increase in body size and an increase in brain weight is connected. I believe I have proven here, for the first time, the influence of body weight and body size on brain weight, and it seems to me to deserve our greatest attention.

Though proud of his discovery, he seemed to learn nothing from it. He allowed his preconceived notions to overwhelm his data.

It is undeniable that the male sex, always and everywhere, clearly has a higher degree of intelligence and mental performance than the female; the male brain is everywhere and at all times one-twelfth to one-ninth larger than that of the female, and that has made a difference. Also, maximum brain weights do not occur in women, but nevertheless minimal weights often do.

In addition to dropping his name, our author seems to have alluded to Bischoff and his work in more subtle fashion. When discussing the female brain, for example, von Bischoff observed, "Among the women, a husband's murderer had the largest, an unusually high brain weight of 1565 grams." He was concerned that criminals seemed to have unusually large brains, and made special note of the murderous wife to emphasize the conundrum. In *The Sign of Four*, Holmes made a similar comment, albeit with more flair.

"It is of the first importance," he said, "not to allow your judgment to be biased by personal qualities. A client is to me a mere unit, a factor in a problem. The emotional qualities are antagonistic to clear reasoning. I assure you that the most winning woman I ever knew was hanged for poisoning three little children for their insurance-money, and the most repellent man of my acquaintance is a philanthropist who has spent nearly a quarter of a million upon the London poor."

In other words, one cannot tell a book by its cover or a genius by her genitals.

Though von Bischoff's data do not categorize the brain weights by the race of their previous owner, that shortcoming did not stop him from pontificating on the inferiority of non-Caucasian races. In his concluding remarks, he took this parting shot, presenting zero data to substantiate his conclusion:

> The Total Area-brain weight is subject to significant individual differences in all adult humans, which can be almost doubled (1000 to 2000 grams). So far, wide-ranging observations indicate the differences are larger in cultivated nations than in non-cultivated. The mean brain weight seems to be pretty much the same in cultivated nations, 1350-1360 grams for men, 1220-1225 grams with the women. In the dolichocephalic prognathous tribes, as far as we know, the average brain weight is lower.

As evidence of having read and understood Von Bischoff's work, our author turned those very words, *dolichocephalic* and *prognathous*, against von Bischoff by providing Holmes those very characteristics. In *The Hound of the Baskervilles* (1902), James Mortimer, former physician to the late Sir Charles Baskerville, appears at 221B Baker Street to discuss mysterious goings-on near Baskerville Hall. Mortimer is quite taken with Holmes's skull.

> "You interest me very much, Mr. Holmes. I had hardly expected so dolichocephalic a skull or such well-marked supra-orbital development. Would you have any objection to my running my finger along your parietal fissure? A cast of your skull, sir, until the original is available, would be an ornament to any anthropological museum. It is not my intention to be fulsome, but I confess that I covet your skull."

Though Holmes is surely seething, he reveals no sign of it. Who would not, after all, be insulted by such insensitive remarks about one's skull? Dolichocephaly is a condition where the head is distinctly narrower than expected, relative to its length. Neanderthals exhibited a marked dolichocephaly, much more so than properly proportioned *Homo sapiens sapiens* of today.

Mortimer's observation regarding Holmes's "well-marked supra-orbital development" only makes matters worse.

The supra-orbital ridge, also known as the brow ridge, is the bony structure just above the eye sockets. In early primates, and in Neanderthals, the ridge reinforced the weaker bones of the face. In most primates, this is necessary because of the large force that powerful chewing transfers to the cranium. The brow ridge was one of the last traits to be lost during the evolution of anatomically modern humans. We no longer need a pronounced brow ridge because we have a pronounced frontal lobe, one that not only withstands the chewing forces, but that evidences our superior intelligence. Most people have a pronounced frontal lobe. Holmes does not, at least not according to Professor Moriarty, so he still needs a "well-marked supra-orbital" ridge.

Somehow, despite his primitive features, Holmes manages to hold his own in matters of the mind. Perhaps his creator was engaging in literary irony when assigning Holmes these features, and when outfitting Holmes with a pronounced jaw.

According to the craniometrists and phrenologists, inferior people could be just as easily distinguished by the protruding of their jaw as by the size of their hat. A prognathous jaw is one that juts forward, and it was, to Victorians, a giveaway of its owner's inferiority. On this point, Gould once again quoted Broca, who wrote that "a prognathous face, more or less black color of the skin, wooly hair and intellectual and social inferiority are often associated, while more or less white skin, straight hair and an orthognathous [vertical] face are the ordinary equipment of the highest groups in the human series."

In his *Anthropology: An Introduction to the Study of Man and Civilization* (1881), Edward Burnett Tylor was just as certain about the significance of the jaw.

> The Australian and African are *prognathous*, or "forward-jawed," while the European is *orthognathous*, or "upright-jawed." At the same time the Australian and African have more retreating foreheads than the European, to the disadvantage of

the frontal lobes of their brain as compared with
ours. Thus the upper and lower parts of the profile
combine to give the faces of these less-civilized
peoples a somewhat ape-like slope, as distinguished
from the more nearly upright European face.

Prominent jaws as character determinants made their way into
the literary fiction of the time. In *The Island of Dr. Moreau* (1896),
H.G. Wells made his Beast People seem even more depraved by
giving them prognathous jaws: "The next most obvious deformity
was their faces, almost all of which were prognathous, malformed
about the ears, with large and protuberant noses, very furry or very
bristly hair, and often strangely-coloured or strangely-placed eyes.
None could laugh, though the Ape-man had a chattering twitter."

Perhaps the most striking image of a person with a prognathous
jaw in literature appears in the first Holmes adventure, *A Study in
Scarlet*, as Watson describes the appearance of the first murder
victim.

At present my attention was centred upon the single,
grim, motionless figure which lay stretched upon the
boards, with vacant, sightless eyes staring up at the
discoloured ceiling. It was that of a man about forty-
three or forty-four years of age, middle-sized, broad-
shouldered, with crisp curling black hair, and a short,
stubbly beard. He was dressed in a heavy broad-cloth
frock coat and waistcoat, with light coloured
trousers, and immaculate collar and cuffs. A top hat,
well brushed and trim, was placed upon the floor
beside him. His hands were clenched and his arms
thrown abroad, while his lower limbs were
interlocked, as though his death struggle had been a
grievous one. On his rigid face there stood an
expression of horror, and, as it seemed to me, of
hatred, such as I have never seen upon human
features. This malignant and terrible contortion,
combined with the low forehead, blunt nose, and

prognathous jaw, gave the dead man a singularly simious and ape-like appearance, which was increased by his writhing, unnatural posture. I have seen death in many forms, but never has it appeared to me in a more fearsome aspect than in that dark, grimy apartment, which looked out upon one of the main arteries of suburban London.

At first blush, Dr. Watson's discussion of prognathism seems an endorsement for Victorian craniometry and phrenology. A closer reading of the story, however, reveals what we have by now come to expect. The author wished to play with our minds. Consider Watson's description of Holmes's physical appearance, from earlier in the story: "His eyes were sharp and piercing, save during those intervals of torpor to which I have alluded; and his thin, hawk-like nose gave his whole expression an air of alertness and decision. His chin, too, had the prominence and squareness which mark the man of determination."

Both Holmes and the murder victim have pronounced jaws. Watson demeans the pronounced jaw of the murder victim as "prognathous," but elevates Holmes's by giving it a "prominence and squareness." Watson suggests the pronounced jaw of the murder victim is apelike, but sees in Holmes's pronounced jaw a mark of strong will.

By the time the author is done with Holmes, his tiny head is a mess. It has an underdeveloped frontal lobe and therefore needs a pronounced brow ridge so he can chew without breaking his face. His head is too long, or too narrow, or some combination of the two, with a jaw like that of an ape. Nonetheless, burdened with all the disadvantages supposedly inherent to women and non-Caucasian races, he is supremely intelligent.

Perhaps appearances do not matter, at least in terms of a person's innate worth. Perhaps there are no substantive differences between the sexes, or among the many races, ethnic groups, or whatever categorization we choose to apply. Perhaps an unknown author of phenomenally popular detective stories has been trying to tell us this for more than a hundred years. Perhaps we have been slow in recognizing and acknowledging the equality of all mankind.

Chapter 11
Opportunity

Among means, motive, and opportunity, the simplifying concept of opportunity assumes that no person can be in two places at once, that time cannot run backwards, that no one can violate the space-time continuum. We can be confident, for example, that Arthur did not write *A Scandal in Bohemia* from his new consulting room on 2 Upper Wimpole Street if he did not take occupancy until after he had sent the manuscript to his agent. Based on similar opportunity-based arguments, we can also realize that Arthur wrote neither the second Holmes adventure, *The Sign of Four*, nor the last of the early Holmes adventures, *The Final Problem*.

The Sign of Four

The Sign of Four was the second Sherlock Holmes adventure, a novella of some 44,000 words. Arthur allegedly began writing it no sooner than 30 August 1889, completing it no later than 1 November, leaving him no more than sixty-three days to write the book. A skeptical review of its origins reveals not only that Arthur had no opportunity to write the book during that two month window, but that it also represents one of Arthur's more spectacular fabrications.

From *Memories and Adventures*:

> Now for the second time I was in London on literary business. Stoddart, the American, proved to be an excellent fellow, and had two others to dinner. They were Gill, a very entertaining Irish M.P., and Oscar Wilde, who was already famous as the champion of aestheticism. It was indeed a golden evening for me. Wilde to my surprise had read [Arthur's own] "Micah Clarke" and was enthusiastic about it, so that I did not feel a complete outsider. [...] The result of the evening was that both Wilde and I promised to write books for "Lippincott's Magazine"—Wilde's contribution was "The Picture of Dorian Gray," a book which is surely upon a high moral plane, while I

wrote "The Sign of Four," in which Holmes made his second appearance.

Regarding Wilde, Arthur added "that the monstrous development which ruined him was pathological, and that a hospital rather than a police court was the place for its consideration." The "monstrous development" of which Arthur so uncomfortably wrote was Wilde's homosexuality. In 1895, after John Douglas, Marquess of Queensberry, referred to Wilde, in writing, as a "somdomite [sic]," Wilde imprudently charged him with criminal libel. Queensberry was arrested and quickly put to trial. The evidence produced at trial, however, established that Wilde did engage in sex with "rent boys," a euphemism for young male prostitutes. Wilde withdrew his charge of criminal libel, Queensberry was freed, and Wilde was prosecuted for sodomy and gross indecency. During the first of his two trials, when asked by the prosecutor about "the love that dare not speak its name," Wilde again responded imprudently, if honestly and memorably.

> "The love that dare not speak its name" in this century is such a great affection of an elder for a younger man as there was between David and Jonathan, such as Plato made the very basis of his philosophy, and such as you find in the sonnets of Michelangelo and Shakespeare. It is that deep spiritual affection that is as pure as it is perfect. It dictates and pervades great works of art, like those of Shakespeare and Michelangelo, and those two letters of mine, such as they are. It is in this century misunderstood, so much misunderstood that it may be described as "the love that dare not speak its name," and on that account of it I am placed where I am now. It is beautiful, it is fine, it is the noblest form of affection. There is nothing unnatural about it. It is intellectual, and it repeatedly exists between an older and a younger man, when the older man has intellect, and the younger man has all the joy, hope and

glamour of life before him. That it should be so, the world does not understand. The world mocks at it, and sometimes puts one in the pillory for it.

Wilde was acquitted of sodomy but convicted of gross indecency, sentenced to two years of what the prison advertised as "hard labour, hard fare and a hard bed." Particularly unaccustomed to such a life, Wilde fainted from illness and hunger, rupturing his eardrum in the fall. Denied books and writing material, jeered and spat at during transport, Wilde suffered far beyond his physical torment. Upon his release, he departed England for the continent, never to return. He wrote of his experience and revival in *De Profundis* (1897).

> When first I was put into prison some people advised me to try and forget who I was. It was ruinous advice. It is only by realising what I am that I have found comfort of any kind. Now I am advised by others to try on my release to forget that I have ever been in a prison at all. I know that would be equally fatal. It would mean that I would always be haunted by an intolerable sense of disgrace, and that those things that are meant for me as much as for anybody else— the beauty of the sun and moon, the pageant of the seasons, the music of daybreak and the silence of great nights, the rain falling through the leaves, or the dew creeping over the grass and making it silver— would all be tainted for me, and lose their healing power, and their power of communicating joy. To regret one's own experiences is to arrest one's own development. To deny one's own experiences is to put a lie into the lips of one's own life. It is no less than a denial of the soul.

For three years, Wilde experienced the pageant of the seasons away from England, before dying of cerebral meningitis in 1900. His body was transported in a cheap coffin to Paris's Bagneaux Cemetery, and a mere thirteen people followed the shabby hearse that carried him to his internment. In 1909, however, his grave was moved. He joined Mademoiselle Rachel and many other noteworthies in the Père Lachaise cemetery, where people now visit him in great numbers.

Wilde was not around to confirm or deny the anecdotes Arthur related of him in *Memories and Adventures*. Evidence, however, casts substantial doubt on Arthur's version of events. Arthur, for example, claimed that, soon after their meeting, he sent a letter complimenting Wilde on *The Picture of Dorian Gray*. Wilde allegedly replied with a letter that Arthur incompletely quoted in his autobiography. "I omit the early part," Arthur added with false modesty, "in which he comments on my own work in too generous terms."

Given Arthur's penchant for prevarication, one might seek supporting evidence of Wilde's "too generous" comments. One would thereby be frustrated. In the 1,200-page *The Complete Letters of Oscar Wilde* (2000), edited by Merlin Holland and Rupert Hart-Davis, the exchange of letters exists only as Arthur's autobiographical excerpt. A footnote reads, "The text of this fragment is taken from *Memories and Adventures* (1924). The original letter seems to have disappeared from the voluminous Conan Doyle papers." Not only has the reply from Oscar to Arthur disappeared from Arthur's papers, the reply letter from Arthur to Oscar is also missing from Wilde's.

More legendary than the exchange of letters is Arthur's dinner with Wilde. During that famous event, each of the two authors struck a deal with J. M. Stoddart for what were to become equally famous books, *The Sign of Four* and *The Picture of Dorian Gray*. It seems exceptionally unlikely, however, that such a dinner ever took place. Consider Stoddart's letter to Arthur, dated 30 August 1889, the same day as the alleged dinner.

> Confirming the verbal and mutually agreed upon understanding of today, we propose to pay upon receipt and acceptance of a story to be written by you consisting of not less than 40,000 words, the sum of one hundred pounds. Our rights to be entire in America in all forms of publication, and to be exclusive in Lippincott's Magazine for the period of

three months in England. It is understood that you
deliver the manuscript by or before January of next
year. Your written acceptance of this will be
satisfactory.

Note that the contract did not call for a Sherlock Holmes
adventure, only that the story consist of not less than 40,000 words,
with the English rights reverting back to Arthur three months after
publication. Note also that Arthur was given four or five months to
write the story, depending on one's interpretation of "by or before
January."

From a letter that was written on 30 September 1899, we get
some sense of the contract offered to and accepted by Wilde.

Dear Mr. Stoddart, I have just returned from France,
and find your letter of 18th waiting for me. You ask
me to try and send my story 'early in October'; surely
you mean 'early in November'? If you could be
content with 30,000 words I might be able to post the
manuscript to you the first week in November, but
October is of course out of the question. If this date,
and 30,000 words, will do, telegraph me on receipt of
this. If not, it will be sufficient to write.

Clearly, Wilde was not granted four or five months to write his
story, as was Arthur. Instead, he received slightly more than one
month, or slightly more than two, depending on whether Stoddart
meant to write "early in October" or "early in November." Even if
granted two months, Wilde felt unable to produce a story of more
than 30,000 words.

From Christopher Roden's introduction to the Oxford edition of
The Sign of Four (1995), we learn that Wilde was more troubled by
Stoddart's insistence that he give up all rights to his story in
perpetuity: "Oscar Wilde, for instance, gave them *The Picture of
Dorian Gray*, and bitterly regretted it, having been told that their 10
per cent was an invariable royalty only to discover that it was not.
Conan Doyle [...] absolutely refused to surrender his rights beyond
the three months."

Though Wilde was already well known and Arthur much less so, Arthur bargained more successfully. By securing the English royalty rights after three months, Arthur eventually earned more than ten times the face value of the contract. His successful negotiation is his giveaway, since we can be confident that Stoddart did not concede to Arthur's demands while Wilde simultaneously dined at the same table. Wilde would certainly not have agreed to deliver his story in two months if he realized Arthur was being allowed five, nor would he have given up his royalty rights in perpetuity, knowing Arthur's would be returned after three months.

Not only did Arthur evidently lie about dining with, and being complimented by, Oscar Wilde, he seems also to have lied, and more substantially so, about writing *The Sign of Four* in September and October of 1889. According to conventional, unquestioned history, Arthur wrote the second Sherlock Holmes novel as a result of the meeting and contract with Stoddart. As noted already, the contract arrived on 30 August. On 3 September, Arthur replied by mail, accepting the terms as stated. On 1 November, Arthur wrote to Stoddart, "I have finished it & sent it to your London agents."

While it is theoretically possible that Arthur could have written *The Sign of Four* in less than two months, it is exceptionally unlikely that he did so. He was, at that time, still a doctor rather than a full-time author. He had a medical practice to maintain, and he supplemented his own practice by working a second job at the Portsmouth Eye Hospital. He had a wife and child. He had ongoing interests beyond medicine, family, and writing. During the same two months in which he was allegedly writing *The Sign of Four*, he helped launch the *Hampshire Psychical Society* and assumed the position of its vice-president.

Arthur lacked not only the time necessary to write a complete Sherlock Holmes novel in less than two months, he lacked the inclination as well. The contract did not call for a Sherlock Holmes story. It called only for "a story to be written by you consisting of not less than 40,000 words" to be completed within five months. Arthur had no requirement to deliver a Sherlock Holmes adventure, much less deliver one in sixty days, and he was busy with his beloved historical fiction.

He had finally started writing *The White Company*. To research that second historical novel, he spent three weeks in New Forest, away from work, family, and friends. He claimed to have read, in whole or in part, 150 books to prepare himself for his masterpiece. He started writing *The White Company* just eleven days before meeting with Stoddard.

In that same month, the one in which he was allegedly at work on both *The Sign of Four* and *The White Company*, he granted an interview to the Hampshire *Echo*. In its 29 September edition, the paper mentioned that Arthur was revising the proofs of his earlier novel *The Firm of Girdlestone*," which will soon commence running in a score of newspapers."

Not only was Arthur working two jobs, launching a paranormal society, and working on his magnum opus, he made himself available for an interview. One might expect that he would have at least mentioned his furious scribbling to complete and deliver the next Sherlock Holmes adventure so that he could deliver it three months ahead of schedule. He apparently made no such remark.

It is suddenly quite clear that Arthur did not write *The Sign of Four* in September and October of 1889. It seems also that Arthur did not write the story beforehand. A stylometric analysis reveals that its function word usage is more akin to that of the early Holmes short stories than to Arthur's non-Holmesian fiction. Consider, for example, the relative usage of the masculine-tending word *the*. In *Sign*, it appears 537 times in every 10,000 words; in the early Holmes short stories, it appears at a similar average rate of 543 times per 10,000 words. Yet, in Arthur's other short works of fiction, *the* appears at an average rate of 596 times per 10,000 words. Arthur used the masculine-tending word 10% more frequently in his short stories than did the author of *Sign*, and that is statistically significant.

Of the seven marker words so distinctive of the early Holmes adventures (*the, that, very, many, another, and, of*), five of them (all but *that* and *very*) point to someone other than Arthur as the author of *The Sign of Four*. The word *the* is used at only 90% of Arthur's rate, the word *many* only two-thirds as frequently, and the word *another* only half as frequently. When all one hundred function words are weighed simultaneously, the result again points away from Arthur.

It seems likely that *Sign*'s author, a woman, had already written the adventure before Arthur agreed to provide a story of at least 40,000 words. Though he was far too busy to write a new story of his own in such a short time, he could have easily made a few adjustments to one already written for him, or had the adjustments made for him.

Other than his name on the cover and the claims of an autobiography, the evidence indicates that Arthur did not write *The Sign of Four*. Examination of the chronology reveals that he did not have the opportunity to do so, and stylometric analysis supports that revelation.

The Englischer Hof
In *The Final Problem* (1893), the last of what we refer to here as the early Holmes adventures, our hero and his companion flee Professor Moriarty. They travel a seemingly random route from London to Switzerland's Reichenbach Falls, where Holmes and Moriarty fight to the death. The circuitous journey, however, was carefully chosen by our unidentified author. During the final week of their unsuccessful evasion, Holmes and Watson retrace a path taken by Mark Twain fifteen years earlier. From *The Final Problem*:

> For a charming week we wandered up the Valley of
> the Rhône, and then, branching off at Leuk, we made
> our way over the Gemmi Pass, still deep in snow, and
> so, by way of Interlaken, to Meiringen.

Holmes's creator tempts us to consider that path, and so we shall. In 1878, Mark Twain tramped through Europe, mostly Switzerland, in the company of his friend Joseph Twitchell. Twain's purpose was to gather material for a travelogue, published in 1880 as *A Tramp Abroad*. During their journey, Twain and his friend travelled from Lucerne, past Meiringen, through Interlaken, over the Gemmi Pass, and along the Valley of the Rhône. In 1893, Louise and Arthur retraced that portion of Twain's trek. Just three months later,

Holmes and Watson hiked that same path, in the opposite direction, in their flight from Moriarty.

The Rhône River forms from the glacier melt of the Swiss Alps. It flows westerly through a valley flanked by parallel mountain ranges along either side. This magnificent region is the Valley of the Rhône. Its eponymous river empties into the easternmost portion of Lake Geneva and re-emerges fifty miles to the southwest, at the city of Geneva. From there, the Rhône heads south to the Mediterranean.

Holmes and Watson hike east from Lake Geneva, up Valley of the Rhône, to Leuk. At Leuk, they make a left turn, to the north, to cross over one of the two mountain ranges that border the valley. From Leuk, they climb the precarious trail leading to the summit of the Gemmi Pass. Mark Twain descended that trail fifteen years earlier. From his *A Tramp Abroad* we gain some insight into its life-threatening nature.

> We began our descent, now, by the most remarkable road I have ever seen. It wound its corkscrew curves down the face of the colossal precipice—a narrow way, with always the solid rock wall at one elbow, and perpendicular nothingness at the other. We met an everlasting procession of guides, porters, mules, litters, and tourists climbing up this steep and muddy path, and there was no room to spare when you had to pass a tolerably fat mule. I always took the inside, when I heard or saw the mule coming, and flattened myself against the wall. [...] More than once I saw a mule's hind foot cave over the outer edge and send earth and rubbish into the bottom abyss; and I noticed that upon these occasions the rider, whether male or female, looked tolerably unwell.

Mark Twain and his friend witnessing a near tragedy,
from *A Tramp Abroad*

After climbing the treacherous path and reaching the summit of
the Gemmi Pass, one imagines that Holmes and Watson must
certainly have taken in the majestic view of the Rhône River Valley.
Though Watson omits this point in his narrative, Twain dwells on it
in his.

> We stepped forward to a sort of jumping-off place,
> and were confronted by a startling contrast: we
> seemed to look down into fairyland. Two or three
> thousand feet below us was a bright green level, with
> a pretty town in its midst, and a silvery stream
> winding among the meadows; the charming spot was
> walled in on all sides by gigantic precipices clothed
> with pines; and over the pines, out of the softened
> distances, rose the snowy domes and peaks of the
> Monte Rosa region. How exquisitely green and
> beautiful that little valley down there was!

Mark Twain and his friend at the summit of the
Gemmi Pass, from *A Tramp Abroad*

From the summit, Holmes and Watson hike across the plateau of the Gemmi Pass, and skirt an alpine lake called the Daubensee. Watson describes their nearly fatal walk alongside that lake.

> Once, I remember, as we passed over the Gemmi, and walked along the border of the melancholy Daubensee, a large rock which had been dislodged from the ridge upon our right clattered down and roared into the lake behind us. In an instant Holmes had raced up on to the ridge, and, standing upon a lofty pinnacle, craned his neck in every direction. It was in vain that our guide assured him that a fall of stones was a common chance in the spring-time at that spot. He said nothing, but he smiled at me with the air of a man who sees the fulfillment of that which he had expected.

Holmes, Watson, and a guide at the Daubensee, from *The Final Problem*

For Holmes and Watson, the descent from the Gemmi Pass to Interlaken is uneventful, as is the final leg of their journey to Meiringen, where they decide to spend the night.

> It was upon the 3d of May that we reached the little village of Meiringen, where we put up at the Englischer Hof, then kept by Peter Steiler the elder. Our landlord was an intelligent man, and spoke excellent English, having served for three years as waiter at the Grosvenor Hotel in London.

In that brief passage is buried the most obscure, most revealing allusion yet to be discovered in any of the Sherlock Holmes tales. There was not then, in 1893, and there is not now, any lodging place by the name of Englischer Hof in Meiringen. Those who whimsically treat the Canon as if every tale has its roots in fact frequently point to the Hôtel du Sauvage as the establishment maintained by Peter Steiler in the adventure.

Hôtel du Sauvage, declared by some to be the Englischer Hof

There was, however, an Englischer Hof in Frankfurt. Mark Twain stayed there upon his arrival in Europe in 1878. It was from that hotel that he began the journey chronicled in his *A Tramp Abroad*.

Designed by Alexandre Nicolas Salins de Montfort, Frankfurt's Englischer Hof opened its doors to the public in 1797. The photograph below, by Karl Hertel, preserves an image as it existed in 1878, the same year as Twain's stay.

The Englischer Hof, Frankfurt, 1878

It is almost certainly no coincidence that the author of *The Final Problem* had Holmes and Watson follow Mark Twain's path through Switzerland before their stay at the Englischer Hof. That hotel is as much an allusion to Mark Twain as are their hike up the Valley of the Rhône, their crossing over the Gemmi Pass, and their descent to Interlaken. The Englischer Hof points to Twain just as surely as does the convenient placement of *Tom* just before *Sawyer* in *A Study in Scarlet*, just a surely as does Holmes's harangue on the German language in *A Scandal in Bohemia*.

It is abundantly clear that Holmes's creator had an abiding interest in Mark Twain. Twain is an allusionary target in the first Holmes adventure, then in the first Holmes short story, and finally what was intended to be the final Holmes tale. In most instances, the allusions are translucent; they are neither so transparent that they are recognized immediately, nor so opaque that they might never be recognized, much less deciphered. The use of the Englischer Hof, however, is of a qualitatively different nature. Until recently, there has been absolutely no chance that a reader could recognize it as an allusion to Mark Twain. So obscure is it that it seems to represent a form of coded writing, to be understood by only a select precious few.

Only recently has information become public that identifies the Englischer Hof as one of Mark Twain's early European stops. The Englischer Hof is mentioned nowhere in Mark's public writings, nor is it mentioned anywhere within the six volumes of *Mark Twain's Letters* (1853-1867), nor were any of his later letters published prior to the publication of *The Final Problem*. The author had no way of anticipating that, more than one hundred years in the future, any such thing as the Internet would reveal the secret.

In 2007, The Mark Twain Project Online (MTPO) opened its website to the public. That site defines itself as follows:

> Mark Twain Project Online applies innovative technology to more than four decades' worth of archival research by expert editors at the Mark Twain Project. It offers unfettered, intuitive access to

reliable texts, accurate and exhaustive notes, and the most recently discovered letters and documents.

Its ultimate purpose is to produce a digital critical edition, fully annotated, of everything Mark Twain wrote.

Of great interest to us is a letter of 4 May 1878, written by Mark Twain, from Frankfurt, to friends William and Elinor Howell. The letter mentions Twain's wife Olivia Clemens, their children, and their governess Rosa. All of them traveled with Twain throughout Europe, staying in hotels as he and his friend tramped about. Twain's letter concludes with a charming anecdote about his daughter, Susie, who was frustrated that the governess, Rosa, spoke only German.

> Susie came to me (from Rosa, in the nursery,) & said, in halting syllables, "Papa, wie viel Uhr ist es?" [Papa, what time is it?]—then turned, with pathos in her big eyes, & said, "Mamma, I wish Rosa was made in English."

The letter was made public much earlier, in the 1917 edition of *Mark Twain Letters*. Comparing the letter from that edition to MTPO's version reveals the texts to be essentially the same. The MTPO version, however, is more faithful to the original. It shows, for example, the strikeouts from the original, which were excluded from the earlier work.

More significantly, much more so, the MTPO version includes the letterhead of the paper on which the letter is written: "ENGLISCHER HOF. FRANKFURT A/M." It is the only reference to the Englischer Hof to be found anywhere within the MTPO, anywhere in publicly available documents, even today.

Our discovery of Mark Twain's brief stay at the Englischer Hof adds hope that we might be able to finally identify the author of the early Holmes adventures. We need only determine who had the opportunity to learn firsthand of Mark Twain's stay there.

Chapter 12
Hot Pursuit

"Hot pursuit" refers to the urgent pursuit of a suspect beyond the jurisdiction of the pursuer. The concept stems from the old English doctrine of *distress damage feasant*, which allowed a property owner to detain trespassing animals to ensure compensation for any damage the animals had caused. The doctrine was naturally modified to allow the property owner to pursue and capture animals that had recently trespassed but had already left the property. The naturally modified doctrine was naturally modified further by peace officers wishing to nab suspects who had just fled beyond the officers' jurisdiction.

In a technical sense, we cannot be in hot pursuit, for any number of reasons. In a figurative sense, however, we finally have a solid lead to pursue. The author of the early Holmes adventures seems to have known Mark Twain, or someone close to him, well enough to learn of the Englischer Hof. Given her established interest in Twain's tramp through Switzerland, we should continue our search there, to see if Twain will lead us to the creator of Sherlock Holmes.

Lucerne

We pick up Mark Twain's trail in Lucerne, a major Swiss city located a bit north of the country's center. We find a photograph of the city, and its Hotel de l'Europe, in a turn-of-the-century postcard.

Hotel l'Europe, Lucerne, circa 1890, from a vintage postcard

The hotel is of interest to us because Arthur and Louise stayed there in 1893, when Arthur was scheduled to give a lecture on 9 August, at the nearby Christ Church. Arthur had been developing two standard lectures for a speaking tour scheduled for England later that year. One of the lectures was "Fiction as Part of Literature," the one he apparently tested before the crowd at Lucerne. The 2 September 1893 issue of *The Critic* suggests it was a success.

> Dr. Conan Doyle, the well-known author of "Micah Clarke" and "The Refugees," has found a more novel entertainment still for his hours of idleness. He has been lecturing at Lucerne, and lecturing on Fiction. It is reported that his discourse was the most largely attended of the whole course of conferences which is being held there, and that he was listened to with rapt attention. Dr. Doyle's view of the fiction of the present day was an optimistic one: he had no tolerance, he said, for the critics who shriek over the decay of literature. "The fiction of the present century," he maintains, "is the most certain and permanent part of England's glory." Rather a high-colored statement!

The 14 October 1893 issue of the same magazine was slightly critical.

> Dr. Conan Doyle's recent address, on "Fiction as a Part of Literature," delivered at Lucerne, has been much quoted by the English papers. Dr. Doyle showed himself to be very diplomatic in speaking of his fellow-craftsmen. He hammered the critics, though, for not admitting that the present generation of writers is equal to the giants of the past, and stoutly maintained that "the fiction of the present century was the most certain and permanent part of England's glory, and would last in the memory and appreciation of the people after the labors of the statesman and the soldier had crumbled away." [...] I do not wish to deprive any living authors of their laurels, but I cannot say that I have yet recognized a Thackeray, a Dickens or a George Eliot in their ranks. But that may be my obtuseness.

Arthur could not have been thrilled to read that later review, since the reviewer was too obtuse to recognize even Arthur as another Thackeray, Dickens, or Eliot.

While in Lucerne, Arthur met fellow lecturer Silas Hocking. Hocking was a Cornish novelist and Methodist preacher. Author of fifty books, Hocking became best known for his novel *Her Benny* (1879), a story of the street children of Liverpool. He took the position of editor of *Family Circle,* and then later helped establish *Temple Magazine.* Interestingly, Hocking places Louise with Arthur at critical points during our pursuit of Mark Twain. In *Out of the Shadows*, Georgina Doyle wrote of Hocking's initial encounter with Arthur and Louise.

> On their trip to Switzerland, Arthur and Louise met Silas E. Hocking, an English minister in the United Methodist Free Church who had turned to writing and whose article of their encounter appeared on January 24, 1895, in *The New Age*. Hocking, who had

not previously met Arthur, described the first meeting in the well-shaded garden of the Hotel de l'Europe, Lucerne: "He was seated with his wife, behind a small table when we came up, a cup of coffee in front of him and a cigar between his lips." Hocking found Arthur to be a large, good-humoured Englishman, such as one would find on any cricket pitch, and not the keen-eyed, sharp featured detective that he was expecting from knowing the Sherlock Holmes stories.

A second person of interest, whom Arthur also encountered at Lucerne, is William James Dawson, English clergyman, author, and co-editor of the Christian based magazines *The Young Man* and *The Young Woman*, who was also a fan of Arthur's historical novels. In his July 1894 edition of *The Young Man*, Dawson wrote a character sketch of Arthur addressing Arthur's preference for historical fiction.

My first acquaintance with Conan Doyle's writings began with *Micah Clarke*, which I esteemed then, and still think to be, his finest book. In this opinion he himself would not agree. It is well known that he prefers the *White Company*. I suspect however, that this preference arises from a vivid memory of the laborious pains by which the *White Company* was begotten, and of the hundred and fifty books of hard historical reading which were needed for its production.

Even Dawson, however, could not completely ignore Sherlock Holmes, who had, by the time of his article, plummeted into Switzerland's Reichenbach Falls some thirty miles south of Lucerne.

I have touched in the main upon Conan Doyle's more serious work, because it is by that he should be judged, and would wish to be judged. It is no sort of secret that the creator of Sherlock Holmes has grown a little impatient of the attention given to that

nimble-witted gentlemen, and that he displayed an
eagerness to hurry him off the stage of action which
certainly was not justified by the impatience or
hostility of the audience. ... No doubt the detective
story can never be other than one of the lower forms
of art, but it is instructive to notice how futile and
feeble all other stories of the kind appear by contrast
with Sherlock Holmes.

The weight of what little historical evidence we have on the
matter is that Dawson was the person who suggested that Holmes be
chucked into the Reichenbach Falls. Henry Lunn, who organized the
conference at which Arthur spoke, explained several years
afterwards how the suggestion came about. "It is curious you should
mention that," Lunn states in the 8 August 1896 issue of *Tit-bits*, "for
it was when Conan Doyle was lecturing us at Lucerne that he turned
to me and said: 'I have made up my mind to kill Sherlock Holmes: he
is becoming such a burden to me that it makes my life unendurable.'
It was Rev. W. J. Dawson who suggested the spot, the Reichenbach
Falls, near Meiringen, where Conan Doyle finished the great
detective, so I was an accessory before the fact."

Meiringen
Dawson, who was quite familiar with Meiringen, the Gemmi Pass,
and the Valley of the Rhône, guided Arthur and Louise on a week-
long hiking tour that approximated the one taken by Mark Twain
fifteen years earlier. Despite her health, Louise hiked along with the
other two. A later article, from the May 1895 issue of *The Ladies'
Home Journal*, entitled "Mrs. Conan Doyle and her Children," gives us
the following excerpt:

Image from *Ladies Home Journal* of Mary, Kingsley, and Louise

It was when crossing the channel on their return from Switzerland one year, where they had done some really hard climbing, that Mrs. Doyle caught the chill, from the effects of which she has suffered so much. To an active, energetic woman the enforced inaction, the long, tedious spell of invalidism has been a great strain, but she has borne it bravely and uncomplainingly.

Led by William Dawson, Arthur and Louise made their way south from Lucerne to Meiringen, of which *Cook's Tourist Handbook of Switzerland* (1876) provides a brief description.

> Meiringen is a charming Alpine village of 2800 inhabitants, with fine views of snow-clad mountains belted with luxuriant woods, [...] If the interest of the visitor is chiefly centred in art, architecture, or exhibitions, he will find little to please him in Meiringen. He may, if he has an hour or two to spare, look into the shops and buy some wood carvings, or sit on the balcony of the hotel and listen to the tinkle of distant cattle-bells, or the strange, weird cry of the peasants calling the cattle home, or stroll to one of the three brooks that leap down into the valley at the back of the village.

In *The Final Problem*, Watson mentions Meiringen only in passing, thereafter referring instead to the Englischer Hof: "For a charming week we wandered up the Valley of the Rhône, and then, branching off at Leuk, we made our way over the Gemmi Pass, still deep in snow, and so, by way of Interlaken, to Meiringen."

Meiringen, 1902; Hotel Sauvage (lower center);
Reichenbach Falls (center)

As we look down into Meiringen, towards the south, we can see the Aare River flowing from left to right across our field of view. Lucerne lies behind us, thirty miles to the north. Interlaken is to our right, seventeen miles to the west, down the Aare River Valley. On the far side of the river, we can barely make out the Reichenbach Falls, its torrent pouring from the low point of the cliff face beyond. The Hotel Sauvage, which some Sherlockians presume to be the Englischer Hof, is the large building at the far side of town.

Arthur, Louise, and Dawson may have reveled in this very view, or one quite similar. Perhaps as Louise stood here, looking down into Meiringen, she may have envisioned Mark Twain travelling down the valley, towards Interlaken, and perhaps Holmes and Watson walking in the opposite direction, entering Meiringen from the right, from Interlaken. Perhaps she decided then and there that Holmes and Watson would spend the night at the Englischer Hof.

Search as you might, however, you will not find the Englischer Hof down below. It sits instead three hundred miles to the north, in Frankfurt, Germany. Mark Twain spent at least one night there before tramping into Switzerland, through Lucerne, and passing Meiringen en route to Interlaken.

While at Meiringen, Holmes and Watson receive advice, from Peter Steiler the Elder to visit the falls. Watson reports:

> Our landlord was an intelligent man, and spoke excellent English, having served for three years as waiter at the Grosvenor Hotel in London. At his advice, upon the afternoon of the 4th we set off together with the intention of crossing the hills and spending the night at the hamlet of Rosenlaui. We had strict injunctions, however, on no account to pass the falls of Reichenbach, which are about half-way up the hill, without making a small detour to see them.

Reichenbach

Following Steiler's advice, Louise Arthur, and Dawson visited the very falls that would soon swallow Sherlock Holmes. Dawson published their experience in his article "Glorious Grindelwald," in the July 1894 edition of *The Young Man*.

> The water pours over a curving precipice into a huge caldron, from whose black depth rises a cloud of vapour, through which the morning sun flashes innumerable rainbows. The eye vainly searches the abyss for any bottom; the depth seems infinite, and the thunder that rises from the boiling caldron is terrific. A narrow path winds along the edge of the abyss, from which the scene may be viewed in all its grandeur.

"It is, indeed, a fearful place," Watson says of the same scene, adding:

> The torrent, swollen by the melting snow, plunges into a tremendous abyss, from which the spray rolls up like the smoke from a burning house. The shaft into which the river hurls itself is an immense chasm,

lined by glistening, coal-black rock, and narrowing into a creaming, boiling pit of incalculable depth, which brims over and shoots the stream onward over its jagged lip. The long sweep of green water roaring for ever down, and the thick flickering curtain of spray hissing for ever upwards, turn a man giddy with their constant whirl and clamour. We stood near the edge peering down at the gleam of the breaking water far below us against the black rocks, and listening to the half-human shout which came booming up with the spray out of the abyss.

Sherlock Holmes, looking into the Reichenbach Falls

Though we can still see Holmes standing on the precipice, Arthur and Louise and Dawson have long since departed. We need to move on, for we are no more likely to solve our mystery by staring into these falls than we were by staying in Lucerne or Meiringen. All that is here is death and sadness.

Gemmi Pass

Everyone's passage through Interlaken was uneventful, so let us pick up Mark Twain's trail as he crossed the Gemmi Pass, a shortcut between the Aare River valley and the Valley of the Rhône. Arthur and Louise had Dawson to guide them, but Mark and his friend were forced to hire one, an elderly one.

> We hired the only guide left, to lead us on our way. He was over seventy, but he could have given me nine-tenths of his strength and still had all his age entitled him to. He shouldered our satchels, overcoats, and alpenstocks, and we set out up the steep path. It was hot work. The old man soon begged us to hand over our coats and waistcoats to him to carry, too, and we did it; one could not refuse so little a thing to a poor old man like that; he should have had them if he had been a hundred and fifty. [...]
>
> As we strolled on, climbing up higher and higher, we were continually bringing neighboring peaks into view and lofty prominence which had been hidden behind lower peaks before; [...] We had been finding the top of the world all along—and always finding a still higher top stealing into view in a disappointing way just ahead; [...] there were much higher altitudes to be scaled yet. [...]
>
> From here forward we moved through a storm-swept and smileless desolation. All about us rose gigantic masses, crags, and ramparts of bare and dreary rock, with not a vestige or semblance of plant or tree or flower anywhere, or glimpse of any creature that had life. The frost and the tempests of unnumbered ages had battered and hacked at these cliffs, with a deathless energy, destroying them piecemeal; so all the region about their bases was a tumbled chaos of great fragments which had been split off and hurled to the ground.

Each and every one of our travellers undoubtedly stopped at the Schwarenbach guest house for rest and refreshment. Mark Twain and his friend certainly did, as he related in *A Tramp Abroad*, and so shall we.

> We stopped for a nooning at a strongly built little inn called the Schwarenbach. It sits in a lonely spot among the peaks, where it is swept by the trailing fringes of the cloud-rack, and is rained on, and snowed on, and pelted and persecuted by the storms, nearly every day of its life. It was the only habitation in the whole Gemmi Pass.

The Schwarenbach

The Schwarenbach was built as a customs house in 1742, destroyed by an avalanche the following year, and rebuilt at a safer location. It remains open to this day, having provided lodging for such celebrities as Alexandre Dumas, Jules Verne, and Guy de Maupassant. Where else would a Maupassant, or a Verne, or a Dumas stay? As Twain himself noted, in 1878, "it was the only habitation in the whole Gemmi Pass."

After refreshing themselves at the Schwarenbach, Twain and his friend continued towards the summit of the pass, as did Arthur, Louise, and Dawson fifteen years later. They all walked alongside the Daubensee, as would Holmes and Watson, though in the opposite direction. Finally at the summit, just before the treacherous descent to Leuk, Twain and his friend found a hotel under construction.

> We skirted the lonely little lake called the Daubensee, and presently passed close by a glacier on the right— a thing like a great river frozen solid in its flow and broken square off like a wall at its mouth. I had never been so near a glacier before.
>
> Here we came upon a new board shanty, and found some men engaged in building a stone house; so the Schwarenbach was soon to have a rival. We bought a bottle or so of beer here; at any rate they called it beer, but I knew by the price that it was dissolved jewelry, and I perceived by the taste that dissolved jewelry is not good stuff to drink.
>
> We were surrounded by a hideous desolation. We stepped forward to a sort of jumping-off place, and were confronted by a startling contrast: we seemed to look down into fairyland. Two or three thousand feet below us was a bright green level, with a pretty town in its midst, and a silvery stream winding among the meadows; the charming spot was walled in on all sides by gigantic precipices clothed with pines; and over the pines, out of the softened distances, rose the snowy domes and peaks of the Monte Rosa region. How exquisitely green and beautiful that little valley down there was! The distance was not great enough to obliterate details, it only made them little, and mellow, and dainty, like

landscapes and towns seen through the wrong end of
a spy-glass.

They were headed for the mountains on the far side of the valley.
Arthur, Louise, and Dawson followed, but by the time they reached
the overlook, the Hotel Wildstrubel had been completed. It stood
precariously at the edge of the overlook, and it offered magnificent
views.

Hotel Wildstrubel at the summit of the Gemmi Pass

Arthur, Louise, and Dawson spent the night. How could they
resist? Arthur's *Through the Magic Door* relates an anecdote about
Guy de Maupassant similarly staying at that cliffside hotel, though
we know that is impossible. Maupassant crossed the Gemmi even
before Twain did. The Wildstrubel simply did not exist then, so
Maupassant stayed instead at the Schwarenbach Inn, as recorded in
their guest register.

Arthur's little "confusion" is monumentally significant. It tells us
that he was oblivious to their following Mark Twain's footsteps.
From *Through the Magic Door*:

> I cannot write the name of Maupassant without
> recalling what was either a spiritual interposition or

an extraordinary coincidence in my own life. I had been travelling in Switzerland and had visited, among other places, that Gemmi Pass, where a huge cliff separates a French from a German canton. On the summit of this cliff was a small inn, where we broke our journey. It was explained to us that, although the inn was inhabited all the year round, still for about three months in winter it was utterly isolated, because it could at any time only be approached by winding paths on the mountain side, and when these became obliterated by snow it was impossible either to come up or to descend. They could see the lights in the valley beneath them, but were as lonely as if they lived in the moon. So curious a situation naturally appealed to one's imagination, and I speedily began to build up a short story in my own mind, depending upon a group of strong antagonistic characters being penned up in this inn, loathing each other and yet utterly unable to get away from each other's society, every day bringing them nearer to tragedy. For a week or so, as I travelled, I was turning over the idea.

Arthur must have been speaking of the Hotel Wildstrubel, since it was the only structure on the summit of the Gemmi pass, at the edge of a huge cliff, with a view of the lights below. It was the only one in which he lodged, the only one that caused him to spend his next week, in the company of Louise, pondering how intimacy fosters animosity.

At the end of that time I returned through France. Having nothing to read I happened to buy a volume of Maupassant's Tales which I had never seen before. The first story was called "L'Auberge" (The Inn)— and as I ran my eye down the printed page I was amazed to see the two words, "Kandersteg" and "Gemmi Pass." I settled down and read it with ever-growing amazement. The scene was laid in the inn I

had visited. The plot depended on the isolation of a
group of people through the snowfall. Everything that
I imagined was there, save that Maupassant had
brought in a savage hound.

De Maupassant's story "L'Auberge" was first published in the
journal *Les Lettres et les arts* in 1886 and then in the anthology *Le
Horla* in 1887, one year before Mark Twain crossed the Gemmi Pass,
sixteen years before Louise, Arthur, Dawson, Holmes, and Watson
did. The very first line of Maupassant's story shows that Arthur
misremembered the words that he claimed caught his eye.

Resembling in appearance all the wooden hostelries
of the High Alps situated at the foot of glaciers in the
barren rocky gorges that intersect the summits of the
mountains, the Inn of Schwarenbach serves as a
resting place for travellers crossing the Gemini Pass.

De Maupassant was specific that he stayed at "the Inn of
Schwarenbach" rather than what Arthur recalled as a small inn on
"the summit of this cliff." Had Arthur ever read *A Tramp Abroad*, he
would have realized that Guy de Maupassant could not possibly have
stayed at the Wildstrubel. Twain would have educated him against
such a foolish claim.

Of the many works Arthur mentions in his *Through the Magic
Door*, *A Tramp Abroad* is not among them. In fact, in Arthur's
comprehensive literary stroll through his personal library, he
mentioned Mark Twain not even once. He offered no comment on
Tom Sawyer, so clearly alluded to in *A Study in Scarlet*. He made no
observation about the peculiarities of the German language, though
Mark Twain and Sherlock Holmes had already done so. He never said
a word about being so taken with Mark Twain that he followed his
footsteps through Switzerland, and had Holmes retrace them in *The
Final Problem*.

Whoever wrote *The Final Problem* not only had carefully read *A
Tramp Abroad*, but also had a profound interest Mark Twain. That
author of *The Final Problem* cannot possibly be Arthur. Of the three
travellers who followed Twain through Switzerland, that author can

only be Louise. She is the one we have been pursuing. Arthur has
delivered her into our hands as we stand on the edge of the Gemmi
Pass and marvel.

Hotel Wildstrubel, at the summit of the Gemmi Pass, circa 1895

Chapter 13
Deliverance

As we stand on the brink, we can imagine Holmes and Watson ascending the last few feet to the summit, and then hiking onwards towards the Daubensee, unaware that Moriarty will soon send a large boulder tumbling their way.

The trail leading to the summit of the Gemmi Pass

Louise stood here, near the recently completed Hotel Wildstrubel, just a few months before *The Final Problem* shocked the world. She would lead Arthur down the trail, up the Valley of the Rhône to Visp, and up the mountain range on the opposite side.

She would deliver Arthur first to Zermatt, then to the foot of the Findelen Glacier. She would explain to him, by her words or her actions, the role of Mark Twain in her Sherlock Holmes adventures.

Zermatt

Perhaps it was during her descent, as she stood near the insubstantial railing, that she gazed down the valley and decided that Holmes would walk here all the way from Lake Geneva.

The descent from the Gemmi Pass, circa 1895

Mark Twain wrote of the path and its rickety fence in *A Tramp Abroad*.

> The path was simply a groove cut into the face of the precipice; there was a four-foot breadth of solid rock under the traveler, and four-foot breadth of solid rock just above his head, like the roof of a narrow porch; he could look out from this gallery and see a sheer summitless and bottomless wall of rock before him, across a gorge or crack a biscuit's toss in width—but he could not see the bottom of his own precipice unless he lay down and projected his nose over the edge. I did not do this, because I did not wish to soil my clothes.

Every few hundred yards, at particularly bad places, one came across a panel or so of plank fencing; but they were always old and weak, and they generally leaned out over the chasm and did not make any rash promises to hold up people who might need support. There was one of these panels which had only its upper board left; a pedestrianizing English youth came tearing down the path, was seized with an impulse to look over the precipice, and without an instant's thought he threw his weight upon that crazy board. It bent outward a foot! I never made a gasp before that came so near suffocating me. The English youth's face simply showed a lively surprise, but nothing more. He went swinging along valleyward again, as if he did not know he had just swindled a coroner by the closest kind of a shave.

When Twain and Twitchell reached the Rhône, they turned left and travelled east, upstream to Visp. When Arthur, Louise, and Dawson reached the Rhône, rather than turn downstream towards Lake Geneva, whence Holmes and Watson later came, they followed Mark upstream to Visp.

At Visp, Arthur once again caught sight of Silas Hocking, who had opted against the arduous trek by taking a train over the Saint Gotthard pass. In *Out of the Shadows*, Hocking was reportedly still on the platform when he heard a man call out from behind.

"Hello! I thought I should very likely stumble across you somewhere on the way" fell on our ears; and turning round, we came face to face with Conan Doyle, and his cheery, plucky little wife.

Georgina Doyle added, parenthetically, "Very plucky, if she had indeed travelled over the Gemmipass." The little wife, as it turns out, was very plucky indeed. She had just done exactly that.

In *The Man Who Created Sherlock Holmes*, Andrew Lycett wrote that Dawson guided Arthur and Louise all the way to Visp, and that Hocking then accompanied them to Zermatt. It is unclear whether

Dawson travelled any further than Visp. There seems no record that he did, so we say farewell to him as we near the conclusion of our pursuit.

Mark Twain and his friend had no train available to them, so they hiked all the way from Visp to the resort town of Zermatt, spending a night along the way in St. Nicholas. "We made Zermatt at three in the afternoon, nine hours out from St. Nicholas. Distance, by guide-book, twelve miles; by pedometer seventy-two."

"Arrival in Zermatt," from *A Tramp Abroad*

At 5,310 feet, Zermatt is almost exactly a mile above sea level. The most distinctive nearby geological feature is the mighty Matterhorn. At 14,692 feet, its peak is nearly another two miles above Zermatt. Three of the major hotels in the town were then managed by Alexander Seiler the Elder, founder and proprietor of seven hotels in the area. That name rings a bell.

In *The Final Problem*, the proprietor of the Englischer Hof is Peter Steiler the Elder, a name tantalizingly similar to Alexander Seiler the Elder and Peter Taugwalder the Elder. Old Peter and Young Peter, as they were called, were the two guides who accompanied Edward Whymper during the first successful ascent of the peak of the Matterhorn. The seven-member ascent team formed at Seiler's Hotel Mont Rose in Zermatt before launching their assault on the mountain. Four of the team perished during the descent. Only Whymper, Old Peter, and Young Peter returned to the Mont Rose.

Grand Hotels Seiler; Hotel Mont Rose at rear

Just a few months before *The Final Problem* went to press, Louise and Arthur took the train from Visp to Zermatt and hiked further beyond, passing Seiler's Hotel Mont Rose along the way, before settling in at another of Seiler's grand hotels at their final destination.

Riffelalp

Before bedding down in Zermatt, Mark Twain relaxed by reading about the "fearful adventure which Mr. Whymper once had on the Matterhorn." He was moved and motivated by the tragic story. He decided to act. He decided to ascend the trail to another of Seiler's hotels, the Riffelberg.

> I was no longer myself; I was tranced, uplifted, intoxicated, by the almost incredible perils and adventures I had been following my authors through,

and the triumphs I had been sharing with them. I sat silent some time, then turned to his friend and said:

"My mind is made up."

Something in my tone struck him: and when he glanced at my eye and read what was written there, his face paled perceptibly. He hesitated a moment, then said:

"Speak."

I answered, with perfect calmness:

"I will ascend the Riffelberg."

If I had shot my poor friend he could not have fallen from his chair more suddenly. If I had been his father he could not have pleaded harder to get me to give up my purpose. But I turned a deaf ear to all he said. When he perceived at last that nothing could alter my determination, he ceased to urge, and for a while the deep silence was broken only by his sobs. I sat in marble resolution, with my eyes fixed upon vacancy, for in spirit I was already wrestling with the perils of the mountains, and my friend sat gazing at me in adoring admiration through his tears. [...]

I went to bed, but not to sleep. No man can sleep when he is about to undertake one of these Alpine exploits. I tossed feverishly all night long, and was glad enough when I heard the clock strike half past eleven and knew it was time to get up for dinner. I rose, jaded and rusty, and went to the noon meal, where I found myself the center of interest and curiosity; for the news was already abroad. It is not easy to eat calmly when you are a lion; but it is very pleasant, nevertheless.

As usual, at Zermatt, when a great ascent is about to be undertaken, everybody, native and foreign, laid aside his own projects and took up a good position to observe the start. The expedition consisted of 198 persons, including the mules; or 205, including the cows.

Twain detailed the 205 members of his party as follows: himself, his friend, twelve guides, four surgeons, a geologist, a botanist, three chaplains, two draftsmen, fifteen bar keepers, a Latinist, a veterinary surgeon, a footman, a barber, a head cook, nine assistants, four pastry cooks, a confectionery artist, twenty-seven porters, forty-four mules, forty-four muleteers, three coarse washers and ironers, one fine ditto (whatever that might be), seven cows, and two milkers.

> I commanded the chief guide to arrange the men and animals in single file, twelve feet apart, and lash them all together on a strong rope. He objected that the first two miles was a dead level, with plenty of room, and that the rope was never used except in very dangerous places. But I would not listen to that. My reading had taught me that many serious accidents had happened in the Alps simply from not having the people tied up soon enough; I was not going to add one to the list. The guide then obeyed my order.
>
> When the procession stood at ease, roped together, and ready to move, I never saw a finer sight. It was 3,122 feet long—over half a mile; every man and me was on foot, and had on his green veil and his blue goggles, and his white rag around his hat, and his coil of rope over one shoulder and under the other, and his ice-ax in his belt, and carried his alpenstock in his left hand, his umbrella (closed) in his right, and his crutches slung at his back. The burdens of the pack-mules and the horns of the cows were decked with the Edelweiss and the Alpine rose.
>
> I and my agent were the only persons mounted. We were in the post of danger in the extreme rear, and tied securely to five guides apiece. Our armor-bearers carried our ice-axes, alpenstocks, and other implements for us. We were mounted upon very small donkeys, as a measure of safety; in time of peril we could straighten our legs and stand up, and let the donkey walk from under.

"All Ready," from *A Tramp Abroad*

Mark's travails were numerous and nearly unbelievable. It turns out that none of his twelve guides had ever before made the ascent to Riffelberg, so the caravan meandered aimlessly. Their path was once blocked by a huge boulder, but a mule fortuitously ate some of the nitroglycerin they had incidentally placed nearby. The resulting explosion replaced the rock with a crater thirty feet across and fifteen feet deep. A half hour later, the residents of Zermatt "were knocked down and quite seriously injured by descending portions of mule meat, frozen solid." One of the porters took a shot at a mountain goat and missed. Fortunately the stray round hit the Latinist instead of a mule. Twain was "utterly unmanned" to hear that one of the bar keepers had fallen over a precipice, then relieved to learn that it had been only a chaplain. They blasted their way through another gigantic boulder, only to discover that there had been a chalet on top. They helped the family from the ground and rebuilt the chalet. After three days of such slapstick hardship, they finally arrived at the Riffelberg pass.

At noon we conquered the last impediment—we stood at last upon the summit, and without the loss of a single man except the mule that ate the glycerin. Our great achievement was achieved—the possibility of the impossible was demonstrated, and [my friend] and I walked proudly into the great dining-room of the Riffelberg Hotel and stood our alpenstocks up in the corner.

Yes, I had made the grand ascent; but it was a mistake to do it in evening dress. The plug hats were battered, the swallow-tails were fluttering rags, mud added no grace, the general effect was unpleasant and even disreputable.

There were about seventy-five tourists at the hotel—mainly ladies and little children—and they gave us an admiring welcome which paid us for all our privations and sufferings. The ascent had been made, and the names and dates now stand recorded on a stone monument there to prove it to all future tourists.

Hotel Riffelberg, circa 1895

We can be confident that Louise and Arthur never saw the plaque commemorating Twain's accomplishments, if for no reason other than they did not stay at Seiler's Hotel Riffelberg. Instead, they lodged a mile and a half away, at Seiler's more recently constructed, even more grand Hotel Riffelalp.

Hotel Riffelalp

Also staying at the Riffelalp that season were the Archbishop of Canterbury, Edward White Benson, his wife Mary, and their fifth son, the novelist E. F. Benson. One morning, the younger Benson, Silas Hocking, and Arthur hiked five miles to the Findel Glacier. In the 24 January 1895 issue of *New Age*, Hocking related the conversation that took place as they walked along the glacier.

> "Whether you like Sherlock Holmes or not," I said, "he's been a gold mine to you."
>
> "Anyhow," he said, "I shall kill him off at the end of the year."
>
> "Nonsense!"
>
> "If I don't," he said with a laugh, "he'll kill me."
>
> We paused on the edge of a gaping crevasse, which gashed the glacier almost from side to side.
>
> "How are you going to finish him?" I asked.
>
> "I don't know; I haven't decided yet," he said thoughtfully.
>
> I stooped over and looked down into the blue treacherous abyss at my feet.
>
> "Why not bring him out here," I questioned, "and drop him down a crevasse? That would finish him off

effectually, and save all the trouble and expense of a funeral."

He laughed heartily. "Not a bad idea," he said.

Louise was apparently not with them. Presumably she was back at the Riffelalp, outdoors, taking in the grandeur of the Matterhorn, or indoors, writing the first draft of *The Final Problem*. As she was apt to do, she incorporated her fellow guest, the Archbishop of Canterbury, into her story: "We shall get out at Canterbury," declares Holmes, as they attempt to evade Moriarty.

Hotel Riffelalp with the Matterhorn in the background

In his *Uncollected* Sherlock *Holmes*, Lancelyn Green reports that, only a few weeks later, Arthur sent Hocking a Meiringen postcard: "Have dropped Sherlock Holmes down the Reichenbach Falls." Louise had chosen to follow Dawson's suggestion.

Chance Encounter

We know that Louise spent time in Switzerland sometime before she married Arthur in 1885, well before she retraced Mark Twain's footsteps in 1893. The evidence of her earlier stay there is buried in an unexpunged letter she wrote to Arthur's mother from Vienna. Louise reassured her mother-in-law that the beds were excellent:

"Yes, dearie, the beds have been most comfortable. I wonder why you should have such a bad idea of the foreign ones. When I was in Suisse, they were very nice, and how well I remember the sweet scent to the linen."

Switzerland has four official national languages: Swiss German, Swiss Italian, Romansh, and Swiss French. Swiss French is predominant in the west and southwest, in those regions adjacent to France. Suisse, the term Louise used to describe Switzerland, is the French name for the country. The most populous region in French-speaking Switzerland, by far, is Lake Geneva and its environs. Simple probability considerations suggest that Louise lived somewhere near Lake Geneva.

We might be able to narrow the location of her residence even further. Consider Holmes's surprising, out-of-the-blue announcement that he is the product of famous French ancestry. That shocking revelation arrives in *The Greek Interpreter*, published the month after Louise's 1893 return from Switzerland.

> "My ancestors were country squires, who appear to have led much the same life as is natural to their class. But, none the less, my turn that way is in my veins, and may have come with my grandmother, who was the sister of Vernet, the French artist. Art in the blood is liable to take the strangest forms."

Vernet is not only the name of a French artist, it is the name also of a tiny community located on the north shore of Lake Geneva. Vernet, also called Vernex, was one of several villages that grew together to form the current city of Montreux. We learn from *Von Ziemssen's Handbook of General Therapeutics* (1885) that Montreux and Vernet were noted for their supposedly curative climate, and their purportedly salubrious grapes.

> Montreux, with the adjacent hamlets of Clarens, Vernet, Territet, and Veytaux, scattered over different elevations, lies nearer to the mountain walls, thereby enjoying better protection and an additional source of warmth, owing to the reflection of the sun's rays.

On the other hand, it is at times exposed to cold winds, and is rather deficient in promenades with sheltered resting-places. Montreux is adapted to many cases as an intermediary station, and may also be used in winter by patients with stationary phthisis. Montreux and Vevey are, moreover, well-known resorts for the grape cure, producing as they do grapes of superior quality.

Emily Hawkins may have brought Louise and John to Vernet. Georgina Doyle makes clear in *Out of the Shadows* that Mrs. Hawkins spent much time transporting her ailing children to destinations that might improve their health. Arthur, in his autobiography, claimed that he first met the three of them when they were visiting Southsea, just before John died horrifically of cerebral meningitis.

Meningitis can be a complication of tuberculosis, caused when the bacteria escape the lungs and attack the brain. When writing of Louise's tuberculosis, Arthur alluded to her family's history in general, and to her medical record in particular.

Within a few weeks of our return [from Switzerland] she complained of a pain in her side and cough. I had no suspicion of anything serious, but sent for the nearest good physician. To my surprise and alarm he told me when he descended from the bedroom that the lungs were very gravely affected, that there was every sign of rapid consumption and that he thought the case a most serious one with little hope, considering her record and family history, of a permanent cure.

Arthur wrote to his mother of the physician's suspicion: "He seemed to think that the mischief must have been going on for years unobserved, but if so it must have been very slight." It seems that Louise's strenuous efforts to follow in Mark Twain's footsteps may have allowed her latent tuberculosis to turn active. After the diagnosis, she returned to Switzerland in search of a restful cure, first to Davos Platz and later to the hillside resort of Caux, overlooking Vernet and Lake Geneva.

Grand Hotel de Caux; Valley of the Rhône to the left, Vernet beneath, Ouchy to the right

Olivia Clemens, the wife of Mark Twain, suffered tuberculosis of the spine, and stayed in the nearby town of Ouchy, also on the north shore of Lake Geneva. She waited there for her husband as he risked life and limb making the treacherous ascent to Seiler's Hotel Riffelberg.

Louise and her family may have, even before 1893, dared a similar excursion. Looking upwards from the foot of the Findel Glacier, one can see a prominent mountain peak, pointed and leaning to the right. It is the Adler Horn. It overlooks the Adler glacier and the Adler pass.

Leading edge of Findel Glacier (left); Adler Horn (right); 1910

It seems to be the origin of the name Irene Adler, the only woman to have ever defeated Sherlock Holmes. She appeared in the first short story, *A Scandal in Bohemia*, the one in which Holmes poked fun at the German language, just as Mark Twain had in *A Tramp Abroad*.

It was Louise, not Arthur or Dawson or Hocking, who delivered the little group here by retracing Mark Twain's route from Lucerne to Zermatt. Arthur had no concern for the man. It was Louise who, for some reason, felt the urge to follow in Twain's footsteps, even at the risk of activating her dormant *Mycobacterium tuberculosis*. It was Louise who urged them from Lucerne, across the Gemmi Pass, up the Valley of the Rhône, through Zermatt and finally to Seiler's Hotel Riffelalp, so near the Findelen Glacier. It was Louise who provided them that view of the Adler Horn.

It might have been during an earlier visit to Zermatt and the Adler Horn that a twenty-one-year-old Louise, along with her mother and brother, happened to cross paths with the already famous Mark Twain. "Made some nice English friends," he wrote to his beloved Olivia from St. Nicholas, "and we shall see them at Zermatt tomorrow."

After recovering from his perilous ascent to the Riffelberg, then descending safely to the Valley of the Rhône, Twain traveled to Lake Geneva, there to meet up once again with Olivia and their children. As he related in *A Tramp Abroad*, he traveled with company: "We left with a family of English friends and went by train to Brevet, and thence by boat across the lake to Ouchy."

Perhaps.

Chapter 14
Surrender

"My heart is sick and sad. From where the sun now stands I will fight no more forever."—Chief Joseph, after the battle of Bear Paw Mountains, Montana, 1877.

The Moss Rose

Louise returned to England early in September of 1893, in time to add new content to what she expected to be her penultimate Holmes adventure. *The Naval Treaty* appeared in the October and November issues of *The Strand*, thereby becoming the first Holmes short story to be published in two parts. The previous short stories had averaged 8,300 words; the longest had barely exceeded 10,000. After Louise's last-moment additions, *The Naval Treaty* ran beyond 12,500.

Three of the late additions stick out like a wonderfully sore thumb. Consider the instance in which Holmes suddenly digresses from the mystery at hand, muses on religion for the first time in the Canon, and then continues with the mystery as if nothing had ever happened.

> "I have no doubt I can get details from Forbes. The authorities are excellent at amassing facts, though they do not always use them to advantage. What a lovely thing a rose is!"
>
> He walked past the couch to the open window, and held up the drooping stalk of a moss rose, looking down at the dainty blend of crimson and green. It was a new phase of his character to me, for I had never before seen him show any keen interest in natural objects.
>
> "There is nothing in which deduction is so necessary as in religion," said he, leaning with his back against the shutters. "It can be built up as an exact science by the reasoner. Our highest assurance of the goodness of Providence seems to me to rest in

the flowers. All other things, our powers, our desires, our food, are really necessary for our existence in the first instance. But this rose is an extra. Its smell and its colour are an embellishment of life, not a condition of it. It is only goodness which gives extras, and so I say again that we have much to hope from the flowers."

Percy Phelps and his nurse looked at Holmes during this demonstration with surprise and a good deal of disappointment written upon their faces. He had fallen into a reverie, with the moss rose between his fingers. It had lasted some minutes before the young lady broke in upon it.

"Do you see any prospect of solving this mystery, Mr. Holmes?" she asked, with a touch of asperity in her voice.

Holmes's reverie plays no role in the story, and it can be excised without any disruption of the plot. Examining the same text again, this time without the reverie, it flows seamlessly and unremarkably.

"I have no doubt I can get details from Forbes. The authorities are excellent at amassing facts, though they do not always use them to advantage.

"Do you see any prospect of solving this mystery, Mr. Holmes?" she asked.

Like the moss rose, the reverie is an extra, an embellishment. It is Sherlock Holmes finally pondering religion, and it is Louise Conan Doyle surrendering to her tuberculosis. She spent her adult life pursuing palliative or prophylactic treatment, but to no avail. Her *Mycobacterium tuberculosis* turned aggressive, "galloping" in the words of her doctor, and her prognosis was bleak.

She accepted her fate and sought comfort in her religion, and she had her creation do the same. In *The Naval Treaty*, his tuberculosis turns wasting; in *The Final Problem*, he accepts his mortality and dies gracefully.

Sidney Paget participated in Louise's plan. In *The Naval Treaty*, he drew Holmes even thinner than usual, the face more sallow than ever before. Then, in *The Final Problem*, Louise and Sidney Paget would leave no doubt that Holmes's consumption was galloping and wasting.

Contemplating a moss rose

The Board Schools

In the second of Louise's late additions to *The Naval Treaty*, Louise envisions a bright future, though not for Holmes or herself. Instead, she has Holmes express their hope for England and its children.

> Mr. Joseph Harrison drove us down to the station, and we were soon whirling up in a Portsmouth train. Holmes was sunk in profound thought, and hardly

opened his mouth until we had passed Clapham Junction.

"It's a very cheering thing to come into London by any of these lines which run high and allow you to look down upon the houses like this."

I thought he was joking, for the view was sordid enough, but he soon explained himself.

"Look at those big, isolated clumps of buildings rising up above the states, like brick islands in a lead coloured sea."

"The Board schools."

"Lighthouses, my boy! Beacons of the future! Capsules, with hundreds of bright little seeds in each, out of which will spring the wiser, better England of the future. I suppose that man Phelps does not drink."

Britain's Education Act of 1870 created localized elected school boards. The boards could levy local taxes to establish schools for the education of all children, both boys and girls, up to the age of 10. In 1881, education became free. In 1889, the London Schools Board established a School Dinners Association, one of the first to offer free or inexpensive school meals, to ensure that the children were adequately nourished. These board schools are the institutions that Holmes declares to be beacons of the future.

The board schools are another extra. They have nothing to do with the plot, and we hear nothing more of them. They are an embellishment, just as is the moss rose. Both embellishments speak to Louise's surrender to her fate, obviously so with respect to the moss rose, more subtly so with respect to the board schools. Louise is going to die, and she is going to take Holmes with her. She is passing the baton to the next generation, and England will be even better for it. It is the natural order of things. It is time to have her creation meet his maker.

A Woman of Rare Character

Early in *The Naval Treaty*, Holmes somehow detects the hand of a woman where Watson can see none.

"A very commonplace little murder," said [Holmes]. "You've got something better, I fancy. You are the stormy petrel of crime, Watson. What is it?"

I handed him the letter, which he read with the most concentrated attention.

"It does not tell us very much, does it?" he remarked, as he handed it back to me.

"Hardly anything."

"And yet the writing is of interest."

"But the writing is not his own."

"Precisely. It is a woman's."

"A man's surely!" I cried.

"No, a woman's; and a woman of rare character."

It makes no difference to the story whether the writing is that of a man or a woman. Holmes, of course, is correct about it being that of a woman, but he never explains how he knows. The author left that mystery to the readers.

Even more mysterious is how Holmes could conclude that the woman is of rare character. On that point, Holmes seems, at first blush, to be incorrect. Annie Harrison wrote the note, but she is only a minor character. After meeting her for the first time, Holmes asks Watson his assessment of her.

"What did you think of Miss Harrison?"

"A girl of strong character."

"Yes, but she is a good sort, or I am mistaken."

That is the extent of any discussion or evidence relating to Annie Harrison's character. Whoever inserted the digression about the sex of the letter writer forgot about, or simply ignored, the fact that Miss Harrison was "a girl of strong character" and "a good sort," but hardly a "woman of rare character."

An alternate explanation is that the digression is an allusion to the woman who wrote the Sherlock Holmes adventures. If those words, with that intent, came from Louise herself, then she seems to have finally lost her modesty just as she humbled herself before her maker.

Perhaps, instead, the digression is just another of Louise's games: her creation describes her as a woman of rare character when, in fact, she is nothing more than a good sort.

Perhaps, more hopefully, the words were inserted by someone else, someone who finally saw fit to acknowledge all that Louise had accomplished.

Chapter 15
Confession

"It is with a heavy heart that I take up my pen to write these the last words in which I shall ever record the singular gifts by which my friend Mr. Sherlock Holmes was distinguished." So begins *The Final Problem*, and so begins Louise's confession.

The Consumptive Holmes

From *The Final Problem* come these words, Louise's words, by way of Dr. John Watson:

> In an incoherent and, as I deeply feel, an entirely inadequate fashion, I have endeavoured to give some account of my strange experiences in his company from the chance which first brought us together at the period of the "Study in Scarlet," up to the time of his interference in the matter of the "Naval Treaty."

She accepts responsibility for the adventures being incoherent and inadequate for their intended purpose. She explains that she wrote each of the Sherlock Holmes adventures, beginning with *A Study in Scarlet* and ending with the story we now consider.

> I alone know the absolute truth of the matter, and I am satisfied that the time has come when no good purpose is to be served by its suppression. It lies with me to tell for the first time what really took place between Professor Moriarty and Mr. Sherlock Holmes.

She informs us that no one, not even Arthur, has been aware of the full depth of her stories. She will therefore be more explicit with her allusions. She will explain that she is dying, and that this story is an allegory for her struggle to persist. She will introduce a new character, one who will be a metaphor for the disease that will take her. He will be called Moriarty.

> I received two notes from Holmes, dated from
> Narbonne and from Nîmes, from which I gathered
> that his stay in France was likely to be a long one.

As she has done many times before, she mentions two geographic locations in close conjunction, thereby inviting us to explore the region between. Narbonne and Nîmes are located near the southern border of France, near the Gulf of Lion. A straight line connecting the two runs directly through Montpellier.

In her first Holmes adventure, she alluded to the fevered murderer Marie-Fortunée Lafarge, both as Lefevre of Montpellier and Leturier of Montpellier. Mademoiselle Rachel, the person whom she had Holmes declare to be a waste of investigative energy, visited Madame Lafarge in the Maison Centrale in Montpellier. Lafarge was being consumed even as Rachel visited her. Lafarge may have even, unintentionally, infected Rachel. Whatever the source of her infection, Rachel later suffered the same fatal disease. Her doctor sent her back to Montpellier for its allegedly recuperative air, but Rachel continued to deteriorate there, as would Holmes, thirty-three years later.

> It was with some surprise, therefore, that I saw him
> walk into my consulting-room upon the evening of
> April 24th. It struck me that he was looking even
> paler and thinner than usual.

Compared to Sidney Paget's sketch in *The Strand*, Watson understates the worrisome condition of Holmes's visage. Holmes is shockingly sallow. His face is even narrower than usual, even narrower than in *The Naval Treaty*. His eyes and cheeks sink into his skull. His robe engulfs his emaciated frame. He is suffering a wasting disease. There is a gun on the table near his hand, as if he might shoot his foe or, possibly, take his own life.

Paget's Holmes (clockwise) from *The Red-Headed League*,
The Beryl Coronet, *The Stockbroker's Clerk*,
The Naval Treaty, and *The Final Problem*

The Threats on Holmes's Life

Holmes nevertheless attempts to keep his terminal condition private.
He recognizes Watson's suspicions and dismisses them.

"Yes, I have been using myself up rather too freely," he remarked, in answer to my look rather than to my words; "I have been a little pressed of late. Have you any objection to my closing your shutters?"

The only light in the room came from the lamp upon the table at which I had been reading. Holmes edged his way round the wall and flinging the shutters together, he bolted them securely.

"You are afraid of something?" I asked.

"Well, I am."

"Of what?"

"Of air-guns."

"My dear Holmes, what do you mean?"

Louise alludes again to the consumptive Madame Lafarge and her not-yet-afflicted visitor Rachel. After observing Lafarge wasting away, Rachel wrote to her sister about the dreadful nature of —

that most terrible of all diseases, consumption. She feels the skein of life's thread unwinding, and, to the very last, she will see, she will feel. It is very dreadful. Better far a bullet in the weak chest, or a tile falling on the aching head some windy day.

Holmes then describes three attempts on his life.

"My dear Watson, Professor Moriarty is not a man who lets the grass grow under his feet. I went out about mid-day to transact some business in Oxford Street. As I passed the corner which leads from Bentinck Street on to the Welbeck Street crossing a two-horse van furiously driven whizzed round and was on me like a flash. I sprang for the foot-path and saved myself by the fraction of a second."

Louise alludes again to Blaise Pascal, previously referred to as Jansen of Utrecht. Legend has it that Pascal was almost killed when runaway horses nearly pulled his carriage off of a bridge. Mary

Shelley described the event in her encyclopaedic work *Lives of the Most Eminent French Writers* (1840): "One day, in the month of October, he was taking an airing in a carriage-and-four towards the Pont de Neuilli, when the leaders took the bit in their teeth, at a spot where there is no parapet, and precipitated themselves into the Seine: fortunately the shock broke the traces, and the carriage remained on the brink of the precipice. Pascal, a feeble, half-paralytic, trembling being, was overwhelmed by the shock. He fell into a succession of fainting fits, followed by a nervous agitation that prevented sleep, and brought on a state resembling delirium."

According to Shelley, that event caused Pascal to abruptly change his focus from math and science to religion and salvation. He took up the defense of the persecuted Jansenists in his *The Provincial Letters*, but the Jansenists were nevertheless forced to flee to Utrecht and elsewhere in the Netherlands.

> "I kept to the pavement after that, Watson, but as I walked down Vere Street a brick came down from the roof of one of the houses, and was shattered to fragments at my feet. I called the police and had the place examined. There were slates and bricks piled up on the roof preparatory to some repairs, and they would have me believe that the wind had toppled over one of these."

Louise alludes again to Rachel's sad letter: "Better far a bullet in the weak chest, or a tile falling on the aching head some windy day."

> "I took a cab after that and reached my brother's rooms in Pall Mall, where I spent the day. Now I have come round to you, and on my way I was attacked by a rough with a bludgeon."

Louise alludes to English editor, critic, and poet William Ernest Henley, one of Arthur's many acquaintances. Henley lost his leg to skeletal tuberculosis acquired during childhood. Against the advice of his doctors, he refused the amputation of his remaining leg, opting instead for three years of hospital treatment and at least one operation on his remaining foot. He is most famous for his 1875 poem "Invictus", in which he describes his refusal to be bowed by the "bludgeonings of chance."

> Out of the night that covers me,
> Black as the pit from pole to pole,
> I thank whatever gods may be
> For my unconquerable soul.
>
> In the fell clutch of circumstance
> I have not winced nor cried aloud.
> Under the bludgeonings of chance
> My head is bloody, but unbowed.
>
> Beyond this place of wrath and tears
> Looms but the Horror of the shade,
> And yet the menace of the years
> Finds and shall find me unafraid.
>
> It matters not how strait the gate,
> How charged with punishments the scroll,
> I am the master of my fate:
> I am the captain of my soul.

The Consumptive Moriarty

Mycobacteria tuberculosis is among the most ancient and prolific killers of mankind. Even today, a third of the world's population carry the microbes latent in their lungs. In ten percent of those people, roughly 200 million of them, the microbes will become active and consume their hosts from the inside out. Louise's family had its history with the disease, and Louise fought against it for as long as she could, but she too was being consumed even as she wrote her *Final Problem*.

> "You have probably never heard of Professor Moriarty?" said he.
> "Never."
> "The man pervades London, and no one has heard of him. I tell you, Watson, in all seriousness,

that if I could beat that man, if I could free society of him, I should feel that my own career had reached its summit, and I should be prepared to turn to some more placid line in life. I could not rest, Watson, I could not sit quiet in my chair, if I thought that such a man as Professor Moriarty were walking the streets of London unchallenged."

"What has he done, then?"

"His career has been an extraordinary one. He is a man of good birth and excellent education, endowed by nature with a phenomenal mathematical faculty. At the age of twenty-one he wrote a treatise upon the Binomial Theorem."

Louise alludes yet again to Blaise Pascal, the first person to describe both the binomial formula and the triangular nature of its coefficients. She soon has Holmes describe Moriarty's physical presence, and we learn that he has the familiar look of a consumptive.

"My nerves are fairly proof, Watson, but I must confess to a start when I saw the very man who had been so much in my thoughts standing there on my threshold. His appearance was quite familiar to me. He is extremely tall and thin, his forehead domes out in a white curve, and his two eyes are deeply sunken in his head. He is clean-shaven, pale, and ascetic-looking, retaining something of the professor in his features. His shoulders are rounded from much study, and his face protrudes forward, and is for ever slowly oscillating from side to side in a curiously reptilian fashion. He peered at me with great curiosity in his puckered eyes.

Moriarty's shoulders are not rounded from decades of hunched study, rather from Pott's disease. *Mycobacteria tuberculosis* can attack any part of the body. When they consume the intervertebral joints, as they do in Pott's disease, as they did with Olivia Twain's spine, the spine collapses into an arch and the host displays a hump or a curved back. Not surprisingly, Louise had Sidney Paget portray Moriarty with symptoms of the disease he represents.

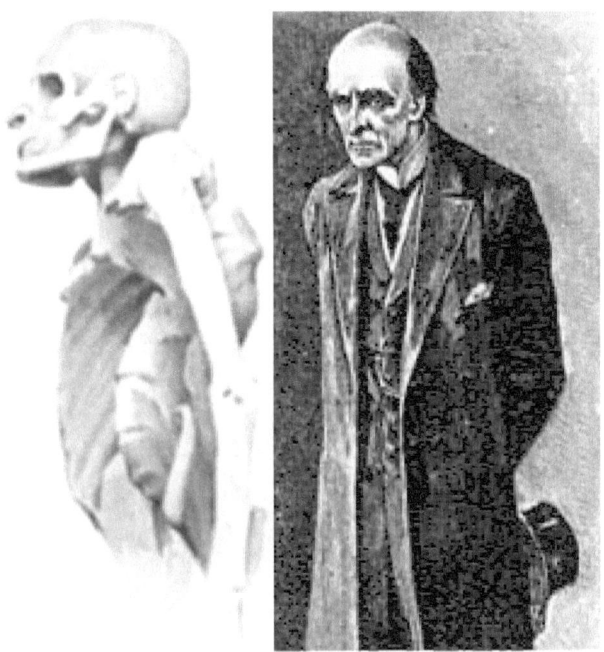

Pott's disease in an Egyptian mummy (left); Moriarty (right)

Holmes and Moriarty engage in verbal combat. Moriarty attempts to insult Holmes, assigning to him an attribute usually, back then, ascribed to non-Caucasian races: "You have less frontal development than I should have expected." Moriarty, now a visual representation of tuberculosis, explains that Holmes can defeat him only by sacrificing his own life.

> "It has been a duel between you and me, Mr Holmes. You hope to place me in the dock. I tell you that I will never stand in the dock. You hope to beat me. I tell you that you will never beat me. If you are clever enough to bring destruction upon me, rest assured that I shall do as much to you."
>   "'You have paid me several compliments, Mr Moriarty," said I. "Let me pay you one in return when I say that if I were assured of the former eventuality I

would, in the interests of the public, cheerfully accept the latter."

"'I can promise you the one but not the other," he snarled, and so turned his rounded back upon me and went peering and blinking out of the room.

A Deadly Escape

Holmes suggests to Watson that they visit the continent and await Moriarty's arrest, which Holmes has already arranged with Scotland Yard. Despite their elaborate efforts to give Moriarty the slip, he appears just as their train departs the station. Holmes anticipates that Moriarty will wait for them in Paris. Rather than continuing to Dover and crossing the Channel to Calais, they depart at Canterbury, divert to Newhaven, and cross over to Dieppe.

> We made our way to Brussels that night and spent two days there, moving on upon the third day as far as Strasbourg. On the Monday morning Holmes had telegraphed to the London police, and in the evening we found a reply waiting for us at our hotel. Holmes tore it open, and then with a bitter curse hurled it into the grate.
>
> "I might have known it!" he groaned. "he has escaped!"

The human body is ill equipped to destroy the rugged *Mycobacteria tuberculosis*. It can, however, imprison the bacteria within nodes of flesh called tubercles. These tubercles, visible to the naked eye during autopsy, give name to the disease. As long as the body contains the bacteria in this way, the host will be symptom-free and noninfectious. When the host is under stress, however, or her immune system falters, the bacteria can escape and wreak their havoc. In what she perceives to be her final adventure, Louise has Moriarty escape. Holmes at this point warns his friend:

> "I think that you had better return to England, Watson."
>
> "Why?"

"Because you will find me a dangerous companion now. If I read his character right he will devote his whole energies to revenging himself upon me."

Once the *Mycobacteria tuberculosis* have escaped their tubercles, they become a public menace. Any cough might send them directly into the air. Coughed or expectorated phlegm will dry, be pulverized underfoot, and sent airborne. Anyone inhaling the bacteria might become a host and future victim. It is therefore prudent and considerate of Holmes to separate himself from Watson once Moriarty escapes. Unlike Arthur, however, Watson will not abandon his friend and partner.

It was hardly an appeal to be successful with one who was an old campaigner as well as an old friend. We sat in the Strasbourg *salle-à-manger* arguing the question for half an hour, but the same night we had resumed our journey and were well on our way to Geneva. For a charming week we wandered up the Valley of the Rhône.

Valley of the Rhône

Watson explains, "branching off at Leuk, we made our way over the Gemmi Pass." The length of the Valley of the Rhône, from Lake Geneva to Leuk, is fifty-five miles. If Holmes and Watson would simply take the train on which Louise had just recently rode, they would cover the distance in just a few hours. Instead, they wander up the valley for a "charming week." The math and the significance are left for us to infer.

Holmes and Watson average less than eight miles a day. This ambling pace should demand no more than three hours each day, allowing them to rest or explore for the remaining twenty-one. We might consider this leisurely pace a confession that Louise, too, took her time traveling through the valley, investigating potential cures along the way. Perhaps, Holmes considers the grape cure, whey cure, or milk cure of Vernet. Perhaps he samples the baths at Bex, or visits their inhalation rooms. Maybe he climbs and descends the mountains lining the valley, hoping that the abrupt change in elevation will overwhelm the bacteria in his lungs. Possibly he visits the elevated Leysin sanatorium, to consider winter quarters, or ascends the Col de Balme to view the glaciers of Mont Blanc, where Victor Frankenstein confronts his own monster.

Alternatively, Holmes and Watson might take the time to explore the valley beyond Leuk, all the way to Visp. From there they may ascend to St. Nicholas, where Louise potentially encountered Mark Twain, then to Zermatt, where they met again the next day. They might spend the night at the Hotel Riffelberg, or the Hotel Riffelalp.

Holmes might, the next day, ascend further, finally to the Findel glacier, from there to see the Adler Horn. He might wonder at the coincidence that he had long ago been defeated by a woman of that same name.

We are left only with surmise, though, for Louise's adventures are forever coy and subtle. She tells us only that Holmes and Watson idle for one week in the valley, when they could have traversed it in a day.

Gemmi Pass

Mark Twain crossed the Gemmi Pass fifteen years earlier, and Louise had followed just the previous August. Holmes and Watson have been tracing their path, in reverse. It comes as no surprise, therefore, when they leave the Valley of the Rhône at Leuk and climb to the Gemmi Pass.

Holmes and Watson clear the summit without incident, pass the Hotel Wildstrubel, where Louise had recently stayed, then hike alongside the mile-long Daubensee. It is here that they are threatened by the boulder that "clattered down and roared into the lake."

Louise alludes to Mary Shelley's *Frankenstein*. As Victor Frankenstein climbs the glaciers of Mont Blanc, he ponders death by falling boulder: "The path, as you ascend higher, is intersected by ravines of snow, down which stones continually roll from above; one of them is particularly dangerous, as the slightest sound, such as even speaking in a loud voice, produces a concussion of air sufficient to draw destruction upon the head of the speaker."

Meiringen

After crossing the Gemmi Pass, Holmes and Watson make their way, without further incident, to "the little village of Meiringen, where we put up at the Englischer Hof, then kept by Peter Steiler the elder." Peter Steiler is, of course, a nearly transparent allusion to Alexander Seiler, the famous Zermatt hotelier.

Nowhere else in Holmes's travels through Switzerland does Louise identify a city in which Holmes lodges. Nowhere else along his entire journey from London to the Reichenbach does she identify a lodging place by name. In *The Final Problem* she mentions only the Englischer Hof, with full knowledge that it exists not in Meiringen, but in Frankfurt.

Of the suspects who might have written this final adventure, one of them seems to know that Mark Twain spent a night in Frankfurt's Englischer Hof. Arthur never exhibited any interest in Mark Twain, seemed oblivious to the various Mark Twain allusions in the early Holmes adventures, and had no opportunity to meet him. Louise, on the other hand, may have been encountered Mark during her earlier trip to Switzerland.

Reichenbach

In August of 1893, Louise and Arthur hiked to the Reichenbach Falls, crossed the Gemmi Pass, proceeded to Visp, and ascended beyond Zermatt. In this adventure, her *Final Problem*, Louise does not allow Holmes to travel any further than the falls.

> It is, indeed, a fearful place. The torrent, swollen by the melting snow, plunges into a tremendous abyss, from which the spray rolls up like the smoke from a burning house. The shaft into which the river hurls itself is an immense chasm, lined by glistening coal-black rock, and narrowing into a creaming, boiling pit of incalculable depth, which brims over and shoots the stream onward over its jagged lip. The long sweep of green water roaring forever down, and the thick flickering curtain of spray hissing forever upward, turn a man giddy with their constant whirl

> and clamour. We stood near the edge peering down
> at the gleam of the breaking water far below us
> against the black rocks, and listening to the half-
> human shout which came booming up with the spray
> out of the abyss.
>
> The path has been cut half-way round the fall to
> afford a complete view, but it ends abruptly, and the
> traveller has to return as he came. We had turned to
> do so, when we saw a Swiss lad come running along it
> with a letter in his hand. It bore the mark of the hotel
> which we had just left, and was addressed to me by
> the landlord.

The note is, of course, ostensibly from Steiler the Elder, alleging
that one of his female guests needs emergency medical care. Watson
is reluctant to leave Holmes's side, but his professional responsibility
overwhelms his caution.

A Shadowy Figure

As Watson makes his way down the trail, he sees someone walking
energetically towards the falls. Foolishly, he ignores the obvious.

> As I turned away I saw Holmes, with his back against
> a rock and his arms folded, gazing down at the rush
> of the waters. It was the last that I was ever destined
> to see of him in this world.
>
> When I was near the bottom of the descent I
> looked back. It was impossible, from that position, to
> see the fall, but I could see the curving path which
> winds over the shoulder of the hill and leads to it.
> Along this a man was, I remember, walking very
> rapidly. I could see his black figure clearly outlined
> against the green behind him. I noted him, and the
> energy with which he walked but he passed from my
> mind again as I hurried on upon my errand.

Louise alludes again to *Frankenstein*. Seventy-five years earlier,
Mary Shelley had Victor Frankenstein narrate this original scene.

It was nearly noon when I arrived at the top of the ascent. For some time I sat upon the rock that overlooks the sea of ice. A mist covered both that and the surrounding mountains. Presently a breeze dissipated the cloud, and I descended upon the glacier. [...] My heart, which was before sorrowful, now swelled with something like joy; I exclaimed— "Wandering spirits, if indeed ye wander, and do not rest in your narrow beds, allow me this faint happiness, or take me, as your companion, away from the joys of life."

As I said this, I suddenly beheld the figure of a man, at some distance, advancing towards me with superhuman speed. He bounded over the crevices in the ice, among which I had walked with caution; his stature also, as he approached, seemed to exceed that of man. I was troubled: a mist came over my eyes, and I felt a faintness seize me; but I was quickly restored by the cold gale of the mountains. I perceived, as the shape came nearer, (sight tremendous and abhorred!) that it was the wretch whom I had created. I trembled with rage and horror, resolving to wait his approach, and then close with him in mortal combat.

While Mary Shelley's book is subject to innumerable interpretations, one overriding theme is that of hubris. Victor Frankenstein had the audacity to create beyond his station, and such impertinence will not go unpunished. He will suffer the consequences of his hubris, as will those he loves.

Watson fails to recognize that which is obvious to Victor Frankenstein: the dark, rapidly moving figure is the nemesis, intent on mortal combat. It is necessary, though, that Holmes confront Moriarty on his own, so Watson must ignore the obvious. The realization settles on him only after it is too late.

> It may have been a little over an hour before I reached Meiringen. Old Steiler was standing at the porch of his hotel.
>
> "Well," said I, as I came hurrying up, "I trust that she is no worse?"
>
> A look of surprise passed over his face, and at the first quiver of his eyebrows my heart turned to lead in my breast.
>
> "You did not write this?" I said, pulling the letter from my pocket.
>
> "Certainly not!" he cried. "But it has the hotel mark upon it!"

Similarly, the 4 May 1878 letter by Mark Twain, supplied at last to the public by the Mark Twain Project Online, has the mark of Frankfurt's Englischer Hof upon it!

The Consumptive Englishwoman

Louise was convinced, as she wrote *The Final Problem*, that she was dying. All her efforts to cure or contain her tuberculosis had failed. Her consumption was once again active, and she was an immediate threat to everyone nearest her heart. Though her doctors gave her but three months to live, she knew she must avoid close contact with her loved ones, isolating herself completely from her two young children. She therefore retired to a location designed for consumptives such as herself: Davos Platz, on the far side of Switzerland, finally completing her earlier travel from Lucerne.

In her final adventure, Louise confesses her responsibility for Holmes and his demise. While Watson is still at the falls, he reveals the contents of the letter that will lead to Holmes's demise.

> It appeared that within a very few minutes of our leaving, an English lady had arrived who was in the last stage of consumption. She had wintered in Davos Platz, and was journeying now to join her friends in Lucerne, when a sudden haemorrhage had overtaken her.

Holmes must confront Moriarty alone because a consumptive Englishwoman was dying alone in Switzerland. That consumptive Englishwoman is none other than Louise herself, who will return to Switzerland to await her fate alone, at least without her husband. Arthur will choose to remain behind to lecture about the state of fiction in English literature.

Louise turns her final story into an allegory for her battle with the disease that, she is assured, will soon take her. She names her nemesis Moriarty. "I write these few lines," reads the farewell note that Holmes leaves for Watson, "through the courtesy of Mr. Moriarty, who awaits my convenience for the final discussion of those questions which lie between us."

Louise knows, as she writes *The Final Problem*, that *Moriar* is Latin for "I die."

Epilogue

Jean

Jean, being the youngest of our suspects, outlived the others. She died on 27 June 1940, at sixty-six years of age. Among her final wishes was that Adrian, her youngest son, burn her love letters to Arthur. Many secrets perished amidst the flames.

Late in life, she believed herself to be a spiritual medium. Between 1921 and 1926, she put Arthur in contact with those on the other side. Through Jean and her spirit guides, Arthur spoke with or inquired about his son Kingsley, his mother Mary, his brother Innes, and other departed relatives, friends, and associates. Jean leaves no record that Arthur ever asked about Louise.

Jean communicated most frequently and most extensively with the spirit Pheneas, an Arab from Ur, who lived before the time of Abraham. Pheneas's insights and advice, as they were recorded by Arthur, seem quite similar to those expected from a loving wife. Pheneas reassured Arthur that his work to promote spiritualism was his highest calling as God's messenger, that those Arthur loved were happy in the afterlife, and that he should get plenty of rest and take care of his health.

According to the stylometric analysis, Jean wrote many works currently credited to Arthur.

In 1926, Jean wrote *The Land of Mist*, in which Arthur's Professor Challenger of *Lost World* fame, accepts spiritualism as a matter of faith and fact.

In 1899, while Louise was still alive, Jean wrote *A Duet with an Occasional Chorus*, in which a female ex-lover threatens a loving marriage. Arthur put his name to that novel, had the manuscript bound, and presented it to Jean, its author, as a loving gift.

On 18 September 1907, somewhat more than a year after the death of the first Mrs. Conan Doyle, Jean married Arthur.

On 15 March 1897, the day after her twenty-third birthday, Jean began a romantic relationship with the famous author, thirty-three-year-old Arthur Conan Doyle.

Between 1903 and 1927, Jean probably wrote twenty-nine of the last thirty-three Holmes adventures. In 1926, she wrote *The Three Gables*, the story in which Holmes mocks prizefighter Steve Dixie for his racial features. In 1908, she wrote *Wisteria Lodge*, the story involving "a huge and hideous mulatto," in which Watson is unable to distinguish between "a mummified negro baby" and "a very twisted and ancient monkey." In 1904, she wrote *The Second Stain*; her handwriting appears in the manuscript.

Arthur put his name to each of her works.

Arthur

Arthur died on 7 July 1930 at age seventy-one. He had been one of the most prolific writers of all time. He wrote hundreds of fiction and nonfiction books, pamphlets, short stories, newspaper articles, and letters to editors. He wrote of life, love, medicine, mystery, terror, war, travel, the occult, and the great beyond. As he feared, he is remembered best for the Sherlock Holmes adventures, only two and a faction of which he wrote.

In his last year on earth, he managed to turn out one final book. It was about spiritualism. In *The Edge of the Unknown*, he addressed how the residual sweat of deceased slaves can move lead coffins about within a sealed vault.

In 1927, he put his name, and his name alone, on the cover of *Pheneas Speaks*. Though he wrote the introduction and posed the questions to those on the other side, most of the content came from Jean, or Pheneas.

In 1926, he put his name, and his name alone, on the cover of *The History of Spiritualism*. Though he conceded that Leslie Curnow contributed substantially to the book, he hoped that Curnow would understand why he could not be credited as a co-author.

In 1922, Arthur put his name on the cover of *The Coming of the Fairies*. Edward Gardner contributed substantially to the book, but Arthur did not acknowledge him as co-author. The two intended that their book would prove the existence of fairies worldwide, focusing in particular on five photographs taken by young cousins Elsie Wright and Frances Griffiths. "The series of incidents set forth in this little volume represent either the most elaborate and ingenious hoax ever played upon the public, or else they constitute an event in human history which may in the future appear to have been epoch-making in its character."

Near the end of her life, Elsie explained the fairies. "What we did was a long hat pin that we put down the back like that, and stuck the tape at the back like that, [...] and then we wormed that down into the earth," she said. "The thing was that they said they could see that the fairies were moving when the photographs were taken, but that's because they were in a breeze."

"I never even thought of it being a fraud," said Frances. "It was just Elsie and I having a bit of fun. And I can't understand why they were still taken in. They wanted to be taken in. People often say to me, 'Don't you feel ashamed that you made all these poor people look fools; they believed in you.' But I don't, because they wanted to believe."

Elsie added, "Two village kids and a brilliant man like Conan Doyle—well, we could only keep quiet."

In 1921, Arthur wrote *The Wanderings of a Spiritualist* wherein he told of a clairvoyant fox terrier. Though the dog failed to perform as advertised, Arthur wondered "how many other dogs have human brains without the humans being clever enough to detect it."

Between 1918 and his death, Arthur wrote eleven books proselytizing spiritualism, plus numerous pamphlets, articles, and letters to make his case. To spread the word, he lectured throughout Britain, the United States, Canada, Australia, New Zealand, and Africa. He opened his own psychic bookstore. He established a fractious friendship with Houdini and refused to accept a natural explanation for the magician's mind-boggling stunts. To Houdini's biographer Harold Kellock, Arthur wrote, "I think, however, that you may take the words 'An Unsolved Mystery' off your cover. It is I who have solved the mystery of Houdini and I have no more doubt that he used psychic powers than I have that I am dictating this letter."

In *Flim-Flam: Psychics, ESP, Unicorns and other Delusions* (1987), James Randi calculated that Arthur "spent some £250,000 in pursuit of this nonsense." Even for Arthur, this was a substantial expense. His need for money made necessary and somewhat more palatable Jean's authorship of the late Holmes adventures.

The conclusions from the stylometric analysis are shocking.

Of the last twelve adventures in the Canon, anthologized as *The Casebook of Sherlock Holmes* (1927), Arthur wrote none.

Of the thirteen short stories in the third series of Holmes adventures, anthologized as *The Return of Sherlock Holmes* (1905), Arthur wrote only *The Empty House* and *Charles Augustus Milverton*.

Of the last two novels in the Canon, *The Valley of Fear* (1915) and *The Hound of the Baskervilles* (1902), Arthur wrote neither.

Of the twenty-four earliest Holmes short stories, anthologized in *The Memoirs of Sherlock Holmes* (1893) and *The Adventures of Sherlock Holmes* (1892), Arthur wrote none of them.

Of the first two novels in the Canon, Arthur wrote only the Utah interlude to *A Study in Scarlet*.

Louise

Louise died on 6 July 1906, at age thirty-nine, succumbing to tuberculosis of her lungs, larynx, and probably of cerebral meningitis. Arthur was at her bedside, crying.

Shortly before she died, while speech was still possible, she called seven-year-old Mary to her. Louise revealed that Arthur would soon marry Jean Leckie, and that it would be with her blessing.

Late in 1893, just before Holmes and Moriarty tumbled into the Reichenbach Falls, Louise ventured to Davos Platz, Switzerland. She had recently been informed that her tuberculosis had turned "galloping and wasting," that she had but three months to live. She lived for thirteen years more, sustained by a religious faith only recently recovered after years of questioning and apostasy.

According to the stylometric analysis, Louise wrote at least one more Holmes adventure after surviving the immediate threat on her life. That adventure, one of the best ever, was the novel *The Hound of the Baskervilles*. Arthur put his name to that novel.

According to the stylometric analysis, Louise wrote twenty-six of the first thirty Holmes short stories to appear in *The Strand*. A separate analysis indicates that she wrote each of her adventures, other than *Hound*, prior to her self-imposed exile to Davos Platz, and that her adventures were not published in the sequence in which they were written. Arthur put his name to each of her short stories.

Sometime before Arthur's alleged dinner with Oscar Wilde, Louise wrote the second Holmes novel, *The Sign of Four*. To fulfill a lucrative contract, Arthur put his name to her novel.

During 1885 and 1886, Louise wrote the detective portion of the first Sherlock Holmes adventure, *A Study in Scarlet*, while Arthur wrote the Utah portion. Arthur excluded her name from the novel.

Louise was a willing partner in all this. "When I have spun the web, they may take the flies," she had Holmes allow in her *Five Orange Pips*. She used another of her adventures, *A Case of Identity* no less, to have Holmes inform everyone that there was far more happening behind the scenes than first met the eyes.

> "Life is infinitely stranger than anything which the mind of man could invent. We would not dare to conceive the things which are really mere commonplaces of existence. If we could fly out of that window hand in hand, hover over this great city, gently remove the roofs, and peep in at the queer things which are going on, the strange coincidences, the plannings, the cross-purposes, the wonderful chains of events, working through generations, and leading to the most outré results, it would make all fiction with its conventionalities and foreseen conclusions most stale and unprofitable."

Author and Contributors

I am an engineer by education, training, experience, and temperament. More recently, I learned from my wife how to program custom database systems. In brief, I am a data junkie, whether those data be revealing numbers or critical facts deeply buried and long overlooked.

I became interested in the issue of wrongful conviction after my fourth stint as a juror for criminal trials. I began my writing career not long after as an effort to mitigate the problem of innocent people living behind bars. I turned away from writing of such cases after failing to stop the execution of a man I believed to be innocent.

I turned then to writing about a subject that has long fascinated me, the authorship of the Sherlock Holmes adventures. The result of that effort is the book before you. By a path that is too circuitous to be detailed here, my work on this book has led me to launch a fictional mystery series that features the actual creator of the Holmes adventures as the lead character. That series has, in turn, prompted me to turn my attention once again to wrongful convictions. You will need to read the books in the mystery series to see how I have merged two such disparate subjects.

For this book and the ones that will follow, I wish to thank Wendy Iverson for her role as production assistant. I wish to thank Dean Williams for his astounding artwork, and Heather Osborn for the final round of formal editing.

I wish to take special notice of Byron Case, inmate #328416 at the Crossroads Correction Center in Cameron, Missouri. He is serving a double life sentence without possibility of parole for a murder he did not commit. We did not know each other when I began working on his case without his knowledge or approval. We have since become friends. I intend to see that he is someday freed so that he may pursue his own writing career unrestrained by bars and lethal fences. He is a more polished writer than I am, and a fastidious editor. If you come across any section in this book that reads particularly well, feel free to assume the wording came mostly from him.

I save the best and most important for last. I especially thank Lynn, my wife of twenty plus years, for everything she has done to support me. A gifted artist and programmer in her own right, she has added book publishing to the skill set at Allen & Allen Semiotics, Inc. She has been always beside me, whether I have been charging heroically forward or tilting at windmills.

For more information regarding the authorship issue, the stylometric analysis, and the fictional mystery series, visit us at **www.louiseconandoyle.com**.

Also by my hand, writing as J Bennett Allen:
The Skeptical Juror and the Trial of Byron Case
The Skeptical Juror and the Trial of Cory Maye
The Skeptical Juror and the Trial of Cameron Todd Willingham
Inferno (A second book on Cameron Todd Willingham)

And look for ***Brimstone***, the first adventure in
the Louise Conan Doyle Mystery series,
to be released in 2017.

First Edition 7/1/2017
Revised 8/17/2017

www.ingramcontent.com/pod-product-compliance
Lightning Source LLC
Chambersburg PA
CBHW020540020726
47494CB00006B/1855